Also by Peter Spiegelman

Black Maps

Death's Little Helpers

Red Cat

Thick as Thieves

Dr. Knox

A SECRET
ABOUT
A SECRET

Peter Spiegelman

Alfred A. Knopf
New York | 2022

THIS IS A BORZOI BOOK
PUBLISHED BY ALFRED A. KNOPF

www.aaknopf.com

Knopf, Borzoi Books, and the colophon are registered trademarks of
Penguin Random House LLC.

Library of Congress Cataloging-in-Publication Data
Names: Spiegelman, Peter, author.
Title: A secret about a secret / Peter Spiegelman.
Description: First edition. | New York : Alfred A. Knopf, 2022. |
"This is a Borzoi book"—Title page verso.
Identifiers: LCCN 2021056371 (print) | LCCN 2021056372 (ebook) |
ISBN 9780307961297 (hardcover) | ISBN 9780307961303 (ebook)
Subjects: LCGFT: Novels.
Classification: LCC PS3619.P543 S43 2022 (print) | LCC PS3619.P543 (ebook) |
DDC 813/.6—dc23/eng/20211118
LC record available at https://lccn.loc.gov/2021056371
LC ebook record available at https://lccn.loc.gov/2021056372

Front-of-jacket images: (woods) Silas Manhood / Arcangel Images;
(keyhole) Imagine CG Images; (sky) Honza Krej; (building) FenlioQ,
all Shutterstock
Jacket design by Ervin Serrano

Manufactured in the United States of America
First Edition

For Sonny

A photograph is a secret about a secret.
The more it tells you, the less you know.

—DIANE ARBUS

A SECRET ABOUT A SECRET

Saturday Evening

The road was long and secret: a tunnel of trees that leaned overhead and wept like mourners in the wind. It ran beneath iron skies, past vacant fields and the lichen-crusted stones of ragged walls. It ran past a farmhouse, dark and empty, and through a stone village with few lit windows and no signs that named it. It ran on then towards the coast, and even in the hermetic car I smelled salt and rotting seaweed.

My driver had excellent posture, a glossy brown ponytail, and perfect silence. I trusted that she knew our destination—what else could I do?—though she had shared nothing about it with me, instead maintaining a near-statuary stillness as she drove. Nor had I any idea of why I'd been dispatched. To examine, to investigate, to discover, to take a confession, to punish, or simply to bear witness? I was authorized to do all of these, though I wondered lately about my qualifications for any of them. If nostalgia was called for perhaps, or distraction, equivocation, worry, longing, or bone weariness, then I might be useful. But in all these years, my masters had never sought such things from me, and I didn't think this Saturday in March would be the first time.

The rear seat was deep and enveloping, the doors were distant, and the windows were tinted. Between the tidal sway of the car's suspension and the thrum of pavement rolling away, I lapsed into a sort of fugue. It was not quite sleep, yet not quite dreamless—an unmooring, a drifting, and as I drifted, I crossed a frontier. There was no razor wire or striped barricade, no skeptical guards or surly dogs, no customs shed for stammered declarations, but a border nonetheless. When I came around, on the far side, it was to another world.

To an uncertain season, neither winter nor spring, under dark, colliding skies—the clouds swollen and malign, obedient to no known physics. To a fading sun pinned wrong in the heavens, casting shadows too long, too dark, and irreconcilable with their antecedent objects. To birds hurtling wildly—careening, tumbling, shedding feathers like confetti, as if they'd been shot from a circus cannon. It was as if the planet had been knocked from its axis, jarred fifteen degrees from true—and not just the planet.

The city, so many miles behind me, seemed even more distant now—a dying ember in my memory. My life there, even my Saturday morning, seemed suddenly remote and abstract—barely a pantomime. The people on my street and in the metro, in the shops and cafés, were like figures in an ancient film—silent, stiff-limbed silhouettes, thinner than smoke. The grocer, the sour man at the newsstand, my garrulous neighbor—it seemed any breeze could take them all into this alien sky. I might've been away from the city for minutes or hours or for a year or more—I had no idea, or any notion of what I'd find when I returned. If I returned. I shuddered and rubbed my eyes, but the feelings of dislocation, strangeness, and dread persisted. It was almost dark when we arrived.

The great house was behind stone pillars and iron gates, down a brick drive bordered with pollarded trees and boxwoods still in burlap, and with brown lawns rolling away. The drive ran for half a mile and rose steeply at the end, to where the house loomed above the sea.

It was an ancient pile of ginger-colored stone, with a massive central section and two long wings that reached towards me. Scrolled and fluted stonework framed dark windows, and stone birds brooded beneath the eaves of a copper roof. The wings embraced a brick forecourt with a fountain in the middle, in gray stone that had fared poorly in the salt air. Its figures were blurred and blunted, and in the failing light I couldn't tell if the squat shapes spouting water were fish or frogs or demons, or if the male form they aimed at was bearing the world or heaving against a boulder. In either case, a thankless job.

The car swept around the court and stopped beneath a columned porte cochere. The driver remained still and mute behind the wheel but unlocked the rear doors. I'd barely wrestled my bag and briefcase to the bricks when she drove off again. The evening air was cold and briny, and a swirling wind raised funnels of stone dust and dry leaves. Beneath the lapping of the fountain and the sound of the receding car I could hear the heavy, restless shift of the sea.

Lights came on in the porte cochere, and one of the massive double doors swung back. A young woman stood there, small in the yawning doorway. She was slender and pale, in black boots, a gray skirt, and a black jacket with a mandarin collar. Her straight blond hair was parted in the middle and bound in a braid that hung over her left shoulder like the business end of a riding crop. Her white hands curled into fists, her lips made a skeptical line, and her large gray eyes narrowed. She looked at me for a long time—my battered luggage, my dark suit and coat, creased from the journey, my creased face and dark hair, tangled by the wind—before she spoke.

"You're from Security?" she asked. Her speech was precise, her voice low and controlled, as if it was perilous to give it rein.

"Yes," I said. "The Division of Security Standards—Standard Division."

"You have identification?" I drew ID from a breast pocket and handed her the case. She flipped it open, studied it, studied me, and flipped it shut. "Agent Myles," she said, and returned my ID.

"'Myles' will do."

"Why is it 'Standard Division'? Why don't you call it 'Standards Division'?"

I looked at her and shrugged. "Even we cannot control how the vernacular develops."

The woman shook her head. "We expected you earlier."

"It's a long drive."

"The cafeteria is this way," she said.

"There's no need, I'm not hungry."

She tilted her head at me as if I'd spoken in tongues. "The cafeteria is where we found the body," she said, and beckoned me on.

CHAPTER TWO

Saturday Evening

She introduced herself as Nadia Blom as she led me in, and told me she was assistant to Piers Witmer, the director of trials at Ondstrand Biologic and one of the company's founders. She walked the way she spoke, with precision and control, and her boot heels were like tack hammers.

We crossed a broad lobby, where the ginger stone walls and floor had been honed and polished to a glossy amber. The space was lit by a vast chandelier—a glowing nebula of interlaced bronze filaments. Nadia Blom's reflection as she proceeded was like the prow of a yacht on a golden sea. We stopped at a long stone counter emblazoned with the company's logo—an *OB* monogram in navy on a scarlet shield. There was a uniformed guard there, with white hair and a drinker's nose, minding a bank of security barriers. He sat up as Nadia approached. She pulled two plastic cards from a pocket and handed me one that read *Visitor.* She pressed her own card to a scanner, and a barrier slid back.

"After you," she said. "You can leave your bag. You'll get a photo pass when we determine what access you require."

I set my bag down, and the guard eyed it suspiciously. "As a rule, I require it all," I said. "Access to everything."

She only just suppressed a laugh. "No visitor gets that," she said, and walked down a corridor to an elevator bank.

I shrugged. "Have you encountered Standard Division before?" I asked.

"Until this morning, I didn't know it existed."

I nodded and followed her onto an elevator. The car was paneled in frosted glass. She pressed *0.* "It's the staff cafeteria," she said as we descended.

"You found the body this morning?" I asked.

"*I* didn't find it, but, yes, it was found this morning. Don't you know this? Dr. Witmer and Dr. Hasp were on for hours with you people."

The elevator doors opened to a white corridor with gray vinyl flooring, and I followed Nadia Blom out and to the left. Ceiling lights shuddered to life as we advanced.

"Who is Dr. Hasp?" I asked.

She stopped short and turned, squinting at me. "Who is . . . ? He's the *head* of Ondstrand—our chief science officer and CEO. He's one of our founders, along with Dr. Muir and Dr. Witmer—really *the* founder. How can you not know *that*? They were on for *hours*."

"They were not on for hours with me."

"Don't your people tell you *anything*? Don't they brief you?"

"As a rule, they find it's best if I hear things for myself. They believe less mediation means less bias introduced. My experience is that bias finds a way. Nevertheless . . ."

Lines appeared across her brow. "So what *do* you know?"

"About your company and what you do here: nothing. About the circumstances that led Dr. Witmer and Dr. Hasp to call on us today: also nothing."

Nadia Blom's mouth opened, but for a while no words came out. "Nothing at all? *Nothing?* Then what good are you?"

"A question I ask myself often. That said, if you'd care to relieve a bit of my ignorance, I might manage something productive. Or at least manage to keep busy."

She looked up and down the blank corridor, empty behind us, and still dark ahead. She sighed and crossed her arms and almost smiled again. "Your ignorance seems so *comprehensive*—which bit shall I relieve first?"

"Let's begin with you. How long have you worked here?"

She squinted. "Me? I joined two years ago."

"Joined from university?"

The squint became a frown. "From a graduate program. Dr. Hasp hired me."

"A graduate program in biology? Chemistry?"

"Business administration. My undergraduate degree is biochemistry."

"But you didn't continue with that. Why not?"

A scowl replaced the frown. "How is this relevant, Agent Myles? How does this possibly—"

" 'Myles' will do, Ms. Blom. Were you no good at biochemistry? Did you lose interest in it? Was the pay not sufficient?"

She leaned back. "I . . . I suppose it was *all of the above.* I realized that I was no better than good enough at the science, and that *good enough* was going to lead me into teaching, or something equally dull. I realized that the science itself was less interesting to me than how the science made its way in the world—the forces that directed that—the market forces. And, yes, I decided I wanted to make some money."

I nodded. "And Ondstrand Biologic fits the bill? You've not been disappointed?"

She uncrossed her arms and stood even more erect. "Not at all."

"No? Despite the fact that Dr. Hasp recruited you, yet two years later you don't work for him—not directly—but instead report to his subordinate. I assume that Dr. Witmer *is* his subordinate."

The frown returned, deeper than before, and pink patches rose on her cheeks, and on her neck above her collar. "Honestly, this is ridiculous—I don't see how my employment history or job satisfaction can possibly be relevant to the body we found in our cafeteria. But, for your information, *Agent* Myles: my employment with Ondstrand has entailed a rotation through *all* of the firm's operating areas—a program designed for me by Dr. Hasp himself, who has mentored me from my first day, and to whom I've *always* had a reporting line. So, no—I've never been disappointed here, the past ten minutes notwithstanding."

I nodded. "Are you his spy, then?"

"What?"

"Do you spy for Dr. Hasp? Do you report to him about goings-on in whatever department you're working in? Inefficiencies, discontents, ineptitudes, malfeasance, conflicts of interest, forbidden liaisons, unseemly ambitions—those sorts of things? I'd think he'd be interested—who wouldn't? Or is Dr. Hasp beyond such mundane concerns?"

The pink patches darkened to red. "You're outrageous and . . . offensive," she sputtered, and then the corridor lights behind us began to blink out. Nadia Blom drew a deep, slow breath. "We have to move; otherwise, we'll be in the dark," she said, and pivoted and walked away.

"I understand completely," I said.

We proceeded along more hallways. There were long stretches of white walls interrupted infrequently by frosted glass doors. The doors were closed, marked only by numbers, and affixed with security scanners. As I followed, I ventured onto less fraught ground.

"Tell me about Ondstrand—what it does, how long it's been doing it—that sort of thing."

Nadia Blom's shoulders relaxed minutely, and her speech fell into the practiced cadences of a tour guide. "Ondstrand Biologic was founded eleven years ago by the geneticist, virologist, and biochemist Dr. Terrence Hasp, along with cofounders Dr. Piers Witmer and Dr. Karen Muir, who today assist him in managing the company. The firm takes its name from Ondstrand Hall, a boarding school that Dr. Hasp attended as a boy, and that once occupied these premises.

"From its inception, Ondstrand Biologic's core business has been the design, development, and delivery of components of biological infrastructure crucial to genetic therapies, including the bespoke design of viral vectors, gene cassettes, and vector delivery systems."

Nadia Blom paused and glanced at me. "Does any of that make sense to you?" she asked.

"I know what 'bespoke' means."

She sighed. "I'll try to make it simple. Say you're treating a disease— let's call it *crippling rudeness*—that arises from a genetic anomaly. To treat it, you need to identify the faulty genetic sequences responsible and replace them with the correct ones. At the level of cells, you need a mechanism that will deliver a payload—in this case the anti-rudeness sequence—to the relevant target site, getting through all the cellular defenses along the way, and without breaking any china. It's a bit like launching a ballistic missile at a building halfway around the world, destroying the building, erecting a replacement, and all without waking the neighbors. Our clients develop the payloads—the genetic sequences—and locate the targets; we provide the missiles—the rockets and warheads—and make sure the payloads hit the bull's-eyes. Make sense?"

"Sounds rather martial for something therapeutic."

"I tried to make it accessible for you."

I smiled. "And your customers are . . . ?"

"By and large, we partner with pharmaceutical companies that are developing genetic therapies."

"By and large?"

"We've developed some therapies on our own, in-house; they're in the pipeline now. And we also partner with some non-pharma entities on special projects."

"'Non-pharma entities' meaning what?"

Nadia Blom sighed again. "Dr. Hasp would be best able to answer that."

I nodded. "And all this missile designing and warhead production and pipelining and non-pharma partnering—that all takes place here, at this facility?"

"Most of it. This is our corporate headquarters, and it's also where the science happens: the location of our research, development and prototyping labs. Some trials are run out of here, too. For production at scale, we contract with labs overseas."

"How many people work here?"

"Employees on-site? At last count two hundred seven, not including any trial participants who may also be here. Right now there are none of those."

"Does that two hundred seven account for most of the people employed by Ondstrand?" She nodded. "Not huge," I said.

"Not at all—our impact far exceeds our head count."

"I was thinking that it wasn't a large number of people in comparison to the size of this facility."

"We make good use of the campus. Besides the offices and laboratories in Ondstrand House, there's a fitness center in the north wing, along with staff apartments and guest rooms."

"Employees live here?" I asked as we rounded another corner.

"A fair number. Fifty here in the main house—mostly younger members of the science and corporate staffs. And Dr. Hasp lives in the Cottage—that's the old headmaster's residence, in the woods just beyond the north wing. And there are the former stables and the former carriage house near the south wing—those were converted to offices and to larger apartments. Another thirty or so staff live there."

"That accounts for eighty or so employees living here. Where do the other hundred twenty or so live? Surely they can't be commuting from the city every day?"

"Of course not. There's Soligstrand, just north of here, right on the coast—a lovely town, very popular for holidays. Many of the science staff and their families live there, and they've done wonders with the local schools over the years, with our help. Then there's Fiskdorp, to the south. Most of our support and maintenance staff live in that area. There's a lighthouse there, some pubs, a fishing fleet out of the harbor, not much else, really. And you probably came through Slocum on your way in—"

"A blink-and-you'll-miss-it sort of place?"

She nodded. "Some of the science staff lives there, too. Dr. Witmer and his wife, Dr. Muir, others."

"And you, Ms. Blom—where do you live? Or do you just curl up under your desk at the end of a long day?"

She stiffened again. "I have an apartment in the north wing."

I nodded. "You don't mind it? Being back in boarding school again? I'm assuming you went to boarding school the first time around."

Her eyes narrowed. "This is hardly boarding school, Agent Myles," she said. "A university campus might be closer, or a research institute, perhaps." We took another turn, passed the door to a stairwell, and, a few paces later, came to three doors quite unlike the others I'd seen since the elevator. They were old, wood-framed, with heavy brass doorknobs and windows of pebbled glass. I stopped, opened the first one, and peered inside.

"This rather undercuts your assertion," I said. It was a classroom, an old-fashioned sort, with one-armed wooden desks arranged in rows before a battered oak writing table and a chalkboard on a wooden stand. There were small windows set high on one wall, with views of window wells and a bit of sky. On another wall was a narrow cupboard door, and above it a clock in a wire cage, with hands frozen at two-fifty-seven.

"You send naughty scientists here to sit detention?"

Nadia Blom was unamused. "They're old Ondstrand Hall classrooms—the only rooms left untouched when the interiors were rebuilt for our purposes. This was a Latin classroom."

I opened the next door and found a classroom that looked very much like the first, but for an array of world maps on the back wall.

"Geography?" I asked, and Blom nodded. Then I opened the third door. It had the same one-armed desks, here facing a long, black-topped table. The table held an assortment of antique labware—clouded flasks, beakers and retorts of mysterious purpose, a stone mortar and pestle, a blackened ceramic crucible, and a gas burner with a hose like dead flesh. There was a scarred oak lectern beside the bench, and behind it, across the room's back wall, a slate chalkboard.

"It's the room where Dr. Hasp attended his very first chemistry lecture," Nadia Blom volunteered. "He says he preserved it as a tribute to the first sparking of his scientific imagination."

I stepped in and caught no whiff of imagination. Instead, I smelled chalk dust, ancient wood, floor wax, and the manufactured lemon scent of industrial disinfectant—the perfume of my own unlovely, itinerant school days. Top notes of tedium and bureaucratic callousness, middle notes of aching loneliness, and base notes of fierce and unpredictable violence. It left me chilled and vaguely nauseated, and I stepped back into the corridor and shook my head.

"It wants wax figures," I said. "A droning lecturer, perhaps some dozing students."

Nadia Blom scowled, shook her head, and pressed on, down a blank hall and around a corner. Then we came to the cafeteria.

CHAPTER THREE

Saturday Evening

There were glass partitions at the end of the corridor that could close to form a frosted wall or open to make a wide passage. They were open just then, and beyond them was a field of white tables awash in chilly white light. Some were refectory-style affairs, with matching white benches, and others were smaller, for two or four people, with angular chairs that would encourage brief meals. The space opened to the left and right into more dining areas, and the walls were hung with paintings—color-saturated geometrics that brought to mind nautilus shells and DNA. Straight ahead was the food-service area—a run of refrigerated cabinets, glass-and-steel serving counters, a curved steel track for trays to slide along, and, behind it all, an industrial kitchen. There were two men at the nearest table, and they rose as we approached. One of them stepped forward.

"Lose your compass, Nads?" the man said. "Forget your wilderness skills?" His tone was bluff and jocular, his undertone needling. He was fortyish, broad-shouldered, heavy with muscle, and tall—taller than me—with an immaculately shaved head, glittering black eyes, a meaty nose, and a carefully barbered scruff. He wore paddock boots, tan corduroys, a chunky brown roll-neck, and a diving watch that bristled with complications and might've weighed ten pounds.

Nadia Blom colored slightly and cleared her throat. "Dr. Terrence Hasp, Agent Myles."

He looked me up and down, nodded slightly, and put out a large hand. "From Standard Division, yes? Never actually met a field agent before. Does one shake hands?"

I nodded back. "'Myles' will do," I said and grasped his hand. His grip had a rubbery strength.

"Myles it is, then. Myles, this is Piers Witmer—runs Trials."

Witmer was also in the neighborhood of forty. He was smaller, with a runner's narrow frame and a wiry build. He had a head of black curls salted with gray, a handsome, clean-shaven face, pale and lean, with deep-set blue eyes. In his rumpled khakis, untucked blue shirt, and shapeless navy sweater, he looked like an aging adjunct professor—underslept, overworked, perpetually insecure. His hand was damp and his grip quick.

"We haven't moved her, or anything else," he said. "Haven't touched a thing." His voice was quiet and deeper than I expected, ideal for hosting an opera broadcast.

"'Course not," Hasp said, annoyed. "Why would we? Your head office told us not to—not to touch anything, not to notify the locals, not to do anything but sit tight and wait for you. And so we have. Waited quite a while."

"Who found her?" I asked.

"Kitchen staff, name of Willis," Hasp answered. "They were cleaning up after breakfast; Willis went to fetch something from the walk-in, and there she was."

"And Willis is where now?"

"Staff lounge in the south-wing basement," Hasp said, "with the other three on his shift and the security guard who they called. Your people told us to isolate them, so that's what we did. Closed the cafeteria, too, with a story about a gas leak."

I nodded. "Then let's have a look."

Hasp led and we followed, behind the service counters and into the kitchen. It was a steel cavern of prep stations, ovens, and cooktops. The back quarter of the space, from one side of the kitchen to the other, was hung, floor to ceiling, with heavy-gauge plastic sheeting, punctuated with several door-shaped passages sealed by zips.

"What's going on there?" I asked.

"Construction," Hasp said. "Just finishing up. Replaced the dishwashers and dryers with more efficient gear. Greener. All this was supposed to come down today, but we turned the clean-up crew away. Guess we'll make do with paper plates a bit longer."

I nodded, and we passed through the kitchen and down a corridor lined with steel shelves stacked with pots and pans. There were walk-in pantries beyond, and then a walk-in refrigerator and a matching freezer. There was a clear plastic glove hanging on the handle of the refrigerator.

"Tried not to add to any prints that might be there already," Hasp said, and he put his hand on the glove and opened the door. A light went on inside, and a wave of cold air rolled out. Blom and Witmer stepped aside, and I followed Hasp to the door.

The refrigerated room was lined with high shelves and stocked with produce, dairy, fish, and meat, in clear plastic bins. It was pin-neat, except for the body on the floor.

The woman was in her middle thirties, trim and fit, with cropped red hair the color of an autumn maple. And she had been pretty—more than pretty—in an elfin way, before someone had dumped her like a sack of laundry. She lay on her left side with her knees drawn to her waist, her left arm tucked beneath her, and her right arm flung out in front. Her upturned face was gray and slack-featured, and she seemed to stare behind her right shoulder through clouded, half-closed eyes. She wore a thin chain of pink gold around her neck—a neck that had clearly been broken.

I knelt beside her. She wore running shoes that looked as if they'd actually been run in, black athletic pants with zips at the bottom and a white stripe down the side, and a matching jacket that zipped up the front. Her hand was limp and gray; the nails were cranberry-red, clipped short, and recently manicured. There was grit beneath them, and around the gold signet ring on her pinky finger, too. I took a closer look at her shoes and found sand in the treads, and also crusted around the zippered cuffs of her pants, on the knees, and on the sleeve of her jacket. I took out my phone and took some pictures.

I stepped out of the refrigerator, waved Hasp out of the way, and knelt in the doorway. No drag marks that I could see, but on this kind of flooring they might not show. I stood again and pointed down the corridor.

"Where does this go?" I asked.

Hasp answered. "There's a washroom down there, closets, lockers, and the loading dock, where the food and whatnot comes in."

I took a pair of nitrile gloves from my pocket and went down the corridor, opening doors. One closet of cleaning supplies; another of table linens and kitchen whites, folded and baled from the laundry; a bathroom; and then a small locker room, with a bench and six metal lockers. At the end of the corridor was a cement foyer and a set of double doors. Beside the doors were three metal-sided dumpsters. They were on wheels, and each was about three feet by four feet, and about four feet high. Two of them were full to brimming with construction debris: bits of drywall and plastic pipe, tangled lengths of hose and wire, dangerous-looking ribbons of sheet metal. The third dumpster was about half full of similar trash, and beside it, in a more or less tidy heap, was enough rubbish to fill up the other half.

Hasp looked at the dumpsters and wrinkled his brow. I opened the double doors and saw nothing but two empty loading bays, an empty stretch of drive, empty concrete steps, and a security camera high up in the corner.

"Are these the only two exits to the kitchen and cafeteria—the way we came in and the loading dock?"

"Yup," Hasp said.

I nodded and returned to the closets in the hall. I looked at the laundry. "These linens—the tablecloths and napkins—you use them in the cafeteria?"

Hasp, Witmer, and Blom glanced at one another, puzzled. Hasp shook his head and pointed up. "They're for the executive dining room, upstairs. The kitchen serves both."

"Is there an elevator between here and there? A stairway?"

Hasp shook his head. "Dumbwaiters. Meals go up, waiters serve them, dirty dishes come down. Same with the linens."

"Show me," I said.

Hasp was momentarily irked. "They're over here somewhere," he muttered, and we followed him back to the kitchen and along a side wall towards the rear of the space, where the construction barrier was hung. He stopped at a large rectangular column that jutted from the side wall and that was bisected down its length by the plastic sheeting. At first glance, I thought there were two oversized wall ovens set side by side on the column, at about waist height, but I was wrong.

I pulled open the steel door of one and stuck my head inside. The dumbwaiters were more vertical conveyor belts than simple up-and-down lifts. Each one had six generous bays, and each bay was divided with racks to accommodate trays. There was a matching pair of doors on the opposite side of the column, so that trays full of meals could be loaded from one side, and trays of dirty dishes unloaded from the other. Beside each door were controls, including a button that advanced the bays one at a time, and another that set them into continuous, slow rotation, with only a brief pause between station stops.

I took a penlight from my breast pocket and set the dumbwaiters to run continuously. I watched the bays pass quietly by until two appeared that had no dividing racks. I hit the *stop* button, flicked on my penlight, leaned in again, and stared at some bits of sand that glistened in the narrow beam. I emerged after a while and turned off the light. Hasp, Witmer, and Blom were staring at me, waiting.

"Has the dining room upstairs been open all day?"

Hasp shook his head. "Executive dining is usually closed on the weekends."

"I'll need to go up there."

Once again we trooped behind Hasp, back through the kitchen and the service and seating areas, past the old classrooms, past a stairwell, to an elevator bank, and up one floor.

The executives, whoever they were, clearly dined in style. Whereas in the staff cafeteria there was a chilly sea of white tables, here was the first-class lounge of a premium air carrier—the kind of space designed to soothe and swaddle long-haul travelers, and to remind them constantly of their privilege. The aesthetic was spare and modern, but warm—muted lighting, blond woods to go with the honeyed stone, thick rugs, big abstracts on the walls suggesting seascapes, and broad windows with expansive views of lawn and wood. There was a lounge area with a gas fire and sleek sofas and chairs. Beyond was a dining room with white linen on the tables and upholstered seats, a full bar along one wall, and on another a stretch of glass-fronted refrigerator cabinets stocked with bottled water, juices, and a variety of healthful and attractive snacks. Adjoining them was a coffee station—whole beans, grinders, automated brewers of espresso and pretty much anything else.

"Who are the fortunate who enjoy all this?" I asked as we made our way through the luxury.

"The corporate office," Hasp said. "Also, the heads of the divisions, their chiefs of staff, admin heads, and department heads. They all have access, along with guests."

I nodded, and Hasp led us through a door by the bar and down a hallway to four bathrooms—identical white-tiled rooms, each with a toilet, a sink, a mirror, a steel shelf holding paper towels, and a trash bin. Beyond the bathrooms was a glass-walled, refrigerated wine room and, at the end of the hall, the dumbwaiters, side by side on the wall.

I opened the dumbwaiter doors and ran my penlight around the edges of the openings and over the floor beneath.

"Would there have been much traffic here today?" I asked.

Hasp, Witmer, and Blom exchanged quizzical glances. Hasp answered. "Shouldn't have been any."

I nodded and slipped my penlight back into my pocket. "Okay," I said. "Tell me about her."

The four of us adjourned to the executive dining room and sat at one of the round tables. Hasp pushed up his sleeves and rested his hairy forearms on the white tablecloth. "Name's Allegra—Allegra Stans. Dr. Allegra Stans. Been with us about seven years—that's right, isn't it, Wit, seven years?" Witmer nodded gravely, and so did Nadia Blom. "She's a virologist—was a virologist—and a damn fine one. Well, all our people are damn fine—wouldn't have 'em otherwise. But Allegra was top-notch. Hired her myself, after her postdoc. Brilliant bibliography for someone that young. Started here in R&D—vector evaluations to begin with, then did a long stint in Special Projects with Karen Muir, and recently came back to R&D, working for Mario Pohl." Hasp looked down at his big hands and shook his head. "Unbelievable, this whole thing," he muttered. "Just unbelievable."

I looked at Witmer and Blom. "Did either of you know her well?"

"Of course we did," Witmer said.

Hasp scowled. "A place this small—everyone knows everyone to some extent. Wit worked with her, back when he ran R&D. She was very talented—very smart, curious, tireless—wasn't she, Wit?"

Witmer nodded absently.

"I never worked with her," Blom offered. "But I observed that she was quite . . . personable."

I nodded. "Was she married?" I asked. "Does she have family?"

"She wasn't married," Nadia Blom said, "and according to our records her closest relatives are a sister in the city, and a brother living overseas."

"Your people said they'd handle notification," Hasp added.

I nodded. "Where did Allegra herself live?"

Blom nodded. "She had an apartment in the north wing."

"And was she particularly close with any other employees? A best friend? A lover?"

Hasp looked at Witmer, who looked at Blom. Their heads shook in near unison. "Dunno," Hasp answered.

"Was she seeing anyone at all—if not here, then from outside?" This time I got shrugs. I sighed and rose from the table. "All right, then," I said.

They looked puzzled. "Do you want to see her apartment?" Hasp asked.

"I'll get to that, but until then, I'd like your security staff to secure it against any entry. Dr. Stans's office as well."

Hasp nodded and looked at Nadia, who nodded back. "And the kitchen staff, and security guard?" Hasp asked. "Will you be interviewing them tonight?"

"I will."

Hasp frowned. "What about the body? Can it be moved? Can we get it out of the kitchen and get the caf reopened? Can we get it moved off-site?"

I raised an eyebrow. "Forensics will see it off, after they've done what they need to do."

Hasp looked as if he wanted to complain, but he didn't. Not quite. "Forensics, eh? Makes sense, though I'm sure you appreciate we don't want to upset the natives round here. Small community, tight ship—great for teamwork and camaraderie, et cetera, but the downside is, any ripple can tip the canoe, if you catch my drift. Got some big deadlines coming, and we want to keep everything humming if we can." He stopped and looked at me and saw something, then added: "Not to be insensitive."

"Of course not," I said.

"These forensics—when will they be coming?"

"I expect they were dispatched soon after I was, so they should arrive presently. Until then, if someone can arrange a room for me—someplace I can wash my face and make some notes."

Hasp looked at Nadia Blom. "Nads, you'll sort that, too?"

She nodded. "We've arranged a guest suite for Agent Myles in the north wing, third floor."

"Once forensics get here, they'll need to walk around—at a minimum around the cafeteria, the kitchen, the loading dock, outside the building, and of course up here. Hopefully, access won't be a problem."

" 'Course not, whatever they need," Hasp said. "Nads?"

"I'll see to it."

"There's the matter of my own access as well," I said, holding up my visitor's badge.

Hasp looked at Nadia Blom. "Is there a problem?"

She colored and stammered, "No problem, just a question of what level."

His jaw tightened. "Whatever the hell he asks for, Nads—this is *Standard Division*, for shit's sake."

Nadia Blom nodded and looked at me. I smiled.

CHAPTER FOUR

Saturday Night–Sunday Early Morning

Jane Wilding's forensics team arrived about an hour later, in three unmarked black vans, and they left the same way well after midnight. Before she departed, Jane spoke with me. We were at the loading dock behind the kitchen, beside one of her vans, under harsh floodlight, and Jane was climbing out of her white jumpsuit. She put a hand on my shoulder to balance as she tugged her foot free. I could smell soap from the waves of her short, dark hair, notes of pear and freesia from her perfume, and the faint tang of her sweat, before the sea breeze carried everything away.

"You look tired," she said. "Did you manage some food?"

"Until just recently, I was talking to the people that found the body. I did manage a few cups of coffee, though."

"Sounds like my meal plan. The kitchen crew tell you anything interesting?"

"Only that everything was as it usually was yesterday morning: They came on-shift at six a.m., turned things on, started prepping for breakfast, which meant going in the fridge. There was no body there then; two and a half hours or so later, there was. Nobody saw anything or anyone out of place the whole time, but they were short-staffed and had their hands full throughout the shift, and may not have noticed if something was amiss. All of them knew Stans by sight; a couple of the people knew her name; none of them knew her any better than that. Is that interesting?"

"Time will tell," Jane said.

"And you?"

She stood up straight, took her hand back, and started rolling her jumpsuit. Her generous mouth curved in a wry grin. "You mean: *How have I been? What do I ponder on those dark, frosty nights? Do my feet still get cold?*" Her green eyes were bright in the floodlight.

"Have you anything to tell me about the body or the scene?"

She brushed off the sleeves of her plaid shirt and the legs of her jeans. "All business, then. In which case, no, I don't have much yet. Her neck is broken—that's clear. Pretty sure we're going to find damage to the C2, the C3 maybe, other bits as well, perhaps—lot of force used. I'd guess it happened fast, though, no time to put up a fight—no sign of it anyway, at first glance. Nothing defensive: no skin under her nails; she didn't bite anything."

"Any thoughts on time of death?"

"None I'll swear to yet—the refrigeration complicates things. But my guess right now it was within two to three hours of when the body was discovered."

"So, as early as five-thirty?"

Jane nodded. "Subject to revision. There is some indication of recent sexual intercourse, but we'll know more about that when we get her on the table."

"Indications of sexual assault?" I asked.

"Nothing to suggest it," Jane said, stuffing her jumpsuit into a plastic bag. "There was sand on her shoes and clothing, even some on her hands. And there were the traces of sand that you found in the dumbwaiter itself, and around the dumbwaiter station in the fancy dining room. I sent my guys down to the beach to collect comparison samples. Had them poke around the paths and the lawn between here and there, too. They did find sandy footprints—too many of 'em, unfortunately. They took pictures of the ones in this vicinity—see if we can match 'em to her treads."

"How about fingerprints?"

"An embarrassment of riches, sorry to say—they're everywhere. At some point we're going to need comparison samples."

"I've got the kitchen and security staff that were there, for starters. Was there anything in her pockets?"

"Besides her jewelry—her signet ring, a chain necklace—her personal effects consisted of: driver's license, company ID, apartment key. I'll send pictures."

"No mobile phone?"

"Not that we found," she said. "We did find the missing racks from the dumbwaiter bays. They were behind a trolley in the executive dining room. No prints on them."

"Did you get those dumpsters?"

"We did, and we pulled some prints, too—some lovely ones from the sheet metal."

"And the pile of rubbish beside them?"

"We processed that as well."

I nodded and was quiet for a while. Jane watched me. "You think someone could drag a body from the dumbwaiter in the kitchen, down the hall, and into the fridge?" I asked finally. "And not be seen?"

"The dragging part wouldn't be hard," Jane said. "It's a short trip—a dozen paces, perhaps—and she wasn't a big person. It's the not-being-seen part that would be tricky."

"But with a small number of kitchen staff on duty, all busy up front with cooking and serving, and with the dumbwaiters being back in the corner, and not in use, and one set of doors being behind the construction barrier . . . it would be a risk, but not impossible."

"This speculative stuff is more your turf," Jane said, "but it seems to me you'd have to be desperate."

"You'd have to be improvising."

Jane shook her head. "Improvising and damn lucky," she said.

"Until luck ran out. Ondstrand Protection reports that the only thing out of the ordinary yesterday morning was a delivery from the kitchen linen service—a delivery that should've been made the day before. The truck passed through the service gate at seven-fifty-nine, and security reports they buzzed open the loading dock doors for them at eight-oh-five. The linen people were in and out again by eight-eleven."

"And your theory is—what?—that they interrupted someone moving Dr. Stans's body?"

I nodded. "I think the refrigerator amounted to *any port in a storm*—the easiest place to dump a body when the loading dock was suddenly out of the question."

Jane squinted and shook her head. "You think the killer originally planned to take the body out through the loading dock? Past the security camera?"

"Not out past the cameras; to a dumpster parked inside, by the doors."

Jane smiled and shook her head. "To that half-empty dumpster?" I nodded. "Put her in there and cover her up, and—what?—let the construction crew haul her off? You think the killer took the trash out of that bin to make room?" I nodded again. "Sounds a bit wild to me, Myles."

I nodded again. "As a plan it is mad—nothing anyone would opt for if they had a choice. But as improvisation . . ."

She laughed. "You spin a lovely tale, Myles—you always have—but better you than me. I'm happy to tend to the known world—or the knowable one, at any rate." I smiled. "Guess you'll be out here for a bit," she said.

"It may take longer than that," I answered.

She gave me a skeptical look, the default setting of her lovely oval face. "For you—the Director's pet and star pupil? Not unless you want to cadge some extra time by the sea." Then she squinted at me and tilted her head. "Though, now that I look more closely, I see you could use a little sun, a little fresh air. You're in rougher shape than some of my customers."

I was about to say thanks when the loading-dock doors swung open and two of Wilding's techs carried out a black body bag.

"Seriously, Myles," she said, squeezing my arm, "get some rest."

I was watching the vans recede along the service road when Nadia Blom emerged from the loading-dock doorway behind me. Her black jacket and gray skirt were rumpled here and there, but her braid was as wicked-looking as ever.

"Your Dr. Wilding seems very capable," she said. I nodded. "She said I should ask you if we could get a cleaning crew in and get the kitchen and the cafeteria up and running again."

"That should be fine," I said.

She nodded and slipped a hand into her jacket pocket. She came out with an Ondstrand ID card. "For you," she said. "Brand-new. It should get you wherever you need to go."

I took it from her. "Thank you," I said, yawning.

Blom looked at me. "Did you sleep in those clothes?"

"Not yet," I said.

"Would you like coffee? The machines in the executive dining room do a fine job."

"Just a bed, I think."

"Can you find your way back to your quarters?" she asked.

"Blindfolded and in the dark," I answered.

CHAPTER FIVE

Sunday Early Morning

My quarters in the north wing were comprised of three rooms: a lounge with a sofa, low table, desk, and chair; a small bedroom; and a bathroom. The floors and walls were the same ginger stone that was everywhere else in Ondstrand House, here covered in pale-gray rugs, and hung with framed photos of microbes taken with an electron microscope. The aesthetic was modern, minimalist, and chilly, and, as with the cafeteria chairs, the intent seemed to be to discourage extended stays. I took off my suit jacket and tie and slung them on a chair. The bed was beckoning—shouting my name, in fact—but I had one more thing to do.

I left my bag by the door and dug into my briefcase for a pad, a pen, and my tablet. Then I dropped on the sofa, switched on my tablet, and called Director Mehta. She answered on the first ring. Her handsome, sharp-featured face and thick, wavy hair—ink-black shot with silver—filled my screen. She reached a slender hand up to touch a chunky silver earring.

"Enjoying the salt air, Myles?" she asked. Her voice was soft, smooth, and dangerous—like honey on a dagger—and a rueful laugh was never far off.

I nodded. "Restorative, Director. I hope I'm not calling too late."

"Not at all."

"The forensics team is on its way home, with Dr. Stans's body. Thank you for sending Dr. Wilding."

Director Mehta smiled minutely and nodded. "You two work well together. What else can I do for you?"

"I'll need a porter."

She sighed. "Of course you will. I've assigned Goss Ivessen."

I nodded. "That's good—he doesn't require much sleep."

"I believe that's more to do with self-medication than his innate qualities."

"Nonetheless, he's the best of them."

"And, conveniently, the only one willing to work with you these days."

"The rest are lazy sods."

She snorted delicately. "Hardly. If you would take a partner, you wouldn't strain the porters so, and they wouldn't be in open revolt at the prospect of working with you."

"All but Ivessen," I said.

The Director ignored me. "And we wouldn't find ourselves having this conversation again and again. It's been two years since we lost Ms. Lake, Myles."

"Not quite two—not yet."

"Near enough. And at one year it was already past time."

I stared into the camera and said nothing.

"You realize I'm indulging you, yes?" she said. I nodded, and the Director smiled minutely. "A small victory, then."

I smiled back at her. "There are next of kin for Allegra Stans," I said. "A sister in the city, a brother overseas."

"Yes, Ivessen is on that already."

"And there's the staff that found her—I'll send their names."

"And we will remind them emphatically of the virtue of discretion. Any initial thoughts, having seen the body *in situ*?"

I nodded and told Director Mehta what Jane Wilding and I had found, and my interpretation.

Her brow wrinkled. "Impulse and improvisation—a crime of passion, then?"

I shrugged. "It's all preliminary."

"How could it be otherwise? What did you make of Terry Hasp? Enjoy him?"

"As I enjoy every strutting ass I meet."

Director Mehta sighed. "So judgmental, Myles. You're nothing if not consistent."

"Have you met him?"

"Only on-screen."

"He wants to maintain business as usual around here. And he doesn't want a trivial thing like murder to upset his applecart."

"Not surprising," she said. "And, of course, we'd like to keep his applecart upright, too, if possible." I didn't answer. Director Mehta sighed again. "It doesn't make him a bad man, Myles, being a strutting ass, wanting to keep his operation running. It doesn't make him worse than other men. Not necessarily."

"Is that all the guidance you have for me at this point? Or is there anything you'd like to add about Hasp or Ondstrand or anything at all, by way of context?"

"It sounds as if you have a specific question in mind."

"The 'non-pharma entities' that Ondstrand contracts with—I assume those include the security services."

She tilted her head very slightly to the right. "Government is a vast and varied enterprise, with many fields of interests and many partners."

I shook my head. "And always complete transparency. You're nothing if not consistent."

Director Mehta smiled. Her teeth were immaculate and bright. "Good night, Myles. Don't be a stranger."

"Good night, Director."

My tablet went dark, and I stretched my arms in front of me and over my head. *It's been two years. . . .* Actually, one year, eleven months, two weeks and five days, and the accretion of days had done nothing to diminish the loss. Tessa Lake—my training officer during my first year out of Conservatory, then my partner, then . . . no more. A rarity, that—a training officer taking on her trainee as a partner—but so it was for us, for eight years. And then, for a few months, we were more than partners. That's rarer still, or so we are led to believe, as it's in contravention of a dozen or more Division Policy Statements. Violation of service oath. Conflict of interest. Destabilization of the chain of command. Undermining of unit cohesion. Conduct unbecoming. Punishable by, punishable by, punishable by. Any worries I might've had about such transgressions were made moot, in the end, by Tessa's death.

Lost on mission overseas, the report read—remains not recovered. Her solo assignment was another rarity, almost unheard of. One year, eleven months, etc., and still the hollow ache. I indulged in a moment of memory: of her lanky frame, her milky skin and thick black hair, which smelled always of patchouli, her wide, skeptical mouth and even more skeptical eyes—cobalt-blue and always looking askance—her speed and unexpected strength. A moment's indulgence was sufficient—just enough to sharpen the pain and lodge it in my solar plexus. I shook my head, breathed deep, and glanced into the bedroom, at the waiting pillows. Instead, I woke my tablet again.

Goss Ivessen had an ancient voice—doleful, exhausted, and hoarse, like that of a paid mourner long past retirement. As usual, his camera was trained on a wall in his porter's lodge—digs so unlike the antiseptic quarters of the other porters I'd worked with. Just then I was looking at a long run of shadowed bookshelves—bowed and laden far beyond safety with mildewed volumes, crumbling journals, and odd bits of stained paper. The papers stirred fitfully in what I assumed was a musty draft, or perhaps at the passage of Ivessen's cat—a creature I knew only by its perpetual irritated mewling.

On the many operations I'd worked with Ivessen, I'd seen little more of him than these perilous shelves, the shadow of his angry cat, the rare glimpse of his surprisingly patrician silhouette, like the profile of an emperor on a crumbling coin, and his terrible hands. They were gnarled, battered things, with ropy veins and swollen joints, and were—from wrists to crushed fingertips—gloved in scars. I'd never learned the story behind those hands, though I was certain the Director knew it. Even so, I never asked, and she was not the volunteering sort.

I heard Ivessen at his keyboard—an impossibly rapid glissando of strokes—and wondered at his fluency. The typing stopped abruptly.

"Myles," he whispered, "for my many sins, I once more find you at my door."

I nodded. "I suppose you have much to atone for. You've spoken with the Director?"

"She spoke to me; mine is but to listen and to serve." Irony was heavy in his weary voice.

"She briefed you?"

"In her fashion. Ondstrand Biologic, Ondstrand House, Dr. Allegra Stans, murder. I am to support you in any and all ways that I am able."

I nodded. "You'll be receiving whatever passes for security footage here, along with the entry and exit logs of whatever they maintain logs for. The first question is: Who was in Ondstrand House at the time of the murder?"

The typing began again. "Do we know what that time was?"

"Dr. Wilding estimates, provisionally, that it might've been as early as three hours prior to the body being discovered. That was at eight-thirty this morning, so that makes our start time five-thirty a.m."

"Understood. Presumably not many people at work at that hour on a Saturday."

"Some of the staff is in residence here—fifty of them in the main building, another thirty or so elsewhere on the campus. That makes eighty or so on a typical day, but, this being a holiday weekend . . ."

"Possibly fewer. A list of resident staff would be helpful."

"You'll get it."

"Anything else for now?"

I nodded. "Background on six. Hasp, Terrence, Doctor. He runs the show here. Witmer, Piers, Doctor. A senior scientist of some sort, runs trials for the company. Muir, Karen, Doctor, another senior scientist, and the deceased's former boss. Pohl, Mario, Doctor, yet another scientist, and the deceased's current boss. Blom, Nadia. Not a scientist; responsibilities vague and administrative. And, of course, Allegra Stans."

"Of course. Anything in particular that you're interested in?"

"Nothing in particular; everything in general. And let's make sure to include financials. Also, I'm given to understand that Ondstrand has a contract—possibly several—with some elements of the security services. That likely means security clearances for some staff. See if those include any of the names on our list. If so, let's pull their clearance packages."

He made a noise that might've been a chuckle. "Very well," he said. "Always a pleasure, Myles." And then the screen went dark.

I shut down my tablet, rose and stretched, and felt rust on every joint. I carried my bag to the bedroom, ran water in the bathroom sink, and sluiced it on my face. Then I opened the bedroom window and leaned out. The salt air was like a blade on my cheeks. My view was of the courtyard and the fountain, lit by ground spots. The plashing water sounded like a whispered incantation, and the shadows of the fountain's weather-worn statues leapt and shook on the façade of Ondstrand House. Neither fish nor frogs, but demons every one.

CHAPTER SIX

Sunday Morning

Nadia Blom met me outside my rooms after my all-too-brief sleep, to escort me to Allegra Stans's company apartment. I had showered and shaved by then and, in a concession to Sunday, traded my dark suit, white shirt, and tie for dark trousers, white shirt, and black pullover. Blom wore jeans and a fawn roll-neck, and her braid was like a lurking familiar as I followed her down the quiet corridors for what seemed a walk of a mile or so.

Blom was less agitated today, perhaps because the kitchen and dining rooms had returned to normal operations, or because she'd been given some marching orders by Dr. Hasp.

"He agreed with your people on the phone yesterday that we could notify staff of Dr. Stans's death—though not of the circumstances, or the particulars of where and how her body was discovered. He agreed also to caution staff that this information, until further notice, is to be treated as confidential—internal to Ondstrand Biologic—in order to minimize interference with ongoing investigations."

I stifled a laugh, and Blom looked at me. "Is that really all it takes here—a word from Dr. Hasp to end whispers and leaks?" I said.

"This is a close-knit community, and very loyal." I shrugged, and she continued. "In any event, Dr. Hasp has drafted a memo and would like you to review it before it's distributed."

She handed me a single page, and I stopped to read. I handed it back. "In that last bit, where he talks about the investigation, instructs them all to cooperate to the fullest, and asks that anyone who saw her in the past forty-eight hours come forward—he identifies me as being from Standard Division. Have him change that to identify me simply as a representative of the security services."

"Why? You are from Standard Division."

"I prefer not to lead with that. It means nothing to people who've never heard of us—they're just confused—but people who do know of us are often made anxious. Neither of those is particularly helpful to me."

"Doesn't 'security services' make people anxious?"

I smiled. "Not in the same way."

Nadia Blom scribbled some notes on the page, folded it, and slid it into her back pocket. As we approached Allegra Stans's apartment, she produced a key. A uniformed security guard was outside the door, sitting in a metal folding chair. He stood when he saw us coming, folded his chair, nodded to Nadia Blom, and departed.

There was a nameplate above the spyhole—*Dr. A. Stans.* Blom worked the lock. "There we go," she said as she turned the key. She held the door for me to enter, and was about to follow when I blocked her way. She stumbled back into the corridor.

"What are you doing?" she said.

"I'll need the key," I said, and she handed it over.

"What are you doing?"

"I'm closing the door, and you are staying outside."

"What?"

"You can wait here, or not. Your choice."

She was saying something in reply when the door swung shut.

Allegra Stans's apartment was filled with northern light that fell in pale beams through three large windows. It fell on the stone floors of the open kitchen to my right, on the dining area straight ahead, and into the living room to my left. Some even made its way to the foyer, where I stood and pulled on nitrile gloves. I took a deep breath and smelled stale air and a vegetal odor.

There was a coat closet to my immediate right, which held—no surprise—her coats. All the pockets were empty save one—the right-hand zippered pocket of a light down jacket in forest green. In it was a receipt, dated last week, from someplace called Sunnyside Salon and Spa, for a manicure. There were a couple of rain-and-wind shells for running on a closet hook, and a couple of pairs of running shoes on the closet floor. They were the same make as those she'd worn in the refrigerator. They had the same grit in their treads, too.

Allegra's kitchen was a sparse thing—barely equipped, hardly stocked, seldom called upon. It had the basic appliances, but they were lightly used, if used at all—the warranty card was still taped inside the wall oven—and her crockery, cutlery, and glassware barely amounted to service for one. Only her coffeemaker seemed to have gotten regular work. Her refrigerator wasn't entirely barren: There were several containers of yogurt that she could have eaten with her one spoon, a carton of orange juice for her single glass, and a small container of cream for the coffee in her lone mug. The nearest thing to solid food was a leftover slice of tiramisu in a container from someplace called Beacon Bistro.

The dining area had never been used for anything close and was where, on a glass-topped trestle table, Allegra had set up a workspace, with a laptop, a pile of notebooks, and a sleek desktop computer that had a massive screen and a label on the back declaring it property of Ondstrand Biologic. I leafed through the notebooks and found page after impenetrable page of organic-chemistry diagrams drawn in ink, in a neat, fast hand. There was also a stack of papers—printouts of articles from journals of virology, biochemistry, and genetics. From the little I could follow, the broad subject matter seemed to be proteins, techniques to fold them, and the implications of folding them this way or that. I took pictures of the title pages and restacked them. Then I powered up both computers but got no further; I had passwords for neither. I closed Stans's laptop, placed it by the door, and moved to the living room.

In which, it seemed, not much living took place. There was a lounge chair, a small sofa, and a credenza with a television on top. A vase stood next to the television, with six shriveled tulips in a millimeter of brown slurry, and a slender tripod in gray aluminum was folded and leaning in a corner. There was a mounting head, but nothing affixed there. I moved to the hallway.

There were more closets there, a linen closet with two pillowcases in it, a closet with a single, spotless broom, and another closet that held a stacked washer and dryer. The next door was to the bathroom.

There was a stall shower with a dry face cloth hanging from a knob, and a razor, a bottle of expensive shampoo, and another of bath gel on a shelf. There was also a sink stained with toothpaste, a vanity with a jar of pricy face cream and used cotton swabs on it, a streaked mirror, a toilet, and a laundry hamper overflowing with clothes.

There was a cabinet behind the mirror, but I found little inside it: the usual dental products, face scrub, moisturizer, and sunscreen, bottles of perfume, deodorant, and something that looked like deodorant but was a lotion that distance runners slathered on to protect against chafing. I closed the cabinet and looked at the hamper. A musty, humid smell emanated from it and dominated the room. I wondered if Sunday was Allegra Stans's usual washing day, or if any day was.

I stepped into the bedroom.

There was a king-sized bed against the wall in front of me, the sheets and blankets twisted as if someone had just thrown them off. It was flanked by an angular nightstand and a matching dresser. There was another dresser on the adjacent wall, with a mirror above it, and next to that, by the window, a writing table and chair. Opposite the bed was a wardrobe, and on the floor a shaggy pink rug, like the pelt of a storybook beast.

I started with the nightstand. It was stacked with papers—more printed journal articles, and just as arcane. Again I took pictures of the title pages. Then I opened the nightstand drawer.

Which was more understandable: two running magazines, a bottle of vitamins, some hair clips, a half-empty box of condoms in green foil wrappers, a tube of lubricant—water soluble and flavor-free—and, in a discreet travel case, a small silver vibrator. Beside the vibrator was a leather pouch, square and weighty, that fit in the palm of my hand. I unzipped it and found a camera.

It was a digital model, with a tiny screen on the back and even tinier buttons. I touched one, and the screen flashed. A little icon told me the camera's battery was nearly drained. I pressed another, and the camera began to display the photos in its memory. I didn't know what I might see, though I suppose the vibrator had established certain expectations. As it happened, they were wrong. There were only two pictures in the camera: one was of the dining area in Stans's apartment, with the glass-topped table and the Ondstrand Biologic computer workstation in center frame; the other was a close-up photo of the same computer—its screen filling the frame. The camera had a port for a tripod mount on its bottom, and a slot for a memory card in back, but when I opened this I found only empty space. I put the camera back in its case and put the case in my pocket.

I closed the drawer and moved to the dresser on the other side of the bed.

The first three drawers were a jumble of running gear. The fourth was racy underwear. Perfume wafted up—a light, spicy scent. It created a sudden intimacy in the room that somehow underscored the violation of my search and sent a chill up my spine. I rolled my shoulders as I stood and took a deep breath.

There were more clothes in the wardrobe and in the other dresser—casual, outdoorsy, athletic wear with disappointingly empty pockets and a lack of any visible stains, from blood or any other bodily fluids. I sat down at the writing table.

This was the place where Allegra Stans dropped her bag and emptied her pockets when she came home. A shallow bowl stood on the table, with coins and a few small bills inside, and another bowl with a dozen or so matchbooks from pubs and restaurants; between them was a small sculpture, maybe six inches long and four inches high: a carving of a deer made mostly of driftwood. It was as light as a cork in my hand, and the artist had used the white and gray lines of the wood grain to define the deer's musculature and the delicate structure of its face. The deer's hooves were made of silver, and its eyes were green agate. I turned the piece over and around, but the only markings I found were three small letters carved precisely on its belly: *JEN*. I took pictures.

Next to the deer was a small purse in soft green leather. Inside were a mobile phone, a tube of lip balm, a wallet with Allegra's bank and credit cards, insurance cards, some larger bills, a few crumpled receipts, and a sheaf of loyalty and membership cards from what I guessed were local establishments: the Sunnyside Salon and Spa, Soligstrand Kaffe, Solig Run, Coastal Fitness, Beacon Espresso, Café Slocum. There was also a set of car keys on a ring with a silver charm attached—a single winged sandal. There was nothing high-tech about the keys themselves, no intelligent or automatic features of any kind, and I guessed that the car that went with them was not a recent model.

I removed the contents of the purse and the wallet, laid them all on the desk, laid out all the matchbooks, too, and took pictures. Then I replaced everything but the car keys and the mobile phone. The keys went in my pocket, and the phone into a ziplock bag and another pocket. I took pictures of the corkboard that hung above the desk.

It was covered mostly in photographs, and most of them were of Allegra, racing. Allegra tensed, leaning and ready at the start, her cropped red hair clipped in place, her face shining and eager in a sea of other faces, a locket hanging about her neck on a short pink-gold chain, like a prize already won. Allegra at the head of a sloppy pack, charging up a hill, her legs and arms streaked with mud, her numbered bib spattered, the locket bobbling behind her on its chain, nearly lost in the sweat-darkened strands of her red hair, her mud-spattered face intent, hungry, straining. Allegra levitating, feather-light, above the tarmac, blue skies above, the finish in sight. Her nearest challenger is a speck in the background; her focus is all forward, and a smile is just beginning to form. Allegra breasting the tape. There were photos from many races, in many conditions, in all seasons, and mementos from some of the races hung on the board, too—medals, ribbons, sashes, tattered bibs.

Not all the photos were of Allegra running; there were pre- and post-race shots as well, and all of these were group affairs. Allegra in a cluster of men and women, younger and older, some kneeling, some standing, all smiling, all in matching running kit, posing beneath a banner proclaiming the finish line of the Soligstrand Half. All the runners looked fresh and clean, and the finish tape was still intact, so I guessed the race hadn't yet been run. Another picture was of Allegra in a gathering of very fit young women—all in singlets and bibs—mugging for the camera at the starting line of the Coastal Women's 10K. And there she was at the center of another group—men and women, faces I'd seen in the first two photos, the faces red now, the matching singlets damp and dusty. There was no indication of what race had just been run, but its winner was clear: Allegra thrust her gold medal at the camera, grinned, and raised a fist in victory. Around her, her teammates did, too. The last group photo had been taken well after a race, after the racers had toweled off, hydrated, slipped on training pants and jackets, and decamped to a pub for a beer. They were in the parking lot—the same set of faces again—bottles hoisted, and they were grinning and leaning in. And again Allegra was at the center.

I took the pictures down and got out my magnifying glass. In all the photos in which I could see Allegra's neck, I could also see her locket. Under the glass, I could see that it was cloisonné, with red and black enamels dominant, and that it depicted a red deer leaping against a black wood. I looked again at the photos I'd taken of Allegra's body, and in them saw her chain clearly. It was clearly pink gold, clearly intact, and clearly not strung with a locket or anything else.

I rose then, went back to the entrance foyer, and conducted another search of the entire apartment, paying even more attention to small spaces: pockets, corners, the backs of drawers, the overfull and aromatic laundry hamper, in her bedding, and under her bed. But there was no locket to be found. I sighed and returned to Allegra's writing table, and sent a message to Jane Wilding.

I gathered up the photos from the corkboard, scanning the other faces in them as I did. I recognized one amongst them: Piers Witmer. His focus, like that of the other men and women in the group, like the camera's itself, was on Allegra. Indeed, they were drawn to her as light was drawn to her glowing limbs and face. I took the photos with me.

CHAPTER SEVEN

Sunday Morning

W hat are you doing with those?" Nadia Blom asked, and pointed to the laptop and the photographs I carried from Allegra Stans's apartment. I didn't know if she'd waited in the corridor the whole time, but she was standing where I'd left her.

"The laptop will go to a tech team at my office, unless you happen to know the password."

"I don't."

"What about the password to the desktop in her apartment?"

"That's an Ondstrand computer. Our IT people can get you in, but I'm not sure what you'll find."

"Mail from her killer? Maybe a folder titled *Clues.*"

She was unamused. "What about those?" she asked, pointing to the photos.

"These I wanted to ask you about. Do you know any of these people?"

Nadia Blom took them from me, studied them, and handed them back. "I know all of them. All of these people work at Ondstrand, and they're all in the running club."

"I'll need a list, and I'll need to speak with them."

She nodded. "Many of them won't be back until tonight or tomorrow."

"That's fine. I have something else you can arrange for today."

"And that would be?"

"I need to meet with your security fellow—Mr. Halsell, is it?"

"I'll call him now," she said.

I nodded, and we set off down the corridor.

I dropped Allegra's camera, phone, laptop, and photos in my room, and followed Nadia Blom to the offices of the Protection Department, on the lowest level of the large central section of Ondstrand House.

We approached Protection down a long corridor and through another anonymous door of frosted glass. Nadia Blom waved her ID at the scanner. The door clicked, and we came into a small reception area with an unattended desk. We followed a corridor lined with gray metal filing cabinets. At the end was an office, and Victor Halsell was waiting.

He was in his mid-forties, and a wedge of a man, tapering from broad shoulders to narrow hips, with legs like cement posts in khaki pants. His head was topped with a thinning blond brush cut, and his features were blunt and watchful. He tugged the sleeves of his black sweater up on his thick forearms as he came around his desk. In his combat-style boots, he was nearly five and a half feet tall.

"Agent Myles," he said, and motioned me to one of the two steel-and-leather guest chairs in front of his desk. His voice was raspy, and softer than I had expected. He looked at Nadia Blom, who was waiting at the threshold. "Are you joining us?" he asked her.

"Not just now," I answered. "And 'Myles' will do."

He nodded at me and at Nadia and shut the door.

I looked around the office, which was spare and functional: the two guest chairs and a steel desk, with a computer like the one on Allegra Stans's dining table. The walls were bare but for a framed pen-and-ink map of the Ondstrand campus.

Halsell settled himself in the other guest chair and leaned forward. "Myles, then," he said. "What can we do for Standard Division?"

I smiled. "To begin, perhaps an overview of your department's responsibilities."

Which were, Halsell explained in his quiet rasp, to protect the physical premises of Onstrand Biologic from fire, flood, locusts, and unauthorized access; to protect the life, limb, and general safety of Ondstrand's employees and visitors while they were on the 120-acre campus, and to protect the equipment and property—including and especially the intellectual property—of Ondstrand Biologic from destruction, theft, and unauthorized use or access. To fulfill this mission, his department had at its disposal twenty stalwart souls and a variety of systems: the usual environmental sensors to monitor heat, cold, moisture, fire, smoke, and noxious gases; specialized systems designed for each lab, to monitor and mitigate potential threats—toxic chemicals, for instance, or explosive gases, radioactive material, biohazards, or other dangers unique to that lab—and an array of access-control systems and alarms to mind and control the comings and goings of people to and from the grounds, in and out of the buildings, and in and out of individual laboratories.

Halsell's summary was clear and efficient. He paused when he finished, and added: "Of course, nothing like this has happened here before—nothing close. It's a stunning thing to everyone here, but it's particularly a shock to me and my staff. It feels *personal* somehow; it feels like a failure. I know that Standard Division is highly self-sufficient, but we stand ready to help in any way we can."

I nodded when he was done, and let an appreciative silence form. Then I looked up at the map of the campus. "Has the company been located here from the start?" I asked.

He shook his head. "The first site was in the city, in a warehouse by the old docks. That was before all the redevelopment down there. Dr. Hasp had had the foresight to have bought then, and he acquired this property not long after. It was in quite a dilapidated state, apparently, and renovations took some time—years, in fact."

"Were you with the company then?"

Another head-shake. "I came on seven years ago, after the renovations were done here."

"Where were you before?"

He paused and looked at me. "Defense Ministry," he said finally. I said nothing—certainly nothing about minimum height requirements—and I didn't tilt my head or wrinkle my brow. Still, Halsell had learned to anticipate the question. "I was a civilian employee—an intelligence analyst in a threat-assessment group."

"Coming here must've been a big change, then. A very different mission, a very different job, and not an easy one, I imagine—a large, complicated site, a fair number of people to herd, and a relatively small staff."

Halsell nodded and smiled. It looked to be an uncomfortable experience for him. "A much smaller staff when I started—less than half the size. And, as you might guess, scientists can be a challenge when it comes to security protocols and procedures. They know how to run their laboratories—always safety first there—but they can't reliably grasp why one shouldn't use the fire exits when there is no fire. Heads in the clouds sometimes, if you follow."

I smiled sympathetically. "Unruly," I said. "Like children at school. Maybe it's the surroundings."

He nodded. "There's a bit of that, and actually it's part of what Dr. Hasp was looking for when he moved the company out here. A 'space for the free flow of ideas,' and the 'latitude to innovate,' 'room to breathe'—those are his words."

I nodded back. "Is there tension between those goals and the imperatives of security?"

Halsell thought about it for a while. "We try to maintain a light touch as we do our job—security needn't be oppressive or intrusive—but we *do* our job. It's a balance, and we try to leverage our systems as much as possible to help us."

"Tell me about the access-control systems."

He leaned back. "Every employee and visitor has an ID; you have one that I coded myself. The IDs are how we control entry to all the buildings on the grounds, and to the laboratories. We track entries and exits, who's on-site and off. And every swipe is accompanied by an image of the transaction."

"A photo of the person coming or going?" I asked. Halsell nodded. "And you do this for the laboratories, too?" Another nod. "And am I right to assume that lab access is granted individually—that not every person can access any lab?"

Halsell grimaced. "That's right—lab access is permitted to authorized staff only."

"'Authorized' meaning . . . ?"

"The staff assigned to a given lab, or the supervisors, managers, or executives overseeing work in that lab."

"So some people may have access to only one lab, while others may have access to several?"

Halsell nodded. "For example, Dr. Pohl, who heads up Research and Development, can access any of the R&D labs, while Dr. Hasp can access all of the labs, across all departments."

"And Dr. Stans—to which labs was she allowed access?"

"I thought you might ask," Halsell said, and he went to his desk and retrieved a sheet of paper. He handed it to me. "She was in R&D, and she worked in South 217. That's on the second floor of the south wing."

"Do you know what sort of work she was doing there?" I asked.

"I could read you the names of the projects, but they wouldn't mean anything to me, and maybe not to you. The best thing would be to talk to Dr. Pohl or Dr. Hasp. They can tell you."

I nodded. "How about a list of the other people working in South 217."

"I checked that, too. It was just Dr. Stans."

My eyebrows went up. "Are all of the laboratories in this building?"

He nodded. "Yes. The south wing is entirely labs, and there are labs elsewhere in the main house, too."

"I understand that, prior to working in R&D, Dr. Stans worked in Special Projects." Halsell nodded but said nothing. "About how long ago did she transfer?"

Halsell frowned and went again to his desk. He sat behind it and tapped at his computer. "Her access was modified just over seven months ago," he said.

"And prior to that, where was she working?"

He typed some more. "All the Special Project suites are on the third and fourth floors of south wing. She was authorized for suites 304, 306, 307, and 310."

"So many?"

Halsell looked at his screen again. "She had supervisory access there. She was overseeing work in those labs."

I nodded. "But after her transfer . . . ?"

"I gather she wasn't supervising. But if you want to know more . . ."

"Ask Dr. Hasp?"

Halsell nodded. "Would you like the names of her co-workers in those labs?"

I nodded. Halsell hit a key, and a printer whined under his desk. He handed me the page—a list of names, eight of them, that I didn't know. I sighed and sat back, and looked up at the map of the Ondstrand campus on the wall.

"Are there other cameras, besides the interior ones?"

"Besides the cameras in the building lobbies and at the lab doors, we have cameras at the main gate, and at various points on the exteriors of this building, the old stables, and the carriage house."

"You archive all your video?"

"Oh yes. We have the most recent six months online, and the twelve months prior to that on the shelf. Just let me know what you need."

I looked again at the drawings of Ondstrand House and at Halsell's computer. "Does cybersecurity fall within your department's mandate?"

The question surprised him slightly, like missing a stair. "In part.

Cybersecurity is part of the IT Department but has a dotted line to me as well."

I sighed and tapped my chin. "You said, 'Nothing like this has happened here before—nothing close,' and I'm sure that's so. But I wonder what sorts of things *have* happened here in the past? What sorts of security incidents?"

Halsell colored slightly and cleared his throat. "Very little, actually. We've had a few kitchen fires over the years—small, smoky things, with no damage to speak of. We had a smoke condition in our fitness center a couple of years back—someone left a towel in the sauna, right on top of the heating unit. Had to have that replaced. We've had small fires in some labs, too—electrical things due to faulty equipment installation. We've had false alarms as well, from bad sensors. Really, nothing major. Lab safety is ingrained in the culture here."

"I imagine. How about outside the lab areas—any incidents in staff housing?"

Halsell thought about it and shrugged. "I'd have to check logs, but, outside of the odd complaint about someone's music being too loud or someone burning incense, nothing comes to mind."

"Nothing involving personal disputes or brawling, or someone who had too much to drink in the executive dining room? No pilfering or vandalism? No jealous lovers acting out?"

Halsell chuckled. "They're not a bunch of undergraduates."

"That sort of thing is not the sole purview of undergraduates, as I'm sure you know. What about break-ins?"

"No, no break-ins or attempts, but we have had trespass problems from time to time. The property is posted, but we have had hunters wander on in pursuit of the occasional deer or grouse, and we have had people—teenagers, mostly—trespass on the beach below the house. It's on a protected cove, but in the warm weather they swim around the rocks, or paddle in to drink or smoke dope or have sex in the caves at the base of the cliff."

"What do you do about it?"

"When we catch them at it—kids and hunters alike—we warn, we take names, we report the rare repeat offender to the local police, and we post more signs. We've talked about installing motion-activated cameras around the property lines, but Dr. Hasp isn't keen on it—he wants staff to feel free to enjoy the grounds. And, honestly, it hasn't been a big problem."

I nodded again, and was about to ask another question when Halsell frowned and raised a finger. "You asked about cybersecurity before. We did have an incident involving that, a while back—a spear-phishing attack. One of the science staff clicked on a link in a quite plausible-looking e-mail—something that seemed to be from an editor at a journal that had published a paper of hers but wasn't. The link loaded some malware—I can't remember what exactly—but IT caught and isolated it right away."

"When was this?"

"I'll have to look up the exact dates, but it was about six months ago."

"The scientist wasn't Allegra Stans, by any chance?"

He shook his head, then bent to his keyboard and typed. "Dr. Georgina Stahlmann, a chemist assigned to Special Projects."

"Did she work with Dr. Stans?"

Halsell squinted at me and typed some more, faster this time. He scanned his screen and shook his head. "No. Dr. Stahlmann is assigned to one of the labs Dr. Stans had been supervising, but they didn't work together. Stahlmann transferred in after Dr. Stans went to R&D. Shall I print the incident report for you?"

I nodded. "Did you know Dr. Stans personally, Mr. Halsell?"

He looked up, and his cheeks were pink. "Not well. I knew who she was, of course, as you do in a small community, but there was nothing that brought her to this department's particular attention. I suppose I knew her a bit better than that, through the running club."

"You're a member?" He nodded. "And what were your impressions?"

The printer whined, and Halsell thought. "A very fit young woman, and a talented runner—I think she ran as an undergrad. Very focused, and a fierce competitor—one of those people who don't so much relish winning as they hate the idea of losing. That was my sense."

"Competitiveness doesn't always make a person well loved, or even well liked."

Halsell laughed. "It was the opposite with Dr. Stans—and no one called her that, by the way, no one on the running team. It was 'Al' or 'Allie.' Everyone who ran with her was very fond of her. She motivated them—pushed them—but she led by example, so they welcomed it. A couple of my staff are in the club, too, and they turned in some of their best times training with her. People were drawn to her, I suppose. She was . . . charismatic."

The word seemed to embarrass Halsell, as if it was one word too many, and he colored again as he handed me the incident report.

CHAPTER EIGHT

Sunday Evening

Director Mehta wore black, as she often did, and silver bracelets on her wrists, and she sipped whiskey from a short, thick glass with a single large ice cube in it. The room behind her was in darkness on my screen, but I heard faint music and muted laughter.

"An inconvenient time, Director?" I asked.

She smiled. "A small gathering, but my wife will hold the fort. How is the seaside, Myles?"

"I haven't set eyes on the actual sea thus far. I've been otherwise occupied."

"Pleased to hear it. Do tell."

And so I told her about my visit to Allegra Stans's apartment, and my conversation with Victor Halsell. "I'll need a courier to fetch her mobile, her laptop, and her camera, and a tech team to get past any passwords," I said in conclusion. Director Mehta nodded absently and tapped on an unseen keyboard. Then her gaze returned to me.

"'Focused,' 'fierce competitor,' 'charismatic,' a leader 'by example'— you didn't hear those words from Hasp or Witmer."

I smiled. "I did not. In fact, I heard next to nothing about her from them—despite the fact that Hasp hired her himself, or so he said, and that she'd worked for Witmer and was in the running club with him."

"And neither one said anything about a change in her professional circumstances several months before. What do you make of that? Had she been demoted?"

"Going from supervising work in four different labs to working by herself in a single lab—it certainly reads that way. It'll be interesting to hear how Hasp describes it."

"Indeed," she said, and sipped her whiskey. "Do you think Mr. Halsell had something of a crush on Dr. Stans?"

"He might've. Of course, I could say the same about most of the people in those photos with her, judging by their expressions."

Director Mehta smiled ruefully. "That's the romantic in you. And speaking of, from the box of condoms you found, it seems Dr. Stans had some sort of sex life. Any idea with whom?"

I frowned. "Not yet."

"Of course, it may be with more than one person." I nodded, and Director Mehta chuckled softly and shook her head. "I know you disdain this part, Myles—who wouldn't?—picking through people's condoms and vibrators. But it is part and parcel of our work."

"And often our bread and butter," I said. Director Mehta sighed and drank some more whiskey. "Nevertheless, Director," I continued, "I will keep in mind that the dead are beyond embarrassment, and that no man is a hero to his valet, much less to an investigator examining his violent death."

"No man *or woman*, Myles. And I'm pleased you've been paying even a little attention. What is your impression of security there, overall?"

"*Adequate*, I suppose, but I'll know better when I've had a chance to look around more, and review some of the footage from their cameras. And, of course, I've requested a download of all their footage and logs to Ivessen. He'll no doubt have a view."

The Director smiled ruefully. "No doubt," she said. "Perhaps 'adequate' is the best Mr. Halsell can do, given Dr. Hasp's priorities and the physical circumstances he has to work with. It's not a campus that was designed for its current use, after all. What do you make of the phishing incident?"

"Spear-phishing, actually—targeted at a specific person. The timing is interesting—an attack like that, that utilized specific information about its intended victim, coming just a month or so after Dr. Stans's transfer. The target was a Dr. Stahlmann. She's a chemist in one of the Special Project labs that Stans had supervised, though she didn't work there during Stans's time. She transferred in after Stans transferred out."

"A coincidence?" she asked.

I laughed. "I'll be talking to the IT director tomorrow, and with any luck I can get a copy of the e-mail and the malware for the tech team."

"And Ms. Blom—did she provide names to go with your group photos?"

"She did. And Ivessen should soon have a report on who was on campus and in the building around the time Stans died."

"Dr. Wilding may also have some news for you tomorrow, or so she tells me." I nodded. "So—a busy day ahead for us both. And, as I'm sure my wife believes that I've ignored our guests for long enough, I shall ring off now. And you, Myles?"

"To bed, I think."

"Wise man," she said, and the screen went black.

I sighed, turned off my tablet, and leaned back on the sofa. I looked around the little living room, and out the window. I could see lights elsewhere in Ondstrand House, in windows that had been dark since I'd been here, and I felt the low-level hum of life returning to the building as people returned from the weekend. I wondered if I would feel the frisson of tension and fear, the clammy titillation, as they learned of Allegra Stans's death. I rolled my shoulders, circled the room, and stepped to the window, but an incipient melancholy followed me.

There were no weekends at Conservatory, which recognized no calendars, no seasons of the year, no passage of time at all except as dictated by Standard Division. Nevertheless, there was always that feeling— a chill in the marrow, a small ache in the chest—that marked a Sunday evening. Before that, at the state homes, weekends existed, but, like much of life in those places, they were variations on central themes of bleakness and steady violence. In the times before those, the short time when I lived with my grandmother, the shorter time when my mother was alive, there were also weekends, but I could barely remember them, and what I could recall I wished that I couldn't. So I had never been partial to weekends—not their beginnings, their middles, or their ends.

My tablet burred softly and pulled me from my reverie. Goss Ivessen's groaning bookshelves resolved out of the darkness, and I heard his rapid typing, and the complaint of his cat.

"Burning the midnight oil, I see," he whispered. "Leadership by example—very inspiring."

"But, sadly, I have only you to lead. What can I do for you?"

"It's all the other way. I have answers to one of your questions."

"Which?"

"The question of who was in Ondstrand House at the approximate time of Dr. Stans's death."

I sat up and leaned towards the screen. "Barely twenty-four hours after the asking—that's quick, even for you."

I imagined him shrugging. "Mr. Halsell was prompt in supplying the data, I have no competing commitments, and, as you well know, people tend to return our calls—if not enthusiastically, then at least with panicked speed. Would you like my results?"

"Pray tell."

Ivessen cleared his throat. "According to Ondstrand Protection's video surveillance and electronic and other logs—and, yes, Myles, that includes actual paper-and-ink logbooks—there were fifty-nine people on the property around the time of Allegra Stans's death—a much lower number than usual, due to the long weekend. That number is mostly Ondstrand staff, but it also includes delivery-truck crews, a cleaning-company crew, a small number of contractors of various sorts, and four company spouses. Without them, the number comes to forty-nine.

"Of that number, thirty-four were in the main building at some point during our window. Of these, twenty-three can account for their time, either because they were with one or more of the others, because they were engaged in some independently verifiable activity such as, for example, participating in a video conference, or because their locations within the main building, say in a laboratory suite, are verifiable during the time window in question."

"If arithmetic serves, thirty-four minus twenty-three leaves us with eleven."

"Impressive," Ivessen said flatly.

I ignored him. "Four company spouses? Do they all live on campus?"

"All but one—Mrs. Dr. Piers Witmer."

I nodded. "Let's add the spouses back in."

A spray of keystrokes followed, and then the sounds of Ivessen whispering to himself in words I couldn't make out. I heard his cat somewhere in the darkness, denouncing something. "Of those four spouses, only Mrs. Dr. Witmer was in the building."

"What was she doing there, or on the grounds at all?"

"Apparently, she paints," he whispered. "The cliffs and coastline there are favored subjects, and she likes early light. Her husband was in his lab. She stopped in at the staff cafeteria twice."

"The cafeteria where the body was found?"

"The very one. She got coffee."

"She told you this?"

"She and the husband. Unfortunately, there are no interior cameras in or around the cafeteria, and exterior coverage doesn't include the seaward terrace. She thinks she might've seen other people in the caf but isn't sure."

"Where was the husband?"

"In his lab some of the time; with Dr. Hasp in Hasp's office some of the time."

"Some of the time?"

"Not enough of the time," Ivessen said softly.

"So our list of eleven—"

"Our *preliminary* list—I'm still not sure how effective their perimeter security and surveillance actually is, how comprehensive their logging is, or if I've missed something by excluding the non-staff."

"Points taken. Our preliminary list goes to twelve, of which the Witmers are two."

"And Dr. Hasp is another, as are Halsell and Nadia Blom."

"You'll send me the full run?"

"Just did, along with the digests of my interviews and the raw audio of the calls."

I nodded. "And let's add Halsell and Mrs. Witmer to the background reports, shall we?"

"Already added."

"How are those coming, by the way?"

"Working as we speak."

"Anything of interest?"

"A notable lack of response from our sisters and brothers in Domestic regarding security clearance packages."

"Is that laziness, incompetence, or uncooperativeness?"

"Could be any or all," Ivessen said.

"I'll talk to the Director. Anything else of interest?"

"Is it interesting that Dr. Hasp and Dr. Muir are step-siblings?"

I raised an eyebrow. "How did that come to pass?"

"In a usual way—Hasp's divorced mother wed Wilbur Jolley, Muir's widowed father. Both of them were faculty members at a boarding school up in the Lakelands—literature for her, physics for him. The kids were grown by then—Hasp was at university, and Muir was in medical school."

"Though presumably they'd have known each other before."

"Presumably," he said. One of those terrible hands made a shooing gesture then—at his cat, I thought, and not at me. Then the screen went dark.

I stood and stretched my arms above my head and tried to work the kinks from my neck. I looked into my bedroom, at the unmade bed, and thought about showering and then climbing in, but did neither. Instead, I opened my tablet and pulled up Ivessen's list of a dozen names.

There were the names we'd discussed—Hasp, two Witmers, Victor Halsell, and Nadia Blom—and seven more I didn't know. I read and reread the names, again and again, as if there was some meaning hidden in them that might emerge with repetition. If so, it eluded me, or I quit too soon.

CHAPTER NINE

Monday Morning

I was the new boy at school on Monday morning, the stranger in the cafeteria, the one uncertain at the hallway intersections, the one followed by glances and whispers as he passed. It was a feeling enhanced by the fact that I seemed centuries older than most of the other kids, and that I wore a black suit and black tie, whereas nearly everyone else wore khakis, yoga clothes, or pajamas.

Nadia Blom was again to be my escort, and met me in the lobby. Together we made our way outside, to the courtyard. Her skirt was black this morning; her close-fitting, buttoned-down shirt was burgundy; and her braid was like a fang. It was chilly out and windy, and the sky was a hard blue behind a scattering of fast, fleecy clouds. The smell of white-caps came with every gust. I buttoned my suit jacket and turned up the collar. Still, my tie escaped, to flap like a sad pennant. Blom slipped into a black raincoat that wrapped her like a cloak. Ondstrand staff crossed the courtyard around us, leaning into the wind and eyeing me furtively.

"I take it they've all received Dr. Hasp's note," I said to Blom.

"It went out last night."

"And the reception?"

"Early signs indicate stress."

I smiled. "Murder does have that effect, especially on the victim."

She winced and checked her watch. "Caroline Drucker is expecting you at nine."

We crossed the courtyard to a brick footpath that led us past the south wing, down a terraced hillside, to a stand of shaggy pines. At the pine trees, the brick became pea gravel, and the trail wound through the wood for maybe seventy yards. Beyond the trees were two slate-roofed buildings made of brick and dressed stone. The far one was the old stable; the near, the carriage house. They faced each other across a wide gravel yard where cars were parked. Both buildings had been modernized with new windows and sleek glass entranceways, and the carriage house had been given an addition: a glass-and-steel annex at one end, which went with the original structure less well than ice cream went with sweetbreads. And the copious ivy did not improve things. Its dull gray leaves shrouded large swaths of both buildings like a family curse, and had found purchase on the new bits as well, draped at the edges of the glass and steel like a caul. I followed Nadia Blom across the carriage-house lobby, through the security barrier, and into the annex.

The IT Department was mostly open space—three long tables, each divided into a dozen workstations, and each one of those outfitted with several large screens. Most of the stations were occupied when we came to the reception desk, and most of the occupants were looking at me. Nadia did not pause but proceeded down a corridor to the largest of the glass offices that bordered the open area. She knocked on the door, and the woman behind the glass-and-steel desk looked up from a screen, waggled a finger, and pointed at her guest chairs. Then the woman returned to her screen and spoke softly into the headset that she wore.

"I'll save you the trouble of dismissing me," Nadia Blom said. "I take it you can find your way back."

"I'll send up a flare if I get lost," I answered, and she turned and left. I took a seat, and Caroline Drucker took off her headset.

This took some doing, as her tight chestnut curls were thick, springy, and anarchic, and fell past her shoulders. She chuckled at her awkwardness, and even that small, self-deprecating smile took ten years at least from her face—transformed it from a handsome, dignified fortyish into something girlish and unguarded. Her dark eyes glittered above high cheekbones, and her teeth were bright and even in a generous mouth. Her skin was an unblemished dark caramel. She wore black pants, a butter-yellow top that zipped up the front, and no jewelry besides simple gold hoops in her ears.

"Agent Myles, is it?" Her voice was low and pleasant—a newscaster voice, matter-of-fact, competent, calm, and friendly. A voice to tell you how the market did today, without provoking mania or panic.

I nodded. "'Myles' will do."

"As 'Caro' will for me."

"You know why I'm here?"

"Nadia called me Sunday night, while I was driving back from the city." She glanced at a framed photo on her desk: Caroline Drucker flanked by two dimpled girls in pink tee shirts, with ice cream on their faces. One looked just school-age, the other not quite. Their brown skins were a shade lighter than hers. "I'd been visiting with my kids. I had to pull over when she told me."

"Your children live in the city?"

She raised an eyebrow. "With their father, my ex. What can I help you with, Myles?"

I nodded. "With a few things. For starters, Dr. Stans has a desktop computer in her apartment. I was hoping you could provide the password." She nodded. "I can reset it right now, if that works." She typed quickly and looked up. "The password is 'C-@-r-o-2-M-i-l-e-s-!'" She spelled it out for me, wrote it on a slip of white notepaper, and handed it to me.

"For future reference, it's Myles with a y," I said.

"Extra security feature," she said, smiling slightly. "Now memorize it, then eat it—that's what you fellows do, right?"

"And sometimes in that order," I said. "Do staff typically keep company hardware in their homes?"

"Most do—and nearly all of the science staff. Besides our e-mail and messaging apps, and our various corporate subscriptions to any biochem, genetics, and virology journal you can name, they all use a virtual laboratory bench application."

"Which is?"

"It's application software that lets a scientist monitor the status of almost any process she might have going on in her laboratory—an assay, for example, or a culture growth, a synthesis, really anything that may be going on—in real time, from anywhere."

I nodded in a way that apparently did not convey comprehension. Caro smiled. "Think of it this way—the software saves her from having to sit in a lab all weekend, watching the pots and waiting for them to boil. It's a window into her lab that she can open anytime from anywhere and see how things are going."

I thought about that for a while and nodded in what I hoped was a more convincing fashion. "I imagine there's a lot of security around that window—just as there is around physical access to the labs. Presumably, you don't want just anybody peeking in."

She smiled. "Quite right. The lab bench software access is organized along lines similar to physical access. A scientist has access to her own bench only, along with the benches of anyone she's supervising. Same principles that determine who gets to walk through a physical door."

"Is this software something you developed here?"

She shook her head. "No, it's an off-the-shelf product, sold by a vendor. There're several packages on the market. This was the one that best suited our needs—the easiest one to customize and for our scientists to use, the best integration of data collection and data analysis, the best integration with the array of documents our projects generate. We've used it for some time—about seven years at this point."

I smiled. "You were here then?"

"I was. I started eight years ago. Dr. Muir hired me to install the virtual-bench software; she was running what passed for IT at the time and wanted to get out from under that chore. I took over as IT director five years back."

"So you predated Dr. Stans here?" She nodded. "Did you know her well?"

"What's 'well'? I worked with her from time to time—initially, in setting up the bench software for her, showing her how to use it, how to configure it for her needs. And I worked with her periodically after that: if she had a new piece of equipment to integrate with the software, or she was doing something new that didn't fit so obviously into the workflow she was used to."

"And? How did you find her?"

Caro tilted her head and thought for a moment. "She was smart—very smart—which is not exceptional around here—you can't turn around without tripping over a very smart person. But her smarts were not confined to her field of expertise. She was curious about everything, really. If she ran across a problem, she wanted to solve it.

"The bench software was a case in point. A lot of science staff—not all, mind, but more than a few—approach this stuff with a kind of theatrical helplessness. They throw up their hands and dither and can't be bothered to learn how to work the software. They want it to be like a teakettle or something—just add water and flick a switch. Al was not like that—not at all. She saw the software for what it is—a tool—and she was determined to master her tools. She was easy to teach—a quick study, focused, tenacious—and she was easy to work with."

"You liked her."

"I did. She didn't take herself too seriously, she was funny. Charming, really—which is *not* something you can say about all of the science staff. After I took over this department and she took on more responsibility, I didn't have occasion to work with her one-on-one, but I was always glad to see her in the dining room or wherever."

"Did she have any close relationships amongst the staff here, or with anyone, that you know of? Best friends, significant others, sex partners?"

Caro laughed. "I'm sure she did, but I didn't know her well enough to tell you who."

"You're sure about which: a significant other, a sex partner, a best friend? And why do you say you're sure?"

Her brow furrowed. "I . . . I can't say about the best-friend part, but about the rest—it was just clear that Al was a sexual person. People responded to her on that wavelength, and she responded to them. It was just a part of her vibe, I guess."

"Do you mean she was flirtatious?"

Caro shrugged. "I'm not saying she was swapping spit in the hallways or anything. Just that she would flirt, in a playful, lighthearted way, and people often flirted back. Maybe I'm just extrapolating from what I saw of her in the workplace to how she might be outside. That's probably a mistake."

I shrugged. "It seems that, around here, there's not much distinction between *in* and *out* of the workplace."

She smiled ruefully and nodded. "Some of the staff enjoy that, I think—particularly those not far removed from university days. Others of us get away every weekend we can."

I nodded back. "Any names come to mind, of who she flirted with?" Caro shook her head. "Was it with men or with women?"

"With both," she said without hesitation.

I pursed my lips and was quiet for a while. "You mentioned Dr. Stans's taking on more responsibility—I assume you meant supervisory or managerial responsibility," I said finally. Caro nodded. "But I understood that, for the past seven months, she no longer had that kind of responsibility."

She nodded some more, slowly. "I guess that's right . . . from when she moved back to R&D from Special Projects."

"Do you know what was behind that? Was it a demotion of some sort?"

Caro raised a graceful eyebrow. "I have no idea. I guess I'd assumed it was part of some larger reshuffling—that her current slot was a place-holder, pending the opening of a more senior position. I can't say I'd given it much thought, though. You might ask—"

"Let me guess—Dr. Hasp?"

"He'd be the one to know." Caro glanced at her watch. "Is there anything else I can help with?"

"Cybersecurity. That falls to your department?"

"Mostly. The technical expertise is here."

"Victor Halsell mentioned a spear-phishing attack several months back."

Caro nodded. "Yes—an e-mail to a scientist in Projects, supposedly from an editor at a journal. She made the mistake of clicking on it."

"And?"

"It tried to install a keystroke logger on her workstation, but it was detected and quarantined. Kind of a primitive piece of software, if I remember."

"Did that strike you as odd—a relatively sophisticated phishing e-mail, well tailored to its target, that delivers only a simple piece of malware?"

She shrugged. "I guess their social engineering was better than their software engineering."

"Whoever *they* were. Does that happen a lot here—spear-phishing attacks?"

"No, not really—not often at all. We haven't had any since then, and that was certainly the most we'd had at once."

I sat up. "There were multiple spear-phishing attempts?"

"Four in total, all within days. But the recipients of three of them recognized what they were and reported them to us."

"I wonder why Halsell didn't mention them?"

"He probably didn't know—he was alerted automatically when the malware was detected, but not when the other three recipients called my department directly. We took care of the problem. I didn't see any reason to alert him. I guess that's an oversight on our part." She jotted something quickly on a notepad and looked back at me.

"Did you evaluate the other e-mails? Did they come from the same place?"

She nodded. "Almost certainly. The servers they were sent from were thoroughly obscured, and the spoofing of the spurious sender addresses was pretty slick—they all had that in common. And there were stylistic similarities— one purported to be from the recipient's former employer, another from a former grad-school adviser, and another from the head of the alumni association at the recipient's university. In all three instances, the messages addressed the recipients by their first names, and they were written in familiar, informal language. And in all four instances, the payload was the same: a keystroke logger."

"The same primitive keystroke logger."

Caro nodded and frowned. "You're making me a bit nervous, Myles. Should I be?"

I shrugged. "You have these e-mails? And the malware?" She nodded. "I'm going to need copies of them, and the names of the other recipients."

"I'm going to put them on a stick for you, okay?"

"That's best."

"You'll tell me if this is something I should be nervous about?"

I met her gaze and held it for a moment. "I'll tell you what I can," I said.

CHAPTER TEN

Monday Morning

Nadia Blom was waiting outside the carriage house when I emerged. She was talking on her phone, and the wind was flicking at her braid and at the hem of her raincoat. There was more cloud in the sky, and the wind was colder and steadier from the ocean.

"Did you get what you needed from Caro?" she asked.

"I got something," I said. "I'll reserve judgment on whether it's what I need. Don't you have work to do for Dr. Witmer, or Dr. Hasp? Or has trailing after me become your job?"

"Dr. Hasp wants to make sure there are no obstacles to your work, and he's asked me to do what I can to facilitate things. If you'd rather that I didn't—"

"I'll make my wishes clear, Ms. Blom."

"No doubt," she said. I smiled and so did she, slightly. "I also know you've arranged a meeting with Dr. Hasp. I wanted to make sure you found your way."

"Advanced though I am in years, Ms. Blom, and lacking a doctorate, nonetheless, I am capable of navigating. Unless it's physical infirmity that concerns you, and you propose to carry me on your back, or perhaps in a sedan chair."

"My sedan chair is at the mechanic's just now."

I shrugged, smiled again, and set off towards the main house.

My meeting with Terrence Hasp took place not in his office in Ondstrand House, but in his studio—an annex to his residence, the Cottage, that made no attempt at reconciliation with the older building, or even recognition of its presence. Whereas the red-brick, slate-roofed

Cottage looked like a cousin to the country train stations that still dotted small towns across the nation, Hasp's studio was a concrete-and-glass bunker bolted to its side.

From my approach along a mossy, uneven brick path, the addition looked as if it had been dropped from the sky—a bullying wedge between the Cottage and what remained of the Chapel—the burnt ruin of a small oratory as old as Ondstrand House itself. The studio had tall windows that rose from its foundations to a flat metal roof, and siding of finished gray concrete, already streaked from water damage and sporting patches of gray mold. Beside the brutal slab, the bones of the Chapel—blackened and crumbling archways and empty windows—were an elegant, elegiac rebuke.

Low concrete steps led twenty paces from where the brick path ended up to the studio's big glass door. Hasp had seen my approach and was waiting there. He wore jeans and a fawn-colored chamois shirt and greeted me as if I'd circumnavigated the globe.

"Found your way—fine work. Excellent. Good man. Come in and recover." He stepped aside and ushered me through.

It was one large room, with a wall of bookshelves that climbed to a ceiling lost in shadow, and a man-sized fireplace bordered in coarse slate. The fireplace and shelves faced the wall of glass I'd seen on my approach, which framed a dramatic view of the Chapel's charred bones and the mossy trunks and black limbs of the surrounding wood.

The furnishings consisted of Hasp's desk, a black refectory table set before the window, with a black chair that kept its back to the view, and a pair of gray leather chairs that flanked the fireplace. The floor was shiny wide-plank oak, the color of dark syrup, and looked older than anything else in the room. A large, bright rug in blue and black stripes lay before Hasp's desk, and there was a fire in the big hearth. The room was warm and fragrant with apple-wood smoke.

Hasp directed me to a fireplace chair and offered coffee. I accepted, and he opened a panel adjacent to his desk. Inside was a small refrigerator and an espresso machine, and Hasp set the machine to chugging.

"'Preciate you making the trek," he said as he fiddled with cups. "Got to have a bit of peace in the day. Quiet the background noise and think straight. The studio gives me that. Much needed today, I can tell you, Myles. Nervous as cats over there, with the news of Allegra."

I looked around some more and nodded. It was indeed a room to take refuge in, a room to impress, a room to envy. And, I thought, a room in which Hasp could be admired, could admire himself, and could enjoy all that regard. Though, I had to admit, he'd done a subtler job than most with the vanity-wall business.

The diplomas—and there were many—were not prominently displayed, and some were mounted high enough up that their elaborate calligraphy and ancient university seals were visible but not legible. And the framed reprints of magazine interviews and profiles—"The Wizard of Ondstrand," "Hasp on the New Golden Age in Genetic Therapies," "Ondstrand Biologic: Enabling the Next Generation of Vaccines," "One-on-One with Terrence Hasp," and others—were not clustered together, but hung discreetly here and there, so that the self-regard was diluted, though never more than a glance away. The award plaques were similarly arrayed, and the textbooks and monographs he'd authored were stacked modestly on two eye-level bookshelves.

Hasp brought coffee in white demitasses and placed a silver sugar-and-cream caddy on the hearthstone. He dropped into the chair opposite mine, crossed his legs, and stirred his cup.

"First thing, I want to make sure you're getting on all right—got all you need, getting the right cooperation and so forth. Anything amiss, you let me know, or Nads; we'll see to it."

I nodded. "If I require anything, you'll know."

Hasp ran a palm over his shaved pate and grinned. "Blunt—I like that. I'm the same." He sipped his coffee delicately and sighed. "Nasty business, all this. Hard to fathom. Be glad to have it sorted."

"As will I. I have a few things I'd like to go over just now. Some you've already discussed with my colleague."

"Ivessen—yes? Odd fella. A bit chilly."

"The access-control system logged your entry into Ondstrand House on Saturday morning at six-fifteen."

Hasp nodded. "Sounds about right."

"And you informed my colleague that you went directly to your office upon your arrival."

Hasp nodded. "Indeed."

"And that you remained there until you were notified by Protection of the body in the kitchen refrigerator."

"Correct. That was at about eight-thirty-five, plus or minus."

"You were alone there for that entire time?"

Hasp frowned. "No, Piers—Dr. Witmer—dropped in. I told your man Ivessen all this."

"Perhaps you can tell me."

"Not much to tell. Piers was in—he often is on Saturday mornings—and he stopped by to jaw on a few issues. Knocked on the door around eight o'clock, maybe a few minutes before. He was getting up to leave when Protection called."

"You said it was not unusual for Dr. Witmer to be at work on Saturday mornings. Is the same true of you?"

Hasp nodded. "Part of what I love about this situation, Myles—being a stone's throw away. I work most of the time, whether I'm in the building or not. But, yes, it's often the case that I wander over early on Saturdays. Piers does, too; so does Karen—Dr. Muir. That's most of our senior management committee right there. Dr. Pohl's a more recent addition, and a fine one, and I expect he'll join our Saturday-morning coffee klatch soon."

I nodded. "But he didn't this past Saturday. Neither he nor your sister was here."

Hasp's brows gathered and he grew very still. "Dr. Muir is my *step-sister*," he said after a while. "And, no, neither she nor Dr. Pohl was here. Dr. Pohl went to the city on Thursday, as did Karen. She's overseas now, at a conference. Flies back this Thursday."

"Did anyone else stop by while you were here with Dr. Witmer on Saturday?"

"No—it was just Piers and me. It was a Saturday, after all, and a bit early, even for the workaholics around here."

I nodded. "Let's discuss Dr. Stans's role here. I understand that she was transferred from the Special Projects Department about seven months ago."

"Yep—over to Dr. Pohl's world—R&D."

"And I understand that in Special Projects she'd had supervisory responsibility. Management responsibility." Hasp nodded. "But she did not have that sort of responsibility in R&D." Hasp nodded again, more slowly. "Had Dr. Stans been demoted in some way?"

Hasp frowned. "Demoted? No—I wouldn't call it that. She was just in a different sort of role in R&D—troubleshooting for Dr. Pohl, looking after odd bits and bobs for him while he gets his sea legs here. Truth be told, R&D was not going to be a long-term assignment for

Dr. Stans—be a waste of her talents unless she was going to run the division for me—and I've already got someone doing that. Point is, been planning a bit of a reorganization around here, a reshuffle, and saw Allegra as a part of that. A big part. More substantial role. This stint in R&D was temporary."

I nodded. "So—there was no issue with her performance?"

"Of course not. First-rate mind, hers."

I let that sit for a while, as the fire settled in a plume of fragrant sparks. Then I asked: "When we first met, I asked about what you knew of Dr. Stans's personal relationships—her friends, lovers, et cetera. I realize that Saturday was somewhat chaotic, and I'm wondering if anything else has occurred to you on that subject."

Hasp frowned. "Allegra's relationships? Don't know that I can add much. I'm sure she had some—personable gal, very sporty, what with her running club and such, very popular with that crew. And very attractive, of course."

"But you don't know any names?"

He shook his head. "I don't."

"Do you know anyone who might?"

"Sorry, Myles."

I nodded. "I understand that Ondstrand Biologic's clients include what Ms. Blom rather poetically referred to as 'non-pharma entities.' As lovely a phrase as that is, I was hoping you could be more specific."

Hasp frowned again. "Well . . . as you may've guessed, it includes government entities."

"Entities of *our* government?"

"Oh yes—our government wouldn't permit anything else."

"And which entities would those be?"

He hesitated. "We have projects ongoing with departments of the Agricultural Ministry, departments of the Defense Ministry, and elements of the security services."

"Which elements?"

He hesitated longer. "Have to forgive me, Myles, but I can't be more specific, not without explicit approvals from the relevant agencies." I nodded. "But I can tell you, if it matters—Allegra Stans was never assigned to any of those projects."

"Thank you, Doctor. One last question, then, and it has to do with this place."

A look of surprise, even fear, flitted across Hasp's face, so quickly I wasn't sure I'd seen it. "*This* place—my studio?"

"I was thinking of the campus as a whole—Ondstrand House, its grounds. It's an impressive facility but hardly an obvious choice for a biotech company's headquarters—so far from the city, from universities, from much of anything at all."

Hasp nodded. It wasn't the first time he'd fielded the question. "It *is* far from everything. And it isn't the obvious location for a company like ours, but we were never interested in building something obvious. If we'd wanted that, we could've stayed in Dockyards and leased a few more converted warehouses. But we always knew we wanted to create a campus like this, something a bit remote, but something *immersive*—a place where our people, our scientists, could focus deeply on their work, without distraction, but with the creative stimulation and cross-fertilization that can only be found in a community of dedicated, innovative people working to a common purpose. That sort of culture doesn't just happen, and that sort of space doesn't just appear out of thin air. Ondstrand Hall and its property presented a unique opportunity. Derelict as it was, the price made it feasible."

"With your prior connection—being an alumnus of the school—it must've seemed—"

Hasp winced. "Don't say 'fated,' Myles—it's much too dramatic."

"I was going to say fortuitous. It must've been quite a project."

He smiled ruefully. "Damned massive."

"And who is 'we'?"

"Pardon?"

"You referred to 'we'—as in 'we always knew we wanted to create a campus like this.' Who is 'we'?"

"The senior management committee—the original management committee—Dr. Muir, Dr. Witmer, and myself. All there at the founding."

CHAPTER ELEVEN

Monday Afternoon

left Dr. Hasp's enviable refuge and walked back to Ondstrand House, to the executive dining room and the coffee bar there, and I filled a tall cup from one of the miraculous machines. I was affixing the lid when Nadia Blom appeared.

"Sedan chair repaired so quickly?" I asked. "I must have the name of your mechanic."

"Rest assured, I'm not following you. But a courier has arrived, and I wanted to let you know. She's waiting in the forecourt."

"Excellent," I said. I stepped past her and headed out of the dining room and towards the elevators. Nadia Blom followed in silence at my side. When we reached the elevator bank, she turned to me. Color rose in her face.

"I think I might owe you an apology. When you arrived on Saturday, I really had no idea what Standard Division was. I still don't, not completely, but I've learned that I should've been more deferential, perhaps."

I laughed. "Deferential—really? I can't imagine what you've heard in the past couple of days, Ms. Blom—or maybe I can. Something like: a shadowy service-within-a-service; accountable to no one; a law unto itself. And, concerning field agents, perhaps: judge, jury, and executioner; or half management consultant, half assassin; or, my own favorite formulation: warrior-monks of the security state. Am I close?"

She cocked her head. "Close enough, though not the 'warrior-monk' part."

I laughed again. "Rumor, gossip, and urban legend."

"And none of it true?"

I shrugged. "It's been months since I've assassinated anyone. Weeks, anyway. C'mon—I don't want to keep the courier waiting."

The courier was my driver from Saturday, though she didn't acknowledge me, or even emerge from her car. We merely exchanged paperwork, and I handed her ziplocks containing Allegra Stans's mobile phone, laptop, and camera, and the memory stick Caroline Drucker had given me, with copies on it of the phishing e-mails, along with the malware package they were designed to deliver. After which she drove off, without a word, but still with perfect posture.

Nadia Blom watched the car disappear down the long drive, then looked at me. "What now?" she asked.

"Now I will pay another visit to Protection, which I am capable of doing all by myself, so you may feel free to do whatever it is you do when you're not following me." Irritation began to blossom on her face, but I escaped into Ondstrand House before it reached full flower.

Victor Halsell found a small office for me in his department, a white, windowless cell. He'd also summoned a rangy young man, barely out of university, or perhaps middle school, to assist me. His name was Gerald, his uniform was a size too large, and his voice broke often, but he was able to show me how to query the logs of Ondstrand's access-control system, and how to search the video archives of the network of external cameras installed around the campus. He offered to run the searches for me and seemed massively relieved when I declined and asked him only for a pad of paper. I took a pen from my pocket when he left and hung my jacket on the back on the chair. Then I took a deep breath.

There's a tedium to this part—the establishment of a victim's where-abouts, movements, and contacts in the days and hours prior to death—which means that there can be, sometimes, a meditative quality to the exercise, a liberation of the over-busy conscious mind from forever playing connect-the-dots, and the achievement of a blissful drifting, in which the data wash over you and leave behind information, like shells glistening on the shore, and the story tells itself. Sadly, that morning in the white room was not one of those times.

It was, instead, like mining coal with a toothpick, an endless scrape,

scrape, scraping in a dark hole, an erosive process in which I played all the roles: the tide, the rock, and the sandy bits that were washed away. Minutes moved like months, but still I scraped on. It was too late for a late lunch by the time I reached a stopping point, but I had filled several sheets of paper with times into the lab, times out of the lab, times out of the lobby, times into the lobby, times out of the gate, and times back in.

I'd started eight weeks back, and Allegra Stans's routines, at least some of them, had grudgingly emerged from the logs and photos in the access-control system—muddy but unmistakable images of Stans entering and exiting her workroom—from video of Stans crossing the main-house lobby, sometimes in running kit, sometimes in a group of people in running kit—and from outside camera video of Stans, with and without her club, embarking on and returning from her runs. There were even videos of her getting into her car—a sporty foreign convertible, a forest-green classic over thirty years old—and driving through the gates, off property, to return several hours later.

So I knew she favored solitary runs in the morning—out by 6:00 a.m., back by 7:00, unless she had a training session with her club that day, in which case she was back by 6:40. And I knew she was early into her lab, typically before 8:00 a.m. most days, and that lunch was usually around 1:00 p.m. and over by 2:00, at least on days when she didn't train with her club. Her training schedule seemed to be Mondays and Thursdays, from 12:30 p.m. to 1:30 p.m., and on Fridays after work, from 6:00 p.m. to 7:00 p.m. Most other weeknights, she was in her lab until around 7:30 p.m., the exception being on Wednesdays, when she was out of the lab, out of the building, and driving through the gate by 3:00 p.m. Where she went after that was a mystery, and would stay such until I could get a tech team to extract some location information from her mobile. Wherever she went, she was never back before 7:00 p.m., and sometimes not till later.

Her weekends were similarly structured, except when they weren't. Typically, on Saturdays and Sundays, she ran early, usually for longer times, and went briefly into her lab. But there were occasions—three in eight weeks—when she drove off after her Saturday-morning run, and did not reappear on campus until Sunday evening.

The week prior to Stans's death saw no variance in her routine, at least not in the low-resolution version visible to me. She kept to her established schedule and was last seen—by the cameras in and around

Ondstrand House, at least— departing for a run at 5:49 a.m. There was no record of her having re-entered the building. A few hours later, she was found dead.

The riddle of how she had re-entered Ondstrand House was far from the only one before me. My notepad sketch of Allegra Stans's routine was like bad pointillism—grainy at best, and more questions than answers. I had no idea yet who, if anyone, she lunched with regularly, or who she dined with. I had no idea who she had worked alongside or who she'd gossiped with, if she'd gossiped at all. If she'd worked alongside of anyone. If she'd even had dinner. And her evenings—like her off-campus sojourns—were all blank space to me.

There was more I could do with data from the Ondstrand systems, I knew, that might improve the resolution. I could look at the people leaving or entering the building with Stans whenever she left or entered, or within five minutes of her, to see if some faces turned up more often than others. I could look at who exited any laboratory at times consistent with Stans's usual lunch times. I could look at who she seemed to be walking most closely to most often when the running club departed on its runs, and when it returned again. With Goss Ivessen's help, I could crunch all those data and more, but not just then.

I stood, stretched, and took a few deep breaths. Just then I had to talk to more people. I still had not spoken with anyone who would admit to knowing Allegra Stans well enough to fill the voids in my sketch—what she did with her evenings, for example, and who she did it with. Perhaps my next appointment, with Mario Pohl, would help connect some dots. If nothing else, it would get me out of this room. I gathered my papers and picked up my jacket.

Dr. Pohl waved at me as I came down the hallway. He was a tall, lanky man, elegantly rumpled, with a square chin and a quick, wide smile. The skin over his cheekbones was smooth and brown, and his graying hair was cut close to his scalp. His deep-set dark eyes presented first as solemn, on closer inspection as skeptical, and then as quietly amused.

He stood before one of the many white doors that lined the second-floor south-wing corridor. This one bore a number plaque that read *S-217*. Allegra Stans's lab. Pohl pushed up the sleeves on his gray sweater as I walked over.

"Agent Myles?" he asked, and nudged his glasses up on his nose. His voice was deep and sonorous.

"'Myles' will do," I said.

Pohl nodded, and lifted the photo ID card that hung by a lanyard about his neck. He touched it to a sensor pad set beside the door frame. "Shall we?" he said. The door made a soft whirring sound, and Pohl pressed down on the door lever. The lights came on as he pushed on the door, and I followed him in.

I hadn't known what to expect—not humming machinery and flashing lights, necessarily, or intricate scaffolds of bubbling glassware—but not this void, either. It was little more than a closet—perhaps ten feet by ten, windowless, with harsh white lights mounted on the ceiling and an ambient temperature barely north of meat-locker. The chilly sterility was relieved not at all by the furnishings: a white metal table with an Ondstrand computer, a white telephone, and a white metal desk lamp upon it; a white plastic chair with wheels and no mercy; two white metal filing cabinets, one small and one larger. *Closet* wasn't the right reference point, perhaps—*cell* might have been closer to the mark.

Mario Pohl leaned against a wall and offered me the single chair. I declined.

"Terry—Dr. Hasp—said you'd want to talk," Pohl said, "and to see Dr. Stans's office."

I nodded. "This is where she worked? No other workspace—no laboratory assigned to her?"

"This was it, until she had a new assignment," Pohl said. He shook his head gravely. "Really, it's just unbelievable, what's happened. I wasn't going to leave the city until Monday afternoon, but when I heard the news, I returned right away. Crazy."

"When did you last see Dr. Stans?"

He scratched his chin. "That was on Thursday, in the late afternoon, just before I left for the city. She was coming out of here, and I'd just left my office, which is down at the end of the hallway. We rode the elevator together and got off at the lobby. I went to my car; I'm not sure where Dr. Stans went."

"Did you speak with her?"

He nodded. "Not about anything of substance, really. The drive to the city, traffic, the weather forecast—that sort of thing. We exchanged wishes for a good weekend."

"Nothing else?" He shook his head. "She didn't mention her plans?" Another shake of the head. "Were you aware of any plans that she had?"

Pohl raised an eyebrow. "Aware? No—we were friendly, but we really didn't know each other well on a personal level."

"No? She'd worked for you for seven months."

"R&D is a large department, and I'm still finding my way around." I raised an eyebrow. "I joined Ondstrand not quite eight months ago, and, between the new job and the move from the city, I've had my hands full. And, honestly, Dr. Stans required very little of my time."

I crossed my arms on my chest. "Do you mean you didn't supervise her? Or did she resist supervision?"

Pohl shook his head. "I mean that she didn't need much of it. Allegra Stans was more than qualified for the position she held. Hell, she was more than qualified to hold *my* position. She handled her responsibilities—all of her projects—with no problems at all. I've told Terry more than once that she was grossly under-utilized."

"To which he answered . . . ?"

Mario Pohl considered, then shrugged. "He didn't, I suppose. He would say something to the effect that he was planning a reshuffling outside of R&D, and that Allegra would be a part of that. He's never mentioned time frames."

I nodded. "What kinds of projects was Dr. Stans working on?"

"A grab bag. There's overlap between R&D work and Special Projects, and some of what she was doing had crossover with work she'd been doing in Projects—work on cassette size, on unintended immunogenicity from some of our viral vectors, on improving yields and purity in our production runs overseas.

"Besides those, I gave her projects I would've liked to have done myself, but couldn't because of my managerial responsibilities. She had a wealth of experience and a deep knowledge of our procedures, having implemented a lot of them to begin with."

I looked around the little office. "She did all that from here?"

Pohl snorted. "She did. It doesn't look like much, does it?"

"It looks like punishment, Dr. Pohl."

He nodded. "This is the space Terry found for her when she transferred in, and if I had something better available, believe me, I'd have given it to her. As far as her assignments went, this space was actually suitable, if not the most pleasant, in that she wasn't doing any bench work at the moment. It was all analysis—evaluating data, running simulations, designing future experiments, that sort of thing. One way or another, it was design and data work."

"Did she complain about her office?"

"No, never, and I do think she was engaged with the projects I'd assigned to her. There weren't many other people I would've let look after those projects."

"So—she was a trusted number two?"

Pohl shrugged. "I would've welcomed that, but, as I said, I was under the impression that Allegra was with me only temporarily—that Terry had other things in mind for her."

"But he never said what."

"He didn't—though, truth be told, we didn't spend a great deal of time talking about her."

"Did you ever talk to Karen Muir about her—about her impressions of Dr. Stans, and her experience with her in Special Projects?"

Pohl leaned back and sighed. "We had a conversation not long after I joined—around the time Allegra transferred." He stopped and studied his shoes.

"And?"

He shrugged again. "I suppose I'd characterize her feedback as mixed. She was unequivocal about Allegra's smarts and capabilities—you couldn't spend ten minutes with Allegra and miss those. At the same time, she questioned . . . I suppose you could say Allegra's willingness to be a team player. Karen seemed to think that Allegra's inclination was to be concerned mainly with her own career."

I raised an eyebrow. "Did she cite specifics?"

Pohl raised a cautious hand. "She didn't, and I want to be careful not to mischaracterize Karen's views. You should talk to her about those."

"And when she gets back I will. But I'm curious about why she would go out of her way to describe Allegra to her new boss in that way. It borders on poisoning the well, does it not?"

"I didn't construe it that way, but if that was her intent, it didn't work with me. I don't know what if anything happened between her and Allegra, but I reach my own conclusions about people. Mine about Allegra were that she was knowledgeable, rigorous, curious, and creative, with the highest professional standards."

I nodded. "But it was your impression that something *had* happened between Dr. Stans and Dr. Muir?"

Pohl took a deep breath. "Really, Agent Myles—"

"Myles," I reminded him.

"I don't want to speculate. I suppose I got the impression that there was history there, but as to specifics—again, I'd suggest talking to Karen."

I let silence settle for a while, and let Pohl relax. When the tension had gone out of his shoulders, I asked, "Has it been a difficult transition, coming from the city to this rather sheltered environment?"

Pohl was relieved to be on more stable ground. He chuckled. "*Sheltered*. I suppose it *is* that—like being back in uni days, or even earlier. It used to be a boarding school, you know."

"So I've heard."

"And it *is* a bit out of the way. Though the towns nearby are pleasant enough, if a little precious. They have all the mod cons."

"I wasn't thinking just of the physical circumstances or the local services. How is it culturally?" Pohl's face clouded again, and his brow furrowed. "A small company on a closed campus, far from the wider world—I wonder if office personalities and politics aren't oppressive sometimes—even suffocating."

He raised an eyebrow and smiled ruefully. "Now you're flat-out inviting me to gossip, Myles."

"While I certainly welcome gossip, Doctor, I'm not seeking it from you. I'm simply asking for your unguarded impressions of the interpersonal environment here. Are people generally collegial? Is it a particularly hierarchical environment? Are the elbows particularly sharp? Does the office org chart weigh heavily on the minds around here? If I was a colleague of yours—a close friend, say from your prior company—and I was thinking about taking a position here, what would you tell me?"

Pohl laughed. "Simply my 'unguarded impressions'? Of my colleagues and employers—who happen to have a certain amount of influence over my professional and financial prospects? And you want me to pretend that you're not an agent of the most intimidating arm of the security services, but instead that you're my close friend. And you just come right out and say all that. . . ."

"I'm simply being forthright, Dr. Pohl."

He laughed again. "I'm sure that's greatly prized in Standard Division. Do you approach everyone like this? I'd have thought you'd just threaten imprisonment and so forth."

"To the occasional chagrin of my masters, I favor a lighter touch where possible. So let us trade like for like—an exchange of forthrightness—and I'll go first. I'm asking you these questions, Dr. Pohl, because you're the new man on the senior management team, and the only one not a founder of the company. And you're mature enough—astute enough, I think—not to subscribe to all of the local folklore concerning the wisdom and general magnificence of the founders. And so I think, perhaps, you might share something useful with me, without unnecessary . . . exertions."

Pohl studied me for a while, an opaque weighing and measuring uncomfortably reminiscent of Director Mehta's. Then he sighed. "If you were my close friend, then I would say that the atmosphere is less relaxed here than at some places, but certainly collegial. There's a good deal of lip service paid to the open exchange of ideas, yes, but there's a good deal of actual exchange as well. Terry Hasp goes out of his way to see that that happens. And while some might see him as overly fond of enforced good fellowship, and a bit self-important— a first-amongst-equals sort, if you will, and a bit . . . *performative* as the big-vision scientist-entrepreneur—he's gathered some fine minds here. A very impressive bunch, not least of which is Hasp himself, who may be a bit theatrical, but is by no means untalented.

"I would also point out—though you'd know this if you'd worked at any biotech enterprise, and especially a privately held one—that, regardless of the collegiality of the environment, or how hierarchical or informal it may seem, what weighs heavily on the minds of many people here is less the org chart and more the stock options. There are reasons the scientists here are not in academia or in the public sector, and one of them is money. There's an opportunity to make a good deal of it at a firm like this, but it's a competitive environment. The waters are rough, and the current's sometimes treacherous. So, yes, there are sharp elbows here, just as there were at every other firm I've worked for or heard about. But perhaps Standard Division is the exception." Pohl smiled again and held my gaze. "How was that for forthright, Myles? Did I hold up my side?"

I smiled back. "So far, Dr. Pohl. Let me take advantage of your candor further and ask you about Dr. Muir."

Pohl stiffened. "Karen? We spoke about Karen already."

"We spoke about her view of Dr. Stans. I'm interested in your view of her."

"You really are pushing things now, Myles."

I shrugged. "I haven't met her yet, but she is a part of the senior management team, and one of the founders, in addition to having been Dr. Stans's boss for several years. My curiosity seems well placed."

"My issue isn't with your curiosity, it's with you asking me to satisfy it."

"Again, I simply seek your impressions. Given in confidence and held that way."

Pohl regarded me again, considering. He nodded. "I'm not sure if I have anything useful to provide. Dr. Muir is a very smart, very able administrator and researcher. A bit of a polymath, as well—besides her degrees in molecular biology and genetics, she has an MD and an MBA. Her scientific interests strike me as eclectic, I'd say. Not necessarily in the mainstream, but by no means frivolous. There's nothing of the dilettante about her. And, obviously, she's very committed to the company."

"Obviously?"

"As you said, she's one of the founders, she's on the senior management committee, and she has a sizable personal investment in the firm."

"Yes?"

"She's the largest individual shareholder."

"A larger shareholder than her stepbrother?" Pohl nodded. "Does that cause friction?"

Pohl smiled. "They playact a kind of friction between them—like an old married couple for whom bickering is the default mode."

"So . . . they're close?"

Pohl considered his shoes again. "I'd say so."

"And who usually prevails in their playacting skirmishes?"

"Karen, nearly always. Always, in fact."

"Despite Hasp being the public face of the company?"

Pohl nodded. "It was a bit confusing for me at first. Last year, when I was considering my move here, they conducted each of my several interviews together. And on the management committee there's never any appreciable daylight between them—not really. Terry might occasionally voice disagreement on some topic, but it never lasts long."

I raised an eyebrow. "And Dr. Witmer?"

"A decent enough fellow. But on the committee, he's very much a lapdog running between them."

"An uncomfortable position for him?"

Pohl shrugged. "I imagine, but he seems used to it."

"And for you?"

He smiled. "Uncomfortable? Not really. My comfort was addressed when I negotiated my contract here—if it hadn't been, I wouldn't have signed on. As far as the management committee goes, the process and personalities may be a bit odd, but I can't say I've disagreed with anything of substance that the committee has decided."

"That *Dr. Muir* has decided—no?" I asked.

"Point taken," Pohl said.

"And if you had disagreed?"

Pohl's smile turned rueful. "What might I have done? I suppose I'd have thought long and hard about that. Dr. Muir can be a bit . . . intimidating."

I raised an eyebrow. "How so?"

He nodded. "There's a temper beneath all that rationality. It's never been directed at me, happily, but I've seen flashes, and, based on those, I suppose I can understand why Terry and Piers are deferential."

"By which you mean intimidated?"

Pohl sighed. "I think that's entirely enough talking out of school, Myles—unless Standard Division intends to *insist*."

I shook my head. "You've been quite helpful, Dr. Pohl. And now, I think, I will search this office."

Pohl stood away from the wall. "Of course. Would you like me to . . ."

"To leave, yes," I said, which Pohl did without further comment, and with evident relief.

My search didn't take long. The tabletop was empty of anything other than company equipment, and the filing cabinets—both the large and the small—held the same, mostly in the form of hard copies of indecipherable tables of numbers, equally arcane bar charts and scatter diagrams, and computer-generated images of DNA segments.

The only personal effects of Allegra Stans that I came across were in the bottom drawer of the small filing cabinet: a well-worn pair of running shoes and a pair of rather fragrant socks.

CHAPTER TWELVE

Monday Afternoon

It was midafternoon by the time I emerged into fresh air—cold, blustery, and threatening, with a low, fast-moving sky. A raindrop hit my cheek, but it was just a warning shot. I didn't care; I wanted to stretch my legs. I wanted to see the ocean.

I crossed the courtyard and followed a brick path around the north wing. The north face of the building rose like a cliff on my left, and the wind hurtled along it and pushed at me as I turned the corner. I leaned into it as I walked. It carried sand that stung my face and caught in my hair. To my right, across thirty or so yards of rolling lawn, there were trees sweeping back and forth across the sky as if in ecstasy. As they moved, I saw lights through the limbs—a lit path and, deeper in the woods, windows. Dr. Hasp in his keep.

I pressed on and came to the small loading dock that adjoined the kitchen where Allegra Stans had been found, and the narrow service road that led away north from it. After the loading dock, the ground rose sharply. The wind strengthened as I rounded another corner and came to the seaward side of Ondstrand House.

There was no courtyard here, or fountain; instead, there was the sweeping semicircle of a stone terrace, with railing and balustrades. The railing was punctuated at intervals by cement planters, pitted by salt air, their contents still bundled in burlap, like ungainly infants. The terrace was empty but for a dozen wooden deck chairs stacked at the north end. They were ancient, peeling things, badly weathered, and looked like artifacts from some mountain sanitorium, long defunct.

I went up to the terrace, to the midpoint of the railing's arc, and looked out.

It was chaos in white and gray: shifting sea and shifting sky, waves, whitecaps, and low cloud careening and shattering against one another, painted with a palette that ran from rime to wet slate. The cliff edge beyond the terrace rail, and the crescent of beach and cove directly below, were all invisible from my vantage, obscured either by the steepness of the cliff or by the same mist that hid the horizon. The wind ran through the balustrades with a low ululation, the surf was an endless clatter, and the movement of water and cloud was a dizzying slide that I felt in my legs. The illusion of being on open water was powerful, but this was no luxury cruise on some unsinkable behemoth. Rather, the sense was of rushing headlong in a ship badly overmatched by the weather, and with a heedless captain at the helm.

I recrossed the terrace to the brick path and followed it towards the cliff. It ended at a chest-high pipe fence that was rusted and leaning where its concrete footings had crumbled. The fence ran in both directions along the cliff edge but was interrupted to my immediate right by a flight of concrete steps. They were steep and narrow, set into the cliff at right angles, and they descended to the beach with nothing between the treads and the gray air but a banister that was mostly rust. The wind sought alternately to shoulder me into the cliff or to pluck me from its face as I picked my way down the eighty or so feet. By the time I reached the sand, it had begun to drizzle.

The beach was an ecru-colored curve perhaps half a mile long from north to south, and as bleak and beautiful as only empty beaches can be in gathering darkness, in chilly air, in an off-season. It was thirty yards from the cliff to the fringe of seaweed that marked the last high tide, where the sand became dark and velvet-smooth, like the flanks of a horse. The southern tip of the beach was lost in haze, but to the north I could see the bend of the cliff out towards the sea. At the base of the cliff were the caves that Victor Halsell had mentioned, where trespassing kids drank, smoked dope, and had sex. I walked north, my feet sliding in cold sand.

The smell of seaweed was strong as I slogged, and there was a tang of salt on my lips. I looked up, but caught no glimpse of Ondstrand House or of the terrace. The stairway had vanished.

The caves were a network of recesses and hollows at the base of the cliff, which began where the beach gave way to rocky outcrops. The largest recess was the closest—a high, narrow band shell carved by surf and weather. It was sheltered from the rain and from the worst of the wind, but the sounds of waves and gusts echoed weirdly from every direction. A pile of charred driftwood stood at its mouth, in a shallow pit, on a bed of blackened stones, and graffiti on the walls nearby was as obscure in its meaning as hieroglyphs. There were cigarette butts around the pit, more than a few beer bottles, and the brown remains of old joints, and all of it was sodden and crusted with sand and looked months old.

The floor of the cave was carpeted in sand that was deeper farther in. I followed it back. It was quieter here, and darker; I found a penlight in my jacket and flicked it on.

If out front was where the drinking and dope smoking took place, this must be where the sex happened. The ragged circular niche, maybe ten feet in diameter, was a dim and chilly spot, but it was private and out of the wind, and some improvements had been made. A low table made of driftwood stood against one rocky wall, holding an empty wine bottle, a box of wooden matches, and a seashell ashtray, and candles—twenty or more—had been affixed to the walls with dollops of wax. Most of them were spent, or nearly so—little more than commas of black wick, with halos of soot above where they'd burned, and surrealist mounds of colored slag below. But there were three new candles on the walls, too, white and barely used.

I ran my penlight over the candles and followed the strands of wax down the wall to small white puddles on the ground. And stopped when the light crossed sets of footprints in the sand—two sets, small and large, and both with treaded soles—and caught on something shiny. I went farther in, crouching and doing my best to avoid the footprints. I knelt for a better view. It was a corner of green foil that became a condom wrapper when I lifted it from the sand. Like the three candles, it, too, was new. The condom was also there, just beside the wrapper, but I didn't touch that until I'd pulled a pair of nitrile gloves from my pocket and found a ziplock bag.

CHAPTER THIRTEEN

Monday Evening

This is a long drive, Myles," Jane Wilding said. "And I don't know that I'd keep making it but for your smiling face and the lovely gifts you have waiting." She held open an evidence bag, and I dropped my two ziplocks—one containing a used condom, the other its wrapper—inside. She marked my name, the date, and the time on it, sealed it shut, and slipped it into her shoulder bag. "Same brand as in her nightstand?"

"Same," I said.

Jane had returned to Ondstrand House with her forensics team an hour before. Her team was in the cave on the beach, where she'd joined them to survey the scene and give them their brief. Then we'd come up to my rooms. I'd conjured coffee, and Jane drank some, then put it on the low table. Her dark hair was damp and tangled from the drizzle, and she ran her hands through it and then pulled her black jumper over her head. She had an orange singlet underneath. She tossed the jumper atop her bulky coat in the corner, stretched, and took a seat. Her pear-and-freesia scent filled the room. She unlaced one boot and then the other, kicked both off, and propped her stockinged feet on the table.

"Decent digs they've given you," she said. "Warm and cozy. All you're missing is the fire."

I nodded. "You think your people will get anything more from the cave?"

"Probably nothing as useful as the DNA gold mine you've turned up. But you never know. You hoping for that locket of hers?"

I nodded. "It has yet to turn up," I said.

"We rechecked her personal effects after I got your message—no joy. But if it's down there, the lads will find it."

"Anything to be done with the footprints?"

She made a theatrical grimace. "Dry sand is not the best medium, and they were already pretty blurred, but they'll do their best. And there may be other bits to pick up—hair, skin, prints on the wine bottle or the candles, what have you."

I nodded, and Jane opened her bag again and drew out a file folder. "But what you found might help us fill in some blanks here," she said, and handed me the folder. "Autopsy of Dr. Allegra Stans. Figured I'd deliver it in person. I've sent a digital copy as well. Copy to your porter?"

"Please," I said. I opened the file and leafed through. "Care to give me the headlines?"

Jane reached for her coffee, drank some more, and wiped her mouth demurely with the back of her hand. "There are three. First, we place approximate time of death between seven and eight on Saturday morning. Her time in the fridge complicates things a little, but we're pretty confident of that range. Second, cause of death is acute spinal-cord injury, in this case a complete injury—a severing—resulting from crushing trauma to the second and third cervical vertebrae, which were themselves the result of blunt-force insult. Death would've been instantaneous, or nearly so. Third, there are signs she engaged in sexual activity not long before death, though nothing to indicate that it was nonconsensual."

"'Not long' in this context means . . . ?"

"Means we can't be more precise. I give it a three-hour window prior to death. So, if our estimated time of death is seven to eight a.m., then the sexual contact might've taken place as early as four a.m., and as late as just before eight."

"The signs you noted . . . ?"

"Dried saliva, traces of dried pre-ejaculate, pubic hairs, all recovered from her body, all belonging to the same person—a person not Allegra Stans."

"You get DNA from any or all of that?"

"We did—all from the same unknown male. If it matches what we get from your discovery, and if we can lift Stans's DNA from that as well, it will tell us where this sexual activity took place."

"Don't forget matching the condom wrapper to the lot in Stans's nightstand."

Jane bared her teeth theatrically. "As if I would."

I smiled. "The crushing trauma—any idea of what it was caused by?"

"The collision of the back of her neck with a rigid object at a high relative velocity."

"And this object?"

She shrugged. "The proverbial blunt one. Smooth surface, no paint or particle transfer, possibly metallic, glazed ceramic, or some synthetic stone. The cross section is a sort of wedge shape, with the edge having a rounded nose. There are diagrams and dimensions in the report. Her skin was intact, so if we do find a candidate there won't be blood on it, but there might be touch DNA."

I nodded. "And now for the grand prize—was this collision accidental, or something else?"

Jane Wilding stood and motioned for me to stand, too. I did. She stepped in front of me, about arm's length away. She leaned over and looked behind me, then placed a hand on each of my biceps and came up very close. In her stockinged feet, her nose came to my lips, and the scent of her filled my head. She tilted her head up and spoke softly.

"Definitely something else," she said. She leaned in then and took a step forward, forcing me to take a step back. She did that four more times, walking me backwards until I was against the wall. Then she pulled me forward, and just as our faces touched, she pushed me away with force, so that my head bumped the wall. She held me there and reached her hand behind my neck.

"The blunt object caught her here," she said, pressing warm fingers to my C3 vertebra. Then she moved her hand to the back of my head. "It snapped her head back with enough force to leave a contusion just here, where her head was stopped by something fixed—either a floor or a wall."

"You think the blunt object was something protruding up from the floor, or out from a wall? Something she hit, not something she was hit with?" Jane nodded. "Maybe she tripped and fell on . . . whatever," I said.

Jane smiled. "A fine theory, undercut somewhat by the fact that it happened twice."

"Twice?"

Jane held my arms again and pulled me away from the wall. Then she pushed me and pulled me and pushed me again, bouncing my head—once, twice—gently against the wall. "Twice," she whispered. "The second blow crushed her C2."

"With sufficient momentum, you wouldn't need a lot of raw strength," I said.

"No," Jane answered. "It could've been a man; it could've been a woman."

"Were there marks on her arms?"

"Bruising, right where I'm holding you, but she was wearing a jacket, so no trace on her skin. And we weren't able to pull anything from the jacket itself."

"Any indication of hand size from the bruises?"

"Nothing useful—a medium-sized hand. Could belong to a man or a woman."

I nodded. Jane leaned closer, and I stood very still. Her breath was warm on my neck. She laid her hands on my chest. They were hot through the fabric of my shirt.

"What are we doing?" I said eventually.

"I believe that, once upon a time, you called it being 'collegial,' no? As in two colleagues passing the time while their teammates complete some work on the beach. Work that should take another couple of hours to finish, at least."

I took a deep breath and put my arms around her, and put my face in her dark, wavy hair. It smelled of salt and the sea, and it made me light-headed. She turned her face up, and her mouth and tongue were soft against mine. My hands were in her hair and at the nape of her neck. She bit gently at my lower lip.

"Jane," I murmured.

"Hmm?"

"How tall was Allegra Stans?"

She stiffened. "What?"

"How tall was Allegra Stans?"

She pushed away from me, shaking her head. "Five feet five inches."

"So—five-six or -seven in running shoes."

"Something like that. So what?"

"So come on," I said, and went to the door.

Jane Wilding picked up her boots and her jumper. "You *are* an ass, Myles," she said, chuckling ruefully. "Without question—an ass."

I found my way to the executive dining room, and Wilding followed. It was empty when we got there, and dim, and we crossed the lounge and the dining room and went through the door that led to the bathrooms, the wine cave, and the dumbwaiters. I went into the first bathroom and turned on the light.

It was as I'd first seen it: a simple, one-person affair of white tiles, a toilet, a sink, a mirror, a shelf with paper towels and a box of tissues on it, a waste can below. I pointed to the shelf, a brushed-steel wedge with a rounded nose.

"That's at about five feet, yes? About the right height?"

Jane looked, squinted, and nodded slowly. "Yes—that's about right."

"There are three more bathrooms back here like this one. It was in one of these."

She nodded some more. "Shit," she said softly. "I'll have the team up here after they're done on the beach."

CHAPTER FOURTEEN

Tuesday Midday

If you hadn't come looking for me, I would have come to you," Sandra Silber said. We were in the corridor outside of the office she shared in the north wing of Ondstrand House, two floors up from the executive dining room. Silber pulled the door shut behind her and set a brisk pace down the hall. If my legs hadn't been several inches longer than hers, I would've had trouble keeping up. We passed an elevator bank, but Silber didn't pause.

"I never take those," she said. "Too slow, especially at this time of day."

I followed her into the stairwell, and down the stairs.

Silber was a biostatistician, a recently minted Ph.D., not yet thirty; though she had been a full-time employee in the Trials Department at Ondstrand Biologic for just two years, she had worked there on a part-time basis for several years prior, while completing her doctorate. Her name was first on the list of running-club members that Nadia Blom had provided me, and she was on Ivessen's list as well—of the dozen people who were in Ondstrand House at the approximate time of Stans's death and who also lacked an alibi.

Silber had a broad, ruddy, freckled face and a snub nose, and there were plentiful red highlights, not naturally occurring, in her cropped brown hair. She wore a black tracksuit with white stripes down the arms and legs. The jacket was snug across her strong-looking shoulders, and I wondered if, besides being a runner and a very fast walker, she also rowed or lifted weights. Her small blue eyes were bright and darting, and there was a darting quality to her movements and her speech that reminded me of an overcaffeinated chipmunk. There was also, I thought, in her hair, her tracksuit—even in her brand of running shoes—an attempt to emulate Allegra Stans.

She trotted down the stairs and across the lobby; when we emerged into the forecourt of Ondstrand House, she paused to turn her face into the sunlight and take a deep breath. Then she led us at a quick march along a trail that ran between a terraced lawn and a manicured wood, headed more or less in the direction of the property's main gate. I felt sweat pricking on my brow as we strode through patches of midday sun and the thin shade of still-bare trees. Silber's head bobbed below my shoulder, and she huffed a little, as if keeping cadence, as she marched along.

"I'm glad we found each other, Dr. Silber, and I appreciate you forgoing your run for me."

She made a flapping motion with her hands. "Do you run, Agent Myles?"

"Only when I must. And 'Myles' will do. Did you train with Dr. Stans?"

She nodded enthusiastically. "Of course—Allie and I ran together *all* the time. At club practices and races, naturally, but also just the two of us—mornings or at lunch."

I nodded. "I understand she was a talented athlete."

"*So* talented. It was as if her bones were full of air—she'd just float above the ground. 'Hollow bones,' I'd say to her, and she'd laugh."

"You knew her for some time."

"Since I started here. I was a part-timer then; even so, I ran with the club."

"Her death must have been a shock."

Sandy Silber came to an abrupt halt and pivoted to face me. "*Shock?* It's been—I don't know what it's been. 'Shock' is too mild a word, though; I couldn't believe it when I heard. And then I heard there were—I don't know—*unusual circumstances.* I don't even know *what* that means, only that her death wasn't accidental. And what am I supposed to think about *that?* If she died here—on campus—and her death wasn't accidental, doesn't that mean that somebody here—one of *us* . . . I mean, why else would you be here?" Silber gasped, dramatically, I thought, and put her hands to her face. Her shoulders shook, and then she peered through her fingers at me. "The thought that someone here could be responsible—it's just *too* awful."

"Let's not get ahead of ourselves," I said, and tried to make it sound comforting. I continued down the trail, and Silber followed. "You first met Dr. Stans how many years ago?"

"Five years."

"But you didn't work together."

She shook her head. "I was helping out on a trial, and she was in R&D. She hadn't been here all that long herself at that point—a few years, maybe. She wasn't any older than I am now."

"Nevertheless, you became friends."

She nodded. "Fast friends, but more than that. She was a mentor to me—an older sister, almost. A role model." Silber paused, clutched her hands together, and put them to her chest. "I could talk to her about anything. She helped me sort through questions about my degree program, my career, a lot of things."

"A friendship—a *relationship* like that—I can appreciate that this must be very painful. To lose someone who knows you well . . . And you must've known her quite well, too."

She wiped at her eyes. "I *did*—as well as or better than anyone, I'd guess."

"I'm glad to hear that, Dr. Silber. Because, while I've learned something of Dr. Stans from people I've spoken to thus far, I don't feel I've yet spoken to anyone who knew her intimately."

Sandy Silber stopped again and nodded furiously. "Because no one did—well, almost no one. She didn't open up to people easily. She was very friendly—and *so* charming—but when it came to vulnerability, to real intimacy, Allie had a hard time with that. She was *guarded*. She didn't let just anyone in."

"But she let you in?"

More nodding. "I like to think it was because we were alike in so many ways. As close as sisters."

I nodded back at her. "Then perhaps you can shed some light on Dr. Stans's personal life. Her sexual or romantic relationships."

Silber drew herself up, tugged at the cuffs of her track jacket, and pulled down the hem. Then she took a deep breath and marched forward again. "To understand that, you need to understand something important about Allie—something essential. Allie has—*had*—attitudes about certain things that aren't always commonplace in a woman. That you might more often find in a man."

"There's no need to be oblique, Dr. Silber. Are you saying that she smoked cigars? Drank beer to excess?"

She shook her head. "Her attitudes about her career, for one thing. Allie wasn't uncomfortable with competition the way some women are—she wasn't ambivalent about it in the slightest. And she was just as comfortable with her own ambition. It's not something she gave a second thought to or apologized for. She didn't worry that it was unseemly or overreaching—not ever. She had a man's confidence in her talents, and a man's certainty that her talents entitled her to things."

"Things like career advancement?"

Silber looked momentarily puzzled. "Oh yes—certainly that, too, without doubt."

"'Too'? I'm not following."

She waved her hand in frustration. "I'm saying that Allie had a *man's attitude,* you understand? She felt she was *entitled* to things. To things, and to *people.* If she was attracted to someone, if she wanted them, then she felt entitled to them and she . . . had them."

"*Had* them?"

"It sounds strange when you say it. It wasn't an assaultive thing . . . not really. But Allie was *so* attractive and *so* charming, and when she wanted something . . . someone . . . she could be very persistent. Insistent, really."

"What you're describing is predatory behavior, Dr. Silber. Did Allegra sexually harass people?"

"No, no," Sandy Silber said, and flapped her hands again. "I don't think anyone would perceive it that way. At worst, they might feel . . . manipulated, if they weren't actually thrilled by her attention. And many people—most people—were thrilled.

"Besides, when a man acts like that, it gets lost in that gray zone of—what?—*seduction.* Yes, when a man does it, it's called seduction. As if all that exhausting pursuit is somehow supposed to indicate the sincerity of his passion? He's sincere, all right—sincere about wanting to fuck you. Yet, when a woman acts that way, when a woman has appetites . . ."

I stopped walking, and so did Silber. She looked at the ground. I heard branches creak in the small wind, and her rapid breath. "What are you saying, Dr. Silber?"

"I . . . I don't . . ." She took a deep breath. "I'm saying that Allie didn't have romantic relationships per se—not intimate ones. But she had sexual liaisons. I'm saying that some people might not understand her—not the way I do . . . did. They might not approve of her attitudes and her appetites. People fear what they don't understand. They resent it.

"And some of the people she was involved with . . . they may have thought there was more to the relationship than there really was. More than Allie thought there was."

I nodded. "Is this what you wanted to tell me? Why you said you would've come looking for me?" Silber nodded back and wiped her nose. "Is there someone in particular you had in mind?" Another nod. "Is there a name?"

Silber shook her head. "I don't know his name. But I know he isn't from campus. He's local—from town."

"From which town?"

"I don't know that, either. Allie didn't say. But I know she saw him often—every week at least. Someone like that could get the wrong idea. Get overly invested."

"Someone like what, Dr. Silber?"

"Someone from . . . from such a different world. And, no, I'm not being a snob. It's just the reality of things. Allie was sophisticated, educated, while someone born and bred in one of the villages around here is likely not. There can be a world of difference between such people. A world of misunderstanding."

"You know this for a fact? Dr. Stans told you these things?"

"I know he lives around here, and that he's from around here. It's only reasonable. Just as it's only reasonable that someone like that would misconstrue—"

I cut her off. "Was this something Dr. Stans worried about?"

"She . . . she *should* have. Who else could've hurt her? It must've been someone from outside."

"Must it? Perhaps you could tell me who else Dr. Stans was seeing, or had been seeing?"

Her ruddy face grew more so. "I . . . I don't . . . I couldn't possibly—"

"*Couldn't possibly say,* Dr. Silber? You, who knew Dr. Stans so well? I have a hard time believing that. Just as I don't believe you'd be foolish enough to obstruct an investigation carried out by Standard Division."

Sandy Silber's face went white then, and she stammered for a while before she spoke.

CHAPTER FIFTEEN

Tuesday Evening

N ot truthful," Director Mehta said, "but useful."

"Yes. Dr. Silber is conflicted—to say the least—in her feelings towards Dr. Stans, and delusional regarding the nature of their relationship, but her fixation made her a close observer of Stans's activities. And some of her assessments of Stans's personality and proclivities—and their impacts on others—are germane."

Director Mehta chuckled, and sipped at her tea. On my tablet screen I could see that she was in her office, drinking from her office tea service—graceful cups and saucers, the porcelain no thicker than an eggshell, sugar tongs like the talons of a tiny silver raptor. I could see the wide window behind her, the late-day light spilling in, reflecting off the river that glowed like another sun.

I continued. "I did go back to the security videos of Stans departing on her runs—with her club and without. I reviewed the two months I'd already watched and went back two months prior. I found no occasion on which Stans and Silber ran together, just the two of them."

Director Mehta shook her head. " 'As close as sisters.' Poor thing."

"Leila Vroman said something less kind about Dr. Silber. 'Pathetic little fool' was the term she used."

"And who is Leila Vroman?"

"A protein biochemist, and until recently another member of the running club. About two months ago, she began a secondment to one of the overseas labs that Ondstrand has contracted with for volume production. I spoke with her this afternoon—this evening for her. She thinks Sandy Silber has been mooning over Stans since Silber was a part-timer at Ondstrand. According to Vroman, Silber's sexual encounter with Stans was Silber's first with another woman. Vroman's read is that Stans was bored and Silber was low-hanging fruit. She thinks also that Stans regretted it afterwards, as the encounter left Silber annoyingly—cloyingly—infatuated."

Director Mehta smiled minutely. "Dr. Vroman was certainly forthcoming with you, Myles. How did you sway her?"

I thought of Vroman's handsome, freckled face on my tablet screen, and the emotions that were plain there, despite the distance and her fatigue. "No swaying was required; she was eager to help. Unlike Silber, she seemed actually to have been an intimate of Stans's, at least in some respects. She and Stans started working at Ondstrand seven years ago, just a month apart from one another, and both in R&D under Witmer. Vroman seemed genuinely shocked by Dr. Stans's death—saddened and angry, too. And while she doesn't hold Silber in high regard, she did corroborate several things Silber told me."

"Such as?"

"That Stans was sexually confident and assertive, that she could be charming, seductive, and even manipulative in her amorous pursuits, and that a less confident person who was the object of her interest might find her behavior to border on the . . . 'inappropriate' was the term Vroman used."

Director Mehta nodded. "Did she corroborate anything else Silber told you?"

"Vroman confirmed that she and Stans had had a sexual relationship, though she characterized it as an entirely casual arrangement, and said things between them had been platonic for nearly a year. She also confirmed that Stans had once had a relationship—and for her, a long one—with Piers Witmer."

Director Mehta sipped her tea and nodded. "How long was long, and how long ago?" she asked.

"Neither Vroman nor Silber was sure. Vroman thought it began while Stans was working for Witmer. Stans worked there for two years before her transfer to Special Projects. Dr. Vroman thought the affair had ended prior to that and had become *messy* somehow. That was the word she chose."

"Isn't Dr. Witmer married?"

"The source of the messiness, perhaps," I said.

"Perhaps. What about the other names Silber gave you: Loring, Geary, and Holliman?"

"Vroman believes that Stans and Loring might've had a fling—Loring is a member of the running club as well, one of the security staff, working for Victor Halsell. As for the other two, she believes it's possible—Vroman claims they're both Stans's type, meaning young, attractive, fit, and emotionally undemanding—but Vroman could neither confirm nor refute the relationships. As Vroman put it: she didn't keep score the way Silber did."

"No scorecard is required to observe that Dr. Stans seemed to use the running club as something like a dating service." I nodded. "And Geary and Holliman—are they both scientists?" she asked.

"Harris Geary is; he works in one of the Special Projects labs. Sylvie Holliman is the number two to Ondstrand's CFO. Interestingly, Geary is one of the people who received a spear-phishing e-mail several months back."

"Another fascinating coincidence," Director Mehta said, smiling. "Did your new friend happen to shed any light on Dr. Stans's apparent demotion last year?"

I shook my head. "All Dr. Vroman could tell me was that it was not something she and Dr. Stans had discussed. She had a sense that it was something Dr. Stans was sensitive about—not surprising, I suppose—and that there was some strain between Stans and Karen Muir."

"Consistent, then, with what Dr. Pohl had to say, though not precisely aligned with Dr. Hasp's characterization," the Director said.

I nodded. "Pohl suggested a certain rancor towards Dr. Stans on Karen Muir's part, while Hasp presented the move as merely a reassignment, pending a promotion."

The Director raised an eyebrow. "I imagine you're keen to speak with Dr. Muir. She sounds a fascinating personality."

I nodded. "Ivessen has me hip-deep in background reports, and even without input from Domestic, Dr. Muir's is certainly one of the more interesting."

"Yes?"

"As Dr. Pohl said, she's something of an intellectual powerhouse, with multiple degrees and academic accolades that more than rival her brother's. More interesting, though, is the money. Ivessen's report answers the question of where Karen Muir got the capital to become Ondstrand Biologic's largest shareholder. The source, it turns out, was Marcus Muir."

The Director smiled and nodded. "Of Muirsoft. Yes, she's his widow—one of them, anyway. The one actually married to him when he died."

"You knew."

"It rings a bell."

"You might've mentioned it."

She sighed. "It was hardly a secret, Myles."

"Yes, well, they weren't married long—less than three years—and there were several other ex wives and offspring with seniority, as it were. Still, Dr. Muir managed to walk away with a sizable chunk when all was said and done—not in percentage terms, but even a small percent of an estate that large is nontrivial. It enabled her to fund the purchase of the Ondstrand property and much of the renovation, and to acquire a controlling stake in the company."

The Director nodded and sipped her tea. "Quite an age gap there."

"Between Muir and her late husband? Thirty-four years."

"Had he been ill long?"

"Ivessen says he had been. The proximate cause was pneumonia, which was not surprising, given the list of Muir's chronic respiratory ailments. The earlier wives demanded an inquiry nonetheless, but nothing came of it, at least not as far as Ivessen has discovered. Again, without any input from Domestic."

She sighed again. "I did hear you before, Myles," she said, and switched subjects. "Has he reported on Dr. Stans's finances?"

"He has, though there was little to report. A straightforward arrangement of checking and savings accounts; four credit cards with minimal balances; equity investments mostly in the form of index funds, with some direct positions in tech; stock and options in Ondstrand Biologic; no real estate; no debt. Net worth estimated at just north of one million. And all very stable—no changes in the pattern of activity across those accounts in years."

"Assuming those accounts tell the whole story," the Director said. "Any progress on Dr. Stans's missing locket?"

I shook my head. "Both Silber and Vroman recognized it, and both offered that it was something she always wore. Leila Vroman thought it was a family piece—a gift from her parents, perhaps."

"But no ideas of what might have become of it?" I shook my head again. "And Dr. Wilding's team has found no trace."

"Not yet."

"So—a mystery."

"For the moment at least. I'm still waiting on the tech team for its assessment of those e-mails. And I'd love to know if they've found anything on Stans's laptop or phone, or on her camera. Location data from her phone could be useful in identifying her off-campus friend."

She swiveled in her chair. I heard a burst of rapid keystrokes, and then she turned back to me. "A fire has been lit," she said.

"Thank you, Director."

She nodded. "Dr. Wilding tells me her visit with you was productive," she said. Her tone was neutral and her expression opaque.

"We've made progress in reconstructing Stans's final hours, but there are still many blanks to fill in, and I have a long list of people to see."

Director Mehta smiled. "Always so measured, Myles. It's one of your many admirable traits: you never oversell. I'll let you get back to it, then."

"Yes, Director."

My tablet screen went blank, and I rose and stretched and walked around the guest quarters' little sitting room. The fading sun struck the stone face of Ondstrand House and fell in dusty beams through the windows. I let out a long breath, and the sound of it made the room seem emptier.

I stood over the coffee table and stared down at my several lists: Allegra Stans's former co-workers in Special Projects; the members of her running club; the recipients of the spear-phishing e-mails; Allegra's current and former lovers; the people who were in Ondstrand House without alibis on the Saturday morning of her death. These were not, of course, disjoint sets: the list of Stans's lovers—a long one, and almost certainly incomplete—included several members of the running club and one of the phishing e-mail recipients. The running club included several members—Piers Witmer, Victor Halsell, and Sandra Silber— who were in Ondstrand House, without an alibi, on Saturday morning.

That particular list—of people in Ondstrand House last Saturday morning who lacked alibis—had recently gotten a bit shorter. Jane's estimate of Stans's time of death allowed me to draw lines through two names—people who'd both left Ondstrand House before seven that morning. I'd also interviewed another pair—a scientist from R&D and a programmer from IT—at first separately and then together, and learned that they did, in fact, have an alibi for that Saturday morning, though not one they were eager to share. Which was not altogether shocking, given that they'd spent that morning, as they had many other Saturday mornings, together, having sex on the floor of her lab—a practice that would likely not have pleased either of their spouses. One of the complications of a murder investigation. Time-stamped images from Ondstrand's access-control system, of the two of them entering and leaving her lab, corroborated their story and I'd taken them off the list as well.

I stretched and returned to my tablet, to wade through more of Ivessen's background reports on Halsell, Drucker, and Nadia Blom. Nothing jumped out from them, or even strolled or stumbled. Drucker's professional credentials were impeccable, as were her computer-science and management degrees. Her divorce had been an amicable one, though expensive for her: she shared custody of her daughters with her violist husband but paid the whole of their school fees and the upkeep on the house in the Cheviot Green district of the city.

Victor Halsell's professional backstory was entirely consistent with what he'd told me, though he'd left out the bit about how his career at the Defense Ministry plateaued in the three years before he'd left. On the personal front, Halsell had never married and, prior to his Ondstrand job, had never lived anywhere other than in his mother's house in Tristedorp.

Nadia Blom on paper was much as she appeared in the flesh—precise, modulated, conventional but for the suggestion of . . . what? Hidden passions? Hidden obsessions? I laughed and shook my head. I was reading too much into her stringent braid, no doubt. Certainly nothing in her CV—an almost boring list of conventionally admirable degrees, test scores, internships, and jobs—supported any such speculation.

I pushed the tablet away and rubbed my eyes. Lists, reports, questions—but they were all crowded aside, as they had been since Monday night, by three stark images stuck in my head: of strong hands locked on Allegra Stans's arms, of Allegra thrashed like a rag doll—once, twice—against a steel shelf and a tiled wall, of Allegra limp, seams burst, and lifeless on a bathroom floor. It had been no accident, Jane Wilding was clear about that, but had that violence been a deliberated act— a calculated solution to someone's problem—or was it a sudden detonation of impulse and rage—an obliterating explosion sparked by hate or by a desperate love?

I sighed again and sat down to work.

CHAPTER SIXTEEN

Wednesday Afternoon

Allegra Stans's car sat alone in the lot, in the watery shade of a young larch, as if it had been shunned by the other cars. The lot was a flat gravel acre not far from the converted stables and carriage house south of Ondstrand House, and the walk over, under a hard blue sky with fast-moving clouds, was a chilly tonic after a Wednesday morning spent talking. Small stones crunched and skittered underfoot, and I reached into my pocket and felt for the key ring with its winged sandal charm.

The green roadster had muddy flanks, a mildew-stained canvas roof, and wiper wells full of brown pine needles. The windows were dim with grime. The trunk key turned without effort, the lid sprang up, and a musty smell rose. The trunk was lined with camel carpet, but apart from the odor, the spare tire, a jack, and a set of rust-spotted tools rolled up in a brittle leather pouch, it was empty. I closed the trunk and moved to the driver's door.

Inside, the car was all leather, walnut, and chrome, and the dash was a museum of analogue measurement: an array of gauges and meters with slender black needles. The sun had warmed the cockpit and raised the scent of old leather from the saddle seats and the scent of violets from an open tin of pastilles in a tray beneath the radio. I peered into the vestigial rear seat and found nothing besides a green woolen blanket with a wide red stripe. It was folded neatly and speckled with pine needles and grains of sand.

The pocket in the driver's side door was empty but for an ancient-looking road map of the county, a packet of tissues, and a pair of small driving gloves in thin brown leather. Beside the gearshift was a narrow compartment with a finicky latch. I pried it open and found a chromed steel flashlight, a small first-aid kit, the contents gummy with heat, and a packet of condoms in now-familiar green foil wrappers. The pack was nearly empty. There was nothing beneath the sun visor. I moved around to the passenger seat.

The passenger door's pocket was empty, as was the sun visor, and I pushed a button latch to open the glove box. I knelt down and looked in. There was a folding leather case inside, holding the car's yellowed owner's manual, along with Stans's registration, inspection, and insurance documents. When I slid the case out, several slips of paper, smaller than business cards, fluttered down. They were white and flimsy, and there was faded black print on them: *Soligstrand Municipal Parking,* along with date and time stamps and three-digit numbers that I thought might correspond to parking spaces. I gathered the fallen receipts and scanned the dates. They went back months, and when I checked them against my phone calendar, I saw that all of the dates fell on Wednesdays. All of the times were in the midafternoon. I looked inside the glove box and found several more, and I put all of the receipts in my jacket pocket. I found no locket in my search, but I did find another camera.

It was in a back corner of the glove box, a silver, palm-sized digital model, identical to the one I'd found in Allegra Stans's apartment. I sat in the passenger seat and flicked a tiny switch, and the rear screen flashed. I pressed the button to display photos in the camera's onboard memory and found that—like its counterpart in Allegra's apartment—it held just two, and they looked in all ways like the two pictures I'd seen on that other camera: the dining table in Allegra Stans's apartment, with the Ondstrand Biologic computer workstation atop, in center frame; and a close-up photo of the same computer's screen. I checked the camera's memory-card slot. Like its counterpart, it was empty. I stood, put the camera in my jacket pocket, and shut the passenger door.

I stretched and checked my watch. It was not quite noon—a few hours earlier than Allegra would typically have made her weekly off-campus sojourns. But it *was* Wednesday, and I badly needed to sweep away the cobwebs. I went around to the driver's side again, opened the door, and slid behind the wheel.

Allegra Stans might not have cared much for car washes, but she'd kept her roadster in excellent shape. The engine purred, the gearshift was silken, the steering was agile, as was the suspension, and the clutch, brake, and gas were responsive but not obnoxious. And the thing was fast. I just made it to second gear as I swooped down the main road, and

I stopped in a dusty skid at the gate. I lowered the canvas top, took off my jacket, rolled my sleeves, and slipped on a pair of sunglasses. Then I headed north, towards Soligstrand, and let it run.

Once it passed beyond the woods of the Ondstrand property, the road to Soligstrand rose to follow a low ridgeline, with views of the headland and the sea on one side, and stone walls, hedges, and unkempt meadows on the other. The sky was bright and immaculate as I drove, the sea air poured down in a frigid, briny wave, and Ondstrand House was for the moment just a shadowed memory. I saw no houses along the way, and the road was empty of cars and all else. The only other travelers I spotted were a pair of gulls, hanging above the headlands, pacing me like shadows. My necktie snapped like a banner behind me, and I laughed and felt my head clear of the detritus of a morning spent with more of Allegra Stans's former lovers.

I'd spoken to Gilbert Loring in a small conference room near Victor Halsell's office. He was long-necked, lanky, blond, and crew-cut—a former soldier, and now a supervisor in Ondstrand's Protection Department. He was just thirty, but his smooth jaw, guileless blue eyes, and unguarded demeanor made him seem even younger. An avid runner, he had met Stans when he joined her club. He was unembarrassed when he spoke of their relationship.

"She liked sex, and she liked having it outdoors—especially after a hard run. That was my experience with her anyway, from that first time. We'd finished a group training—a six-miler with lots of hills—and it was starting to rain. I was feeling spry and asked if anyone was up for a final loop along the beach and through the woods—another three miles, maybe—and Dr. Stans was the only taker. She set a fast pace, and I barely kept up. We were in the final stretch—in the woods by the Cottage, where Dr. Hasp lives—when the sky really opened up: buckets of rain, lightning, the works. Dr. Stans says, 'Follow me,' and I do, to that addition on the Cottage that Dr. Hasp uses as an office. It's beside the remains of a stone chapel, and one of the walls and arches left standing is attached to the studio. It makes a little courtyard there, with an overhang, and there was a dry patch where we could wait out the storm. It was getting dark, and getting cold standing still, and I started jogging in place, doing jumping jacks. I joked that we might have to share body heat to survive, and Dr. Stans said that, with the way the temperature was dropping, we might have to share more than that. I laughed and said I was game, and she said, 'All right, then,' and grabbed hold of me. I was worried, being where we were, but not her—not at all. Really, I think the chance of being caught made it better for her. Almost every other time we were together it was outside, and when we weren't, we were in her car."

He wasn't sure if they'd actually stopped having sex, or if they'd merely paused. "The last time, I guess, was five months back or so. There were stretches when we didn't get together—sometimes long ones—and then we would. I don't know what made her decide. It was like every time could've been the last time—and then there'd be a next time. We didn't talk about it a lot. Or at all." When I pointed out that it had almost certainly stopped now, he thought for a moment, looked a bit sad, and nodded agreement.

Loring had gotten off duty an hour before the earliest estimated time of Stans's death, and video showed him driving off campus minutes after his shift had ended. According to him, he'd driven home, to a bungalow in Slocum, and gone to bed, though only his dogs could verify that.

Harris Geary was a version of Loring—a few years older, not quite as tall, not quite as blond, more guarded, and decidedly more embarrassed when he spoke of Allegra Stans. We'd sat in a corner of the staff cafeteria, and there was much hemming, hawing, and furious blushing before he'd actually formed words.

"Our labs were down the corridor when she worked in Special Projects. We didn't talk about our projects—we couldn't—but she'd read my dissertation on vectors for oncolytic viral therapies. She had done some work in that area, too, so we had that in common. We would occasionally go to lunch at around the same time, and I guess that's how we started talking. She was very smart—widely read and very creative. We talked a lot about my dissertation, but the leaps she made—just keeping up with her was a challenge.

"She invited me to run with her club, which I did. I guess that's how . . . things started with us—after an evening run. She said she'd locked herself out of her apartment, which was one floor up from mine, in the north wing. She was really muddy and asked if she could use my shower before she went to Protection to get them to open the door. She said she didn't feel like going down to the fitness center. I said yes, and . . .

"Mostly, we were together after practices. She'd come to my place; I never went to hers. And it happened . . . when she wanted it to happen. I didn't ask; I wouldn't have—I have a fiancée, in the city." To Geary that had seemed to explain something.

Conveniently for Geary, that same fiancée could confirm his where-abouts at the time of Stans's death: she had come to visit Geary, and they were together all weekend at an inn in Soligstrand.

He'd been surprised when I asked him about the spear-phishing e-mail. "That was weird. Sitting in my inbox, it looked fine—an e-mail from my former dissertation adviser. It looked entirely plausible. But when I opened it, I knew right away that something was wrong. It said, 'I thought you'd want to see this ASAP,' or something like that, and then there was a link. 'ASAP'—he'd never use that phrase. I didn't click on the link, and I called IT right away." Geary seemed more troubled after telling me that story, as if he'd connected some dots he wished he hadn't.

Sylvie Holliman and her boss had returned only that morning from a week in the city, meeting with Ondstrand's accountants, and the news of Stans's death seemed to have struck her like a sudden frost. She was in her late twenties, small, small-boned and fair, with large blue eyes and a mouth that, in other circumstances, might have been generous or warm or comic, but just then was wholly dedicated to hoarding syllables.

Yes, she'd had a sexual liaison with Dr. Stans. No, it hadn't lasted long—less than a month—and had ended six months ago. Yes, Holliman had broken it off. No, the relationship had not ended amicably. Promiscuity had been the issue. No, they hadn't spoken since. No, it wasn't an easy situation on such a small campus. "Is that all? May I go now?" Her face had burned as she spoke, and she'd stared mostly at her hands, which moved constantly over her gray skirt, smoothing nonexistent creases.

Allegra's roadster crested a hill, and I breathed in a great lungful of marine air.

The road turned and descended towards the sea as it approached Soligstrand, and it widened when cottages appeared. They were of stone, dark and mossy at the foundations, and had small windows, roofs of green tile, and compact front gardens whose walls abutted the road. As I neared the town center, narrow sidewalks developed, and the cottages were larger. Their plastered walls were whitewashed or painted in pastel blue, pink, yellow, or green. I downshifted as people and traffic appeared, and then there were intersections, wider sidewalks, and a whole town unfolding.

CHAPTER SEVENTEEN

Wednesday Afternoon

The road became Soligstrand Front Street, and it ran alongside a promenade that followed the wide, curving beachfront for nearly two miles—from one end of town to the other. There were long piers at either end, with marinas dangling off that were still buttoned up for winter. And bordering the promenade was an arc of pastel-striped pavilions—shops and food stalls, wine bars and cafés—an optimistic few of which were opened for early-spring business, though technically it was not yet spring. There was much ornamental stone and plaster on the buildings along Front Street, and generous helpings of fountains, flower beds, and ancient, black-painted naval artillery pieces nearly everywhere I looked—all of it lovingly maintained against maritime conditions. Still, without a summer crowd, Soligstrand had the forlorn look of an undressed stage.

Other streets—a bit busier, a bit less twee—emptied into Front Street, and I was near the north end of town when I turned onto one of them. Half a block down, I found the Soligstrand Municipal Parking garage.

It was a semi-enclosed concrete structure, half a block long and three levels high. I drove in and upwards, in search of the numbered parking spaces that matched the receipts I'd found in Stans's car. Each of the eight slips bore one of five parking-space numbers—202, 203, 204, 205, and 206. Those numbers corresponded to a row of five spaces on the second level, along the north wall. Two of those slots, 202 and 206, were occupied. I pulled nose-first into 204 and killed the engine.

I had no idea if Allegra Stans's preference for that row of spaces was by happenstance, mindless habit, superstition, or design, but, regardless, I sat for five minutes and waited and watched. Ahead of me was a metal rail affixed to the masonry half-wall, and beyond that, empty space and the blank wall of a building across the alleyway. Only one vehicle appeared while I sat, a blue sedan that pulled into a space well away from mine, on the south wall of the garage. I saw a woman emerge, walk to one of the automated payment kiosks, walk back with a white ticket that she placed in her front window, lock her car, and walk off towards the street exit. A few minutes later, I raised the top on Allegra's car and did the same things.

The breeze was chilly on the sidewalk, and I donned my jacket and pulled out my phone. I had pictures of the loyalty cards I'd found in Allegra's wallet, and a picture of Allegra from her Ondstrand ID card, and I walked back to Front Street and turned south.

My first stop was three blocks down and two blocks off of Front Street, at a pale yellow building with elaborate cursive lettering across its frosted glass front: SUNNYSIDE SALON AND SPA. When I pushed through the glass door, I found myself at a reception counter—a chest-high curve the color of butter. It was unattended just then, as was much of the rest of the place—a vast plain of hair-washing stations, hair-cutting stations, manicure and pedicure stations, and stations for reading magazines while waiting for hair chemistries to reach fruition. Everything was drenched in shades of lemon and cream.

The only company I had there was a willowy young woman in expensive-looking maroon yoga garb, with shiny black hair and feline eye makeup, and two older, thicker women with weathered, country faces and brassy blond ponytails, who wore knee-length yellow smocks. One had *Penny* written in green cursive on it, over the left breast; the other read *Celia*. They all sat in a waiting area that adjoined the entrance and stared at me. After a while, the young woman sighed theatrically, unfolded her slender limbs, rose, and strolled languidly behind the reception counter.

"Can I help you?" she drawled, and her question was in earnest, as if it seemed entirely possible to her that I was beyond any help.

"I certainly hope so."

She squinted at me. "We don't do men."

One of the blondes stifled a giggle; the other didn't bother. "Speak for yourself, Audrey," Penny said, and she and Celia guffawed.

"Do you all work here most Wednesday afternoons?"

"If you can call this working, dearie," Penny said.

"Wednesdays aren't busy this time of year," Celia added. "But things will pick up nicely in a month or so."

Penny nodded agreement. "Honestly, it's a wonder Georgie opens up at all on the weekdays this time of year. I suppose one day he'll realize it's costing him money."

Audrey scowled at Penny and looked at me more sharply. "That coward didn't send you around, did he? Are you making some sort of survey for him—see if he can save a few pennies by cutting my hours?"

Celia giggled. "You needn't worry, hon—it's not *your* hours Georgie would be cutting."

"Not as long as you keep wearing your yoga costumes round the shop," Penny added, smiling.

Audrey made a rude gesture in their direction, but there was little force behind it. I smiled. "I assure you, I'm not from Georgie, whoever he is, and I'm not here with a survey."

"Then why *are* you here?" Audrey said, turning her scowl to me.

"I'm looking for some information about her," I said, and I took out my phone and showed her a picture of Allegra Stans. Audrey leaned across the counter for a closer look, and, unbidden, Penny and Celia joined her. In silence they looked at the picture, at one another, at me, and back at the picture.

"That's Allie," Penny said, and Celia put a quieting hand on her arm.

"Yes, it is—Allegra Stans. You know her?"

"You're not the police," Celia said. "Not the local."

I made a motion that might've been a nod. "Not the local," I said.

"Is she in trouble?" Penny asked.

Audrey balled her fist and pressed it against the countertop. "We don't want trouble here."

"She's not in trouble. We're trying to locate her, actually."

"You should try the school," Penny suggested.

"The school?"

Audrey sighed. "She means the company where Allie works. It's down the coast, halfway between here and Fiskdorp."

"Used to be a boys' school," Penny said. "That's why we call it that. Creepy old pile."

I nodded. "I've just come from there. How so 'creepy'?"

Penny frowned. "Growing up round here, you'd hear all sorts of stories about what they got up to there—the things they did to 'em."

"Did to who?" I said.

"To the boys. Some of them ran off or threw themselves in the sea."

Celia shook her head. "Jesus, Pen, you sound like my old gran. Those are just stories kids told—like ghost stories."

"Some, maybe," Penny countered, "but that old bastard weren't no ghost. He was a flesh-and-bone bastard."

I looked at Celia and raised an eyebrow. She shook her head. "She's talkin' about the old headmaster over there."

Penny nodded. "The last one they had. He's why they shut the school down—the things he did to some of those boys. He'd still be behind bars now, like as not, if he hadn't jumped off that cliff. I tell you, that place is—"

"Jesus, Pen!" Celia said again. "That was ages ago—if any of it was even true—and, besides, he's not here to talk about that. He's asking about Allie."

I nodded. "I take it she's a regular here on Wednesdays."

Celia nodded slowly. "Like clockwork," she said. "Start of the month is a haircut; the next week is a mani-pedi; the week after is hair conditioning; then a facial; then massage; then time for another haircut." She ticked the items off on her fingers, and Penny nodded agreement.

Audrey was less pleased. "I'm not sure we should be talking to you like this about our clients."

I smiled. "I'm fairly certain that haircutters don't enjoy the same privileges as doctors or clergy."

Penny laughed. "Maybe we should. You'd be surprised what we hear, dearie—it's just like the confessional sometimes."

"I've no doubt," I said. "Is Dr. Stans one for confession?"

Penny's expression turned theatrically haughty. "*Doctor* Stans? She's never *Doctor* to us, is she? Not like some from the school—stuck-up prigs."

Celia shook her head, smiling. "She's just plain Allie to us, and there isn't much she won't chat about." She glanced at Audrey and chuckled.

Audrey reddened. "You shouldn't be gossiping, you two. I think I should call Georgie."

I looked at her. "I assure you, Georgie will be upset by the waste of his time, and even more upset by my attentions. Best to leave him be."

Audrey looked back, colored more deeply, and stalked off, disappearing through swinging louvered doors in the back. Celia and Penny giggled. "She's blushing still over what happened in the massage studio, when Allie was getting ready for a treatment one day, and Audrey was seeing to the towels," Penny said. "Months ago, it was, but she still sweats and stammers."

Celia smiled. "It was just Allie playing games, being bold. It was kissing and barely anything else."

"Though it went on for five minutes or more before that skinny thing started worrying about Georgie finding out," Penny added. "Or so Allie said."

Celia nodded. "It *was* naughty of Allie to tell us, I suppose. But that's her—she likes to mix it up."

"What other things did Allegra tell?"

"What didn't she?" Penny said. "Her love life is an open book. She goes on and on about her conquests—the latest one or the one she's planning next—men and women, young and old. She's shameless, that one, and much better than the television."

"She isn't crude, mind," Celia added. "She's never graphic—well, not *too* graphic—and she never names names."

"But she's got little nicknames for 'em. Professor, Copper, Nanny, and what was that other one, Cee?"

"Bubble Gum," Celia said, "'cause 'once you've stepped in it, you can never get it off your shoe.'"

Penny looked down. "She can be a bit harsh, I suppose," she said softly.

Penny and Celia shared some of Allegra Stans's anecdotes about her love life—mildly cruel tales of her lovers' embarrassing sexual antics or of their emotional neediness, and self-deprecating ones about her own appetites—but they knew nothing of the actual people behind the nicknames Allegra used. After a few stories about one paramour weeping like a baby when he climaxed, or another cursing like a sailor, Penny and Celia both grew quieter, aware that they had said too much, and that I had said too little. Still, I had another question.

"Has either of you ever seen any of Allie's friends—in a picture she might've shown you, or perhaps with her, here at the salon?"

"Never," Celia said. Penny was silent but shook her head.

Celia looked at me and squinted. "Allie's booked for this afternoon, you know—in an hour or so. You could wait—maybe you'll see her."

I nodded slowly. "If she does come in, or if you happen to think of anything she might have said—about worries she might've had about people or about situations, possibly at her job, don't hesitate to give a call." I handed them each a card and left one for Audrey as well. I was halfway out the door when Celia called to me.

"You don't think she's coming in, do you?" she asked.

I turned and looked at her. "If she does," I said eventually, "ring me."

CHAPTER EIGHTEEN

Wednesday Afternoon.

Soligstrand Kaffe was a block south of the Sunnyside Salon and Spa. It was a subdued, contemplative spot with excellent coffee, ethereal music, and pale flowers in glass vases—like the anteroom to a nondenominational funeral chapel. The café staff was efficient and agreeably reserved, but sadly unable to recall ever having seen Allegra Stans. I drank up and moved on.

Solig Run sold running shoes and other related kit and was several blocks south of the Kaffe. But it was still operating on wintertime hours, so its windows were dark and its doors locked. Fortunately for me, Coastal Fitness was just next door.

It was a bright, well-equipped gym, with a shiny weight room, a fleet of treadmills and stationary bikes, and mirrored studios for yoga classes. But for her fair hair and sunnier disposition, the young woman at the desk could've been Audrey's twin. Her name was Kari, and, perhaps because things were quiet there and she was bored, she asked no questions about the nature of my inquiries. She recognized Allegra Stans's picture immediately.

"That's Stans, A.," she said. Her voice was bright.

"That's what you know her by—Stans, A.?"

She laughed. "That's how the names come up when I scan membership cards—last name, first initial—so that's how I think of people."

"Does Stans, A., come in often?"

"Not for a while now. She used to come regularly, usually for a yoga class or for stretching. I know because I help out with the classes. She's in great shape—puts some of the gym rats around here to shame."

" 'Not for a while' means how long?"

Kari processed for a moment. "A year or more? She used to come in all the time with Witmer, P." I thought about that, nodded, and asked her to repeat the name. Then I wished her a pleasant afternoon and left.

A mass of cloud had pushed in from the sea, and it was windier and colder when I emerged from the gym. The other cards I'd found in Allegra Stans's wallet—for Beacon Espresso and Café Slocum—were from establishments in other towns—Fiskdorp and Slocum, respectively. There seemed little else for me to do in Soligstrand just then, and I turned north again. The walk back to the garage was through streets even emptier than before, even more forlorn. With each damp gust, it seemed the whole enterprise that was Soligstrand might just blow away, like a child's birthday party in a summer squall. I turned my collar up and leaned into the wind and tried, with limited success, to imagine Allegra's Wednesday outings—a drive, perhaps with the top down, a haircut or pedicure or something at the Sunnyside Salon and Spa, a nasty chin-wag with Celia and Penny, and then what? A yoga class at the gym? That was unlikely; she hadn't been seen there for a year, and back then she'd been with Witmer. Had their relationship been going on then, despite whatever *messiness* had developed?

I was still chasing Allegra's shadow through imagined Wednesday afternoons as I climbed the cement steps at the Soligstrand Municipal Parking garage, and my footsteps echoed in the stairwell. The second level was darker now, and colder, and all the parking spaces there were empty but for the one in which Allegra's car was parked, and where a man now crouched in the open passenger door. I took a deep breath, closed the stairwell door quietly, and unbuttoned my jacket. I walked softly.

He had short, dark hair and wore jeans, running shoes, a short black jacket, zipped, and disposable gloves on his large hands. When he stood I saw that he was tall and broad-shouldered, and when he turned I saw that he was forty-something and that his face was tanned and craggy— handsome, in a thin-lipped, pale-eyed, brutal sort of way. If he was startled by my presence, he hid it well, and he took his time shutting the car door and locking it with a key.

"Help you with something?" he said. His voice was deep and dismissive. "You forget where you parked your car?"

I shook my head and looked at Allegra's car. "I was wondering the same about you."

He smirked and held up car keys on a ring. "I'm where I'm supposed to be, pal, so why don't you fuck off elsewhere to hunt your car."

I held up Allegra's key ring with its silver charm. "I'm pretty sure I've already found it," I said.

The man peeled off his gloves and slipped them and the car keys into his jacket pocket, zipped his pocket, and smiled nastily. He rolled his shoulders and stretched his neck. "Now you're gonna introduce yourself," he said softly.

I put Allegra's key ring away and patted my right breast pocket. "I've got a wallet full of ID right here," I said.

The man shrugged. "Have it your way," he said, and came at me.

Somewhere, sometime, someone had trained him, and they'd done a pretty good job of it. He set up well, moved well, his balance was good, and he was quick and strong—so there'd been some natural aptitude to build on. But perhaps he hadn't kept up with his training or had become accustomed to facing untrained opponents. Perhaps he was just arrogant and stupid. Or perhaps it was simply that his instructors hadn't come as close to killing him as mine had me, or not on so regular a basis. In any event, he was in over his head, and one of the sure signs was that he had no idea until it was much too late.

So he smiled as I backed up, and smiled wider when his jabs landed on my shoulders and forearms. And he was practically grinning when his knees and elbows made what might've felt to him like good contact. But he didn't seem to notice that his blows were glancing, that I'd rolled away from all the heavy strikes, that I was always up on my toes—moving him, leading him—and that my breathing hadn't changed at all, even as his became ragged and loud.

And then it was over—a knee hard into his thigh, a solid elbow to his temple, a stiff-fingered strike below the sternum and another to the throat, a rip to the kidneys, and then an ankle sweep that landed him on his back like a sack of cement: choking, breathless, with surprise, fear, and nausea on his ashen face. I grabbed his collar, dragged him to Allegra's car, and let him lean against the front tire as he sat and retched, legs splayed, on the oil-stained cement.

I brushed my sleeves and pant legs and straightened my shirt cuffs while he caught his breath. "Put your head between your knees if you think you might vomit," I said.

His face reddened, but he bent his knees, rested his elbows on them, and let his head hang down. "Fuck off," he muttered after a while.

"We've done that already," I said. "This is where you show me some ID and explain what you're doing with keys to a car that is not your own."

He unzipped a jacket pocket, took the car keys out, and tossed them at my feet. "You want the keys—take 'em."

"That's not what I asked for; I asked for ID and an explanation."

He straightened out his legs, raised his arms above his head, and sneered. "I have no ID, asshole. I'm not stupid enough to carry it when I'm working." He patted his legs and his torso theatrically. "You want to check—come ahead."

"A professional—I see. Apologies for not recognizing it sooner."

"Fuck off," he said again.

"If you're a professional, you work for someone. You can add that to the list of things I want to know."

"You're looking for answers, check the trunk—that'll tell you what you want to know." And he tossed a thumb at the car keys still at my feet. I didn't reach for them or make any other move, but my eyes flicked down and that was enough.

The man sprang up, not towards me, but scrambling towards the low metal barrier and the garage's half-wall. Before I could reach him, he'd vaulted over, out into empty space. There was a hollow echoing boom a moment later, and I reached the barrier in time to see him roll off the top of a metal dumpster and sprint down the dark alley. He held up both arms as he ran, and flipped me off with both hands.

"Shit," I whispered. Apparently, he was professional enough.

I found a glove in my pocket and used it to pick up the car keys and put them in a ziplock. Then I fished out my own set of keys and got behind the wheel.

CHAPTER NINETEEN

Wednesday Evening

I kept the top up on the drive back to Ondstrand House, in deference to the colder temperature of dusk, and to my own chastened spirits. I thought about the dark-haired man as I drove, about how relaxed he'd been in the garage, checking Allegra's glove box. I imagined that he'd had a lot of practice, and I wondered if his was a weekly appointment there, or a less frequent arrangement. Perhaps he came as needed.

I clenched my teeth until my jaw ached, and only then did I notice that I was strangling the steering wheel and that I had reached an intersection—the point at which the coast road met the road to Slocum. I pulled over before the fork and shook out my hands. Then I looked up at the road sign and thought about Kari at Coastal Fitness, and about Stans, A., and Witmer, P. I put the car in gear again, returned to the road, and turned at the sign.

A bit of daylight, even fading daylight, did wonders for Slocum. It wasn't as small as it had looked when I'd first seen it, and not nearly so flinty. It had sidewalks, albeit narrow ones, and shops along a compact high street: a butcher, a bakery, a grocery, a wine shop, a café, and a property agent. Their windows were lit, and they were tidy and discreetly prosperous-looking.

Piers Witmer's home was on a narrow lane off the quieter end of the high street: a rambling stone cottage, with dormers and a shingled roof. It sat behind a gray stone wall and was flanked by a stone garage on one side, and a conservatory whose panes were mostly clouded. Cottage and outbuildings faced a cobblestone courtyard on which was parked a battered blue station wagon, a mud-spattered green sedan, and an array of children's toys—tricycle, bicycle, plastic wagon, toddler-sized soccer ball, pink plastic scooter—all muddy and in states of disrepair or outright breakdown. I pulled onto the lane's shoulder and climbed out of Allegra's car. By the time I stepped into the courtyard, Witmer was standing stiffly in the cottage doorway, staring not at me but at the car.

He wore jeans, a blue buttoned-down shirt, and a bottle-green sweater, and had a look of rigid anger on his pale, lean face. I was nearly at the door when he shifted his gaze to me and spoke. "You had to drive that car?" he said. His deep voice was taut and low, and his eyes were rimmed with red. I had no reply, and he seemed to expect none. "You might have called first," he said.

"We don't call first, Dr. Witmer," I said quietly. As I stepped onto the small porch, a wave of childish clamor—shrieks, laughter, complaint, running feet—surged out of the open door, along with a cloud of warm air. "If you like, we can speak outside," I added.

Witmer glanced behind him, as if he'd only just noticed the noise or that he had children. "No, no—you might as well come in," he said, and made an impatient ushering motion devoid of welcome.

I was in an entrance hall with a stone floor, rough stone walls, and the smells of damp stone and old food. There was a bureau straight ahead, painted in bright blue that was peeling along the sides, and laden with heaps of unopened mail and a large pottery bowl that held keys, loose change, and pocket lint. One of the bureau drawers was misaligned, canted in its tracks; the pink fingers of a child's glove reached through the thin opening, and were somehow alarming.

A painting hung above the bureau, and others, some askew, were on the foyer's stone walls: small, unframed oils, impressionistic, marine in their colors, maritime in their subjects—a lighthouse, a pier, a cliff above a beach—and bleak and unsettling in their atmospheres. I liked them.

Witmer led me down a narrow corridor. The sounds of children diminished as we went, and vanished when we came to a study with white plastered walls and a low, black-beamed ceiling. A small stone fireplace stood on one wall, cold and empty but for soot, and on another wall were bowed bookshelves that reminded me of Goss Ivessen's shelves. There was a window at the far end of the room, with blue velvet drapes drawn across it, and a desk in front, black and intricately carved, like something from a church. It was covered with papers, journals, and a large computer workstation that was a twin of the one in Allegra's apartment. Witmer took up a standing post behind the desk, his hands on the back of a high black swivel chair. He motioned me toward a straight-backed chair that seemed designed for use by those receiving remonstrations. I opened my jacket, sat, and crossed my legs.

"Terry—Dr. Hasp—said something about you making appointments to see us. That's why I thought you'd call first."

I nodded but said nothing.

Witmer swallowed. "I spoke to your colleague, you know. I don't recall his name—Ives, maybe? He sounded elderly. At any rate, I spoke to him about where I was on Saturday morning, and he seemed satisfied. I thought that was the end of it."

I shook my head. "No, Doctor." There was another small oil on the study wall, and I pointed at it. "Is that your wife's work?"

Witmer nodded absently. "Well, what can I do for you?"

"To begin with, let's go over your movements at Ondstrand House last Saturday morning, from the time you arrived until, say, eight-thirty."

Witmer seemed relieved by the question and told me what he'd told Ivessen: that he'd driven to the campus with his wife, though in separate cars; that he'd gone to check on the latest batches of trial results that had just come in from a hospital in the city, and catch up on some administrative work; that he'd been in his office in the south wing until almost eight, when he'd gone to Hasp's office; that they'd been talking there when the call came through from Protection just after eight-thirty.

"So, if that's all . . ."

I shook my head. "Now I'd like you to tell me all of the things you've thus far neglected to mention about Allegra Stans. We can start with your relationship with her."

Witmer took a deep breath. "I told you when we first met—"

I held up a hand to silence him, then wagged a finger. "No, Doctor, we won't waste time with that. You told me that she worked for you for a period of time when you ran the R&D division and she had just started at the firm. You did not tell me about your affair with her, when it began, the nature of it, how long it lasted, the circumstances of its ending, or what your relationship with her was in its aftermath. So—shall we start with those things?"

His shoulders slumped, his pale cheeks burned, and he sputtered for a moment. "I didn't . . . It was . . . It was *nothing* in the scheme of things—trivial. And it was *years* ago."

I held up a hand again and sighed. "Not so trivial that it wasn't worth a lie, however. Really, Doctor, I am being exceptionally patient with you, and exceptionally civil. So far. So—a bit of respect please. Now, have a seat and tell me."

Witmer looked at me for a moment, then sat. The chair seemed to swallow him. When he spoke, his voice was low. "I thought I had embarrassed myself enough over this; apparently not. It really *is* old news, you know—years old. It's something that happened and then stopped happening, and life went on. Like running a fever, and the fever breaking." He paused, searching for something in my face. He thought he found it and continued.

"She came seven years ago, following right from an overseas postdoc—a very impressive program. And that was her, all-around: impressive. Top schools, top marks, top prizes, publications—an amazing CV for someone her age. But in person, Allegra was something else altogether. She was amazing."

Witmer paused and shook his head. "But you've heard this all before, no? From everyone you've spoken with, I imagine—how smart she was, how quick, how driven. How charming she was, and funny, how . . . *electric*. Well, I can tell you—it's all true. I was focused on my work, as I always have been. I wasn't looking for anything. But from her first day, I couldn't look away. She made sure of that. It was barely over a month later that we . . . But it began between us much sooner than that.

"She was doing vector evaluations to start with, which go on endlessly here. After a week of working with our procedures, studying them, learning them, she bursts into my office—it wasn't even seven in the morning—and she pitches me a redesign of all of our evaluation protocols—soup to nuts, incorporating techniques she'd used in her postdoc, but adapting them for our needs. She said she could increase the speed of our evaluations and increase the number we could perform concurrently.

"It was a hugely risky move, you understand—to come in, still wet behind the ears, and propose a sweeping change like that. The risk that you might be talking out of your arse, or that people would think you were; the risk of making the sale but not being able to deliver the goods; the risk the boss would just say, 'Fuck off, new girl.' Risky, ballsy—but that was her, absolutely fearless. She had an implementation plan all worked out as well, and she was ready to pull the trigger then and there if I'd said yes. It was all I could do to get her to wait through the weekend while I went over her proposal in detail and reviewed it with Terry. After that, I worked with her twelve, sixteen hours a day for the next month on that redesign. In the end, it was a big step up for us—in efficiency, in throughput, really by every measure. And in the end, we were lovers."

The more he spoke, the less Witmer seemed to speak to me. He sat up straighter in his chair, and his voice grew softer. "I didn't think I was looking for something, but maybe I just didn't realize it." He paused and sighed heavily. "Perhaps I was. At any rate, it was heady stuff. Her clarity and drive, her creativity—they were contagious, at least for me. The work we did together . . . I felt at the time that it was some of my best work. Maybe it was, or maybe I was just kidding myself. It's hard to see it clearly now. Hard to see her clearly."

Witmer sighed massively. "We were together for over a year, and I was happy, though that doesn't seem the right word for it. It was a drug—like being high on a drug for that time. Perhaps it was all the dopamine—between the running and the sex, my brain must've been flooded with it. It was thrilling, dizzying, exhausting. And while I don't think I'd ever been more productive at work—and why not, I spent days at a time in the lab—my judgment outside was impaired, to say the least. My family never saw me, and, honestly, they became unreal to me; I didn't give them a thought. I didn't give a thought to discretion, either. I didn't care who knew, and in the end nearly everyone did, including, eventually, my wife."

Witmer fell silent then, and I watched his gaze wander his desktop and bookshelves and light on a cluster of framed photos there: race-day pictures of the running club, some of them duplicates of the ones I'd found in Allegra's apartment.

"What happened when your wife found out?" I asked.

Witmer snorted. "She confronted Allegra."

"Confronted her how?"

He shook his head and ran a hand down his face. "On a street corner, for God's sake, in Soligstrand. Allegra and I had just had coffee, and we were walking back to her car."

"And?"

"And it was bad theater—the wronged wife faces the other woman. It was absurd. As if Petra actually gave a shit."

"She didn't mind the affair?"

"The affair, not particularly; the embarrassment, the supposed impact on the children, on her fucking work—those were different stories."

"And how did Allegra react to this confrontation?"

Witmer propped his elbows on the desk and cradled his face in his hands. "She was as she always was—cool and in control. She listened to Petra's silly rant and then apologized and explained that she was appalled to have caused another woman such upset, and that she never would have, had she not been misled by me. A lot of swill about sister-hood and solidarity."

I nodded. "Had you misled Allegra?"

Witmer looked up, and a petulant look crossed his face. "Misled how? She knew I was married, and knew I had children. I told her that Petra and I had discussed divorce, and we had—even if it had been years before, and the conversation had been somewhat theoretical. It wasn't a lie that I'd withdrawn from my marriage—that we both had—that our lives had become quite separate. I called what Petra and I had arrived at an 'understanding,' and perhaps that was a mischaracterization. Appar-ently, I was the only one who understood anything. I didn't mislead Allegra; at worst, I was mistaken."

I nodded at his labored defense. "So Allegra offered apologies to your wife. What did she offer you? Was she angry with you? Upset?"

The petulant look became one of sadness. "Upset? No. And not angry, either. If I had to call her one thing, I'd say she was relieved. Relieved to have a reason to end things with me—something I couldn't argue with."

"Had she sought to end things with you before this confrontation?"

"She had been . . . pulling away. Reminding me more frequently that she wasn't looking for a permanent commitment, or, indeed, any com-mitment at all. Reminding me that monogamy had never been a part of her constitution. The end was coming, I suppose, but that scene with Petra was a turning point."

"Had Allegra been seeing other people while she was with you?"

He gave an exhausted shrug. "How would I have known? She was so . . . expert."

"Expert at . . . ?"

"Deception."

I nodded. "How long after the incident with your wife did things end between you and Allegra?"

"It wasn't long—two or three weeks, perhaps."

"Was that an acrimonious scene?"

He laughed bitterly. "Acrimonious? No, it wasn't acrimonious. If anything, it was ludicrous——even more so than that pantomime in Soligstrand, though it featured the same players."

I squinted. "You, your wife, and Allegra?"

He nodded. "They dictated terms to me, together, right here in this room. They told me it was over between Allegra and me, but that we would remain cordial, productive colleagues, running teammates, and would in all other ways be friendly towards each other, even if we were not precisely friends. All would be forgiven, as far as Petra was concerned, provided there was no retaliation against Allegra, no dejected mooning, no refusal to accept the end of the affair, no awkwardness at all. I was to return home and stay there, doing my part with the children, and things were to return to normal. Except that they weren't at all normal, not remotely so. The idea of my wife and my mistress making common cause—it was thoroughly bizarre. And then the idea that they would . . ." He stared down at the desk and massaged the back of his neck.

"That they would what, Dr. Witmer?"

He shook his head. "That they would become such fast friends. Bizarre."

"Did things transpire according to their program?" I asked. "Did you indeed stay home? Did you and Allegra return to being cordial colleagues, and so forth?"

"Yes, and yes. She continued in R&D for another year and handled all her work with her customary brilliance. Then she transferred to Special Projects, under Karen Muir. And we continued to run together and race together. All very cordial. Friendly but not friends."

"But she and your wife were friends. Were they still?"

He waved a dismissive hand. "As far as I know. You'd have to ask Petra."

I nodded. "And do you know how things worked out for her in Special Projects?"

"Quite well for most of her time there, from what I heard. I was moved—one might say *removed*—to Trials not long after Allegra went to Projects."

"Why was that?"

"As I told you, eventually, everyone knew about Allegra and me. That included Terry—Dr. Hasp. He was not pleased. Even after all these years, he's not pleased."

"So, if I asked you why Dr. Stans returned to R&D, and why she went from having supervisory responsibilities in Projects to not having them . . . ?"

"I'd refer you to Dr. Hasp."

"And that would be all? You have no other information? No speculation? It seems an uncharacteristic—a unique—stumble, in a career that was otherwise without a misstep."

He shook his head. "Maybe there was some tension between Allegra and Karen, but I don't know over what. Maybe it was just idle gossip." Witmer sighed, closed his eyes, and rubbed his temples. I tapped my chin.

"What was the threat, Dr. Witmer?"

He opened his eyes, puzzled. "What threat?"

"You said Allegra and your wife dictated terms—that you would be forgiven if you complied with their instructions. The way you described things, it doesn't sound as if your wife's forgiveness would've been a great motivator for you. So—what did motivate you? What would have happened if you were noncompliant?"

Witmer's cheeks burned, and he began to sputter out some lies. I stopped him. "Please, Doctor—we were doing so well. Let's not spoil things now."

He colored more darkly and leaned forward in his chair. Then he sank back. "Allegra threatened a sexual-harassment suit against me personally and against the company, and Petra threatened to corroborate any and all of her claims. The charges alone—especially if Petra had substantiated them—would've ruined me professionally and likely cost me my equity stake in Ondstrand Biologic."

"Is it a large stake?"

"Large then and larger now. Low eight figures." I nodded and stared at him, and after a few moments his cheeks reddened again. "It *wasn't* harassment," he bleated finally. "And it wasn't coercion—no one could coerce Allegra into anything. What we had was *a relationship*—a consensual relationship. I wanted her—wanted to be with her. I was in love with her, and she . . ." He shook his head. "Well, I suppose I have no idea how she felt about me. As I said, it's difficult to see her or that time clearly now. There was an unreality about it—about her. Until this happened, seeing Allegra around Ondstrand was like seeing a stranger walking past. It was as if I didn't know her and never had."

"And since her death?"

He shut his eyes and shook his head. His voice was very low. "Now I remember everything."

Witmer sank into his chair again, as if speech and the act of memory had deflated him—emptied him of anger, grievance, and wounded vanity, and left behind a listless husk. I stood, and my movement frightened him. He shrank away as if I might strike him. I turned to the study door, and then turned back. I pointed to the running-club photos.

"Who took those, Dr. Witmer?"

He was momentarily puzzled, then followed my finger to the bookshelf. "Those? Petra took 'em. After she and Allegra became friends, she came to all the races."

I nodded and made my way down the corridor towards the front door. On the way, I passed the lounge again. Three somewhat grimy children were in there—a dark-haired girl of perhaps ten, and twin towheaded boys of seven or eight. A skeptical-looking teenage girl was minding them, chattering with them, and sweeping some of the broken toys into a corner with her foot. They all fell silent as I passed, and the little girl leaned against the teenager.

CHAPTER TWENTY

Wednesday Evening

Witmer, P.—Petra Witmer—was in the courtyard when I emerged, sitting in the dark, on stone steps that led to the conservatory's door. She was barefoot, despite the chill, and she was smoking. I walked over and stood before her.

She was a small woman, with dark, wavy hair that shone in the milky light from the conservatory panes. Her face was soft, with rounded, mobile features—a snub nose, a wry, generous mouth, large blue eyes, freckles overall—the face of someone who, when she was young, might've often been muddy and scuffed, and been called a *pistol* or a *firecracker* by her laughing parents. But that fuse had long ago fizzled, and now, when she was forty-something, her face was worn and exhausted, lined around her mouth and on her forehead, red and swollen around her eyes. She wore black, and her pale, strong, paint-stained hands and slender white feet floated in the darkness like a ghost's appendages. She blew a stream of smoke in my direction.

"You're the security toad they're all so scared of?" Her voice was raspy and intimate, a secret shared in a bar, or someplace more private. I was fairly sure she'd been drinking.

"I am indeed a security toad. As for the scared part—I'm not sure which 'they' you're referring to."

She snorted. "You know damned well who. You've got them soiling their lab coats over there." She tossed a white thumb in the general direction of the coast and Ondstrand House. Then she pointed at her own front door. "There's a coat hereabouts that could use a washing, too."

"All I've done so far is ask some questions."

"Questions you can make 'em answer. What's scarier than that?" She took another drag on her cigarette and sent a silver cloud into the night.

"Do they have so much to hide?" I asked.

She didn't bother to answer. "You finish your chat with him?" I nodded. "You hear it all, then? The self-pity, the whining, the rationalization, the melodrama? He give you the full show?"

"He answered my questions."

"Questions about Allie?" I nodded. "Think he told you the truth?"

I smiled. "I think I'll keep my own counsel on that for now."

She shrugged. "I know which way I'd bet."

"You could give me your version, allow me to triangulate."

She snorted. "I'm no science whiz, but aren't there three sides to a triangle?"

I nodded again and counted on my fingers. "There's what he said, what you say, and whatever I already know."

She laughed. "Clever toad."

"One tries. I asked him to tell me the story of his relationship with Allegra. I wonder if your story would be the same."

"Wonder on; I'm not playing that game."

"It's not actually a game, Mrs. Witmer."

She frowned. "I suppose not. I suppose you can compel my testimony, one way or another. That's what they say about you people, isn't it—all the terrible things you can do. Basically, whatever you want."

"I understand you and Allegra were friends. I'm trying to find out what happened to her. I would think you'd be interested in assisting."

"Would I, now?"

"Wouldn't you?"

She sighed and breathed more smoke. "Not sure I can be much help. All I know about their relationship is how it ended. Or, rather, how I ended it."

"You?"

"He must've told you—it's a key tenet of his victimology: how I destroyed the only real happiness he'd known in his lonely life of science. He loves to tell it that way."

"What's the other way?"

"The other way was that I was tired of enduring stares and snickers and voyeuristic compassion from everyone who knew what was going on—which was everyone up and down the coast, apparently. And I was tired of dealing with all of that while keeping his house and cooking and cleaning and making sure the three monsters didn't kill themselves or each other and having not a minute in the day for my own work. I finally got fed up—not with his extramarital sex, mind, I was happy to be relieved of that particular chore—but with being his fucking unpaid servant. Which is basically what I said to him. Allie just happened to be there when I said it."

"Was that the first time you had met her?"

She stiffened. "We'd been introduced before—probably a dozen times—at various gruesome Ondstrand events. We'd never said more than hello, though."

"This was a bit more than hello."

Petra laughed, and drew on her cigarette. "Just a bit. Of course, I wasn't talking to her. But, as it happened, she was the only one actually listening to what I had to say. Piers didn't seem to hear a word of it."

"And you appreciated what Allegra had to say."

"Oh, he told you about that, did he? I can only imagine his bullshit misogynist gloss. The truth is, she didn't say anything elaborate. Allie simply heard me, understood me, and answered me like a human being—genuinely and from the heart. She just apologized for any part she had played in my situation and my unhappiness. That's all."

Petra stubbed her cigarette on the stone step and watched the cinders fade to black. Then she flicked the butt into the darkness and stood. A gust of wind blew across the courtyard, and she rubbed her arms. "I've got to get back to work," she said, and pointed over her shoulder. Then she turned and opened the conservatory door. She didn't seem surprised when I followed her through.

The conservatory had been converted to a painter's studio, with easels and canvas stretchers and a scarred oak counter, running the length of the space, that was covered with paint tubes, charcoal sticks, blocks of paper, colored pencils, soup tins full of brushes, and a whiskey bottle beside a chipped white teacup—all bearing signs of hard use. The air smelled of paint, turpentine, and fresh cement.

Petra made her way to an aluminum easel. There was a canvas on it, stretched on a wooden frame. It was small, like the paintings in the cottage foyer, but its back was to me, and all else about it was obscured. She switched on an electric space heater beside the easel, and the elements began to click and glow and cook the dust.

"You became friends after that encounter, you and Allegra?"

Petra took a brush from a stand on the easel and picked up a sheet of stiff white plastic that was studded with a dozen thick slugs of paint. She perched on a rickety wooden stool and studied the blobs and the canvas and nodded. "She called me the next day and invited me to coffee. Coffee became a three-hour heart-to-heart. We saw a lot of each other after that."

"So I gather. It must've taken you a few of those sessions to come up with your approach to Allegra's breakup with your husband."

She looked at me from behind the easel. "He told you all that, too? Good on you, toad—you *are* convincing."

"Hers was quite a novel approach."

She smiled wider. "Was it not? It was very much a win-win from our standpoints."

"Though not from your husband's. He maintains that the claims of harassment and coercion were complete fabrications."

"He would. But, in fact, he was pressuring Allegra, threatening—subtly but no less definitely—to retaliate against her professionally if she ended things with him. She had entered into the relationship thinking Piers was all but divorced, and that he'd wanted what she'd wanted: an uncomplicated, uncommitted sexual relationship, and nothing else. What she got, soon enough, were his gushing and clinging attempts at manipulation—all his controlling bullshit, dressed up in his usual nonsense camouflage of *romance*. She could deal with it for a while—she was seeing other people, and I suppose for some reason she did like him, at least at first—but, the clingier he became, the more she saw the writing on the wall."

I nodded. "That's a lot of ground to cover, even in several heart-to-hearts. Especially for two people who didn't know each other and had nothing in common besides a cheating husband."

Petra laughed. "Don't kid yourself, toad—a cheating husband is quite a bit to have in common." She picked up the whiskey bottle, poured a healthy shot into the teacup, and took a sip. She proffered the bottle. "Take the chill off? I'm sure I have a cleanish jar around here somewhere."

"Thanks, no. Your husband notwithstanding, it still seems like a lot of intimacy very quickly."

Petra sipped again from the teacup and looked at me over its rim. "That's how it was with Allie. We connected fast, and once we did, she didn't hold back, and neither did I. It'd been a long time since someone had listened to me and understood me; maybe it had been a long time for her, too. You look so dubious, toad—have you never felt that? That feeling of recognizing and being recognized all at once? That feeling of being *known*?" She returned to her canvas then, and I was glad to be free of her gaze.

I breathed deeply. "Whose idea was the harassment suit?"

"The lawsuit? That was Allie—she'd already been considering it."

"Did she suggest that you corroborate her allegations?"

She looked around her easel again. "Why does that matter?"

I shrugged. "It was a show of force—overkill, one might argue—but it was decisive. The threat to your husband's career, to his equity stake in Ondstrand, certainly convinced him. Of course, if he hadn't been convinced, and you'd made good on the threat, it would've harmed you and your children nearly as much—his earnings and assets being in part yours. I'm curious who came up with the idea. It helps fill out the picture."

Petra squinted at me and shook her head. "I don't know. Allie, I guess, though I'd already told her about Piers's equity, how proud he was of it, how paranoid he was about the various contingencies that allowed Terry and Karen to strip it away—his 'behavior unbecoming' clause included. How afraid of them he was generally. I guess she turned all that into tactics."

I nodded. "And you stayed friends, even after your victory."

"Of course we did—why not?"

"So it wasn't simply a marriage of convenience—banding together to defeat a common foe, or at least to leash and muzzle him."

She frowned, and her weary face became hostile. "He brought us together in the way our cars might have if we'd touched bumpers. That's the full extent of his involvement in our relationship. Of course we stayed friends—we became closer friends, in fact."

I nodded and glanced around the studio again. My eyes lit on a corkboard with yellowed postcards, a child's stick figure in crayon, and several curled photos. "I saw your photos of Allegra," I said. Petra looked at me, her face tense and eyes wide. "Your road-race photos," I continued. "They're compelling. They capture something."

Petra colored beneath her freckles, and her eyes were wet. "She was an amazing athlete. An incredible competitor. And the camera adored her, besides."

I nodded. "Were you and Allegra lovers, Mrs. Witmer?"

Her eyes didn't flicker from mine, and her face was still. "Two women can't be friends?" she said softly. "They can't be close without exciting speculation?"

"Two adult people can do whatever they care to do. I'm simply asking a question. Though, when I consider your lovely photographs, it hardly seems necessary to ask."

She brushed her sleeve across her eyes and smiled tightly. "You're a flatterer, toad."

"When did it start?" I asked.

"A month or so after that first coffee. She invited me on a drive up the coast—in that same car you came in today. It was one of those warm autumn days that pretend to be still summer, all soft and yellow, but the light's not quite right. We put the top down. There's a quiet beach up north—Alskarestrand. She packed a lunch, a bottle or two of wine. I brought my sketch pad and a camera." She laughed bitterly. "To say it now . . . it sounds like a seduction scene from a bad film. Perhaps all seductions are slightly ridiculous."

"Perhaps. How long did it go on?"

"The sexual part—a long time. Until about a year ago."

"That's five years by my reckoning."

She nodded. "I suppose it was five years, on and off. But it wasn't an exclusive thing, by any means—not for her—and it certainly wasn't continuous all that time. We'd see each other at most every week or two, much of the time less often. And there were breaks—months long sometimes. It was an arrangement she liked."

"Casual, without commitment?" Petra nodded. "Is that how you wanted things?"

She shrugged. "It's what worked. Anything else wouldn't have worked."

"For her."

She sniffled. "Don't judge, toad. But I forget—that's what you do, isn't it?"

"When the sexual part of your relationship did end, what was finally the cause?"

She shrugged. "I suppose I just got tired of being unhappy, of wanting what ultimately was not on offer. I couldn't do it anymore. It's exhausting, you know."

I nodded. "Did you two remain friends?"

Petra shook her head. "We tried, but, honestly, it was hard for me, being around her. And I don't think she much enjoyed spending time with me when I was unhappy. So—not a great basis for friendship."

"Then you hadn't seen her much this past year?"

"Around Ondstrand—at those horrid fêtes—but not much besides. The last time was maybe six months ago. We ran into each other in Soligstrand and had a quick coffee."

"How was she then?"

"She was Allie. A little more stressed about her work—maybe some unhappiness there."

"Unhappiness over what?"

"She didn't say, and I'm sure I didn't ask. Goings-on at Ondstrand are the last things I ever want to hear about." She raised her teacup again and drained it this time, and she shuddered as the whiskey went down. She looked at me. "You think this had something to do with Ondstrand?"

"It's not much of a leap, is it—considering the circumstances of her death?" Petra nodded slowly but made no reply. "What were you and your husband doing there so early that morning?"

"On Saturday? I was sketching and taking photos from the terrace and the cliffs, for a painting I'm working on. I go there often for that. I don't know why Piers was there. Something going on in one of his labs, no doubt. You'd have to ask him."

"He didn't mention it?"

"No, and we didn't drive over together. We arrived at the same time, entered the building together, but we traveled separately—in separate cars."

"And you went off to paint—"

"I went off to get coffee first; then I went off to sketch and shoot some photos."

I nodded. "And your husband went to his lab."

"Presumably."

"You saw nothing of Allegra that morning?"

"You do know that the man who called from your office asked me these same questions." I nodded, and Petra sighed. "No, I saw nothing of her."

"Did you see anything at all from the terrace or the cliffs?"

"That's what I was there to do, toad: to see."

"Anything out of the ordinary—anything you hadn't seen before?"

She waved me over. "Would you like to see my sketches? Then you can see for yourself what I saw and decide on the relevance."

I raised an eyebrow. "Thank you," I said.

I joined her on the other side of the easel and looked at the painting she was working on. It was of the beach below Ondstrand House, from a vantage point neither quite that of the terrace nor precisely from the cliffs—the perspective, perhaps, of a gull hanging in the wind. Like the paintings I'd seen in the house, the colors were chilly grays, blues, and whites—a winter coast—with dashes of bottle green and sable. There was pigment at the corners of the canvas, and in much of the foreground, but the body of the piece was still white space and faint sketch marks. Petra took a spiral-bound pad about the dimensions of a tabloid newspaper from where it leaned against the easel. She flipped to the last dozen sheets and handed it to me.

The sketch paper was rough, and the drawings were done in charcoal and colored pencil, quick and sure: a graceful little skiff beached above the tideline, near the rock outcroppings and caves below Ondstrand House. The skiff was white with black gunwales, and a band of gray, the color of a gull's wing, just below that. Its oars were shipped, and it was made fast to a boulder by a thick line that ran from its bow.

"You did these on Saturday?" I asked. Petra nodded. "You took photos as well?" Another nod, and she walked along the oak table and extracted a laptop from beneath a black camera and a general wreckage of art supplies. She opened it and clicked something, then handed it to me.

"Those are my photos from that morning," she said.

There were fourteen pictures of the skiff, all taken from above the beach. Some caught the craft from afar, others held it in a tight zoom, but all were much like the boat in Petra's sketches. "The skiff in the photos has a motor," I said. "And the paintwork is different."

"Artistic license," she said. "I prefer oars to outboards, and that blue-and-yellow braid was garish to me."

I nodded and scrolled through the photos again. "Had you seen this boat before?"

"I've seen boats a few times before, always in the early morning. Local kids like to party on the beach, and I guess some of them keep going till dawn. Or they get too wasted and end up sleeping it off there. Sometimes the Ondstrand dragoons chase them away."

"Had you seen *this* boat?"

"I . . . I'm not sure."

I looked at the time and date stamps on the photos. "Is your camera clock accurate?"

"Check for yourself," she said, and retrieved the black camera from the table. She pressed a button beside the rear screen and handed it to me. I looked at it and at my watch. They matched to the minute. "I'll need copies of these."

Petra nodded and took the laptop from me. A moment or two and several keystrokes later, she handed me a memory stick. I thanked her and dropped the stick into my pocket.

"What did you do after you took these?" I asked.

She picked up her brush again and stared at it for a moment. "I packed up and went inside. I went to the cafeteria and drank more coffee. While I did, I looked at my pictures and my drawings, and then I left."

"According to the logs, you re-entered the building at seven-sixteen a.m., exited again at seven-forty-three a.m., and exited the grounds at seven-fifty. Does that sound right?" She nodded. "And you learned of Allegra's death when your husband called you at eight-forty-nine a.m."

Petra looked at her canvas but seemed not to see it. Tears welled in her eyes. "I hadn't been home long when he called. He broke the news like he was reading a shopping list. The prick." The tears fell then, down her cheeks, onto her hands, onto the plastic palette, onto the floor. I heard them strike like the softest footsteps. I gave her a minute of silence.

"Did he know about your relationship with Allegra, either while it was going on or afterwards?"

She wiped a sleeve over her face and shrugged. "You'd have to ask him that."

"You never discussed it?"

She shook her head. "No, and I have no idea what he thought, but we were a damn sight more discreet than he had been."

"And Allegra, after you two broke things off—did she continue to be discreet?"

"Delicately put, toad, but there's no need to tiptoe. Are you asking if she was fucking someone, or if I knew who?"

"Both."

"I assume she was fucking someone, probably more than one someone. That was her way. As to who—I have no idea."

"One last question: Are you familiar with a piece of jewelry that Dr. Stans owned—a cloisonné locket—"

"With a deer on it. Of course I know it. She wore it all the time."

"So, if I were to ask where she might keep it when she wasn't wearing it . . ."

"I wouldn't be able to help you. She never took it off—not once that I saw, anyway." Then Petra straightened on her stool and turned her attention back to her canvas. "And now, toad, unless you wish to clap me in irons, I must work."

"We'll save the irons for when we know each other better," I said, but Petra Witmer had already dismissed me from her focus and was bent to her work.

I walked down the long counter and out into the night and was grateful for the cold air. The wind had sent plastic toys—a ball, a pail, a green spade, a pink bowling pin—careening across the courtyard like flotsam on an unseen tide. They clattered on the stones as they skittered about and made a sound like hollow bones.

CHAPTER TWENTY-ONE

Wednesday Night

It was late when I drove through the gates of Ondstrand Biologic, and a cold rain had joined the lashing winds in buffeting Allegra Stans's little car and clawing at its cloth top. The main house had a battened-down look as I drove past on my way to the parking lot. By the time I walked back up, I was mostly soaked. I crossed the lobby, passed through the security turnstiles, and saw Nadia Blom on my way to the elevators. She raised a tentative hand; though she looked as if she were about to speak, she said nothing, and I boarded the elevator alone and undisturbed.

In my room, I traded wet clothes for dry and switched on my tablet as I toweled my hair. I heard Goss Ivessen's aggrieved cat before I saw his skewed bookshelves.

"Been for a swim?" he asked.

"Not exactly," I said, and told him of my afternoon and evening. He listened in silence and was silent for a while after I'd finished.

"Ah, youth. So much living packed in a day."

"I was hoping for something more insightful than a lament for your younger days."

Ivessen laughed. "Hardly a lament. I barely survived being your age the first time through; I have no desire to do it again. As for insight, I doubt mine is much different than yours. The obvious conclusion regarding the fleet fellow in the garage is that he was clearing a letter-box, no? That box being Dr. Stans's car. He had a set of keys, he knew where the car was parked—likely because it was agreed that she would always park in one of those spaces—and he knew what he was looking for—the camera—and where to find it. Do you read it differently?"

"No," I said. "And the fact that he turned up there at all—"

"Meant that he thought Allegra was still alive."

"And so was not her killer."

"Not her killer, but perhaps someone with knowledge of what might've gotten her killed."

"I look forward to discussing it with him."

Ivessen chuckled. "Ever the optimist. And why not—you remain a fortunate fellow. Those hairstylists being a case in point. Makes me wonder why you need me."

"I wonder myself from time to time."

Ivessen ignored me. "They weren't lying to you about Ondstrand Hall's last headmaster—Roeg was his name. It was quite the scandal in its day. Nothing original, mind, not even back then—just a wretchedly familiar tale of an abusive head of school and many helpless boys. Apparently, his abuse spanned years, and predated his appointment as headmaster. During that time, several of the boys he molested ran away from school, but whatever stories they might've told were either disregarded or covered up. Then one of the runaways attempted suicide, followed by another, several weeks later, who was, sadly, more successful: he ran only as far as the cliffs and flung himself over. The ugly truth of things came boiling out after that—students and old boys, some faculty members, too, coming forward with grisly tales of Headmaster Roeg, complete with all the gothic flourishes: ghostly apparitions, midnight visitations, dungeons and secret passages, threats of death, all quite lurid. And your stylists were not wrong about Roeg's ending, either—he, too, went off the cliff, just weeks after that student did."

"I don't recall this being in the papers."

Ivessen sighed. "It was over two decades ago, Myles—you were but a child. Though even back then coverage was quite limited—*curtailed,* one might say. There were several ministers' sons at Ondstrand Hall at the time, as well as several ministers who were themselves old boys. None of them wanted the grim details plastered across the tabloids, and so they weren't. The story got some local attention at the time—it was the obsession of a reporter at the *Soligstrand Courant* when that still existed, and he self-published a book about it that I'm trying to lay hands on. Otherwise, the powers that be were very effective in shutting down any wider coverage. Though not the local gossip, apparently."

I nodded but said nothing for a while, and Ivessen's grating cat provided the only accompaniment to my thoughts. "The sordid history of the place makes the choice of Ondstrand House as the site of a corporate headquarters all the more unlikely, no? One might imagine Hasp wanting to get as far away from this place as possible."

Shadows shifted on my screen in what might've been a shrug. "Perhaps it's nothing more complicated than the history of the place depressing its price."

"Perhaps. Has Domestic produced those security clearance packages yet?"

"Not yet."

I tapped my chin. "Their silence is getting loud."

"Positively deafening," Ivessen said. "Do you want me to press harder? Or to go around them?"

I shook my head. "Let's hold off on that for the moment, it being technically illegal and all. Do you think my postman in the garage was one of theirs?"

"Anything's possible—he certainly turned tail quickly enough. Are you *sure* you don't want me to press?"

"Now you're being subversive," I said, and Ivessen laughed.

I changed the subject. "The Witmers—theirs is quite the marriage. A hearty recommendation for the whole institution."

"Isn't it? But your Mrs. Witmer provided some interesting information."

I nodded. "Dr. Stans was not subtle in her approach to problem solving. At least not to solving problems of human relationships. Once she found out where Witmer was sensitive, she wasted no time in applying the knife."

"Yes," Ivessen said, "and she was quick to enlist Petra to help drive it deep."

"She left little to chance, and ultimately she left them both brokenhearted."

Ivessen chuckled. "*Brokenhearted?* Really, Myles, you *are* a sentimentalist. From your telling, Dr. Witmer seems petulant and bitter—wounded in his vanity if anywhere. As for his wife—perhaps there was some cardiac trauma, but it sounds as if there might also be something a bit darker."

I nodded again. "Anger, certainly—and something else. Something . . .

unreconciled, brooding. But make no mistake, whatever else is going on with them, she and her husband are grieving."

"And each alone," Ivessen said, "with no solace from the other." There was no irony in his voice.

I sighed. "That said, Petra's pictures are useful. If we assume that the skiff she saw belongs to whoever Allegra met in the cave, and if we believe Petra when she says that she saw no sign of Allegra while she was outside, then the time stamps on the photos give us a better accounting of Allegra's movements before her death, and a better idea of time of death."

From Ivessen a considering silence. "Unless of course Dr. Stans had already departed the beach when Mrs. Witmer took her pictures, leaving her paramour behind, in postcoital cave bliss. And that's *if* the skiff had anything to do with Allegra in the first place. If not, then Allegra and her friend may both have decamped before Mrs. Witmer arrived."

I shrugged. "The skiff suggests a local; one of Allegra's several lovers was a local, according to Sandy Silber."

"The skiff suggests someone with access to a local boat, which is not quite the same as a local."

"Granted. But perhaps you can provide more specificity. I'm sending you Petra's photos."

I plugged the memory stick into my tablet and dragged the photos. A burst of keystrokes followed from Ivessen's end. "I take it that you found Mrs. Witmer plausible when she said she saw neither hide nor hair of Dr. Stans that day."

I tapped my chin. "Her grief is real."

"Perhaps it is; perhaps it's enhanced by guilt. I don't need to tell you that grief does not bestow absolution. Do you think she'd seen that boat before?"

"I don't know."

"You said yourself there's something brooding there. Perhaps that morning she was brooding about whoever Dr. Stans was with in that cave. And perhaps not for the first time."

"Not the first time Stans met her lover in the cave?"

"Nor the first time Petra watched and brooded."

"You're speculating."

"Wildly. As are you, Myles."

"If it's all the same, I'd prefer that you spend your energies finding out more about that boat."

Ivessen snorted, his cat mewled, and my screen went black. I ran my hands through my still-damp hair and looked out my window at the fountain below. Then I turned my attention to Ivessen's background reports.

CHAPTER TWENTY-TWO

Thursday Morning

The Major will be pleased to hear that you've kept fit," Director Mehta said, and made no attempt to hide her amusement. She wore a black jacket over a white shirt, and a black-and-gray scarf at her elegant throat. Early-morning light fell in clear, pale shafts through the window behind her, and everything on her desk—and she herself behind it—was washed in grays and blues.

"The Major is a bastard of the first order," I answered.

"Now, Myles, be charitable—she's getting on in years, and you were always one of her special favorites at Conservatory."

I shook my head. "Special favorite target, perhaps. And she's never been other than ancient. I stand by my characterization."

"You say this fellow had some training?"

I nodded. "Some. Military, perhaps. Perhaps Domestic Security."

She smiled tightly. "I am assured he wasn't theirs."

I sighed. "You spoke with Ivessen?"

"I did."

I nodded. "Then I take it he told you about the rest of my afternoon and evening as well."

"And the excellent report I received from you early this morning filled in the blanks. I believe we all agree that this fellow was clearing a letterbox. The use of the car and the garage was simple but effective tradecraft, and not at all beyond Dr. Stans. She had but to park and walk away."

I nodded. "The camera in the car is identical to the one I found in Stans's apartment, and there are only two photos in its memory, and no memory card—like the apartment version. About which I've yet to hear anything, by the way."

"Freja Berg will be with you shortly and will remedy that. She'll go over the tech team's findings and retrieve the new camera you found and the car keys your postman tossed. Perhaps Dr. Wilding can lift a print."

"You've seen the tech report?"

The Director nodded. "Best to let Ms. Berg do the honors, and then we can talk. Suffice it for now to say that Dr. Stans's tradecraft may have extended well beyond this simple postbox."

"Any thoughts on the Witmers, or on Mrs. Witmer's pictures?" I asked.

"I'll be curious to see what Ivessen comes up with regarding that boat. If it belongs to one of Allegra's lovers, and if Petra Witmer was telling you the truth, then those pictures could establish more precise timing and help cross some names off your list. But those are significant ifs. As for the Witmers . . ." The Director sighed heavily. "Allegra Stans didn't hesitate with Dr. Witmer, all those years ago. She was a hammer."

"And Petra helpfully pointed out the most useful nail."

"Yes," the Director said, "Witmer's equity stake in Ondstrand Biologic."

"'Large then and larger now' is how he described it."

She nodded. "If his equity was valuable enough then to compel Dr. Witmer's compliance, what might its larger size compel now?"

I smiled. "My thoughts have wandered in a similar direction. His equity interest is a blade above his head; the more its value increases, the sharper the edge."

"You do enjoy speculation, Myles."

"I'm not alone in that," I said.

It was her turn to smile. "And so we must be mindful of overindulgence. Nevertheless, we should remain alert to the possibility that the equity stake that motivated Dr. Witmer once, years ago, may have motivated him more recently as well."

"I remain alert," I said.

Director Mehta rang off then, and I went down to the executive dining room, where Thursday breakfast was well under way. I queued at the coffee bar and ignored the discreet and less-than-discreet stares as I wrung a latte with four shots of espresso from the gleaming hardware.

I had pressed the lid onto my paper cup and was on my way out when Nadia Blom waved from across the dining room. She was sitting at a table by a window, accompanied by Dr. Hasp. I paused for a moment, and then made my way to them.

Nadia Blom wore blue, a shade not-quite-navy. Her skirt was longish and tailored, her tunic top had a high collar, and the overall impression was of a novice in a stern but stylish order. The tray before her held cottage cheese and sliced fruit, undisturbed. Dr. Hasp was in jeans, a soft white shirt, and a black cardigan. He sipped from a café-au-lait bowl and smiled stiffly in my general direction.

Nadia Blom caught herself before she said "agent." "Myles, I didn't see you yesterday. I take it you've been getting what you need."

I nodded. "I'm keeping busy."

"So I hear," Hasp said. "Very busy, apparently. Talking to all sorts, I hear."

"Information flows from all quarters."

"No doubt, and no doubt you're moving things along quick as you can. That said, any idea of time frames?"

"Are you asking me how long it will be until I conclude my investigation?"

Hasp colored. He made a little chopping motion with his hand. "You're plowing right ahead, no question, but . . . Well, naturally, we're eager to get things back on course here."

"In that spirit," I said, "I'd best return to my work." I turned towards the exit.

Nadia Blom gulped, and Hasp's face grew darker. He put a hand on my arm. "Full docket, I'm sure," he said, his voice low and impatient. "But any idea if you're gonna need more from me? You spoke with me, with Wit, I understand, and you'll talk to Karen when she returns to the office tomorrow, no doubt. Just seems like you must be done soon." I said nothing but looked at his hand. After a moment, he withdrew it. "The calendar's always tight," he continued. "Want to make sure you've got a place on it."

"I trust that you'll make room as necessary. And in the interests of efficient use of time—mine and yours—I think it's best if we speak again after I've interviewed others on my list. Then, in addition to addressing whatever questions I have for you, you can help to resolve any inconsistencies that may have arisen in prior interviews."

Hasp nodded eventually, then looked at Nadia Blom as if she'd spilled milk. "You're making sure he gets what he needs?" he said. His tone was brusque, and Blom's cheeks burned. I carried the coffee outside and waited under cloudless skies for Freja Berg.

Freja drove a company car—black and shiny—and she parked it under the porte cochere. She unfolded her lanky frame from behind the wheel, brushed off her jeans, rolled her shoulders, and pushed up the sleeves of her black jumper. Then she slung a messenger bag across her body and stepped into the sunlight. She sighed and turned her dark, handsome face to the heavens.

"My god, Myles, that is a *fucking* long drive," she said after a while. "Let me stretch my legs and look at the ocean. And, for fuck's sake, that had better be coffee, and it had better be for me."

"Right both times," I said, and her smile was wide and bright against her brown skin. As we walked around the north wing, her paddock boots made a hard sound on the stone.

She sighed again when we stepped onto the terrace above the beach, and she gazed out at the ocean. It was tranquil just then, with curving ranks of waves marching beneath pristine skies. She closed her eyes and let the salt breeze brush her cheek and her tight black curls.

She put her coffee cup on the stone rail. "Rough duty, this," Freja said.

"It's not all sun and fun."

"So I heard," she said, chuckling, and she raised her hands in a pantomime of boxing. "Which reminds me . . ." Freja dug in her messenger bag and came out with two evidence bags, which she unzipped and held open. "Jane will fucking slay me if I forget."

"Can't have that." I dropped the car keys into one, the camera into the other; Freja zipped the bags and replaced them in her own. She picked up her coffee and finished it off. "The Director tells me you have the tech team's reports," I said.

She nodded. "I do indeed: regarding her phone, her laptop, her camera, and the spear-phishing e-mails. Which do you want first?"

"Dealer's choice," I said.

"Let's start with her phone and her laptop. Dr. Stans bought the phone about six months back—a new device, with service from a new carrier. At the same time—on the same day, in fact—she also bought herself a brand-new laptop. I don't suppose you've come across their predecessors—have you?"

"I haven't."

Freja nodded, unsurprised. "It'd be interesting to have a look at them, as Dr. Stans, for whatever reason, chose not to port any data from her old equipment over to her new. No e-mails, texts, or documents; no browsing history or bookmarks; no calendar entries or contacts."

"Nothing?" I asked.

"It's as if life began anew," Freja said. She let that land, then took a deep breath. "And these six-month-old models have had what my techs call 'gentle use.' In fact, one of them said they reminded her of the displays in a furniture store—not really living rooms but plausible facsimiles, if you don't look too closely."

I shook my head. "She didn't actually use her phone or her laptop?"

"No, no—she used them. She shopped with them, made appointments, sent and received e-mails and texts, maintained her calendar, read news and articles from professional journals, looked up information about road races—those sorts of things. But those were the *only* things she did on her phone and her laptop—and the patterns of usage, especially for her phone, just don't align with the things an actual person actually does with her phone, day to day. There was no checking social media, no aimless browsing, no time lost watching adorable animal videos or checking the weather forecast, no game play, no repeated scanning for new texts or e-mails.

"We have extensive statistical data on mobile-phone use broken down by gender, age, income, race, education, and geographic region, and Dr. Stans's activity makes her an outlier across the board. Even the number of times a day she simply lifted up her phone was drastically less than average for someone in her cohort. It's as if she was expecting someone to be monitoring her usage, and so restricted herself to only the most benign activities."

"So you're saying what—that her usage was so mundane as to be suspicious? That's absurd."

"Is it?" Freja said, frowning. "Scoff if you like, but I'll show you the data."

"She was a scientist, Freja—a dedicated one, from all reports—who more or less lived at her office. On top of which, she was a runner, and she never took her phone with her on her runs. Might those facts not explain the difference between her phone use and that of some city shopgirl's, with a phone glued always to her hand?"

She smiled again. "'Some city shopgirl'? Nice condescension, Myles. But we factor that into our analyses; she just doesn't tally. Then you consider the location data, and it's difficult not to conclude that something odd was happening with Dr. Stans and her phone."

"The location data?"

"You see, all your skeptical sneering distracted me, and I nearly skipped some of the best bits. Yes—the location data. The doctor did, as you say, spend much of her time in the halls of this great pile, with excursions to Soligstrand on most Wednesday afternoons, and other outings on occasional weekends."

"Other outings where?"

"Patience, Myles—I'm getting there. During the six months she had this phone, besides her trips to Soligstrand, we find Dr. Stans in and around Fiskdorp on four Saturdays, in Vinkadorp, south of Fiskdorp, on four Saturdays, in Slocum on three, and on three occasions we find her somewhere out at sea."

"At sea?"

"Not far out, mind—just off the coast, no more than half a mile or so—off of Fiskdorp and points to the north."

"North as far as Ondstrand House?"

Freja nodded. "Perhaps she liked to fish."

We were quiet for a while, looking at the ocean. A gull glided above the cove, and Freja made a gun of her thumb and forefinger and tracked its arc.

"You said she went to Soligstrand on 'most Wednesday afternoons.' My information says she went every Wednesday."

Freja nodded. "Yours may be better than mine. What's interesting about mine are the holes in it."

"Holes?"

She turned her gaze back to me. "Every third Wednesday afternoon, when, I understand, she departed this property, Dr. Stans left her mobile behind. She went somewhere—perhaps to Soligstrand, perhaps other places—but her phone stayed home. Hence the holes."

"What do you make of it?" I asked.

Freja shrugged. "Why might you leave *your* phone at home, Myles? A longing for a bit of peace and quiet? A wish to be unreachable for a time? Or perhaps because you'd like your movements and whereabouts to be untraceable for a few hours. Which do you think was Dr. Stans's motive?"

"Every third Wednesday?" I asked. Freja nodded. "You have the dates? And the dates and locations of her weekend trips?"

"The report has it all."

I nodded. "Tell me about the camera."

"There's little to tell, honestly. It's a pricey model—metal body construction, long battery life, high-resolution photos. As you know, no memory card was installed, and without one the camera's own storage capacity is limited. We pulled eight images from its memory."

"Eight? I saw only two."

Freja nodded. "The other six had been deleted, though not overwritten on the camera's drive."

"Don't leave me hanging, Freja."

Her smile was playful. "They were nothing exciting—just six more pictures of the desktop computer in her company apartment. From slightly different angles, with slightly different lighting, some closer, some a bit farther away. Perhaps we'll find something more on this new one."

"And that's it?"

Freja nodded. "That's it in terms of the images. The only other thing about that camera, or its apparent twin, is that we find no record of her having purchased any cameras. Of course, she may have paid cash, or they may have been gifts, but so far . . ."

"Are you tracing the serial number with the manufacturer?"

Freja's brow furrowed. "Don't be a dick, Myles—of course we are. Nothing's come back yet."

I turned my back on the sea, leaned against the stone rail, and looked up at the looming façade of Ondstrand House. It was gold in the clear light, and the windows were golden mirrors. "That leaves the phishing attempts," I said.

"The best for last," Freja said. "Let's begin with the e-mails. Your Ms. Drucker was correct in her assessment that they were all from the same source. Aside from the stylistic similarities in the contents, she was spot-on in that the address spoofing used the same techniques. We were able to back-trace further than she was, so I am able to tell you that the server that all of these originated from pinged to a location in the city, or seemed to. It was brought online five minutes before these e-mails were sent, and was taken offline three minutes after."

I squinted. "There and then not-there?"

Freja nodded. "And never heard from again."

"And the server was in the city?"

"*Seemed* to be, but I put no stock in that."

I nodded. "What do you make of it all?"

She shrugged. "It's definitely professional. A state actor would be my first guess—maybe military or an intelligence service. Or possibly an alum of one of those, gone private."

"One of ours?"

"Maybe."

"That doesn't narrow things much."

"I know, but, as with the camera, we're still digging. Now let's talk about the package."

"The keystroke logger."

Freja smiled and shook her head. "Yes, let's dispense with that. As Drucker told you, it was a primitive keylogger, the kind of crap any schoolkid might find on one of those bullshit sites that claim to be hacker marketplaces. There was nothing mysterious or subtle about it; that shit was old when I was in nappies."

"Which leads one to ask: What was the point? Why put so much professional, maybe state-sponsored, lipstick on such an unsubtle pig?"

"Because the keylogger wasn't the package. It was misdirection."

"Then what . . . ?"

"You know what clickjacking is?" she asked.

"You know I don't."

Freja smiled. "I just like hearing you say it. Clickjacking is a way of getting some unsuspecting boob to click on something he didn't mean to click on and do something he didn't mean to do—usually without him realizing he's done anything at all. There are lots of techniques employed to work the trick. In this case, there was effectively a transparent screen layer—invisible to the user—over these e-mails once the users opened them. It was built specifically for the operating system and the browser that Ondstrand runs on its desktops, and for the e-mail application it uses. Whoever did this knew the playing field, and was able to turn the entire body of the e-mail message into a single, undetectable button, so that if a recipient touched anything at all on that screen she'd be clicking on that button. And in doing so, she'd load the malware package—the actual malware package."

"Not the keylogger."

She shook her head. "As I said, that was misdirection—a distraction, an easy explanation in case someone had suspicions about these e-mails. By which time it would be too late."

"And the real package?"

"Was something sneakier, and also custom-built. The target was something all of the scientists here use—the virtual-lab-bench software. The malware was designed to subvert the security measure that restricts access to a given virtual bench only to authorized users on authorized devices."

I tilted my head. "Subvert how?"

"Your pal Drucker told you that security for the virtual-bench software is organized more or less along the lines of physical security for the labs themselves, right? Well, there's actually an additional layer. A given user can only access her virtual lab bench from *specific* Ondstrand computers that have been assigned for her use—for example, the desktop computer she's been given for use at home. This malware is designed to subvert that security: it scoops up user IDs, passwords, *and* the authorized-device IDs associated with an individual user."

"It scoops up these IDs and does what with them?"

"Something pretty clever. It renders them in an optical code—similar to a bar code—and sends them to a printer on the Ondstrand network."

"Which printer?"

Freja shrugged. "I can give you the device ID; you'll have to ask Drucker where the printer is actually located."

I turned and looked at her. "How would anyone know just when these codes would be printed? A person would become rather conspicuous, orbiting around a printer all day. And you wouldn't want to leave this kind of material out in public for long, would you?"

Another shrug. "In this case, it would be low-risk. The optical code used is an obscure one, and you'd need a special app to read it. On the page, it would simply look like a cluster of colored dots. People might not notice them at all, or might think it was a test page from the printer's own recalibrations. And before you ask—no, we did not find an app on Stans's phone that could read those codes."

I nodded. "Once someone retrieves these pages—then what?"

"Now we enter the realm of speculation. Presumably, this someone would scan the optical codes, translate them into something human-readable, and use the information to access the virtual lab benches of the people who'd received the phishing e-mails."

"*Use them*—just like that?"

"Not just like that. Our someone would need a hack—a minor one, really—to the lab-bench application, to force the device IDs in. But once that was done—presto, all doors open. We got hold of the lab-bench software from the vendor and managed it ourselves without a problem."

"I'm sure the vendor was pleased to hear that. I'm sure the Ondstrand people will be, too."

Freja shook her head. "We haven't notified the vendor yet; the Director wants to wait. And she'd prefer that you say nothing to the Ondstrand people, either, until you speak with her."

I nodded again. "What's the prize here, Freja? Is someone after Ondstrand's intellectual property? And if that's all it is, why do we care?"

She squinted at me and made a rueful laugh. "I'll leave it to you to ask the Director, Myles; she tolerates those kinds of questions from you. Not that she'll answer any of them, of course."

Freja turned back to the sea, and so did I. There were clouds on the horizon, distant but roiling, and the breeze was gusting and shifting this way and that. The ranks of waves had broken. After a while, Freja sighed and opened her messenger bag. She pulled out a transparent plastic file folder and passed it to me. It was thick and weighty.

"That's all of it," she said. She rolled her shoulders and closed her bag.

"Copy to my porter—the report and the raw data?"

"Yes, yes," she said, shaking her head. "I can't believe I have to make that fucking drive again. Walk me to my car."

We made our way in silence, and when we reached the car, I opened the door for her. "Of the four recipients of the phishing e-mails," I said, "how many clicked on that invisible button?"

She smiled as she climbed behind the wheel. "All of them, Myles. It had a one-hundred-percent hit rate."

CHAPTER TWENTY-THREE

Thursday Afternoon

I walked for a long time after Freja drove off—around Ondstrand House, back to the terrace, down the long stairway to the beach. The wind was calmer at the shore, but the waves fell heavily—each one like a collapsing house—and the sounds of calamity and calling birds followed me as I trudged south along the crescent shore and then north again, until the sand gave way to shingle and rocky outcrops and I came to the caves at the base of the cliff. I found a large rock by the makeshift firepit, sat on it, and opened the plastic file folder that held Freja's report.

I scanned the table of contents and the list of tables, graphs, pictures and other exhibits, and then I leafed through the body of the document, hopscotching from section to section, hoping that these new puzzle pieces would fall into place alongside what I'd learned of Allegra Stans thus far, and that a sharper picture might emerge.

It did not. Instead, I heard, above the falling waves, Director Mehta's voice. "Dr. Stans's tradecraft may have extended well beyond this simple postbox." And I saw, not a clearer picture of Allegra, but several pictures at once—distinct and hard to reconcile. There was the dedicated, ambitious scientist—committed to her profession and passionate in its pursuit. There was the gifted athlete—spirited, disciplined, and relentlessly competitive. And there was the sexual adventurer—a woman of robust appetite, unreliable impulse control, and catholic tastes. And now, besides those, there was another identity: spy.

Or something like that. Certainly Freja's reports, along with the fellow I'd encountered in Soligstrand, suggested something clandestine. And what else to call patterns of behavior like some of Allegra's, if not tradecraft? Not the most refined examples, perhaps, not entirely expert, but apparently suitable for her area of operations.

Again, I heard the Director's voice, a lesson from long ago, oft repeated: "People are never monoliths, Myles; they are divided and divided again, into many parts, and many of them hidden, one from another." It was hard for me to picture Allegra Stans as a mystery to herself, though perhaps that was my failing. It was a simpler matter to imagine when her division into Allegra the spy might've occurred: seven months ago, when she'd returned to the R&D division from Special Projects. Returned or been sent back.

One could mark that date on a calendar and afterwards find the phishing attack, Allegra's new, well-scrubbed phone and laptop, and the recurring holes in her location data. And though I had no evidence of when the man in the garage had made his first appearance in her life, I was willing to bet it was sometime in the vicinity of seven months back.

A gust of wind riffled the pages on my lap, and nearly carried them off. I caught them and tucked them into their plastic folder, then stood and looked out at the whitecaps. I thought about Allegra's weekend travels—the ones that had taken her out on the water. What were those excursions about, and which of her several selves had undertaken them? I had no idea. Maybe Freja was right; maybe she liked fishing. I sighed, tucked the folder under my arm, and headed to the steps. I had a call to make.

M s. Berg is on her way home?" the Director asked. Her jacket was off now and draped on her chair, and her scarf was loose around her neck. Her reading glasses were perched at the end of her nose. By her elbow was a daunting stack of paper.

In my rooms I shifted on the sofa and adjusted the tablet on my lap. "She left about an hour ago," I said.

"And she went over her report with you?"

"She did."

"And?"

"It tells a story, I suppose, or part of one, at any rate."

She let out a long breath. "I know that tone, Myles. Do you have another interpretation of Dr. Stans's actions—something other than that she was scrubbing her communications and her digital footprints, cloaking her movements, and using her car as a mail drop?"

"There's nothing that links her with the phishing e-mails."

"Nothing *yet,* though I trust you'll find it if it's there."

"I appreciate your confidence, but I feel at something of a disadvantage—not knowing our particular dog in this particular fight."

Director Mehta pushed her reading glasses up, into her dark hair. She pinched the bridge of her nose between her thumb and forefinger. "Myles," she said, sighing.

"If Dr. Stans was stealing intellectual property, and her theft led to her death, it might be useful to know what Ondstrand Biologic has that's worth stealing."

"I'm sure Terry Hasp could give you a long list," the Director said quietly. "Or he might simply say: 'Everything.'"

I ignored her. "And if she was engaged in something beyond simple corporate espionage—something with wider security implications— then it might be useful to know that as well."

"Your assignment there isn't a clear enough indication of that?" she said, and a chill entered her voice. "Are you under the impression that this is a training exercise? I should think you'd be well beyond Conservatory lessons at this point. But perhaps not." Even through the screen, she seemed to look right past me.

"So that's it, then? You have nothing less opaque to offer?" I waited, but silence was my only answer. It was my turn to sigh. "And the breach Ondstrand appears to have suffered? Am I authorized to discuss it with anyone here?"

Director Mehta sat up and retrieved her reading glasses from above her hairline. She dropped them onto her nose again. "We must understand the extent of it, of course, but do keep the circle small for now—to Hasp, to Ms. Drucker if you must. But don't discuss—"

"*Don't discuss Allegra's cameras*—yes, I know. I have no intention of mentioning those."

Director Mehta nodded. "In which case, I believe we're done for the moment."

"For the moment," I said, but by then I was talking to myself.

CHAPTER TWENTY-FOUR

Thursday Afternoon

There were a half-dozen young people in Caroline Drucker's glass office when I arrived, showing her things on a large wall-mounted screen and eager for her approval. Drucker glanced at me, and I walked back to the reception area and took a seat and tried to pay no attention to her assistant's staring. I watched the clouds sail like dreams across the sky and thought about how much to tell Drucker. I'd decided nothing by the time she appeared. She was wearing jeans and a gray roll-neck, and she smiled at me.

"I wasn't expecting you," she said.

"Do you have time to speak?"

She checked her watch. "I have another status meeting in ten minutes."

"We'll be longer than that."

Caro looked at her assistant, who nodded, and then she waved me back to her now-empty office. She shut the door. "What's going on, Myles?"

"A few things. But, first, do you know where the printer associated with this device ID is located?" I passed a sheet of notepaper to her.

She squinted at me and at it, and then turned to her keyboard. "Not off the top of my head, but I can look it up," she said, and tapped away. "Care to tell me why you're interested?" I didn't answer. Caro scanned her screen and looked at me. "It's a shared printer located in the main house, just outside the executive dining room. Why?"

I looked at her. "The virtual-lab-bench software—I assume it maintains user-activity logs of some sort—records of access to lab devices, documents, whatever."

Caro nodded. "Yes," she said slowly.

"I need access to those logs, for the recipients of the phishing e-mails, for activity on all dates after the e-mails were received."

Caro pushed back from her desk and stared at me, silent, for several moments. "What's going on, Myles?" she said, finally. "I've been told to provide you with whatever you ask for, and of course I will, but you're making me quite nervous. Has our network been compromised?"

I sighed. "It appears so. The phishing e-mails you provided us were more sophisticated than they initially appeared, and the keystroke logger that was the putative payload was in fact camouflage. The e-mails employed something called clickjacking, which I won't pretend to understand, but hope you're familiar with. The actual package was malware designed specifically for the Ondstrand environment, to attack the virtual-lab-bench application. In each instance, it seems to have deployed successfully."

Caro sat back in her chair, and her mouth opened and closed again. She shook her head and touched her hand to her throat, and finally she said: "Clickjacking. Fuck," quite softly.

"Indeed."

She leaned forward again and locked her dark eyes on mine. "Attacked the bench software how? To what end?"

"Apparently, it was designed to collect the user IDs, passwords, and authorized-device IDs of its targets. Having done so, it converted that information to an optical code—an obscure one, I'm told—and sent that information to a printer on your network."

"The printer you asked about."

I nodded. "Someone then collected those pages, translated the colored dots into something readable by a human, and used the IDs to access the bench software of the four scientists."

Caro thought about that for a while, her head tilted slightly to the left. Then she put a hand on her forehead. "Fuck," she said again. "*Someone*—you said *someone* collected the pages. Someone here, at Ondstrand? Someone who? Allegra? Is that what her death is about?"

"I don't know yet."

She squinted at me and tilted her head again. "But who here would have the kinds of skills to create this malware? The only people who come to mind are on my staff—and me, of course. Is that what you're thinking?"

"Should I be?"

"Of course you should—you'd be a fool not to, and you're no fool."

"I appreciate the sentiment, but I also try not to get too far ahead of the facts. While it's possible that one of your staff—or you—might have been involved, right now the indications are that the technical expertise necessary for this came from outside Ondstrand. Hence my decision to seek your help."

"I suppose I should be appreciative. I'll get to it as soon as I get over the indignation."

I smiled. "Sorry."

"I'm sure. And what did they want, these intruders? To sabotage experiments?"

"I don't know yet. That's why I want to look at those logs."

"Well, you're going to need help with that. Without it, you'll never make sense of them."

"The help will have to come from you, then. I'm not sharing this information with anyone else at this point. And neither are you."

"Not even with Dr. Hasp?"

"Is that a problem?"

Her smile was thin and chilly. "I'm helping Standard Division—how could that be a problem?"

Caro led me to a conference room with a glass-topped table and two large workstations. When she tapped a button, the room's glass walls went opaque. I hung my jacket on the back of a chair, and Caro sat at one of the workstations and typed rapidly. In a moment, both screens were filled with a dense mosaic of windows, each tile of which framed row upon row of text in a font so small as to be nearly illegible.

"The software logs everything, which is good, but there really isn't a decent user-interface to search and filter it all, which is bad. So—we're going to whip something up on the fly, with you telling me what you're looking for, and me doing the looking. Okay?"

I nodded. "As I said, I'm interested in the activity logs of the four scientists who received the phishing e-mails, for any date after the e-mails were received."

She sighed. "Yes, I heard you the first time—that's what all these little windows are. I color-coded them: blue for Geary, gray for Garza, orange for Li, and purple for Stahlmann. But we need to refine things a bit more."

I nodded again. "Each line item in a window represents some activity—some action—one of the scientists performed on the system?"

She sighed again. "The way I've organized them here, every window represents activity by a scientist on a date. So . . . within each window is a heterogeneous grouping of activities. For example, a log entry representing a check of values for a given instrument, say from a qPCR machine, would be mixed in with entries for the creation of an experiment note, the generation of a graph from a particular data set, the initiation or termination of a phase of some process, and the review of a lab report. Right now, the only thing the items in a window have in common are their dates and the ID of the scientist who performed the action. But I can sort them differently, if you like. All instrument-related activities on a given date by a given scientist, for example."

I studied the screens for a moment. "Can we look at document-related activities? Every instance where a user viewed a document on a given date?"

Caro squinted at me. "Documents? I thought you were thinking sabotage."

"*You* were thinking sabotage. Let's start with Dr. Geary. Let's have a look at his document access for the week after the e-mails were received."

Caro started typing again. "Maybe you want to pull in data from the week before as well," she said, glancing at me. "For context." I nodded, and Caro smiled and typed on.

It quickly became clear that her call had been a good one. In the week before receiving the phishing e-mail, there were numerous document-related activities logged for Dr. Geary by the virtual-lab-bench software: the creation and review of various notes, the generation and insertion of tables and graphs, updates and more updates to a summary of findings. There were dozens of document-related log entries on each day of that week, but all of them had to do with sections of the same two large documents. Geary's activity the following week told a rather different story. The dozen or so daily log entries related to his work on the two documents appeared that week as they had the week before, but alongside them were entries concerning many dozens of other documents as well.

Caro shook her head slowly. "It's as if someone was rummaging through his desk," she said, and I nodded. It was indeed.

During the following week, in addition to activity in the documents Geary had been engaged in drafting, there were nearly a hundred other log entries recording access to nearly a hundred other documents. None of these documents was modified, and some were accessed for only brief periods of time—less than a minute in some cases. In no instance was a document accessed for longer than fifteen minutes. In every instance, the access took place at night, between the hours of 9:00 p.m. and 1:00 a.m., and, according to the log entries, from a workstation located in Geary's lab.

"Do you think he was late in his lab on all these nights?" Caro asked, and her fingers flew across her keyboard to answer her own question. It took only seconds for her to create a new window, one that included all of Geary's activity-log entries for that second week, regardless of type, as long as they bore time stamps after 9:00 p.m. Interleaved with the document-access entries we'd been looking at were dozens of others, mostly instrument checks, all initiated from a workstation in Geary's apartment in Ondstrand House's north wing.

"Guess he's made a breakthrough in the field of being two places at once," Caro said.

"Apparently so," I said quietly.

We expanded our time frames out to a month after the phishing attack and turned our attention to the other three scientists: Garza, Li, and Stahlmann. And found similar episodes of nighttime activity, each one several days apart. Less than three weeks after the phishing expedition, the document files of all four scientists had been thoroughly ransacked.

I sat back in my chair, and Caro turned to look at me. "Who did this? Was it Allegra?" There was urgency in her voice, and anger.

I sighed. "What do these documents have in common?"

"You'd have to ask a scientist," Caro said, squinting at me. "Obviously, all of Geary's documents were written, or co-written, by him. He specializes in viral therapies, so I'm assuming that some or all of these documents are somehow related to that field. I assume that the same holds true for the other scientists and their documents—all of them by the same author, all related to the author's field of specialization. Beyond that, I'm out of my depth. As I said, ask a scientist."

"I'll get to that," I said, staring at the screens. "Whoever accessed these documents seemed to spend longer with some than with others."

Caro nodded and then typed rapidly. Another window opened, with a table in it, then another, with a graph. "It's based on the length of the document—the more pages, the more time."

"I suppose that makes sense."

She shook her head. "No, it doesn't. Whoever was accessing these things was spending on average less than fifteen seconds per page on a document. That's certainly not long enough to read these things. So what were they doing?" Caro looked at me and took my silence for puzzlement. "They weren't reading these things, probably not even skimming them. They weren't printing them, either—there would be log entries for that. And of course they couldn't send them anywhere."

"'Of course'? Why of course?"

"Because we don't permit attachments in outbound mail from our e-mail system, not without explicit permission from a manager, and all those are documented and logged. That restriction covers attachments of any kind—documents, images, audio files, video files, what have you. And if an attempt is made—either accidentally or otherwise—to send a company document without authorization, we prohibit it, flag it, and log it. It's part of how we safeguard intellectual property."

"What are the other parts?"

"We don't permit the forwarding of company e-mail to personal e-mail accounts. We don't permit the storage of company documents on anything other than company servers—which is why staff workstations outside of this department don't have local hard drives, nor do they have ports to accommodate removable media of any kind. And the printing of documents is closely monitored: all print requests are logged, printing is done only on network printers, and the documents themselves are watermarked."

"That last bit didn't stop whoever from printing those optical codes."

Caro nodded, frowning. "And I'll be looking into that—into every fucking aspect of this hack—trust me."

I smiled. "You'll have to wait your turn," I said.

She made a harrumphing noise. "You haven't answered my question: If they weren't reading these documents, what were they doing?"

I looked at Caro and thought not about her question but about the tripod I had found in Allegra's apartment, the cameras I had found there and in her car, and about the pictures on those cameras—of the workstation on her dining table. I wondered if, with a bit of practice, fifteen seconds was enough time to photograph a document page on that big screen and then flip to another page, and I wondered, too, about the empty slots in the backs of the cameras, and about the memory cards they might once have held.

"I have no idea," I said.

CHAPTER TWENTY-FIVE

Thursday Evening

It was purple dusk when Caro and I emerged from the conference room and walked outside. We stretched, rubbed our eyes, and gulped the cool air greedily, as if we'd woken from an overlong and unrestful sleep.

"I keep asking you if Allegra was involved in this," Caro said, "and you keep not answering."

"Because I can't say."

"Can't or won't?" I looked at her and didn't speak. She smiled bitterly. "So now what? Where do you go from here? And what am I supposed to do?"

I held up the memory stick Caro had given me. "To start, I'm going to send these documents to my people in the city."

"You're welcome for that," Caro said.

I nodded. "Perhaps they can tease out a common thread."

"And me—what shall I do?"

"Return to work. Business as usual."

"Business as usual? Knowing that the ship is leaking like a sieve? That, every moment, we may be bleeding intellectual property? Am I supposed to ignore that?"

"If it eases your mind, I don't think the leak is ongoing."

"No? Well, maybe that answers my question about Allegra's involvement. But what about what's already slipped out the door? Do you think these were the only documents that were stolen?"

"I doubt it. Now that you know what to look for, do you think you could find other instances of this pattern of access?"

She nodded. "And if I find them?"

"You tell me. And only me."

"Not Dr. Hasp?"

"I understand your concern, but this investigation takes precedence."

"Not for Dr. Hasp, I assure you."

"I'll worry about him."

Caro gave another tight smile. "Small comfort. It's not you he'll be looking to sack."

"He'll have other things to think about," I said. "You were helpful today. That will be noted."

She smirked and pushed up the sleeves of her sweater. "I earn a gold star for cooperation—excellent. I'll be sure to include it when I'm updating my CV. Which will probably be this evening."

I smiled. "Thanks again," I said, and started up the shadowed path to Ondstrand House.

In fact, beyond forwarding the scientific documents to the Director, Freja Berg, and Ivessen, my plan of what to do next was a jumble. When I considered the phishing expedition, the malware, the rifled documents, the cameras, Allegra's patterns of behavior, and her digital footprints, or lack thereof, and of course the man in the garage, it was hard to escape the conclusion that Allegra was engaged in corporate espionage—though what exactly she was intent on stealing, and on behalf of whom, were still unknowns. An analysis of the plundered documents might help answer those questions, as would some line on Allegra's postman, but until those came my way, Allegra's activities were motion without meaning. Still, I was all but certain that the meaning—the event that had incited all this—was to be found seven months back, when Allegra's career had foundered on the rocks of transfer and demotion.

I powered up my tablet when I returned to my rooms, and Director Mehta's profile soon appeared. She was in her office, and I saw lights moving in the window behind her, across the glittering city. They seemed thousands of miles and many years distant from my dreary coast. She'd all but packed up for the day, but sat down again at her desk, unwound her scarf, and pulled off her gloves as I told her what I'd learned in my hours with Caro Drucker. She was quiet while I spoke, and quiet for a while afterwards.

"Well," she said eventually, "Dr. Stans was nothing if not industrious." I nodded. "And, like all good spies, she needed but little sleep.

You'll send along the documents?" I nodded. "They'll be useful, though likely they represent just the tip of the iceberg."

"Agreed," I said.

"Your friend from the garage would provide a shorter path, I think."

"Yes, direct to a buyer, or buyers."

"Or even more direct to thieves who fell out."

"I'm certain he had no idea that Allegra was dead."

"No, but this fellow might not have been her only coconspirator. And he may know of others. I'll make sure those keys and the camera get Dr. Wilding's attention."

"Thank you."

"And, for now, we'll keep news of this leak in the family, yes?" I nodded. "And your Ms. Drucker will observe that?"

"She will, though she's worried about her job."

"As well she should be—she and any number of other people out there."

CHAPTER TWENTY-SIX

Friday Morning

Karen Muir, long awaited, returned to the Ondstrand campus on Friday morning, and received me in her office before noon. She was in the south wing, on the topmost floor, at the farthest end of a long white corridor flanked by many well-sealed laboratories. Karen Muir's door was glass and unfortified, and the plaque beside it read: *Dr. Karen Muir, M.D., Ph.D., Executive Vice President and Managing Director—Special Projects.*

Beyond the door was the kind of waiting area that one might find in an investment bank or an architecture practice—sleek leather, steel, and glass furniture, a similarly sleek and chilly assistant, and, behind her desk, a glass wall, with Karen Muir's office on the other side.

I had been up late the night before, with Director Mehta, with Freja Berg, with Goss Ivessen, and I would've welcomed an offer of coffee, but such was not forthcoming. Muir's assistant made no greeting and looked at me without expression but reached out a graceful finger and touched a key on her phone console as if caressing a newborn's cheek. On the other side of the glass, on the far side of the room, Karen Muir looked away from one of the several monitors on her white standing-desk and beckoned to me. The assistant touched another button, and a door slid open in the glass wall. I went in.

Karen Muir was a tall, slender woman with white-blond hair, pale, smooth skin, and pale gray eyes set far apart in an oval face. It should have been a pretty face, even a beautiful one. Certainly its parts were lovely—a firm, compact chin; full, well-drawn lips; a straight, delicate nose; ears like white petals; those wide gray eyes beneath straight, silken brows—and all of it set in perfect oval equilibrium. But somehow the whole was less than the sum. Perhaps it was all the symmetry that threw things off, or the pallor, or that it seemed somehow a face unmarked by emotion, experience, or even the trials of age, fatigue, or weather. Whichever, there was an odd stillness to it, even when it moved, as if it were a simulacrum, an idea of a face, the product of algorithms and theory.

Her body, by contrast, was quite authentic, even in her yoga wear—snug-fitting, expensive shades of gray on gray on gray, with matching gray slippers, like the costume of a superhero whose powers had something to do with fog or shadows. There was strength in her long limbs—litheness and agility—and she seemed to know her physical capabilities and to be secure in them.

Karen Muir nodded at a pair of white leather chairs before her desk and tapped a toe on a discreet floor pedal. Her desk began to descend, and by the time I took my seat, she was seated, too, in a space-age module of white webbing and brushed aluminum. She made minute adjustments to several items on her desk—a pen, a mouse, a tablet of paper with the Ondstrand logo on it—and then looked at me. Her voice, when she spoke, was perfectly modulated and unexpectedly deep.

"I understand you've wanted to speak with me. I was, as you know, at a conference overseas, delivering a paper and participating in several panels—not to mention meeting with strategic partners and dining with clients and potential clients. It would've been entirely impossible for me to return here any earlier, or even to get away for what I'm sure would have been—quite understandably—a lengthy call. I did make my assistant, Ms. Mundt, available to your colleague—a Mr. Iverson, I believe—"

"Ivessen," I corrected.

She nodded. "I believe she was able to answer his questions concerning my itinerary and so forth satisfactorily."

I sat in silence for several moments, looking at her, and drummed my fingers slowly on the soft leather arm of my chair. I counted to thirty. "Is that Ms. Mundt, out there?" I asked.

"Yes."

"Ms. Mundt provided answers, it's true, though none were satisfactory—through no fault of hers, mind. What I'm looking for, Dr. Muir, what Standard Division is looking for, is first-person testimony. And in this case, that person is you. As for the impossibility of you having returned sooner, let us agree that we operate under different definitions of that word. If I'd believed that your presence here sooner was vital to my investigation, then, rest assured, you would have been here sooner. All by way of clarification."

Karen Muir's symmetrical lips pursed. "That was certainly clear."

I nodded. "Now, let's discuss Dr. Stans. I understand that, prior to seven months ago, she worked for you in Special Projects."

"She did, for nearly five years."

"And during that time, what projects did she work on?"

She tilted her head. "Do you have a technical background?"

"I do not."

"Not to be condescending—but I'm not sure how useful a list of her projects might be to you, then. Their names alone would be incomprehensible."

"Can you render them in layman's terms?"

She made a fist with her right hand and tapped it lightly on her desk. "Dr. Stans spent much of her career studying viral vectors—the viruses we sometimes use to deliver genetic packages into cells. Specifically, she studied adeno-associated viruses—AAVs—a class of viruses often used as vectors. Some of the projects she worked on involved techniques to increase the size of the genetic packages—measured in base pairs—that could be delivered by these vectors. Others involved the study of unintended immune responses to AAVs. As you might imagine, those can severely impact the effectiveness of genetic therapies that utilize these vectors. A related area she worked in involved the so-called off-target effects of genetic therapies mediated by AAVs."

"'Off-target effects' meaning . . . ?"

She cleared her throat. "Unintended genetic modifications."

I frowned. "Ouch," I said. "And Ms. Blom made it all sound so precise."

"Nadia Blom is hardly a scientist."

"I suppose not. In any event, it sounds as if the work Dr. Stans was doing was important. Important enough that she continued with at least some of it when she returned to Research and Development."

Muir nodded. "It was important—though, honestly, *all* of the work we do here is important. There are no dilettantes at Ondstrand."

"Was Dr. Stans good at her job?"

Karen Muir leaned back in her futuristic chair and sighed. "I suppose this is what you're mainly interested in, then." I raised an eyebrow but said nothing. "Why I transferred Dr. Stans back to R&D."

I nodded. "And why you demoted her along the way. I've asked these questions of several people here and have yet to get anything resembling an answer."

Muir clenched her fist again. "Have you asked Dr. Hasp?"

"I have."

"I'm curious about what his answer was."

"And I'm curious about yours, Doctor."

She nodded. "Well, let me say first that there's no question that Allegra Stans was a first-rate mind and a first-rate scientist. She was diligent, creative, focused, and tireless. I may not have approved of everything about her, and certainly not of what I've heard about her rather chaotic personal life, but she was a talent, and her loss is a loss to the whole community. That said, I found Dr. Stans to have certain . . . *judgment issues,* shall we say, that I believe would have seriously limited her contributions to this firm at levels much above that of an individual contributor."

"That's a fairly tortured construction, Doctor. Are you saying that you didn't believe Allegra could rise to management here? Wasn't she already managing scientific staff?"

"She was, yes. I was referring to a senior leadership position, on our management committee, which is what Allegra aspired to. But to join the committee is to be an *owner* of this company, not simply a shareholder. It means putting the interests of the firm—its clients, partners, employees, and other stakeholders—above one's own interests. It means commitment to something larger than one's own career, and that is something I believe was beyond Dr. Stans."

I was quiet for a moment, looking at Dr. Muir. Her slender frame was stiff with anger or something like it. "Was there some incident or incidents that led you to this conclusion?" I asked eventually.

"There was a pattern of entitlement that expressed itself in increasingly obvious ways over the five years of her work for me." I raised an eyebrow again. Karen Muir sighed. "Allegra Stans made it increasingly clear—explicit, one might say—that she thought she should have my job. That she was entitled to it, in fact."

"Why—"

"Why would she think that? Well, not to speak ill of the dead, but there was her innate arrogance—her belief that her desire for something meant that she should have it. For reasons beyond that, you should speak with Dr. Hasp."

"Why would your brother be able to tell me more about someone who worked for you than you would yourself?"

Her eyes narrowed. "Dr. Hasp is my stepbrother, as I expect you know, and I don't believe it's my place to report on conversations that I was not a party to."

"As I said, I'm interested in first-person accounts, Doctor. What is *your* understanding of the basis for Dr. Stans's expectations—beyond simply her 'innate arrogance'?"

Her eyes narrowed and her head tilted slightly. "I was given to understand, by Dr. Stans, that Dr. Hasp had led her to believe she would succeed me in Special Projects. Why Dr. Hasp would've said that—if in fact he did—is something you'd have to discuss with him. He and I have certainly never spoken of anything of the kind."

"But that was Dr. Stans's understanding, and she shared it with you?"

"In increasingly confrontational and disruptive ways. As talented as she was, I simply couldn't keep her around. Not around here, at any rate."

"And so Dr. Hasp moved her."

"He did. He had in mind a position for her in setting up our own production facilities overseas, but I don't see her ever having taken that. From my standpoint, he was going to have to manage her out. That said, it was his concern—his and Dr. Pohl's—not mine. I was very clear about that with him and with Dr. Stans."

Karen Muir glanced at something on one of her screens, then looked back to me. "Now, if that's all, I have—"

"That is not all, Doctor. What sort of terms were you on with Dr. Stans, following her transfer?"

She squinted. "*Terms?* As in, *Were we on friendly terms?* Of course we weren't. There was tension between us. We didn't meet over coffee for a chin wag. That said, Dr. Stans knew how to behave professionally when we did meet, as did I. We were able to interact as colleagues when called to do so."

"And were you called upon often?"

"Not often. But there are intersections between Projects and R&D,

and she took some of her projects with her when she transferred. We would discuss those occasionally."

I nodded. "When was the last time?"

"That we met? Let me check." She turned to one of her monitors and clicked several times on her mouse. "That would have been three weeks ago—three weeks exactly. She came by at seven-thirty."

"In the morning?"

"In the evening."

"Rather late."

"Not here. Our staff—especially those who live on campus—spend a lot of time in the lab."

"And your meeting with Dr. Stans?"

"Was unremarkable. We discussed several of her projects. She had sent me updates on them; I had sent her questions. At the meeting, she addressed them all. Unremarkable."

"There were no arguments, no hostility?"

"As I said, we both knew how to behave professionally."

I nodded. "Turning, then, to your itinerary over the past several days. Ms. Mundt told my colleague that you left campus for the city on Thursday of last week, at approximately two-forty-five p.m. And security logs confirm that."

She nodded. "Yes, and . . . ?"

"She also informed him that you were scheduled to fly overseas from there early on Saturday morning. As it happened, you didn't actually depart until Saturday in the late afternoon."

"Yes, and . . . ?"

"And why?"

Muir sighed. "Why did I take a later flight? Truth be told, I had been out too late the night before with . . . an old friend. I was feeling a bit worse for wear in the morning, and I rescheduled my flight. There's no reason Ms. Mundt would've known; I made the arrangements myself."

I nodded. "And your friend's name?"

She frowned. "Really?"

"Really, Doctor."

"Hanro. Dr. Jacob Hanro. H-A-N-R-O. He lives in the city, at—"

"We'll find him," I said, and stood. Karen Muir looked relieved for a moment, then less so when I didn't bid her farewell. "I'm curious, Dr. Muir, how Ondstrand Biologic came to be here, in this place."

Her very straight brows came together. "Our headquarters? I don't see how that possibly—"

"Considering the history of the place, and how I imagine it might figure in Dr. Hasp's personal history, not to mention how remote the location is, and the costs of acquiring the property and outfitting it for the company's needs, it seems a less-than-obvious choice for your headquarters."

She leaned back, as if I'd just suffered a bout of noisy flatulence, then tapped her fist against her desk again and shook her head. When she spoke, her voice was low and steady. " 'How I imagine it might figure in Dr. Hasp's personal history' . . . How can you have the slightest idea of how it *figures* for anyone? You know nothing about him, or what he experienced here—how can you possibly imagine what this place represents?"

"Why don't you tell me?"

"No, I don't think I will; I will leave that to Dr. Hasp. But neither will I give you grounds to call me uncooperative. So—I will tell you that, from the time the company was founded, its leadership always envisioned a campus setting for it, a cloistered environment, academic in its atmosphere, admission to which would be highly selective and competitive. And that is what we've created. And though the capital expenditure has indeed been substantial, the returns on that investment have been no less great, despite lending themselves less readily to quantification."

I nodded slowly. "The founding leadership that envisioned this ivory tower—that would be you and your brother?"

Her mouth tightened again. "Dr. Hasp and myself, yes."

"And Dr. Witmer?"

Her expression turned sour. "If you already know the answers, why ask the questions?"

I smiled. "Scientists all, businesspeople all, and yet you all seem to have been taken with a romantic vision—a fantasia, one might say."

"You subscribe to a popular notion of scientists as automatons of some sort. Science is a creative endeavor, first and foremost. No one ever discovered anything without an act of imagination first."

I nodded. "That's true in my line of work, too, Doctor. I'm just surprised that, as a business leader, you would be comfortable justifying large outlays of capital for benefits that are intangible. But I suppose it's an owner's privilege to indulge in sentimentality."

Karen Muir opened her mouth as if about to speak, but then thought the better of it. She tapped her fist on her desk again and said: "If this has anything to do with any sort of investigation, I can't imagine how. Now, if that's all, I have a lot to attend to here."

I nodded but made no move towards the door. Instead, I drew a sheet of paper from my jacket pocket. I unfolded it and looked at Muir and began to read aloud. She was silent as I read the first five items on my list—the names of documents that had been accessed as a result of the spear-phishing attack—but her hands became fists, and the fists were paper-white. As I read the sixth, she spoke.

"What is the point of this? To demonstrate that you have access to some of my department's documents? Perhaps you have access to them all. Are we simply to trust that you—that Standard Division—will take the same care with our intellectual property as we do?"

I smiled. "Not the same care at all, Doctor, I assure you."

Color rose in Karen Muir's face then—two faint pink patches across pale cheeks—but she said nothing. I turned and left.

CHAPTER TWENTY-SEVEN

Friday Afternoon

take it you found Dr. Muir's office," Nadia Blom said as I emerged from an elevator in the lobby.

"Yes, and all by myself."

"I trust she was helpful."

"Listening to people is always helpful, regardless of their intent," I said, heading towards the main entrance. Blom followed.

"Are you suggesting she intended to be unhelpful?"

I shrugged. "She did point out that you were not a scientist."

Her brows came together. "That's hardly a secret."

"I suppose not," I said, and took out my phone. "Now, if you'll excuse me . . ." I left the building and walked out from under the portico. The sky was leaden and threatening, and the still air smelled of low tide. I called Goss Ivessen.

"If you're expecting feedback on those papers you sent, it's a bit soon even for me."

"No," I said, "I have someone to locate. The name is Dr. Jacob Hanro, and he lives in the city. Apparently, he can corroborate Muir's explanation of why she wasn't on her scheduled flight on the morning of the murder."

I spelled Hanro's name, and Ivessen recorded it in a burst of keystrokes. "How was Dr. Muir otherwise?" he asked.

"Minimally cooperative. She answered questions, many grudgingly. The question I most wanted answered was the one she answered least satisfactorily."

"About why Dr. Stans was demoted?"

"Yes. According to Muir, it was because Allegra had the temerity to covet Muir's job—a temerity perhaps encouraged, or at least not actively discouraged, by Hasp."

"Karen Muir has a major equity stake in that company. Why should she feel threatened by the ambitions of a mid-level employee? Of any employee, for that matter?"

"That's what I've been asking myself. Any more on that skiff?"

"Not yet."

"And those car keys, and the camera I found in Allegra's car? Do you know if Dr. Wilding was able to pull prints or DNA from them?"

"I've heard nothing from her yet, but you might have better luck in speeding her along," Ivessen said, and rang off.

I crossed the forecourt to the edge of the fountain and looked at the blurred statuary. Up close, they were even harder to identify, and decidedly more sinister. I called Jane Wilding.

"I was about to message you," she said when I asked about the keys and the second camera. "I'm afraid it's no joy. No prints came off the keys, and no useful DNA but yours, and we already have plenty of that. The camera too was of no help—no photos beyond what you saw in its memory. Sorry."

I pocketed my phone and sat on the fountain's coping. The stone was cold. I sighed. Waiting was not my strong suit, but that's what I found myself doing: waiting for information about the skiff, about Karen Muir's friend Hanro, about the documents that had been stolen from Ondstrand, presumably by Allegra Stans, about the still-unidentified man in the garage. And I continued to wait for a reason—one that I believed—why Allegra had been demoted and transferred.

I could have chased down Hasp, listened to what he had to say about the derailment of Allegra's career, seen if he would corroborate his stepsister's story, seen how he might explain his failure to mention Witmer's affair with Allegra to me. But not yet—I wanted more information in hand before I sat down with him again.

I thought once more about Allegra and her maximalist approach to solving her problem with Piers Witmer—her deft use of Witmer's equity stake, and perhaps of Mrs. Witmer, too. I heard the Director's voice then, as if she were beside me at the fountain: "Nevertheless, we should remain alert to the possibility that the equity stake that motivated Dr. Witmer once, years ago, may have motivated him more recently as well."

"I remain alert," I said to the misshapen statuary. And then I thought about the impulsivity that seemed to inform the intimate aspects of Allegra's life, and the impressive self-discipline that characterized so many other aspects—the professional, the athletic, even, apparently, her efforts as corporate spy.

I thought about what Freja Berg had said of Allegra's phone use: "It's as if she was expecting someone to be monitoring her usage, and so restricted herself to only the most benign activities." And I thought of the strange gaps—every three weeks—in the phone's location data, when she apparently left it behind at Ondstrand House and went off—where? To Soligstrand, according to Penny and Celia at the Sunnyside Salon and Spa—she was in there every week. And every week, presumably, the postman found her car in the garage and cleared the letterbox. So what was happening every three weeks, when she left her phone behind? Why did she take pains to obscure her location then? I ran my hands through my hair, damp now from the fountain's spray, and stood and laughed aloud. Then I pulled out my phone.

"Freja," I said when she answered. "I want to have a look at mobile-tower data for the towers that service Ondstrand."

She snorted. "Meaning, you want me to have a look at tower data."

"Well . . . yes."

"As if we don't have enough to do for you, what with the small bio-tech library you just dumped here. And what would I be looking for in this tower data? And for what date and time?"

"Multiple days—I'm looking for a pattern. I'm interested in the every-third-Wednesday gaps in Allegra Stans's mobile-location data. We know her routines on those missing Wednesdays—the times of her comings and goings from the Ondstrand campus, at any rate. I'm interested in whether any mobile phones come up on the network at around the times of Allegra's departure from the campus on those days, and if any of those same phones go offline at around the times of her return. And if you can tease out information on whether Allegra's own phone was co-located with any of these other phones, that would be interesting, too."

Freja laughed. "Shit, yes, it would be interesting! You want to know if Allegra kept a burner phone that she used when she didn't want her own phone tracked, yeah?"

"If she did and we can identify it, maybe we can find out who she called on it."

"You're kind of a clever bastard, Myles."

"High praise."

"Don't let it go to your head. I'll get back to you." Freja was off before I could say thanks.

I got more coffee after that and carried it to my rooms, where I paced and read over my interview notes. When my tablet burred, it wasn't Freja Berg, but Goss Ivessen.

"I have something for you," he said from the shadows.

"About the documents?"

"About the skiff," he answered, and then his bookshelves were replaced by two satellite photos. "I got these from Signals, who had them from Coastal and Fisheries. The time stamps place them solidly in our window. All concerned, including our own analysts, believe the photos are of the same craft."

Two photos, taken from far above: two small white open boats, both powered by outboard engines, leaving small, unremarkable wakes. In both photos, a figure was visible in the stern, beside the tiller; in both photos, the figure was a dark blob.

"Both photos were taken last Saturday morning. The first, with the craft headed north, was taken at five-forty-seven a.m. It was 2.86 miles north of Fiskdorp Marina at that point. The second, with the craft headed south, was taken at seven-forty-seven, at which time it was 1.09 miles south of the Ondstrand beach."

"Same boat?"

"So everyone thinks, and of a size and shape consistent with your skiff."

"No registration markings visible?"

"No."

I was quiet for a while, looking at the images. "So . . . Fiskdorp," I said. "Are there harbor cameras?"

"Almost certainly, but that will take longer. That blue-and-gold band beneath the gunwales is distinctive enough, though. It shouldn't take you long."

So . . . Fiskdorp.

CHAPTER TWENTY-EIGHT

Friday Afternoon

It was south along the coast, about six miles or so, a rugged stretch of road with crags, stunted pines, grasses barely holding on in stony earth—less postcard-scenic than the run into Soligstrand, but somehow more bracing. A glass of ice water to the face, or a sermon about an unforgiving deity. It was all cliff, cliff, cliff under gray, scudding clouds, until the road dropped sharply and the village was at the bottom of a long, steep hill.

There was a marina at one end, compact, with a hodgepodge of small, sea-beaten pleasure craft whose pleasures were mostly behind them. At the other end, at the tip of a rocky finger thrust into the sea, was an old-fashioned lighthouse, white with a red-topped lantern room. The waterfront in between was for working—long, scruffy piers, and, moored there, a fishing fleet. They were small and medium-sized craft, hard-used but hardy-looking. There were trawlers, some long-liners, a few seiners, and an assortment of colorful crab boats too numerous to count. There were warehouses nearby, and around them, like barnacles, a sprouting of maritime business—boat brokers, machine shops, tackle suppliers, a couple of cafés, and more than a few bars. It being later in the afternoon, the fleet was mostly in and buttoned up, and the bars were packed. I had the windows and the canvas top up on Allegra Stans's car as I drove into town, but the scents of salt and seaweed were nonetheless strident.

The town of Fiskdorp proper unraveled in weary arcs away from the waterfront, blocks of low stone and clapboard buildings, stained and weathered, the older ones leaning together like refugees, the newer ones more upright but decidedly uglier. They faced cracked sidewalks and pitted roadways, and the gritty monotony was relieved only occasionally by a church spire or a patch of green that may have been a park or a cemetery.

I made for the harbormaster's office at the far end of the waterfront, near the lighthouse. As I approached, I passed through a few blocks of unexpected gentrification: streets stripped down to their original cobbles, scrubbed stone storefronts, new glass in the windows, and shiny paint and gleaming brass on the doors. There was a cheese shop, a coffee roaster, a bistro with six tables, a wine bar, and an art gallery. I wondered what the locals made of it all. I found a cobbled parking spot for Allegra's car and walked to the harbormaster's office. The smells of brine, old fish, and diesel were powerful.

The office was in a square clapboard building, one-story, white-washed, with windows all around, and it commanded views of the waterfront, the lighthouse, and a small parking lot. It was a stone's throw across a stretch of macadam to a short pier where no boat was tied, but where a sign with a gull-and-lighthouse insignia declared it the harbor-master's mooring. But there was no harbormaster to be found. I tried the office door and peered through the many windows. I saw a snug-looking room with a big desk, an ancient radio, and bookshelves stacked with maritime reference volumes, but no signs of life. I knocked to no avail. I sighed and started walking towards the fishing fleet.

The number and variety of craft there were daunting, but I was about to try my luck on the first of the piers when I heard the thrum of an engine. I turned to see an orange rigid inflatable boat approaching the harbormaster's pier. It had a large black outboard and a center console, and bore the same gull-and-lighthouse insignia that was on the moor-ing sign. I walked back and watched the harbormaster tie up. Which he did quite deftly for an old man with a grizzled beard, a jutting belly, a drinker's nose, and one arm amputated below the elbow. He slung a duffel across his chest as he headed for the little office.

His walk was precise; his dress was otherwise. He wore much-mended deck shoes, stained khakis, a sweatshirt torn at the neck, a yel-low windbreaker stiff with salt, and a long-billed cap the color of spit that barely contained his tangled white hair. He stopped walking when he saw me and looked me up and down, his bloodshot blue eyes linger-ing on my suit and tie.

"You need something?" he asked. He sounded like he'd just smoked a pack.

"Help in finding a boat."

"Plenty around. A fishing charter?" I shook my head, and he squinted at me some more. "You police?" he asked.

"Not exactly."

"I'm gonna need something more than that. An ID would save trouble."

I slipped my ID case from my inside pocket and sailed it to him. He hitched his duffel up and caught the case in one smooth movement, furrowed his brow, and opened it. Then he looked at me some more and sighed.

"You might as well come in," he said, and sailed the case back to me.

His name was Anders, and he'd been harbormaster for over a decade. He was once a soldier—a para, he told me—and he'd served overseas, several wars back. He'd left his arm back there. He'd grown up in Fiskdorp. His family was here; he knew the local waters and the local fishing. He knew a little something about Standard Division, too.

"Back in my war, you lot were doing things behind the lines—very far behind. The talk was sabotage and assassinations. Didn't bother me—the whole business was sabotage and assassinations, weren't it, but in volume and without the niceties. A few times, my unit escorted you lot in—some of the ways, anyway. Always at night, usually in rain or snow, and always the same routine—we'd slog along through the dark, and at some point one of mine would notice that your lot had disappeared. Just like that—not a sound, not a word, no goodbye. No one ever saw them depart; they were just gone. Then we'd turn round and slog back to base. Very weird."

I nodded. "Before my time."

Anders laughed. "But still just as talkative," he said. He poured two mugs of coffee and handed one to me. I poured in some milk. The room was warm and smelled of paper, tobacco, wax, and whiskey. He took a seat behind his surprisingly tidy desk.

"This is the boat," I said, and offered him my phone.

He took it and studied the picture of the skiff. "This your only photo?"

"Swipe right."

He did and nodded. "Belongs to Neumann— Jens Neumann. He runs a seiner out of here, the *Bonny Nora*, tied up on Pier Three. That's his dinghy."

I took back the phone. "You see him today?"

He nodded. "Most days. He's a working fisherman, and most days are workdays."

"Would he be around now?"

"Doubtful."

"Can you give me a description?"

He squinted. "Lean like you, but taller—maybe an inch or two. Gray eyes, pale skin, ruddy cheeks, short hair—what's left of it, and with a bit of black still in it. Got a limp from some kind of back problem, but he gets around his boat pretty good, considering."

"Considering what?"

"Considering the bastard's even older'n me. Three years ahead of me in school, Jens was."

I squinted at him and thought about the lovers' anteroom in the beach cave. Anders saw my confusion. "Not what you expected?"

I shook my head. "Anyone else use his boat. Anyone younger?"

"Might be his boy—though not so much a boy these days. Jens-Edvard. He just graduated the secondary in town. Tall and lean like his pa, bigger through the shoulders, dark eyes, scruffy beard, shaggy black hair, wears it in a ponytail sometimes. He helps out on the boat, does other jobs around town."

"Around town where?"

"That scrubbed-up neighborhood around the corner. The developers want to call it Beacon Square; maybe you passed it on the way. Jens-Edvard waits tables at a restaurant there, works in the coffee place, too, sometimes."

"Industrious."

Anders shrugged. "Like most of the young ones, he wants out of Fiskdorp. Expect he's saving his pennies."

I drank my coffee, put my mug on the desk, and stood. "Thank you for your help," I said.

"He in some trouble, Jens-Edvard?"

"Not that I know of. I just have a few questions."

Anders squinted. "I know how that can go with you lot."

"It doesn't always."

"Hope it don't with him. He's a good kid—just a head-in-the-clouds sort."

I nodded and closed the door behind me.

The shadows were lengthening as I stepped outside, and the waterfront felt cooler after the coffee and the warmth of the office. I turned up the collar on my suit jacket as I walked down to Pier Three and out along it. I passed a long line of craft, mostly dark, mostly quiet but for the creaking. The *Bonny Nora* was halfway down the pier, a small seiner, painted in the same way the skiff was—white with black gunwales, and with a blue-and-yellow braid beneath. And there was the skiff itself, tethered alongside the mother ship. Both were as quiet and empty as every other boat on the pier.

I made my way back to the harbormaster's office and saw Anders inside. Then I pressed on to Beacon Square, and to Beacon Bistro and Beacon Espresso.

I remembered the names from the odds and ends I'd found in Allegra's apartment, and now they took on new significance. I crossed the cobbled square and followed the fresh stone sidewalks to Beacon Bistro. It had an appealing menu and what seemed a charming ambience, but it had not yet opened for dinner. Beacon Espresso, just two doors down, was open, but the sole employee was engaged in an excruciating phone conversation with a customer-support rep about a malfunctioning coffee-bean grinder. The exchange appeared to have been going on for some time, but even two minutes' exposure was more than I could bear. I stepped outside and considered waiting it out in the cheese shop, or simply tearing the phone from the wall. As it happened, I did neither.

Across the street from the coffee place was a gallery—The Mariner's Chest Fine Arts—and something in the window caught my eye. At first, I wasn't sure what it was, and I gazed at the collection of . . . Well, "fine art" was probably a generous term, or at least aspirational.

With a few exceptions, it was neither fine nor art, though it wasn't quite garden gnomes, either. And the maritime theme was relentless: overlarge seascapes featuring the Fiskdorp lighthouse amidst a visual pablum of seagulls, waves, buoys, and sails; garishly enameled seashells that I was certain came from nowhere on this coast, but looked as if they might've been parts of a mermaid's brassiere, if the mermaid was also a stripper; elaborate sculpture made of lobster traps, fishing net, seagull feathers, and beach tar. But none of that had brought me across the street. What had drawn me, I realized, was a fish—a nearly life-sized carving of a cod done in driftwood, with silver at the edges of its gills and its dorsal and ventral fins, and green stones for eyes. The artist had used the grain and coloration of the driftwood to suggest the cod's scales, the color gradient across its flanks, the muscle beneath, and the fish's motion through water.

When I walked through the gallery's door, the woman in back looked at me as if I were the first person ever to have done so. I was out the door again before she'd crossed the room, but not before I'd had a closer look at the fish, and at the three tiny letters carved neatly on its belly: *JEN*. Jens-Edvard Neumann.

CHAPTER TWENTY-NINE

Friday Evening

I wondered where I might find the young artist, though I wasn't worried about it—finding people was something we were good at in Standard Division. I needn't have spent even that much effort. When I returned to Allegra's car, he was there, and he wasn't alone.

I recognized Jens-Edvard from Anders's description: tall, lean, broad-shouldered, dark, dark-eyed, and shaggy. He was handsome but looked barely eighteen. He wore black jeans, frayed at the knees, work boots, a black tee shirt with washed-out skulls and flames on it, and a faded green field jacket tattered at the elbows. His skin was pale, though pink patches burned at his cheeks, and his gaze, fixed on me, burned with intelligence and rage and something else—an agitated worry.

His friends were a few years older than he, dressed more or less like him, and were more or less his size, but that's where the similarity ended. Two were fair with bad skin; one was a ginger with a poorly healed broken nose. The overly broad, thin-lipped faces of all three were stamped with that ever-winning combination of stupidity, meanness, and bad dentistry. I sighed as I approached the car.

Jens-Edvard's dark eyes narrowed. "What're you doin' with this car?" he said. His voice was young, at odds with his imposing physical presence and with the unselfconscious ease of his carriage.

"Lately, I've been driving it."

"Why's that? It's not yours."

The ginger one snickered. "Yeah, you boost that car, or what?" The other two morons giggled. Jens-Edvard glanced at them, and they fell silent.

"Where's the owner?" he said, as if all depended on the answer. "She say it okay for you to drive around?"

"We should talk, Jens."

His look turned angry again. "How you know me? Why you asking up and down the waterfront about me?"

Fucking Anders. "We should talk," I said again.

The ginger one stepped towards me, the other morons close behind. Their fists were balled. "Why he should talk to you? What you want with him? You think he's on the stroll? That what you want?" The three of them laughed and stepped closer.

I sighed and looked at Jens-Edvard. I spoke softly. "Do you care if these idiots get hurt?"

The two fair-haired ones were not so dumb that they couldn't hear something in my voice, even if they didn't know quite what it was. The ginger one wasn't that bright. He colored and sputtered and slipped his right hand into his coat pocket. He looked at Jens-Edvard. "The fuck's he sayin', man?"

"He's sayin' he gonna mess with you, Billy," the smaller of the fair-haired ones said.

Billy took another step forward. He glanced at Jens-Edvard and then back at me. "That what you're sayin', old man?" He was friendly now, easy, laughing, smiling. "Why you need to say—" And then he lunged—if you could call something that slow a lunge—leading with the box cutter in his right fist, following with a left the size of a holiday ham. It couldn't have been more predictable if he'd sent a memo. I leaned aside to let the blade pass, pulled his arm forward, and pulled Billy into a stumble, then put my palm on the back of his head and drove his face into my rising knee.

The wet crunch was nauseating, and the silence afterwards complete. The two other morons went white and stared at Billy, motionless and boneless on the cobblestones. Jens-Edvard stared at me.

"You kilt him," one of the morons said.

"Not yet," I said. I dug in my pocket and fished out Allegra's car keys. "You drive?" I asked Jens-Edvard. He nodded. I tossed him the keys. "Then drive."

He drove us south, out of town, past the lighthouse, up a hill steeper than the one I'd descended into Fiskdorp, and along a road even bleaker than the one from Ondstrand House. It carried us out of sight of the town and the sea, to a more barren, lunar place.

Jens-Edvard knew the road and knew the car, and he breathed in its smell in gulps. Being in the car, driving, facing the oncoming rush of the darkening roads seemed to take the edge off his restless fear. We were maybe five miles out of town when the road rose up again and a patch of ocean reappeared—distant now, a bolt of shifting silver fabric under the rising moon. Jens-Edvard pulled off the road onto a flat gravel turnaround. It had a couple of benches, a lamppost, a metal trash bin, and a view of the rock-strewn landscape and the faraway water. The silence was heavy when he killed the engine, every tick of cooling metal adding to its weight.

His voice was quiet, as if air could barely pass his lips. "She's dead, in't she? Allie—she's dead." He stared straight ahead, his eyes locked on the trash bin.

"Yes," I said.

Jens-Edvard rested his forehead on his hands, which gripped the steering wheel at twelve o'clock. His broad back shook, but he made only small, choked sounds. After a few minutes, he opened the car door, staggered out, and fell to his knees beside one of the benches. I left him to his tears for a while, and when he had managed a sitting position on the bench, I joined him. The night air was cold, and the smell of the sea was faint behind the scent of wet earth and stone, and garbage in the bin.

Jens-Edvard was staring at his shoes. "When did she ... When?"

"Last Saturday, in the morning."

He turned and his face was paper white. "Saturday? But I saw her on Saturday, in the morning. Early."

"I know."

"Was it an accident?" he asked. "Something while she was running? Something in her lab?"

"No."

"No, it wasn't an accident?"

"It wasn't."

"So she was ... Somebody did it? Somebody killed her?"

"Yes."

"At the school?"

"Yes."

He looked at me again, whiter somehow. "You don't think that I ... ?"

"I don't," I said.

"Then who? Do you know who?"

I shook my head, and Jens-Edvard dug in the pockets of his field jacket. Eventually, he produced a crushed pack of cigarettes and a box of matches. He lit one, breathed in deeply, and let out a long plume of smoke into the sky. After a while, he offered me one. I shook my head.

"Anders said you're not police. He said you're something worse."

"I'm not police."

He smoked in silence after that, one cigarette and then another. He was about to light his third when I caught his arm and took the match from his hand. He didn't resist, but looked at me, puzzled, impossibly young. His eyes were red and wet and bottomless.

"What you want from me?" he asked.

"Help," I said. Jens-Edvard stared at me for a while and then nodded.

He told me first of how they met. It was six months earlier, and she'd come into the bistro where he waited tables. She'd spent the raw, gray weekday walking around Fiskdorp. Jens-Edvard had seen her pass by the window more than once.

"Hard to miss her, really. She's like a lit match anyplace she goes, but especially in this town. I see her crossing Beacon Square, looking in the shops. Truth was, I couldn't take my eyes off her. Her face was red from the cold, her nose was running, her hair was damp, but she didn't care. And why should she, the way she looked. I couldn't believe it when she took a seat. I was shakin' so, I nearly dropped the water in her lap."

The attraction had been instantaneous and mutual, and she'd made no attempt to hide her side of things. "She said I was beautiful. Can you believe it—that she talked that way? But she said what she meant, and no apologies—that's her way. She laughed after she said it, though, 'cause I guess I turned so red—like a hot coal, she said. It was funny to her."

She'd lingered over a glass of wine until he got off; then they'd walked. She'd asked how old he was. He'd lied. "I said nineteen, though I was still two months shy of eighteen then. Later, when I owned up, she laughed. Said she'd been pretty sure I was lyin'."

Which apparently hadn't stopped her. Their first time was that same night, in her car. Jens-Edvard blushed when he told it, and Allegra had been right—his cheeks were like coals.

He didn't see her for some time after that and was uncertain whether he'd ever see her again. Which made him pine all the more keenly.

She'd told him she lived at Ondstrand House—"the school," as he called it—and he'd thought about going there to catch a glimpse. He'd run his little skiff up onto the beach there plenty of times before, as many of the locals had, and some of those times he'd hiked up onto the grounds. But he'd sensed that Allegra wouldn't welcome it, and already he craved her good opinion. So he pined, and while he did, he carved the little deer from driftwood.

"Three weeks later, to the day, she shows up at the restaurant window, five minutes before closing. I thought my heart was gonna jump outta my chest—like maybe I was gonna die. I had that deer with me— I'd been carrying it around since I finished it—and, soon as we got alone, I gave it to her.

"At first she looked at it like it scared her. Then she asked where I'd got it and said I shouldn't be spending my money on that kinda thing. I told her I made it—that I'd been making things like that for years. I had to show her pictures of some of my things on my phone before she believed it. When I did, she was quiet for a long time. Then she said they were beautiful—that I was more beautiful than she'd thought."

They saw each other often after that—usually every weekend. But that night, their second together, Allegra set the ground rules of their relationship. They were few and simple. They would get together when she said so; she would call him to tell him where and when; if he needed to contact her, he would do so only with the mobile phone she gave him and using only her mobile-phone number. There would be no e-mails and certainly no visits.

"The only other thing was the club."

"The club?" I asked.

He managed a tiny smile. "She said we were going to be a club, her and me, and we'd be the only two members. That didn't mean we were sworn to each other or anything—she wanted that clear—I could go with whoever I wanted to, and the same for her. But what went on between us—the fact that there was an *us*—was private. Nobody else need to know—that was the rule. She wouldn't talk to anyone about me, and I wasn't to talk to anyone about her, and if I couldn't abide by that, I should say so up front. As if I would talk. As if there was anyone in this place I'd talk to about her."

"Not even those friends of yours I met earlier?"

He laughed. "The *idiots,* you called 'em, and that's what they are. They don't know anything except fightin'. You could get them to fight mud for a couple of ciggies each."

I smiled. "I imagine you two didn't stroll around Fiskdorp much, or Soligstrand."

He shook his head. "Or anywhere after that. We kept to ourselves. Which was fine with me. Sometimes we'd go to a place down the road, in Vinkadorp. There was a little inn there. A few times, on the weekends, we spent the night. Other times, if the weather was right, I'd take the skiff and pick her up at a swimming pier not far from the lighthouse and we'd motor along the coast. Sometimes we'd just be in the car."

His throat closed around the memory, and his body shook for a moment with silent sobs. He took a deep breath and wiped his forearm across his nose.

"And you went to the cave sometimes," I said. "On the beach."

Jens-Edvard smiled sheepishly and nodded. "That was her idea. When I told her about partying at the beach, in the cave, she wanted to see it."

"Despite all the talk about being private—that no one else needed to know? Seems a bit of a risk."

He smiled some more and nodded again. "I said that to her. But Allegra, she wanted what she wanted, and I think she liked the risk of it. I . . . I think that made it better for her." Again his cheeks burned. He wiped his eyes again and perched the unlit cigarette on his lower lip.

"Okay if I smoke this now?" he asked.

I struck the match for him and let him puff away for a while, silent but for the sniffling. Then I asked him another question. "Besides the obvious, what did you two do when you got together?"

It took him a moment to understand what I meant by "the obvious," and when he did, he blushed again. "We . . . we did the usual things that people do. We walked sometimes, we ate, we drove around sometimes, and all the time we talked."

"About what?"

Often it was about his art and his future. It was Allegra who encouraged him to sell his work through the gallery in Fiskdorp, to limit the number of pieces he sold there to only two at a time, and to insist that the prices charged for them be set steadily upwards. She also encouraged him to demand a higher percentage of the revenue for each lot he sold there.

"They fetch the top prices at that place, and they sell out right away. I never met anyone smarter than her," Jens-Edvard said, sniffling. "But you must know that."

He'd mentioned art school to her, little more than a daydream to him, as it seemed a million miles from Fiskdorp and his life there, but Allegra wouldn't hear of it.

"It was the first time—the only time really—that she got angry with me. I'd told her about this program overseas, an art school down south, in Playa Arcadia, how I'd looked into it, the artists who taught there, the artists who'd gone through there, how great it seemed. But then I said that, between the cost and the hassle of putting together a portfolio and getting recommendations, I just didn't think it was possible. She practically tore my ears off.

"She said that was *defeatist bullshit*—that if I was unhappy with the here and now, I shouldn't fantasize about something else, I should get off my ass and change the here and now. She said, if I really believed the defeatist crap, I should right now stop wasting time making things, and instead talk to my pa about taking over the *Bonny Nora*. And while I was about it, I should stop wasting time with her, but find myself some local cow who'd make me a good fishwife. Then she said, if I *didn't* really believe all that—if it was just smoke I blew up my own ass because I was too afraid to see how my work stood up—then I should get out of my own way, and start working the problem."

"What did she mean by that?"

"She said I needed to break the problem down into its parts, find what she called the critical path—the things I had to do to get where I wanted to go, and the order that they had to be done in. Then I had to start doing those things, one by one, until they were done. No excuses, no bullshit, no smoke."

"Hard truths."

He smiled. "Like I said, I never knew anyone smarter."

"Did you take her advice?"

"She didn't give me much choice," he said. "I hate fishing, I hate that fuckin' boat, and I don't much care for the local girls." He chuckled ruefully and his voice grew quieter. "Besides, I . . . I didn't want to lose her."

"How did it go—working the problem?"

"Okay. She helped me with the portfolio stuff, and with the application. And she helped me figure out what I could do about recommendations. I made the mistake of mentioning that, even if I did get into the school, I'd never be able to pay. After she bit a chunk out of my ass, she told me that admission and financing were two different problems."

I nodded. "Was that mostly what you talked about—art school?"

"Mostly."

"Did she ever talk about herself? Her work, her plans?"

Jens-Edvard became quite still for a moment, then stood, stretched, and took several paces from the bench. It was full dark now, but far away the sea gave up a glow. His silhouette, against it, was black and angular.

It was one of those caesuras that arise sometimes in an interview, when the subtle back pressure of conscious resistance first appears, and with it the interviewer's certainty that *something* is there, just on the other side. An injury guarded, a weakness protected, a shame hidden. Something secret. One had to walk softly towards it, as if towards a deer in a clearing.

"Did she talk at all about Ondstrand?" I said quietly. "Was she happy there?"

Jens-Edvard stiffened, and for a moment I thought I'd lost him. But no. "I . . . I don't think so. Not always." He was facing the sea, and spoke softly, and I strained to hear him.

"No?"

"Sometimes she was angry, I think, or worried. Both."

"What did she say?"

He turned around then, and in the light from the lamppost I could see he was blushing again. "She didn't say. It was the way she was—the way she acted when we were together. She was more . . . intense—almost in a frenzy sometimes. Like she wanted to blot out something. It reminded me of my pa when he used to drink—the way he'd pound down whiskey when he'd first get home." He shrugged and wiped his nose. "Allegra liked to be in charge of things, and when she wasn't, I think it made her a little . . . crazy maybe. I think there was something going on at the school that made her feel that way."

I nodded. "Did she say what?"

"She never talked about her work."

"Did she ever talk about people—people she worked with, perhaps?"

"Never. But whatever bothered her, she must've worked it out. She hasn't been that way for a while."

"How long a while?"

"Weeks. Three, four weeks at least."

I nodded. Jens-Edvard sighed deeply and slumped down on the bench. He sank into himself, and once more I felt the faint pushback.

"So—she'd been happier the past few weeks," I said. "Not worried, not scared. That's nice." He nodded slowly. "What did she talk about when she was happy?"

He leaned forward and rested his elbows on his knees, and his face in his hands. His voice was suddenly gruff, and the pushback was more frank. "I told you already, we talked about that art school. We talked about that, we fucked—I don't know what else to say."

"Besides art school—what else did she talk about?"

Beside me, a grunt and a petulant shrug.

I stood and sighed. "Really?" I said. He stayed still and silent. "Okay," I said, walking towards the car. "I'll run you back to town."

Jens-Edvard looked at me. "What?"

"I said I'll run you back to town. As we seem to have reached an impasse. For reasons known only to you, you seem to have given up on helping me find whoever it was who killed your friend. Which is a pity, as, until now, you were being quite helpful. I suppose I could try threatening you or perhaps beating you, but neither approach seems promising. Though, please, correct me if I'm wrong. Might a beating help?"

He pinched the bridge of his nose and shook his head. "Jesus, I . . . I want to help. I just don't know."

"I believe you know *something. Something* changed with her in the past few weeks. Tell me what that was."

"She was happier. She was like . . . *lighter* somehow. She said she was ready to make a move."

"A move of what kind?"

He squinted at me. "From here. She was going to leave the school. She'd decided to move."

I walked back to the bench and sat beside him. "She was leaving her job?" He nodded. "To move where?"

He blushed again. "To Playa Arcadia. With me. She was going with me."

I nodded slowly. "You'd been accepted to the art school?"

"I found out five weeks ago. I told her the day I heard, and she was happy for me—really happy. She said nothing then about going anywhere herself, but she'd been thinking about it since then, she told me, and she'd decided to go. She said she'd been talking to someone at the university there—about lecturing at the medical school or something. She said she was ready for a change. She told me the last time we were together."

"That Saturday, in the cave?"

He nodded. "She told me she had a few more things to wrap up, but that we'd be going soon. She said I should pack a bag."

"And that was the first time she mentioned any of this?" Another nod. "That would've been a big step for her—for the two of you, no? A bigger commitment than simply getting together every week or so." He shrugged. "Had you actually made the decision to go to the school?"

He blushed again. "I wanted to. But I didn't get the money—not all I needed. They were waiving tuition, but as far as everything else . . . I didn't know what I was going to do. And then Allegra told me she would take care of it."

"She was going to subsidize your expenses?" He nodded. "And she told you this last Saturday, too?" Another nod. "She'd never said anything to you before about any of this—about leaving Ondstrand, about going with you?"

"I told you—no."

"Were you surprised?"

"Surprised? Of course I was surprised. It was . . . it was like finding out you'd won the lottery or something. Like you were getting . . . everything."

"Going to art school, getting out of Fiskdorp."

Jens-Edvard glared at me. "Not just that."

"No, of course not. Did she say anything else about wrapping up? What she meant by that, when she might be doing it? Anyone she might be doing it with?"

"Nothing, except I got the impression it was happening soon, maybe that day. When she told me to pack a bag, she wasn't just talking. She said I should go home directly and pack, that I should travel light. So that's what I did. She said she'd be in touch later in the day."

"That was the last time you spoke? The last time you saw her?"

He nodded. "I got in my boat and she went up those stairs from the beach."

"Do you know what time that was?"

Another nod. "It was seven-twenty. I looked at my watch."

"And when you didn't hear from her later?"

"I knew something wasn't right. I got worried."

"You called?"

"First I texted. That's what she'd told me to do—just to text my initial and she'd get back to me. And she always did, usually pretty quick."

"But not on Saturday."

He shook his head. "I texted her a half-dozen times that day, and more the next, and got nothing. The day after that, too. Then I started calling. Till you showed up, I didn't know what to do. I just kept staring at those bags I packed."

Jens-Edvard leaned forward again, held his face in his hands, and sobbed. It sounded like a deep cough and was painful to watch. As I did, I couldn't shake the feeling that there was something still hidden.

When the shuddering had subsided, I said: "You were reluctant to tell me about her plan to leave. Why?"

He seemed to shrink from me. "Because it was my fault, for fuck's sake. Her decision to go to Playa Arcadia was because of me. Because of me, she decided to make a change, to quit her job, to *wrap things up* here—whatever that meant. And it got her killed. I feel like it's 'cause of me."

Was that the bottom of it—the final scrapings from the jar? Or was there something else?

I put a hand on his shaking shoulder. "There's something I want you to look at," I said, and I showed him my phone, and a picture of Allegra's cloisonné locket. "Have you seen this before?"

Jens-Edvard swallowed hard and nodded. "It's hers. Her locket. She had it from her da, she told me. Only thing of his she had, that and the car."

"You saw her wear it?"

He nodded. "She never took it off."

"Do you remember if she was wearing it the last time you saw her—that Saturday?"

He nodded again. "She wore it all the time. That day like every other I saw her."

I was quiet for a while. "If she wasn't wearing it, do you have any idea where she might keep it?"

He shook his head. "She wore it all the time," he said again, and a shudder went through him.

I put a hand on his shoulder again. "I'll run you back to town now," I said.

CHAPTER THIRTY

Friday Night

The lobby of Ondstrand House was like an empty chapel when I returned—dim, silent, dreaming—and my footsteps were like sacrilege across the stone floor. The security guard's glare said that he thought the same. When I was back in my rooms, Goss Ivessen answered right away. Or his cat did. Its tail—a dark whip from the ambient black—lashed at the camera, and it hissed evilly.

"Home from the sea, Myles?" Ivessen said. "Any luck catching something? That skiff, perhaps?"

"Luck and more," I said. "I found another of Allegra's lovers—her last one, I think."

I told him about Jens-Edvard Neumann, the story of his relationship with Allegra, and her plan to resign from Ondstrand Biologic. He was quiet for a while after I finished.

"If her 'wrapping up' was simply a matter of resigning," he said, "I'd imagine a number of people would've welcomed it."

"Karen Muir for one, Piers Witmer for another, and perhaps Terrence Hasp. It certainly would've saved him some personnel headaches. And Petra Witmer might've felt relieved to see her go, too. It might've been easier than seeing her around all the time."

"If resignation was *all* Allegra had in mind," Ivessen said.

"It appears she'd stolen more than a few documents from Ondstrand. Perhaps she was concluding their sale. Or perhaps she was offering to sell them back before departing."

Ivessen chuckled softly. "Hard to imagine either of those arrangements going wrong."

I nodded. "Jens-Edvard gave me the phone Allegra had given to him. It should make it easier for Freja's people to trace Allegra's phone."

"Another burner," Ivessen observed. "More tradecraft. She was certainly committed."

"She took pains to keep her relationship with him private."

"Because she was tired of being the subject of gossip? Because he was more than just someone she had sex with?"

"Perhaps because he was underage," I suggested.

"There's that," Ivessen said.

"If you accept Jens's story, though, Allegra was preparing to make some significant changes in her life—changes that included him. Of course, it's impossible to say if Allegra's relationship with Jens actually drove any of those changes—if running off to Playa Arcadia with him was the point, or merely a sunny by-product."

"I'll confirm with the medical school, but—if she did make such arrangements—that's planning, not impulse," Ivessen said. "And, by the way," he asked, "do you accept Jens's story?"

I nodded. "His shock was real; so were his grief and his guilt."

Ivessen made a skeptical noise. "He did fill some blank spaces, though. We know a bit more about Allegra's off-campus excursions."

I nodded. "And he tightened the time line on last Saturday morning. Jens got into his skiff at seven-twenty a.m. He knows because he checked his watch when he did. And he knows Allegra had left the beach by then, because he saw her from his boat as she was climbing up the stairs."

"And sometime after," Ivessen said, "she re-entered Ondstrand House—via a route still unknown—and was killed. I'll recheck the interviews and alibis of the people on the premises, and I'll recheck the security logs as well. We'll see what a better estimate of time-of-death does to our list."

My screen went black then, and whatever I'd been running on all day flickered out, too. I let out a long breath, fell back on the sofa, closed my eyes, and thought not of Allegra and her escape to the tropics, but of Jens-Edvard and of Petra Witmer.

Their grief clung to me like smoke from a house fire—something trapped in clothing and pores. But these fumes had found purchase not in my skin but on the fabric of my own grief—a dark bolt I kept folded away, on the highest shelf I could find. Grief for my mother, whose features and form were largely lost to me—just a fall of pale hair across a paler face, downcast eyes, hollow cheeks, and hungry arms—heavily inked and terribly scarred. For my grandmother, whose bitter-lipped, ever-simmering resentment I wished were more thoroughly forgotten. For the squad of my own pale selves: small, darting shades that haunted a long line of state homes, for which Van der Wees, the last of them, was the paradigm in my memory: a breeze-block cavern of drafty corridors painted hideous green, a pervasive reek of mold and grubby bodies, and an abundance of unpredictable violence—after which the abundant predictable violence of Conservatory was a relief. And, of course, for Tessa. One year, eleven months, etc. I shook my head, opened my eyes, blinked away the memories, and found my bed.

CHAPTER THIRTY-ONE

Saturday Morning

Director Mehta woke me on Saturday morning, just before dawn. She was in her home office, and she wore a gray tunic with a high banded collar. It gave her the look of a cleric on my tablet screen. An underslept and irritated cleric.

"I've just spent too long on the line with Elkort," she said. "A director from one of our sister services."

I rubbed my eyes. "Domestic Security?"

"The same. In the Science and Technology Division."

"And?"

"And Director Elkort is unhappy, Myles. She is unhappy in *so* many ways."

"Anything in particular—beyond the basic human condition?"

"As it happens, she is unhappy with you in particular."

"As I've not heard of her before this moment—"

"Karen Muir, Myles—Director Elkort had heard all about you from her Minister, who'd heard it from Karen Muir."

"I hesitate to ask what 'all about you' entailed."

"I discount the noises about being *hostile* and *impertinent*—it's part of what I pay you for, after all. What kept me on the line so long was the noise about those documents. Apparently, you waved them in Dr. Muir's face—"

"Hardly a wave."

"Still, not quite the level of discretion we discussed. Not quite keeping the circle small."

"I read her some document names; she recognized them. I said nothing about them having been stolen, though I believe that would not have been news to her. If she did know, that constitutes a motive."

"It might, but how do you plan to establish that? Besides provoking her."

"My provocation seems to have elicited a response."

"Is that much of a surprise? The assets of that company are mostly in the form of intellectual property. Is it a shock that she wouldn't want people rifling needlessly through it?"

"That's one explanation. It didn't seem to take much to send her running to her tame Minister."

"The Minister is hardly tame. She was on the line as well."

"Would I be wrong to assume that this same Minister is sponsor to whatever research Ondstrand is conducting for the government?"

Director Mehta managed a tired smile. "Suffice it to say, we've agreed for the moment to sequester the documents you sent us. Of course, we want to know of any other documents that Dr. Stans liberated from Ondstrand, but for now we will not be circulating the ones you've identified. Not even within our own shop."

"Which is, if I may point out, a ridiculous handicap to this work."

"Point it out till your heart's content, Myles," she said. "Just don't expect that anyone is listening." And then my screen went blank.

CHAPTER THIRTY-TWO

Saturday Morning

You get a paddling, Myles?" Freja Berg asked, chuckling. "Word is, the Director was a bit irked with her favorite lad after having to sit through some long ministerial harangue. We got instructions to wash our hands—and everything else—of the documents you sent us. You get yourself on the wrong side of the wrong people?"

"*Wrong side,* without question," I said. "*Wrong people*—to be determined."

Freja laughed. "Well, now that my in-tray is a bit lighter, is there something else I can do for you?"

"The mobile-tower data."

"The victim's burner phone—assuming she had one."

"Yes—any progress?"

"Still sifting. There's a lot of data out there, Myles."

"Perhaps I can make the job easier. I have the number of a phone—another burner phone—that only ever communicated with Dr. Stans's burner. Pull this phone's history and you'll have the number we're looking for."

"We always welcome an easier job," Freja said. "By all means, send it."

I did just that, then slipped my phone into my pocket and returned to my coffee and the view from the terrace. The sky was clear just then, the ocean calm, and the brown curve of the Ondstrand beach empty but for ropes of seaweed that marked the last high tide. It was early, but there was the promise of warmth in the air, and the scent of softening, opening earth.

Ondstrand House and its grounds were quiet still, and I scanned the cliffs above the beach, and the paths that wound along them, but saw no one. How different, I wondered, had they looked a week before, when Petra Witmer was out here with camera and sketchpad, and Jens-Edvard's skiff had been grounded down below?

The time Jens-Edvard had provided for his departure from the beach was minutes after the Ondstrand security logs had recorded Petra re-entering the main house, and so her testimony to me remained intact. But I knew that the terrace and the cliffs were favorite spots of Petra's, and that she had visited there on many other early Saturday mornings. Had the little skiff been down there on any of those visits? And had Petra lingered up high, and watched who had emerged from the cave? If she had, she hadn't mentioned it to me.

I pulled out my phone, looked at the photos Petra had given me, and tried to work out where she had taken them from. It was highly imprecise—as much guesswork as anything else—but I thought her spot might've been at the south end of the terrace. It afforded some view of the beach, including the spot where Jens-Edvard had landed his skiff, as well as a glimpse of the caves. It also had decent sight lines of the cliffs above the caves, and of the trails along them leading north.

I imagined Allegra climbing the cement stairs from the beach. She would've seen Jens-Edvard's skiff in the cove, heard its motor. Would she have watched the little boat push out into the sea? Would she have waved? I thought not.

I pictured her climbing at a brisk trot, her quads and calves and arms working, her pulse steady, her breath even, her face raised up, her mind focused on . . . what? On what came next—on wrapping up a few things. But where and with whom? I pictured her reaching the top of the stairs to face three choices—the paths north, along the cliff or into the woods north of the house; the paths south, across the terrace or along its footings; the path east, which ran along the side of the north wing. Which way?

Whichever route she took, it eventually brought her back inside of Ondstrand House—somehow undetected by the access-control systems there, unseen by anyone willing to say so. It brought her to that bathroom in the executive dining room and face-to-face with . . . who? I stared at the top of the cement steps and the iron rail, as if staring and sheer force of will might reveal some piece of what happened there a week ago, and I would know which way Allegra had turned. I stared until what remained of my coffee was icy, and my phone burred in my pocket.

It was Freja Berg.

"You're always in such a god-awful hurry, but you don't answer your phone," she said.

I put down my coffee and ran a hand over my face. "What can I do for you, Freja?"

"It's what I'm doing for you. Turns out the phone number you sent me was in fact a big help, and so much faster than searching for a needle in a haystack. We pulled the phone's history. As you thought, we found only one number in it, and traced that number. It's a mobile that shows up on the logs of the towers that service Ondstrand House, and with a usage pattern that fits your prediction."

I felt my pulse quicken. "Can you get a fix on its current location?"

"That's the best part, Myles—the phone switched off last Saturday morning, but it came on again this past Thursday. It came on in the early evening, in Soligstrand, at six-fifty-five p.m., and went off eight minutes later. It started broadcasting once more later that evening, at eight-oh-seven, from north of there, and hasn't moved from its location since."

"Where the hell is it, Freja?"

"Best we can tell, it's about fourteen miles north, northwest, as the crow flies, from where you're standing."

CHAPTER THIRTY-THREE

Saturday Afternoon

It was north of Soligstrand and inland, in a wooded swath off a road that became, just out of town, mostly ruts and crumbling shoulders. I had the top down on Allegra's car, and the sun was bright as I drove, but it lost its warmth as I left the coast behind.

The road bumped past some cow barns that had seen their last residents a decade before, a filling station blanketed in rust and faded graffiti, and what had once been a small settlement—a store, a post office, a pub with a faded sign that read *The Guardsman's Doubt*—where the yawning doors and broken windows of the buildings were like the faces of baffled drunks. I glanced in the rearview and saw a deer behind me in the roadway, stock-still on the white line.

Freja directed me to an overgrown drive a mile or so past the pub, the entrance to what was once a small horse-farm. It, too, had a sign, also faded: *Little Storping Equestrian*. I rolled along a gravel track, past weedy paddocks and fallen fences, to a turnaround before a farmhouse and a stable building that were mostly kindling. I got out there and went on foot another half-mile, down a long-neglected bridle trail into the woods. The cold, silence, and shadows gathered quickly, and I stumbled more than a few times until I came to a clearing, and a small tractor barn that was subsiding into itself.

"From what we can see, you're very close," Freja said in my ear, "no more than a few meters."

I stood on the trail and looked at the sagging heap of the tractor barn, mostly rot and rust and weeds springing up. The few windows were empty of glass, and the cobwebs were shaggy with dust. The trail itself veered away from the barn and ran up a gentle slope, before vanishing about fifty yards from where I stood into a tangle of vines and fallen branches.

"Do you see anything?" Freja said. I did not, but just then the wind shifted, and my stomach turned. "Myles?"

"Shush," I said, and stepped off the trail. I walked around the barn, to where the ground fell away into a hollow about ten meters across. At the bottom was the decaying trunk of a good-sized pine, and alongside it a gray sedan. Its driver's door hung wide, and the smell that had turned my stomach was coming from the body slumped in the opening. I remembered the short, dark hair, matted now with blood and tissue, and the black jacket and running shoes—the same ones he'd worn in the garage. The rest of him was not easily recognizable.

Jane arrived with a full contingent—two vans, their crews and kit—before noon. She knew I wanted ID quickly and took the prints herself as soon as it was possible to touch the body. She sent them back to her lab and to Freja.

"If he is ex-military or ex-government, we should be able to match his prints fast," she said. "As for the rest"—she made a sweeping gesture in the direction of her crew, swarming in their moon suits—"this will take a while, and you're in the way. If you want to go back to Ondstrand House—"

"Got it," a young woman on her crew called out. She held up a clear plastic bag with a mobile phone inside.

"We'll print it and swab it immediately, and courier it back to Freja. She'll have it in a few hours."

I nodded. "I'll be in the car."

Jane's vans were parked near Allegra's car by the stable, and the drivers nodded as I approached but otherwise kept to their own low conversation. I settled in for a long wait, some of which I spent watching fast clouds cross the sky and talking to Freja Berg.

"With the location history from Allegra's burner, we were able to fill some gaps," Freja said. "Specifically, those every-three-week gaps. Those Wednesday afternoons when she left her own phone behind were in some ways like her other Wednesdays—she went to Soligstrand, she went to the salon—but after that things diverged. Every third Wednesday, after beauty time, she'd drive north, up to Hemligstad, to an inn on the edge of town called The Dold Hus. She'd spend between two and three hours there, and afterwards head back to Ondstrand House."

"And that began when?"

"Nearly seven months ago."

"I'm fairly certain that the prints Jane sent you belong to the same fellow I met in the garage a few days back. Any wager on whether he, too, was a regular at The Dold Hus?"

"I'll save my coin, thanks," Freja said. "Now let me see how those prints are coming." She rang off.

The sun was fading and the air was cooling fast, and I was desperately wanting coffee and a sandwich, when Jane came down the bridle trail. Her scene-of-crime garb was over one shoulder, stuffed into a blue plastic sack. Over the other was her messenger bag. Her gray tee shirt was damp, and there was a sheen of sweat on her cheeks.

"Still here?" she said.

"Where else should I be? Done?"

"Nearly. They'll be bringing him out soon."

"And?"

She smiled wearily and swept damp hair off her forehead. "You want name, age, occupation, and cause of death, do you?"

"Not necessarily in that order."

"He has a gunshot wound to the head—entry through the roof of the mouth."

"I noticed that."

"We found no weapons at the scene."

I nodded. "And . . . ?"

She shook her head. "You know the drill—I'm not going to say more at this juncture. He's been outside for close to forty-eight hours; the bugs and animals and elements have had their way with him, not to mention inexorable chemistry; so, until I get him on a table . . ." She made a lip-zipping motion. "It does appear that the victim had been carrying a handgun, though. He wore a holster behind his back, and it's a custom model, tailored to a semiautomatic. I sent pictures to Freja."

"And no sign of his phone?"

She shook her head. "The only phone we found was the one you saw—the one we sent to Freja. And, yes, we searched the car, the body, and the surroundings for a hundred meters around, and that includes that hazard of a barn."

I nodded. "Anything else in the surroundings?"

"Not much in the immediate area, besides signs of your stomping about. And, by the way, I'll need those shoes, and fibers from your trousers and jacket, for elimination."

"I was hardly stomping. And what about the footprints I saw?"

"We saw them too. They're quite blurry, and with no discernible sole pattern. We know they're not his, but otherwise it's hard to tell much."

"No markings from the soles?"

"No. They could be from some sort of moccasin, or a gum-soled shoe or boot perhaps. But, given the composition of the soil, the forest canopy, and the weather recently, it's hard to gauge their size or even their age. They could've been laid down when he died, or days earlier."

I nodded again. "Is it possible that there were coverings over the shoes?"

"Coverings—of the sort we wear at a scene?" I nodded. "Yes, it's possible," Jane said.

"How about another vehicle? Any sign of another car out there?"

"Not out there, but we found some tread marks not far from where the victim's car pulled off the road. They leave the road about thirty meters from where his car pulled off, but stop at some trees there, about ten meters from the shoulder. There are tracks of the car turning about and rejoining the road, too. They're decently clear marks, but it's hard to say when they were made or how long the car was stopped. Now let me see those clothes."

Jane had just finished bagging the threads she'd snipped from my clothing when my phone burred. It was Freja Berg.

"His name was Ian Stiles," she said. "And he was ex-military."

CHAPTER THIRTY-FOUR

Saturday Evening

Ian Stiles had left the military ten years back, as a colonel, and had spent all of his time in the service assigned to Army Intelligence. He'd married in his early twenties, but it didn't take and had produced no children; his ex had moved overseas shortly after the divorce. Goss Ivessen sent photos of him from the time of his discharge, and they were without doubt of the man I'd scuffled with in the garage. A bit leaner, and a bit less louche, but the same.

Since his separation from the army, Stiles had been the chief executive and, as far as Ivessen could determine, the sole employee of Stiles Risk Advisers, a firm based in the city that pitched itself—discreetly—as a corporate security consultancy and executive recruitment specialist. What that actually meant, according to Ivessen, was corporate espionage with a focus on high-tech companies, and he reported that Stiles had previously been engaged by companies in semiconductors, video-game development, financial technology, pharmaceuticals, and telecoms. Ivessen had yet to find an instance of him working in biotech.

"Not something that any firm would advertise, of course," he said, "given the flagrant illegality of it all. That said, I did manage a contact at a fintech house—a former Stiles client—who summarized the business model.

"Basically, a client firm would identify a senior technologist—an engineer, a designer, a scientist, et cetera—at some competitor firm whose services they wanted to procure. They'd put together a compensation package—typically, quite a generous one, including stock options and pay for any mandatory gardening leave specified in whatever non-compete agreements were applicable—and hand it to Stiles to make the approach. But that package was only the public part of the pitch.

The other part—the part for which Stiles served as both cutout and coordinator—was an inducement to steal intellectual property. That part would include significantly more lavish compensation—all of it laundered, untraceable, undeclared, and tax-free.

"Apparently, clients would leave it to Stiles to make the solicitations, negotiate the terms, seal the deal, and handle the nuts and bolts of the thefts, thus keeping everything nicely deniable on their sides."

"That sounds consistent with what Allegra was up to," I said after a while. I was sitting in her car, one of a few in the small dirt lot of The Dold Hus. It was full night now, and chilly, and the lights in the windows of the rambling stone house were warm and inviting. The manager, a potato-shaped fellow named Carew, had been less so, but had responded readily to my ID and thinly veiled threats.

"The manager identified their photos and confirmed that Allegra had been meeting with Stiles there for months—every third Wednesday afternoon," I told Ivessen. "Stiles would arrive first, sign in, and go up to the room he'd booked in advance. Allegra would arrive about twenty minutes after and go directly up. Always the same room, always the same routine. They'd stay for between two and three hours, at some point during which they'd order tea and sandwiches. Then Allegra would leave, followed in short order by Stiles. The manager volunteered that the bed was always untouched, and that all the maid had ever had to do was clean up the tea things and change the hand towels."

"No one else ever asked after them?" Ivessen asked.

"No one."

"And neither of them ever brought a third party along?"

"Not that the manager saw," I said. "And he's the type to have been on the lookout."

I put Ivessen on speaker, put the car in gear, pulled out of the lot, and began the dark drive back to Öndstrand House. Ivessen stayed silent for the first half-mile or so.

"One can construct a narrative," he said eventually, "in which Ian Stiles approached Dr. Stans—either before or after her demotion—made his pitch, and won her over. After which he coached her in the necessary tradecraft, supplied her with cameras and burner phones, made arrangements for the spear-phishing attack, likely with information supplied by Allegra, and then handled her take—the photos she took of the stolen documents—by clearing the letterbox in the garage every week. The meetings every third Wednesday might be to discuss other information his client—her future employer—might want, or to confirm payments, or both."

"I told myself much the same story," I said. "And while it covers how things might've begun between the two of them, it doesn't account for the endings."

He made a noise of assent. "What do you make of Allegra's phone being at the scene?" Ivessen asked.

"That is the glaring question—one of them, anyway. How would Stiles have come into possession of her phone—which we know from Jens-Edvard that she'd had with her on Saturday—and yet not know that she was dead? And if he didn't have it and bring it out to the woods . . ."

"Then someone else did," Ivessen said.

"And turned it on and left it with his body."

Ivessen was quiet for a while, and all I heard for a mile or more were tires hissing on the tarmac, the wind insinuating itself beneath the car's canvas top, and Ivessen's cat, bleating. "What are the other glaring questions?" he asked eventually.

"One is: What happened to Stiles's phone? The other is: Where is his gun?"

"His killer likely has the gun, unless it's been dumped already. And presumably, whoever brought Allegra's phone out there took Stiles's phone away."

"Because there was something on it that they wanted," I said, "or didn't want anyone else to have. But why leave Allegra's phone there—and why leave it turned on?"

"We wouldn't have found Stiles's body without Allegra's phone," Ivessen said. "Was that the point?"

"It served as a beacon and established a link between Stiles and the doctor. Why someone would want to do those things, I have no idea."

"Stiles's wound—through the roof of the mouth—is odd, too."

"More consistent with suicide," I said.

"Which seems unlikely. Unless Jane tells us a squirrel carried off his gun."

I smiled. "The wound suggests someone who could get very close to Stiles."

"And someone who wanted to be certain," Ivessen said. "Have you updated the Director yet?"

"Not yet."

"Give a ring after you do. I'll have finished applying our refined time of death to the list of staff on the premises last Saturday."

"It may be late," I said.

He laughed. "I suppose I'll have to cancel my plans for the ballet."

CHAPTER THIRTY-FIVE

Saturday Night

Nadia Blom was waiting for me when I returned to Ondstrand House, directly in front of the door to my rooms, and there was no avoiding her.

"I've been getting calls all afternoon and evening with nothing but questions from Dr. Hasp, Dr. Muir, Dr. Witmer. They all want to know what is going on after a full week of investigation. Are you close to a conclusion? Have you taken anyone into custody?"

She wore black jeans and a black roll-neck jumper and looked like an advertiser's idea of a bohemian artist. I reached around her to open the door. "Why have they decided to spin themselves up about this now? Simply because a week has passed? And why are they asking you?"

"That's an excellent question. Perhaps it's because you were nowhere to be found, and the people at your headquarters were entirely unhelpful. Perhaps it's because none of the other people they've called have a single clue of what's going on. Or perhaps it's because they take some pleasure in yelling at me when I have no answers for them." I stepped around her and into my room. She followed. "Whatever the reason, I want it to stop."

For an instant, I felt something akin to sympathy for her. "Yelling? At you? Not Dr. Hasp? He wouldn't."

"I don't find this—or you—amusing. Has there been a development in your investigation? Is there ongoing danger here? We have a right to know what's going on."

"Actually, you don't, Ms. Blom. I am charged with managing this investigation as I see fit, and that includes managing the flow of information about the investigation. I suppose I can appreciate that rampant gossip amongst your staff might contribute to the ambient anxiety here, and perhaps degrade productivity, but the emotional well-being of your staff is not my primary concern. Or even my tertiary concern. I can tell you that I don't believe anyone at Ondstrand is in imminent danger just now. Though, of course, I can't guarantee that."

"So you can't say if you're close to concluding things?"

"Who exactly is suggesting *that*, Ms. Blom?"

"People are speculating—"

"That's not actually an answer. People *who*? Dr. Hasp? Dr. Muir? Dr. Witmer?"

"I don't know. All of them."

"Well, if it's helpful, you might suggest that all of them keep their mouths shut."

Nadia Blom looked at me for a while and said nothing. Then she shook her head. "No—it's not at all helpful."

I went in search of food after she left, and managed sandwiches and coffee from the staff cafeteria. The sandwiches were somewhat aged and the coffee was less than fresh, and yet it was all exquisite. I carried a carafe of the old coffee through the dim, quiet corridors back to my rooms, and called Director Mehta at home.

She had just gotten in and was unwinding a scarlet scarf from around her neck. She had spoken to Jane and Freja, and knew what we'd found in the woods, and in the logs of the burner phones. I filled her in on what I'd learned at The Dold Hus. I heard music from her end as she considered what I told her. A string quartet with a mournful cello dominant.

"Two bodies in eight days," she said eventually. "Rather profligate."

I smiled. "I don't suppose Dr. Wilding has anything to report yet."

She shook her head. "I, too, look forward to hearing. I assume you're most interested in what she makes of the circumstances of the body."

"I am."

"I share your curiosity," Director Mehta said. "That type of wound, inflicted, it would seem, by the victim's own gun, would suggest suicide, though of course you found no gun at the scene. And, anyway, Mr. Stiles hardly seems the type. Not to mention the obvious question of why in hell anyone would go to—what's the name of the place—*Little Storping*, for God's sake—if not to meet someone." She disappeared from the screen for a moment and returned with an Old Fashioned glass that held an ice cube and two fingers of whiskey. She took a sip.

"I saw Nadia Blom earlier," I said. "She told me that her masters at

Ondstrand have grown quite restless, and that they'd been calling everyone they know in the city. Apparently, they feel I've overstayed my welcome."

The Director smiled wearily. "They haven't managed to get through to me directly, though not from lack of trying. I did hear from Director Elkort more than once, though, as well as from several ministers."

"And?"

"'Restless' doesn't quite cover it. They're rather frantic about productivity there, the smooth functioning of their operation, et cetera."

"And I don't suppose they have much faith in me."

She took another sip. "None."

"And?"

Director Mehta arched a graceful eyebrow, smiled minutely, swirled her drink. "And carry on, Myles."

CHAPTER THIRTY-SIX

Saturday Night–Sunday Morning

The rest of that night was a bleary-eyed grind of rereading statements and interview notes, cross-checking them, yet again, with Ondstrand security logs and mobile-phone logs and location information, and reviewing it all against our improved information—thanks largely to Jens-Edvard Neumann—about Allegra's movements on the morning of her death. My company in this exercise was the shifting silhouette of Goss Ivessen, the grievance of his cat, and the carafe of old coffee. By the time we finished, Sunday was dawning, and we had winnowed our original list of a dozen names down considerably.

"Dr. Stans was last seen by Jens-Edvard Neumann," I said, "at a few minutes past seven-twenty a.m., climbing stairs from the beach. We believe her body was dumped in that refrigerator at around eight-oh-five a.m.—when the killer was interrupted in disposing of it by the arrival of a linen delivery at that time. In the roughly forty-five minutes between, Dr. Stans re-entered Ondstrand House and made her way to the executive dining room, where she was killed in a bathroom. The tighter time frames leave us with five people on the premises then with no alibis for that window: Drs. Hasp, Witmer, and Silber, Victor Halsell, and Nadia Blom."

Ivessen's shadow nodded. "A shorter list feels like progress," he said. "Or at least feels more manageable, no?"

I sighed and rubbed my eyes. "Perhaps, if certain assumptions weren't so . . ."

"Squishy?" Ivessen suggested.

"As fine a word as any. We still don't know exactly when or how Dr. Stans re-entered Ondstrand House. And, if she could enter undetected, or at least unnoted by Ondstrand Security, then—"

"So could others," Ivessen said.

"And so much for the usefulness of our list. And aside from the *how* of her re-entry, there's still the *who* and the *why* of her murder."

"The *why* is likely related to her work with Ian Stiles, is it not? That's certainly our most productive avenue at the moment."

"I suppose, but that seems a somehow . . . inadequate motive. The people who stand to lose the most from her theft must be the sharehold-ers of Ondstrand Biologic, yes? And if her espionage had been discov-ered, any one of them would've had recourse to remedies other than murder—two murders—wouldn't you think? They could've sued Stans and Stiles, stripped them of every asset down to their socks, compelled them to reveal their employer, and sued *that* firm to the marrow. Hell, they might've wound up with ownership of another company in the bargain."

Ivessen laughed. "Your faith in our legal system is touching, Myles, not to mention surprising, but I take your point. And it makes sense if the only thing Dr. Stans put at risk was the intellectual property of Ondstrand. But who knows what else she might've dug up in all her digging around. More than she bargained for, perhaps."

I rubbed my eyes again, drank the last of the coffee, as cold as sea-water, and nodded at Ivessen's shadow.

CHAPTER THIRTY-SEVEN

Sunday Morning

Sunday was not usually a workday for Caroline Drucker, and yet there she was, behind a precarious berm of paper amidst the wreckage of several meals—a half-eaten muffin, sandwich wrappers, several water bottles, a cylinder of wax paper that might once have held crackers, a coffee carafe and mug. She jumped when my shadow crossed her desk, and looked up. There were dark patches beneath her eyes and lines around her mouth; her hair had broken loose of its tie and was like a storm cloud about her head. There was a coffee stain on her orange tee shirt.

"Have you moved in here?" I asked.

She smiled wearily and brushed muffin crumbs from her desk. "Maybe you have, too. I was just about to call you."

"And the devil appears. What were you going to call me about?"

"Documents—malware and documents," she said, and waved me to a chair.

"I'm all ears."

Caro pulled her hair back and wrestled it into its tie. She took a deep breath and sat up straight. "I took what we found last week—the malware, the hijacked credentials, the users who seemed magically in two places at once, the documents that were accessed—and used that as my template to search through activity in the virtual-workbench logs. Time-wise, I started where we ended in our initial search, and I found . . . Well, frankly what I found is terrible. She basically stole *everything*—everything from the Special Projects section, anyway."

"She?"

"C'mon, Myles—who else but Allegra are we talking about?"

I nodded in concession. "And by 'everything' you mean . . . ?"

"I mean basically *everything*—nearly every document from every active project. I'm talking about project proposals, lab reports, progress notes, logbooks, management presentations, a half-dozen other things I'm leaving out. If it described a project, its sponsors, its objectives, its deliverables, its timetables, its staffing, its commercial prospects, its plans, progress, or status—she stole it. Systematically, project by project."

I squinted at her. "That must've taken her—"

"Months. Several months."

"But I thought you'd suffered no more phishing attacks. Did people just not recognize or report them?"

Caro's jaw clenched. "Yes and no. After those initial e-mails, she dispensed with the spear-phishing business. Instead, if she wanted to steal someone's credentials, she sent them an e-mail herself—an internal e-mail, designed like the spear-phishing prototypes, as one big clickjack. I don't know if it was laziness or a calculated risk on her part; whichever, in the limited time she used them, no one noticed."

"Limited time?"

Caro nodded. "I suppose it eventually occurred to her that she could do away with the person-by-person credential theft, and just steal the credentials of someone who had access to everything she was interested in."

My stomach dropped. "And who was that?" I asked, though I knew the answer.

"Dr. Muir," Caro said.

I sat back in my chair and let out a long breath. "You haven't told anyone else about this?"

She frowned. "Of course not."

"Not about the stolen documents or any of it?"

"I said *no.*"

I nodded. "Has anyone been asking about document access or Allegra's activities or about anything related to Special Projects?"

"No one's asked me anything like that, and I'd know if they'd asked my staff."

"Have you a list of the documents she accessed?"

She gestured to the hillocks of paper on her desk. "That's what all this is. Believe it or not, it is organized—according to project."

"And it includes the material she accessed using Dr. Muir's credentials?"

Caro nodded. "It does. She started using those nearly three months ago."

I looked at the reams of paper and sighed. "You said she worked systematically, project by project." Caro nodded. "Does that mean she went after the same kinds of materials for each project?"

Another nod. "Yes, which isn't surprising. All of the projects are organized and managed according to the same methodology, which means there's a standard, consistent set of documents generated for every one of them. The contents vary, of course, and there may be additional materials—annexes of one sort or another—but every project has the same protocol of documentation as every other one."

"No exceptions?"

"Not that I know of."

I thought of what Goss Ivessen had said last night: "But who knows what else she might've dug up in all her digging around. More than she bargained for, perhaps."

"And that's the set of materials she always went after for each project?" I asked. "No exceptions there?"

Caro stared at me and tilted her head, and I leaned forward. "Maybe. Maybe one exception."

"Yes?"

She swiveled to one of her screens and unleashed a torrent of keystrokes. "Special Project 1107. It was one of the last projects she accessed—about six weeks back." Caro typed more, then scanned her screen. "She swept up the usual complement of project documents, as she had with all the other projects, and then she went back for . . . more."

"More what?"

"More everything. She accessed all the annexes that existed, and then she went after correspondence."

"What kind of correspondence—between who and who?"

"She accessed e-mails and texts—between the researchers and Dr. Muir, and even between Muir and other members of the senior management committee—Dr. Hasp and Dr. Witmer." More typing, more squinting at what came back. "She even accessed correspondence between Dr. Muir and the Financial Control Department concerning the project, and between Dr. Muir and the project sponsor."

I sat back and looked out of Caro's windows, at the restless pine boughs against the empty sky. "Did this happen all at once? Did she access the additional material immediately after going through the standard project documents?"

Caro went back to her screen. "No, it wasn't right away. There was a gap of nearly a week."

I nodded. "And what is Special Project 1107? Does it have a name, or some description to go with the number?"

Caro leaned back in her chair and shook her head. "The number is the only identifier, and I don't really know what it is. What I can tell you is that 1107 is work on behalf of a non-pharma client. A state client."

"A state-security client?"

Caro shrugged. "That's always been my assumption—that or the military—but no one has ever said. In fact, no one discusses it at all. I know it's been under way for years—over six years—and that it's big, at least in terms of budget, though not in terms of staffing. I can tell you also that it's organized rather differently than other projects."

"How so?"

She tapped her chin and thought for a moment. "Information is compartmentalized there in a way that it isn't on our other projects. We've got plenty of projects that are run by multiple scientific teams that work in parallel—on sub-projects, if you will, of a larger whole—and there's always a lot of sharing of information back and forth across those groups. Members of one team are able to look at what their colleagues are doing—their progress, their results, data sets, and so forth—and vice versa. But 1107 isn't organized that way. It's much more segregated—entirely segregated, in fact. The teams on 1107 can look at their own materials, but only Dr. Muir sees the whole picture."

"Dr. Muir and, apparently, Allegra Stans. Has the project always been organized that way?"

She nodded. "From the start."

"Well, let's have a look, then. I'm sure I won't understand much—but let's start with something that describes the project's objectives."

Caro looked at me and tilted her head again. "I can't, Myles."

I sighed. "I thought we'd moved past this nonsense. The barn door has been blown to smithereens, Caro, and your cherished corporate secrets are running wild over hill and dale. It's a bit ridiculous at this juncture to deny access to the investigator. If it's security clearances you're concerned with, don't be. I'm authorized by Standard Division to access—"

"It's not that, Myles," she said, shaking her head. "It's not that I *won't* give you access, it's that I *can't*—I don't have access myself. All materials related to Project 1107 were wiped from the corporate servers."

I leaned forward. "When did *that* happen?"

"Three weeks ago."

"Who did the wiping?"

"Dr. Muir. Of people outside of IT, only she and Dr. Hasp have the necessary access to do that."

"Would she know how—without help from you or one of your staff?"

Caro thought about it for a moment, then nodded. "It's not complicated if you know the volumes the data is stored on, and all of that is well documented here. And Dr. Muir is more than conversant with the technology."

"So she never asked you for help in doing it, or mentioned it? You didn't know anything about this?"

Caro frowned. "No, no, and screw you. Let me point out, Myles, that I only just discovered this myself at around one a.m. today, not long before I called it quits for the night and went home. I was a little tired then, oddly enough, and I suppose I didn't immediately make the connection with what Allegra had been doing. Forgive me for that."

"You said that everything was wiped from your servers. Does that mean—"

"Everything. The project proposals and objectives documents, the project schedules, the status reports, all the annexes, including the budget and billing information, all of Dr. Muir's private annexes, and, it seems, all of her correspondence about the project with the management committee and project sponsors."

"Surely there are backups of these materials."

She nodded. "For every other project—yes. For 1107—not anymore."

"Since when?" Caro swiveled again and typed like mad. While she did, I sat back and thought about calendars. Six weeks ago—Allegra plundering the documentation of Project 1107. A week after that—Allegra rifling through Karen Muir's private files on the same subject. And then, three weeks ago—Muir scrubbing much of that information from the Ondstrand servers. Special Project 1107, on behalf of a non-pharma entity. On behalf of a state security agency.

Caro Drucker turned to me. "Did you say something?" she asked.

I looked up at her. "Did I?"

She nodded, still typing. "I believe you said 'Fuck.' A sentiment I share entirely." She pointed to the screen. "And in answer to your question: since three weeks ago. As of three weeks ago, all of the Special Project 1107 backups—going back to the project's start—are unavailable."

CHAPTER THIRTY-EIGHT

Sunday Afternoon

Special Project 1107," Director Mehta said. "It sounds portentous when you say it aloud." She was in her home office, with gray light streaming in, just a shade paler than her gray jumper.

I raised an eyebrow. "You know of it?"

She chuckled. "It's the object of Director Elkort's considerable stress, which I hear too much about lately. I suspect she's a generally anxious person."

"Is she the project's sponsor?"

"Her agency is."

"Does she know that materials related to her project have been stolen?"

"Do *we* know that? We know that Dr. Stans accessed them improperly, but we actually don't know yet what she did with them. Or do you?"

"I don't."

"Then it would be perhaps premature to say that they were stolen—at least in the sense of them having been passed to a third party."

"We do know that Dr. Stans paid them special attention, though—attention she didn't pay to any of the other materials she accessed."

"Which indicates what, Myles?"

"I'm not entirely sure. Perhaps it reflected her employer's priorities; perhaps it reflected her own assessment of their potential value."

"These materials didn't seem to be her first priority," the Director said. "She didn't go after them until late in the game. According to the time line Ms. Drucker provided, they weren't even the first things Dr. Stans accessed after she'd stolen Dr. Muir's credentials."

I nodded. "But once she had a look, she went back for more, as Ms. Drucker tells it."

Director Mehta's features seemed to sharpen. "Yes. What do you make of that?"

"That she found something in the Project 1107 information she initially accessed that either piqued her curiosity or whetted her appetite. Or both. If I knew more about what was in those materials, I might have more insight."

Director Mehta smiled. "Is this where you ask me for a copy, and I regretfully decline to provide it?"

"Is it?"

Another smile. "Director Elkort and her Minister have so far withheld that material from me, Myles, and I haven't yet pressed the point. But perhaps you'll save me the trouble."

"I can request them of Dr. Muir; I can . . . insist."

The Director shook her head. "You can certainly try, but I suspect Dr. Muir would refer you to Director Elkort, which might be an amusing interlude, but not terribly productive. No, it is simply my hope that, should you, in the course of your work, come across documents that pertain to Project 1107, you will send them my way."

I nodded. "Are you surprised that they're so hard to come by—denied to you, removed from the Ondstrand servers by Dr. Muir?"

She smiled again, a chilly one this time. "Not entirely," she said. "Director Elkort and her Minister continue to cite the project's extreme sensitivity, and I won't be shocked if Dr. Muir says something along those lines when you ask her why she scrubbed Ondstrand's servers. I assume you will be asking."

"I will, and I'll also ask why she chose three weeks ago to remove that information from the servers, when the project has been ongoing for six years. Did it become suddenly more sensitive, or did she become aware of some specific threat three weeks ago?"

"I look forward to the answers."

I frowned. "Why should Domestic Security or their ministers stop our access to this material? Certainly those people haven't worried us in the past."

The Director sighed. "It's less a question of our ability to get what we want, and more a question of timing and cost. At this juncture, our own Minister would prefer to hold her fire." I said nothing but stared at the Director. She smiled. "Wheels within wheels, Myles," she said softly.

CHAPTER THIRTY-NINE

Sunday Night

Y ou saw the autopsy report?" Goss Ivessen asked. His voice was disconcertingly fresh for late on a Sunday night. "She just posted it."

"No, I haven't seen it. I've just now seen the inside of my eyelids for the first time in what seems a week."

He snorted. "I'll give you the highlights while you pull it up."

I took a deep breath, rubbed my face, and swung my legs out of bed. The cold of the stone floor sent a shock up my calves. I groped for the lamp switch.

"Fine," I muttered. I propped my phone against the lamp and reached for my tablet as Ivessen read.

"Decedent is Ian James Stiles, age forty-two years, seven months. Approximate time of death is Thursday evening between the hours of seven and ten p.m. Cause of death was massive cerebral trauma due to a single gunshot wound, the entry point of which was the victim's hard palate. The bullet entered at a roughly sixty-degree angle and followed a path upwards, into the brain, causing extensive damage to the temporal and parietal lobes, and exiting through the parietal bone of the skull. Death would have been instantaneous.

"The bullet, a nine-millimeter, was recovered from the interior roof lining of the car's passenger compartment. Its caliber and the rifling marks on it are consistent with a Voda Nine semiautomatic handgun. As a point of interest, there is a Voda Nine registered to Ian James Stiles and permitted to him for concealed carry.

"There were no other visible marks of violence or struggle on the body, no defensive wounds, no marks of restraint. There's a description of stomach contents, blah, blah, blah, and then we come to the toxicology and histopathology reports."

I had my tablet on and was opening Jane's report. "And I assume there's something interesting there."

"If you consider neurotoxin to be interesting," Ivessen said merrily. "Which, for my part, I do."

I scrolled through the postmortem. "What kind of neurotoxin?"

"That's the most interesting part—Dr. Wilding is a bit in the dark there."

"I find that hard to believe."

"Surprising, I agree. She knows it's a synthetic; her closest guess is that it's a compound based on, of all things, cobra venom."

"Cobra venom?"

"That's what the report says. It's definitely a paralytic agent of some sort, and, like cobra venom, it binds to acetylcholine receptors. But Dr. Wilding notes differences between this compound and naturally occurring venom, mostly having to do with the shapes of some of the molecular bonds. She—"

"I found it," I said, and Ivessen gave me a few moments to skim the section. "Well," I said when I finished, "synthetic cobra venom it is—definitely not your run-of-the-mill. Jane says that the compound wasn't injected. Not at any site she could find."

"She thinks it might have been ingested," Ivessen said, "but that's still a guess."

I nodded in the dark. "If it's a paralytic, then it could explain how the killer relieved Stiles of his gun and got close enough to stick it in his mouth, all without a struggle. Is it anything you've heard of before?"

"No. And neither have our R&D people. I will say that their enthusiasm for the idea was a bit unsettling."

"No doubt. If I run across some, I'll bring them back a souvenir."

"Is it the sort of thing they cook up out there?"

"No one has mentioned anything like that, though I've gotten the airbrushed version of their work. I'll add that to the list of questions I put to Hasp when we meet tomorrow," I said.

"That, and whether he can account for his time on Thursday night," Ivessen added.

"That, too. I'll take Hasp, Witmer, and Muir. You take Halsell, Silber, and Blom."

"Good luck," Ivessen said, chuckling, and my screen went dark.

CHAPTER FORTY

Monday Morning

Terrence Hasp's office suite was in the center section of Ondstrand House, on the main floor. It was off a broad corridor, flanked by the Financial Control Department on one side, and Human Resources on the other. I was in the waiting area outside of his office, ignoring the stares of his PA, when his meeting broke up, just before lunch. Hasp was surprised to see me standing by the high windows, looking at the ocean view, and so were the other members of the Ondstrand Senior Management Committee: Mario Pohl, Piers Witmer, and Karen Muir. Only Mario Pohl smiled.

Pohl had a laptop and a stack of folders under one arm, and he came over and shook my hand as if we'd run across each other at the squash club. "Still with us, I see. Things moving ahead?"

I nodded. "They're moving."

He nodded sympathetically. "Well, if there's anything I can do . . ." Then he strolled out, whistling tunelessly.

Hasp, Muir, and Witmer were in the open double doorway to Hasp's office. Muir was in yoga wear again, today a steel-blue rig with matching jacket and slippers, and a look of chilly irritation on her symmetrical face. Witmer wore a white button-down, a brown cardigan, and a look of fear and embarrassment. His eyes slipped away from mine. Hasp was in jeans and a ropy fisherman's sweater and was missing only a sou'wester and a harpoon to complete the fish-cakes billboard. I saw Karen Muir's assistant, Ms. Mundt, moving about behind them, collecting the coffee service and errant documents from Hasp's conference table, and she was no more pleased to see me than they were. Possibly less. Hasp squinted at his colleagues and then at me.

"Mornin', Myles," he said. "You looking for one of us? Or you here to take the lot of us in?" He chuckled at his joke.

"For you," I said.

"Don't remember you in my book."

"No," I said. "Shall we go in?" I didn't wait for an answer but stepped around Piers Witmer, into the office. Witmer practically sprang back, and Ms. Mundt froze at the head of the table.

"Terry, would you like me to sit in on this?" Karen Muir said.

I didn't wait for Hasp's answer. "Just now it will be Dr. Hasp and myself."

Muir stiffened, but Hasp waved her off. "Not to worry, Karen—makes perfect sense. Besides—it's not so much a meeting as another interview. Isn't that right, Myles?"

"That's correct," I said.

Hasp's office was a dark, cavernous affair, with a black eight-seat conference table at one end, near the double doors, and a huge, intricately carved ebony desk at the other, before another run of tall, sea-facing windows. On one wood-paneled wall was a dark rectangular patch where a large portrait might once have hung. The suggestion of a portrait was enhanced by a bronze plaque below the portrait silhouette. It was small and tarnished and read: *Jerome Roeg.*

Despite its size, or perhaps because of it, the office was an oppressive, almost suffocating space. The walls and furnishings and black beams on the ceiling seemed to absorb the gouts of daylight that poured through the windows and snuff them out before they reached much beyond Hasp's desk.

A pair of ancient-looking leather chairs stood before the fireplace, and I took a seat in one. Hasp motioned Ms. Mundt out, and she closed the doors behind her. He took a tumbler of water from the head of the conference table and carried it over and sat in the other leather chair. He leaned back, crossed his left ankle to his right knee, and smiled equably and wide.

"What can I do for you, then?"

"There are questions that have come up over the past week that I want to address with you."

He nodded. "Splendid, but before you get started, I want to clear up a thing from the last time we met. Something I might've muddied up a bit."

I lifted an eyebrow. "By all means, Doctor."

"It's got to do with Piers—Dr. Witmer. You asked when we met last if I knew anything about Dr. Stans's relationships—her *personal* relationships. I said that I didn't, but that wasn't strictly the whole of it. 'Fraid I stayed mum on the subject of her relationship years back with Dr. Witmer. S'pect you might've heard of it already—it wasn't much of a secret, truth be told."

I nodded. "I have heard a good deal about it, Doctor. And as it happens, this was one of the things I'd wanted to discuss today. I wanted to know your perspective on it, and why you neglected to mention it."

Hasp ran a big palm over his shaved head, wrinkled his brow, and concocted a sheepish smile. "It was foolish, agreed. After all, that business is long over now, and no harm done. I mean, Piers is well over it and all. Didn't want to spread gossip, though, if you see my point, and old gossip to boot. S'pose I saw it as ancient history. Just didn't see it as relevant."

"Generally, we prefer to have our questions answered honestly and in full; relevance is something we judge for ourselves."

He nodded. "Makes perfect sense. *Mea culpa.* But Piers had made such a mess of things at the time, and he's done so much to get his life, his marriage, and so forth, back on course. Just seemed a pity to dredge it all up again."

"When you say he'd made a mess of things at the time—what does that mean?"

Hasp drank some water and wiped his mouth with the back of his hand. "Piers was less than discreet about Dr. Stans—made something of a spectacle, if you follow. Bit of a schoolboy-in-love sort of thing—all moony. Embarrassing to all concerned, really—his wife, Allegra, Piers most of all. S'pose he was too besotted to see it at the time. Lucky for him, Allegra had the sense to break things off." Hasp paused, rubbed his chin deliberately, and peered at me. "You're not thinking that Piers . . . ? It's not possible, Myles."

"What's not possible, Doctor?"

"Don't know what you've got in mind, but if you think he had anything to do with this—well, it's ridiculous. Off base, completely."

I nodded. "Really?"

"I mean, yes, he went through a rough patch, was maybe a bit *unsettled* for a while, but he's pulled himself together over the years. And he's always been a solid contributor here, a founder and a valued member of the management committee. Now he's steady as ever—a rock. Specially these past few months—he's been better than ever."

"How so?"

"He's been more focused, more energetic, more driven. Even-keeled now, confident—more like his old self. But it's crazy, Myles—Piers and I were together that morning."

"As I know you're aware, Doctor, you and Dr. Witmer were together for only a part of that morning. Neither one of you has independent verification for the entirety of the time lines you've provided. Nonetheless, I'm glad we got that cleared up. I'll certainly keep what you've said in mind. Now, if we could get to my other issues . . ."

Hasp took a deep, relieved breath. "Fire away."

I nodded. "Perhaps you can explain to me why Dr. Stans was demoted seven months ago, and why, when we spoke initially, you characterized it otherwise."

Hasp frowned. "I stand by what I said, Myles. It was a transfer, nothing else, and it was a temporary assignment, in anticipation of something bigger."

"Seven months seems a lengthy 'temporary.' I come back to the fact that Dr. Stans went from having a defined portfolio and management responsibilities to having neither of those things."

He grimaced. "You've been listening to gossip."

"If so, it's gossip that came to me from your sister."

Hasp's face grew keen, like that of a dog who's heard something his master can't. "Dr. Muir is my stepsister."

"Stepsister, then. She told me that she insisted Dr. Stans be removed from her department, and that Dr. Stans's undisguised ambition to take over that department was entirely unrealistic. She also stated that Dr. Stans had told her that you had stoked those ambitions. Is all of that simply gossip, Doctor?"

He sighed wearily. "Oil and water, Myles—oil and water. Karen and Allegra simply didn't get along. Not sure why, really—quite similar minds. Incisive. Creative. Focused."

"Dr. Muir characterized Dr. Stans as a careerist, an opportunist, not a team player. Would you agree with any of that?"

"I agree that that's Karen's view. Not my experience with Allegra, though. First-rate mind there—like Karen's."

"And Dr. Muir's contention that Dr. Stans was angling for her job?"

"Again, not my experience. And ridiculous on its face: Karen is on the senior management committee—one of the leaders of this company. One of its owners. Maybe Allegra made mention, once upon a time, of what she might like to do someday, but she was spitballing. I dunno why Karen would feel threatened."

"You and Dr. Muir never discussed it?"

An irritated wrinkle spread across his brow. "She might've said something. Can't say it had much traction with me."

"So . . . Dr. Stans stood no chance of promotion?"

"Nonsense. Had a great future here. Moved her to R&D to position her for it."

"What were you going to promote her to?"

"Had a few things in mind. Opening up our own production labs overseas—thought she might like to run with that. Also thinkin' about a research institute at a med school in the city—thought she might like a hand in that. Plenty of things for her. Plenty."

"You spoke to her about these things?"

"'Course I did," Hasp said.

"And?"

"And she hadn't decided yet; she was giving 'em a think. My impression, anyway."

"You never tried to reconcile things between them—Dr. Stans and Dr. Muir? Clear the air between your stepsister and business partner, and one of your most talented employees? It seems like it might've been a worthwhile effort, no?"

Hasp's laugh was like a bark. "*Reconcile?* Ha! Might as well try reconciling a match and gasoline, Myles. Just no point to it. Get a damn big fire and a mess to clean up after. Too much alike, those two." He looked discreetly at his watch.

I nodded slowly. "Let's move on, then, to Special Project 1107."

Dr. Hasp refrained from going white or fainting, or breaking out all over in a cold sweat. Instead he gazed blankly at me for a while and nodded. Finally, he said: "I won't ask about your sources—s'pect you wouldn't say—but if you know enough to ask about that project, then you know I can't tell you anything. Not without a go-ahead from our sponsors, and they've not said so."

"Are you referring me to Director Elkort, then?"

Hasp shook his head regretfully. "I'm not saying anything other than that I can't say anything. Sorry." He checked his watch again, less discreetly this time.

"How about adjectives, Doctor—are you permitted those? Can you say if Special Project 1107 is, for example, *long-running*? How about *large*? Or *profitable*? Can you say if it's *financially important* to the company? Can you say if it's been *successful* thus far?"

Another head shake, with less regret. "I can tell you again that Allegra Stans had nothing whatsoever to do with 1107. Never worked on it, never contributed to it. No involvement. Beyond that . . ." Hasp looked at his watch again, elaborately now. He stood, brushed off his jeans, and looked down at me. "If that's all, Myles, I have a lunch."

"Sad to say, it's not all, Dr. Hasp. I have two other items. First, has Ondstrand Biologic ever been involved in the manufacture of synthetic neurotoxins?"

Hasp strode to his desk and stood behind his chair. He looked down at his desktop as if his memory lay there. "Synthetic neurotoxins," he said after a while, "yes, that was something we looked at a number of years ago—had to be six years back or longer. Lots of interest then on the potential of compounds found in certain snake venoms as the bases for analgesics, chemotherapeutic agents for some cancers, and so forth. 'Course, it's not easy stuff to come by in nature, not in quantity, and not without risk, so we looked at engineering some stem-cell lines that could synthesize the stuff. Looked at antivenins, too. Actually, grew some venom sacs—in a test tube, as it were. Even tweaked the genome a bit to fine-tune the behavior of the compounds. Interesting stuff, but it didn't prove out commercially. Too expensive, and it could never scale. Why?"

"Who conducted that research?"

"That? That was an R&D project, which was under Piers at the time. Why do you ask?"

I shook my head. "Now just one more thing, Doctor: I'd like to run through your activities and whereabouts this past Thursday, from four that afternoon until eleven that night. As thoroughly and accurately as you can, and do leave the assessments of relevance to me, please."

CHAPTER FORTY-ONE

Monday Afternoon

Caroline Drucker was at her desk on Monday afternoon, looking none the worse for the many hours she'd spent there over the weekend. The remnants of food and drink were gone, as were the stacks of paper, and her desktop was strict in its order. Caro's expression, when I walked through her office door, was likewise. She glanced behind me, through her glass walls, out to where her assistant and staff were studiously ignoring my presence. I closed the door behind me.

"You know," she said in a low voice, "I'd resolved myself to forgetting about everything we discussed this past week, pretending I don't know anything, just doing my job until someone comes to tell me I no longer have it—and that's been working for me so far today. No stolen documents to contend with, no malware, none of that. And then you waltz in again."

I smiled thinly and took a seat. "I hardly waltzed. And by all means, continue with your denial—I'm not here to disrupt it. I merely have what I hope is a simple request."

"Is it about that fucking project?"

"As it happens."

She leaned back in her chair and folded her arms across her chest. "I have no access—you know that. The data is gone."

"I don't want project documents. I want data from your Human Resources Department." She squinted at me. "I want to know what staff are, or were, assigned to work on the Special Project 1107. Can you get me that—names and dates of assignments?"

"HR data?" she asked, and raised an eyebrow. I nodded, and Caro took up one of her keyboards. "Yes, that I can get."

· · ·

The clouds were a heavy gray lid by the time I left Caro in her office and walked back to Ondstrand House, and a cold, gusty spatter had begun. I buttoned my suit jacket and turned up the collar, but in truth I barely felt the rain: between my conversation with Hasp, and the information Caro had provided, I had gathered a few more coins, and for the first time I thought my collection might add up to something.

I hung my jacket and dried my hair when I returned to my rooms, and before I could ring Goss Ivessen, he called me. The screen, when it came into focus, showed another row of overloaded bookshelves, different from the usual run, with ancient-looking textbooks dominant. Ivessen's battered hands skittered across a keyboard at the edge of the frame.

"You read my mind," I said.

"If, as a change of pace, your mind was wondering what you could do for me."

"What might that be?"

"I'd like someone to pay Jacob Hanro a visit. He seems to think he can avoid answering our questions by not returning calls. Location services place him in the city—occasionally at his home, more often at the hospital where he practices, or the medical school where he lectures. I'd like someone to knock on his door and remind him that we are not optional."

"How many times have you tried him?"

"Three times at home, twice at the medical school, and four times at the hospital, including today's calls. I could get an odd-job to do it, but I thought, if we were going to have actual eyes on, you might want to pick the eyes."

I nodded. "I'll have a think."

"If you weren't calling about Hanro, what did you want?"

"I saw Hasp today," I said, and then told him what I'd learned. When I finished, Ivessen was quiet for a while, and I could hear his cat muttering somewhere in the darkened room.

Ivessen took a deep breath. "Is it my imagination, or did Hasp go out of his way to point you at Piers Witmer?"

I nodded. "There was something of the sandwich board to it. His confession of having withheld information about Stans and Witmer became a less-than-subtle insinuation that Witmer might have had a motive for murder, and with all that talk of newfound energy and focus and confidence, he seemed to be suggesting that Witmer's behavior has changed in the past several months."

"Perhaps he's been taking testosterone," Ivessen said dryly. "Or synthetic venom. Did your question about that rattle Hasp?"

"Hard to say. He did inquire as to why I was interested, which was more curiosity than he showed about my other queries. My questions about Stans's demotion elicited the same sort of pablum I've gotten from him thus far. Her demotion wasn't a demotion at all; her future at Ondstrand was bright; she and Muir had irreconcilable conflicts due to their being too much alike. It was just mush. Better, though, than his answers to my questions about Special Project 1107, which were nonexistent."

A tapping sound came from Ivessen's end—the deliberative drumming of his fingers. "It's hardly dispositive, though," he said after a while, "his lack of curiosity about your line of questioning, his evasiveness about Project 1107."

I nodded. "And his ham-handed implication of Witmer?"

"Perhaps he genuinely suspects him and didn't know what to do with his suspicions."

"Perhaps."

"What about Thursday—was Hasp able to account for his time?"

I nodded. "He left here in the morning, not long after I'd seen him in the dining room, and drove to the city. He met with bankers there, had lunch with the CEO of a biotech start-up, and then drove back. On his way, he stopped at the airport and met Karen Muir's flight from overseas. He dropped her off at her house in Slocum and then returned to Ondstrand House, first to his office, where he worked for several hours, and eventually to the Cottage, where he ate some eggs, drank some wine, and went to sleep.

"His sister's flight arrived at two-thirty that afternoon. Hasp reports dropping her at her house at around five-thirty. Ondstrand's access systems marked him present in the main house at five-fifty-eight and recorded his exit from the building at eleven-oh-nine."

Ivessen made a noise of consideration. "Sounds plausible, and confirmed by the logs, too. So your meet with Hasp wasn't entirely a waste of time."

"It wasn't a waste at all," I said. "When Hasp pointed out again that Allegra had never been assigned to Project 1107, it gave me the idea to check on who *had* been assigned to that project. Caroline Drucker was able to supply that information."

He chuckled. "Do tell."

"It turns out that quite a large number of people have been assigned to that project since its inception, though never very many at once, and never for long. Project 1107 maintains a small staff—never more than five researchers assigned, and always relatively junior ones—but it has the highest turnover rate by far of any project in the company. No one has stayed on it for longer than eleven months before being reassigned, with the average assignment period being nine months. The exception being Karen Muir herself."

"That *is* rather interesting."

"I thought so, too. More interesting still is the case of Alan Prather, a young researcher—a geneticist—who was reassigned after only five months."

"A very short time."

"Yes. He was moved out of Special Projects to Trials. Two months after that, he left the company."

"Terminated?"

"The HR records don't say so."

"When did all this happen?"

"That's the most interesting part. Dr. Prather was transferred off of Project 1107 seven months back."

"That's when—"

"When Allegra Stans was transferred from Special Projects back to R&D."

Ivessen's shadow nodded. "Correlation, causation, or mere coincidence?"

"Those are the questions. I have no contact information for Prather—"

"I'll take care of it," Ivessen said.

"And I'll call Leila Vroman again."

"That friend of Stans's who was posted overseas?"

I nodded. "It turns out I have some follow-up questions."

"About Prather?"

"Amongst other things."

"You can discuss him with Dr. Muir and Dr. Witmer, too, when you ask after their whereabouts last Thursday."

I nodded. "I haven't forgotten. Have you spoken with Halsell, Silber, or Blom?"

"Halsell and Silber had credible stories. He was in his office until six-thirty in the evening, then spent an hour or so accompanying members of his team on a segment of their nighttime rounds—a new configuration of patrol areas. He left the campus at nine-oh-two and arrived at his house in Soligstrand at ten-fifteen or thereabouts, having stopped at a nearby grocery first, to purchase milk, tea, granola, yogurt, and toilet paper. He paid with his bank card.

"Silber was in her office until eight-forty-five or so, with a break for dinner in the staff cafeteria. The Ondstrand access system has her leaving the main building at eight-fifty-two and entering the old stables, where she has an apartment, at nine-oh-four. There's no record of her leaving the building after that until the next morning."

"And Ms. Blom?" I asked.

"Thus far, no story at all from Ms. Blom."

CHAPTER FORTY-TWO

Monday Night

There were hours until Leila Vroman's morning, and aside from excursions for coffee and sandwiches, I spent them drawing diagrams. They were nothing elaborate: some were a kind of flowchart, with circles for people, rectangles for places, arrows for the movement of people between places, and, in the white spaces, my annotations of dates and times and questions; others were time lines—recent and not-so-recent events in the life of a person of interest, strung out chronologically, also with notes and questions. Plenty of questions—decidedly more than there were answers.

Who had Allegra met that Saturday morning, after she left the cave, and where had she met that person? How had she re-entered Ondstrand House undetected by the access-control systems? Who had Ian Stiles expected to meet in the woods behind the abandoned equestrian center? Why had his killer switched on Allegra's phone again, almost certainly knowing the authorities would notice the signal and track it? And why had his killer taken Stiles's phone away? What had Allegra found in the Special Project 1107 documents that had sent her back for more? And what more had she found, and what had she done with it? And what had prompted her to decide, just a few weeks back, to leave Ondstrand Biologic, to forgo whatever murky arrangements she had made—presumably through Stiles—with another employer, and instead to leave the country altogether—to go with Jens-Edvard to Playa Arcadia?

I laid my sheets on the sitting-room floor and wandered around in stockinged feet, looking at them from different angles. Regardless of vantage point, the flowcharts seemed still to depict motion without meaning—or at least insufficient meaning. Petra Witmer sketches on the cliffs above the beach. Terrence Hasp picks up his half-sister at the airport. Alan Prather is reassigned, then departs. The linen service delivers its load a day late. Still just free-floating facts. I needed a narrative to make sense of them all, and thus far I had none. Or perhaps I had too many, but not one of them satisfying.

I raised the shade and looked out at the sleeping façade of Ondstrand House. Lit windows were few and far between, and the plashing of the courtyard fountain more distant than the sea. The fountain statuary were hunched in uneasy slumber, dreaming of conspiracy. My watch pinged, telling me it was time to call Leila Vroman.

Though perhaps, from her perspective, it was not quite time. In semi-darkness, her lean, freckled face was blurred with sleep, and her large gray eyes were mostly shut. She brushed straw-colored bangs from her eyes, wrestled for a moment with bedsheets and the tee shirt that was her nightgown, sat up against her pillows, and squinted at me.

"Agent Myles?" she said, fumbling for her glasses. Her voice was a smoky rasp.

"'Myles' will do."

"Yes, yes—'Myles' will do—I remember. I just need some coffee. Can you give me a sec?"

"Please," I said.

Vroman heaved herself from bed and carried me along to her kitchen. Her image lurched and bounced, and I saw over her shoulder the large bare windows of her apartment and, beyond, a dense cityscape of new towers, tangled roadways, and a harbor already bustling under a barely risen sun.

"I assume it's about Allie," she said. "Have you made progress? Do you have someone in custody?" She leaned me on the kitchen counter, and I saw the underside of cabinets and the lights on her ceiling, and heard the sounds of coffee being scooped, water running, a brewer doing its important work.

"Not yet," I said. "I'm hoping you can help me again."

Vroman returned to the frame, looking straight down into her phone's camera. "Tell me how."

"Let's start with Alan Prather. Do you know the name?"

She thought for a moment. "Genetics, right? Wiry, blond-haired guy—a cyclist, I think. Left the company several months back. Worked in Trials, and in Projects before that—on one of those engagements no one could talk to anyone else about. Which seems like half of the projects in Projects."

"That sounds right."

"What about him?"

"Do you know if he and Allegra had any sort of relationship?"

"You mean: Did they sleep together?"

"Any sort of relationship. Sleeping together qualifies."

"Hang on a sec," Vroman said, and disappeared from my screen. In a moment she was back, steaming coffee mug in hand. She took a sip and sighed deeply. Color came into her face. "Yes, I remember Allie saying something about him. It was last year—back when she was still in Projects, I think."

"What did she say?"

"Not very much, really. That he was training for a triathlon and wanted to run with the club—that's how they got together. That they had slept together a few times. That he was eager to please, smart—though not as smart as he thought—and a bit annoying. I don't think it was much of a relationship—certainly not anything that lasted more than a couple of weeks, if that. Not an unusual circumstance for Allie. As I said, it was a while ago—before she was sent back to R&D. Do you think Prather had something to do with her death?"

"No, not directly."

Vroman drank some more coffee, picked me up, and carried me over to a window. "'Not directly'? What does that mean?" She drank more coffee, and even on my screen I could see gears turning in her head. "Her episode with Prather was just before she went back to R&D," Vroman said. "And, if I remember right, it was just before he went to Trials. Do you think those were related?"

"Do you have reason to think they would be? When I asked you last week about her transfer back to R&D, you weren't able to tell me much. You said that you and Dr. Stans didn't discuss it."

"We didn't, but I've been thinking about it since you asked. It *was* out of the blue, that transfer, and, prior to it happening, Allie had never mentioned having problems with Muir. Not that she would have, of course."

"What does that mean?"

Vroman drank some more coffee. "Allie wasn't a big one for sharing, not about things that were important to her—emotionally important, I mean. If something meant a lot to her, in a good way or a bad way, she wasn't one to go on and on about it. Or to go on at all, actually. If she'd had a significant problem with Karen Muir, she wouldn't have complained. She wouldn't have brooded on it, either—that wasn't her way."

"What was her way, then?"

"Allie would've found a solution to whatever her problem was, some way to deal with it."

I nodded and watched a jet climb into the brightening sky over Leila Vroman's head. I thought about what she'd said: "If something meant a lot to her, in a good way or a bad way, she wasn't one to go on and on about it. Or to go on at all, actually."

"Do you think you would've known if Dr. Stans had had a lover in the area?" I asked. "A local, I mean."

"You mean, would Allie have told me if she was sleeping with a cow farmer in Soligstrand?"

"Yes, that's what I mean."

"I suppose so. Why not?"

"If it was someone she cared about—a relationship that was important to her?"

Leila Vroman squinted. "Maybe not," she said. "Probably not. Why— was there someone? Was that person involved in her death?"

I shook my head. "Not to my knowledge."

Vroman pursed her lips. "It's all a one-way street with you, isn't it?"

"I'm afraid so. Do you know the name Ian Stiles?"

"Is he the local?"

"Please, Dr. Vroman."

"Sorry. No, I don't know an Ian Stiles, and don't think I've ever heard the name."

"How about Jens-Edvard Neumann?"

She thought for a while. "Also not a name to me. Sorry, Myles. Anything else?"

I shook my head. "I'll leave you to your coffee."

CHAPTER FORTY-THREE

Tuesday Morning

The equinox was more than a week away, but, nevertheless, Tuesday morning felt like the first morning of spring. The breeze off the ocean was capering and scrubbed clean, and as it came onshore, it spread the scents of new grass, freshly turned earth, and rising pine sap. The sky was cornflower, the climbing sun a polished yellow glass. It promised warmth by midday, and when I pulled into the Witmers' courtyard, before noon, it had already delivered. I left my jacket in the car, loosened my tie, and rolled up my sleeves. I hadn't slept much since my talk with Leila Vroman—hadn't slept at all, really—but I was full of eggs, coffee, toast, and a sense of forward motion. I had hold of a thread; I was tugging at it gingerly, and I could feel it unraveling, one stubborn stitch at a time.

The green sedan was parked in the courtyard, still muddy, and so was the blue station wagon. Its hatch was open, and Petra Witmer, in paint-spattered jeans, tee shirt, and trainers, was loading cardboard boxes. She paused when I pulled in and watched me lower the canvas top and fasten it down. Her face was pale and exhausted.

"You here for me, toad?" she said.

I shook my head. "Not this visit. I'm looking for your husband. They told me at Ondstrand that he was out ill today."

She made a mirthless laugh. "Out ill, eh? Guess that's one way to say it."

"What's the other?"

"Getting over one hangover by working on the next."

"Is that a usual thing?" I asked.

"It didn't use to be. But since you got here . . ." She loaded another box into the car.

"Are you going somewhere?" I asked.

"To my parents in Fredligstad. I took the kids last week. I'm just picking up a few things. I have to set up a new studio."

"Is your move permanent?"

She nodded slowly. "I think so. It's just not worth it anymore. Why—is leaving town forbidden?"

"Not as long as I know where to find you."

She shrugged. "Well, now you know, toad." I nodded, and she turned back to her boxes. "He's inside," she said.

Piers Witmer was in his study, sprawled in the rolling chair behind his desk, with his bare feet on the windowsill and his head lolling back. He wore jeans, unbuttoned and partially unzipped, an unbuttoned blue-striped shirt with sweat stains at the armpits, and a whiskey-spotted tee shirt beneath. He had the velvet drapes and the window open wide, and he was staring blankly at the lovely sky.

The wreckage he drifted in was the work of days. There was a whiskey bottle on the desk, open, half empty, and two others, entirely empty, in the waste bin. Despite the ample ventilation, the room smelled of liquor, sweat, old food, and fear. And perhaps a touch of vomit. His desk was littered with paper, except for a swath by his computer where papers had been swept aside in what looked like a single angry stroke. The Director's voice was with me again as I took it all in: "If his equity was valuable enough then to compel Dr. Witmer's compliance, what might its larger size compel now?"

Witmer was still for a moment after I entered, then swiveled in my direction.

"God," he muttered. "You."

I sat in one of his guest chairs. "Forgive me for interrupting your—what?—self-indulgence?"

"Screw you, Myles." I stared at him and said nothing, and he went paler. "What—will you have me killed now?"

"Is there a particular reason I should?"

He waved a dismissive hand. "I'm not going to do your job for you. Come up with your own damn reasons."

"What's the matter with you, Dr. Witmer?"

"You haven't heard that my wife has left me? Took the kids and all."

I nodded. "I saw her outside."

Witmer stumbled on the words. "There you go, then—doesn't that explain what's wrong?"

"So . . . all this is about the state of your marriage?"

Another dismissive wave, and he swung back to the window. The movement compromised his balance, and he leaned and lurched dangerously for a moment, as if in an unsteady canoe. "What do you want?" he said when he'd recovered.

"I have questions," I said. "On several topics."

"I'm not sure I have answers on any topic. And if I do, I'm not sure I'm in any shape to give them."

"I don't mind that you're drunk; it works to my advantage. Please, feel free to have more."

"You know, you're a fucking prick, Myles."

I nodded. "Alan Prather—you know the name?"

Witmer wobbled again. He brought a foot to the floor but did not turn towards me. "Prather?"

"Alan Prather. He used to work for you in Trials."

"For me?" Witmer said, and performed a moment of thought. "A young guy? Geneticist?"

"That's him."

"He worked three or four layers down from me, and not for long. He transferred in from Projects and left the company a couple of months later."

"Why did he leave?"

Witmer shrugged. "A better job? Better prospects? Why're you asking me?"

"His prospects at Ondstrand were not promising?"

"You'd do better talking to Karen—Dr. Muir—about him. He worked in Projects longer than he worked in Trials."

"She transferred him out of Projects. Do you know why?"

He shrugged again. "Talk to her. I assume she didn't think he belonged there."

"I understand he worked on Special Project 1107."

His other foot found the ground, and he steadied himself with a hand on the windowsill. "If you're asking about it, you know I can't answer."

"Which is a curiously similar response to one I got from Dr. Hasp."

"Is it surprising that we'd have a consistent response?"

"It just makes me wonder who that answer best serves. Perhaps you should have a think about that, too."

He swiveled to face me, and his cheeks were red. "What the hell does that mean?"

I shrugged at him. "Let's leave that for the moment and talk about Ian Stiles."

Witmer was still for a moment and then swiveled back to the window. "Who?" he said quietly.

"Ian Stiles, Doctor. A recently dead man."

"I don't know him."

"*Didn't* know him. As I said, he's dead now. By the way, is his death really news to you?"

"I told you, I don't know him—*didn't* know him. How would I know that he died?"

"I expect we'll get to that, Doctor. But before we do, I suppose I should clarify: Mr. Stiles didn't simply keel over dead of some natural cause; Mr. Stiles was murdered. Did you really not know?"

A shudder went through Witmer's frame, and for a moment I thought he might vomit. He didn't. "How would I know? How would I know anything about that—I didn't know this person."

"Perhaps you'd seen him with Dr. Stans—they were acquainted, after all. Perhaps you had some other mutual acquaintance. Perhaps you met him or spoke to him without ever having learned his name. Do you think that's possible?"

Witmer shook his head, which seemed to make him dizzy. He leaned forward and gripped the windowsill again. "I didn't know anyone Allegra knew, unless they worked at Ondstrand, and no one by that name worked at Ondstrand. How . . . how did he . . . how was he killed?"

"Someone took his gun from him—he carried a gun, by the way—stuck it in his mouth, and blew the back of his head off. Does any of that strike a chord, Doctor?"

His gaze still out the window, his back to me, Witmer shook his head. "What . . . what are you saying?"

"It's what you say now that matters, Doctor. I'd like you to account for your time on Thursday last, from four in the afternoon until eleven in the evening. I'd like you to be as specific and detailed as possible."

Witmer's voice was choked when he answered. "Do I need legal counsel?"

"Feel free, Doctor; it makes no difference to me. But understand that whether you have legal counsel or not has no bearing on my questions, or on my authority to compel you to answer them. Which, believe me, I will."

Witmer turned to look at me. He wiped a hand across his mouth. I crossed my ankles, and he twitched. "I . . . I was at the lab until around five or so," he said. "Then I left and drove to Soligstrand. I went to the bookstore there—I'd ordered some volumes, and they'd called to tell me they were available. I browsed in the store for a while, until . . . I'm not sure what time. Then I had dinner in town—at a place called The Sun Spot. I drove home after that. I'm not sure when I got back—maybe at eight or eight-thirty. I was here for the rest of the night."

"Can anyone corroborate that? Was your wife with you at all?"

"No, I was alone."

"Your wife wasn't here?"

"She was at her parents' place, with the children."

"How about in Soligstrand? Did you see anyone or speak with anyone?"

"I saw people in the bookstore—other customers, the booksellers. They can confirm that I was there. And the waiter at The Sun Spot—he'll remember me."

"And you left there at what time?"

"I told you, I'm not sure—seven-thirty maybe, maybe seven-forty-five. I'm not sure."

"How did you pay for dinner?"

"With cash."

I nodded. "Did you make any calls on Thursday, or take any, either before you left your office, while you were out, or at home? And bear in mind, Doctor, we will check your phone records."

Witmer colored and ran a hand through his hair. "I spoke with Terry—Dr. Hasp—before I left for Soligstrand. He was calling from his car. He was on his way back from the city."

"What did you talk about?"

"Several things: trial results we're due to release, a new trial we're planning, a lunch he'd had with the head of a start-up. Karen was on the call, too—she was in his car."

"How long did you speak?"

"Twenty minutes—no longer than that."

I nodded. "And you made no other stops that evening, and saw no other people? You spoke to no one?"

He colored again and looked at his naked feet. "Before the bookstore, I stopped at a wine store. Strand Spirits. I bought three bottles of this." He pointed at the whiskey bottle on his desk. "They'll remember me there—they know me."

"I'm sure," I said. "Just to make certain I understand, Doctor, you're saying that no one can corroborate your whereabouts from roughly seven-forty-five Thursday evening until—when?—your arrival at work on Friday?"

Witmer looked at me as his thoughts shuffled through a fog of fear and alcohol. "I . . . I suppose so. I didn't see anyone until I got to campus on Friday."

"And that was when?"

"About nine. I was later than usual. I wasn't feeling well."

I tapped his waste bin with the toe of my shoe. The whiskey bottles clinked. "No doubt."

His eyes flashed. "Screw you."

"Have a care, Doctor."

"Is *this* where you threaten my life?"

"Not just yet. But some caution on your part is warranted, I think. Do you know the children's game of musical chairs?"

He squinted at me. "What the hell are you talking about?"

"Surely you know it: the music plays, the children parade around a line of chairs—always one chair less than there are children—the music stops without warning, the children race to claim a seat, and the child not quick enough is *eliminated*, let's say. You must know it."

Witmer squinted more. "I don't know what you're talking about."

I shrugged. "No? Perhaps I've been too opaque. Let me be more direct: You're in a game of diminishing seats, Dr. Witmer, playing with someone who is not observing the rules. Your fellow player controls the music, Doctor, and knows when it will stop. And when it does, you may find yourself alone, standing in the cold."

Witmer swiveled away from me, towards the window again. "I don't understand you," he said, putting his bare feet up. "And I don't have time for this."

I stood, stepped behind the desk, and kicked his chair out from under him. It careened into the wall with a crack and fell on its side, one arm broken. Witmer was on his ass, his face a white mask of shock, confusion, and fear. I grabbed his collar, hoisted him upright, and threw him against the window. It was like throwing a rag doll. He slumped on the sill, shaking. I dusted my palms and leaned next to him.

"Do you understand now, Doctor? No place to sit." Witmer gulped for air but said nothing. "You've put a lot into Ondstrand Biologic, and have much to lose there. But make no mistake, Dr. Witmer, you have considerably more than money at risk now."

"I . . . I don't know what you want me to say." His voice was small and shaky, close to tears.

"Right now? Right now that's simple: I want you to talk about synthetic neurotoxins."

CHAPTER FORTY-FOUR

Tuesday Afternoon

Petra Witmer was still in the courtyard when I emerged from the house, smoking a cigarette now, and kicking the toe of her trainer against a car tire.

"I have more boxes than space," she said.

"It's often the way with moving."

She nodded. "I heard a crash. Did you kill him?"

I smiled. "Not yet. Not even grievous bodily harm."

"I suppose that's good."

"As it happens, I have some questions for you now."

She took a drag on her cigarette and nodded. "If you help me with these." She kicked a box.

"That'll depend on the answers. When did you take your children to your parents' farm?"

She squinted at me. "Last week. Thursday afternoon, after school."

"And when did you next return here?"

"Today, early. Why?"

I shook my head. "And that boat you saw on the day Allegra was killed, the skiff, you'd seen it before, yes?"

Petra's cheeks colored. "I . . . possibly. Probably."

"Do you know who it belongs to?"

"No! I didn't know then and I don't now."

"But you knew that Allegra was in the cave the morning she was killed."

"I didn't! I didn't *know*."

"You suspected, then."

She nodded slowly. "I suppose. But I didn't *see* Allie that Saturday, not at all!"

"On another Saturday, though?"

Petra breathed out smoke and looked at her cigarette. "I wasn't following her, toad, if that's what you think—that's *not* something I go in for. She just happened to be there when I was up on the cliff—at least I think it was her. It was two months ago or more, and I only caught a glimpse of someone going into the cave. The skiff was up on the beach already, and there were footprints from it leading to the cave. I didn't see anyone else, and I certainly didn't wait around or go snooping."

"But you didn't see fit to mention any of this to me."

Her cheeks colored again. "I didn't want you to think I was stalking her, or anything like it. I'm not like some—it was a *coincidence* I saw her out there when I did, nothing more. And it was *months* ago. Besides, I *did* tell you about the boat—I even gave you pictures."

I nodded, and some of the tension went out of Petra's face. "'Not like some'—what did you mean by that? Who are you thinking of?" The tension came back. She dropped her cigarette, made a production of grinding it into the cobbles with her heel, but said nothing. "Was someone else out there the day Allegra died," I asked, "on the cliff or the beach or anywhere nearby?"

"Not on that day, not that I saw."

"On other Saturdays?"

She kept her eyes on the stones. "That Sandra somebody. I didn't see her on the Saturday Allie died, but she was out there most of the Saturdays I was there. She was jogging, I suppose. But she was also scanning for Allie, like she had radar, and shooting me dirty looks whenever she noticed me."

"Sandra? Sandy Silber?"

Petra nodded. "Sandy. Allie slept with her a few times, years back, when the girl was working part-time at Ondstrand, and couldn't shake her afterwards, or so she told me."

"Like bubble gum on her shoe," I said, recalling Celia in the hair salon.

Petra squinted at me. "That's just what Allie used to say. She said Sandy was borderline obsessed with her."

"Is that what earned you the dirty looks?"

"I suppose. There was a time or two, when Allie and I were in Soligstrand, that she saw—or thought she saw—Sandy. Allie thought she was following us."

"And you'd seen her on the cliffs before?" Petra nodded. "But not the Saturday in question?"

"If I had, I would've told you. But just because I didn't see her doesn't mean she wasn't there."

I thought for a while, then nodded. "True enough," I said.

Petra smiled, relieved. "You gonna lend a hand with these boxes, then?"

I was driving through the main gate of the Ondstrand campus when Ivessen called, and I propped my phone on the dash and watched his tiny shadow while I sat in Allegra's car, in the gravel lot.

"I'm really not sure what to make of it," he said. "Domestic guarded these clearance packages as if they were the bloody orb and scepter— I honestly expected to find something that would sear my eyes out when I read it. And I suppose it is shocking in one way—surprising, at any rate, while possibly having no relevance at all."

"I'd be pleased to offer up a view, if I knew what the hell you were talking about."

Ivessen chuckled to himself. "Of course. Well, operating under the principle that forgiveness is easier than permission, I decided to forgo waiting any longer for Domestic to produce the Ondstrand security clearance packages, and to ignore the Director's suggestions about discretion and patience—"

"Those weren't actually suggestions."

He laughed. "You say potato . . . Let's agree that, one way or another, the packages were liberated, and I had a look."

"*Shit*, Ivessen!"

"Don't fret, Myles—I'm too old and damaged to waste punishments on."

"I was worried more about me, thanks—I *am* responsible for your antics. But what I'm mostly fretting about is when you'll get to the punch line."

He chuckled again. "Patience, Myles—foreplay is one of the few pleasures left to the aged. So, as for punch lines—with the exception of a couple of driving-while-impaired charges and a murky domestic-violence report, there wasn't actually too much of interest to look at. Until I got to Hasp and Muir."

"Yes . . . and?"

"And it turned out that Terrence and Karen didn't meet first at that private school in the Lakelands."

"No?"

"No, they met years earlier, when they were still schoolchildren, when Muir's father and Hasp's parents were on the faculty of Ondstrand Hall."

"They were *here*—together? Both faculty brats?"

I heard the smile in Ivessen's voice. "Yes, indeed. Wilbur Jolley taught physics there; Meriam Hasp taught literature."

"And Hasp's father?"

"He was there, too—chemistry master and head of the science departments until his big promotion."

"Promotion to what?"

"To headmaster, of course," Ivessen said, and let it sit there for a while.

"But Hasp—"

"'Hasp' is his mother's maiden name. He had his changed after his parents divorced and his mother became his sole guardian. Prior to that, he was Terrence Roeg, and his father was Ondstrand Hall's last headmaster, the notorious Jerome Roeg."

I let out a long breath. "Hasp was in university when the scandal broke at the school, no?"

"He was, and he'd left Ondstrand Hall, and his father's house, five years before."

"So he didn't actually graduate from Ondstrand Hall?"

"No. He left three years prior to graduation, when his parents parted ways. He and Meriam decamped to the Lakelands, and so did Jolley. Daughter Karen was just starting university then."

"Was his mother's relationship with Jolley the reason for the split?"

"That's one possibility, I suppose, though the record is silent on this. It is worth noting, however, that the divorce action was brought by Meriam Hasp, and neither it nor the custody of young Terrence was contested by Roeg."

"So, another possibility is—what?—that Meriam suspected something was amiss with Roeg?"

"Suspected or discovered? In addition to not contesting anything, Roeg agreed to a rather large monetary settlement, to help mother and child start afresh. To me that suggests *discovered*."

I thought for a while. "I tend to agree. How long were the Jolleys here with the Hasp-Roegs?"

"Jolley came a year after Hasp, and they were together at Ondstrand for four years."

"And so, too, were their children."

"Yes," Ivessen said, "from when young Terrence was ten and Karen was fourteen. Vulnerable ages. Impressionable ages."

"I believe they're all vulnerable, impressionable ages."

"Yes, of course," Ivessen said, as close to apologetic as I'd ever heard him.

"And Domestic had a cordon around all this why?"

"I don't know. It could make things awkward for Hasp, especially amongst investors, bankers, and prospective customers. I suppose it might make some of them skittish. Perhaps that's why Domestic had an interest in suppressing this—all a part of not upsetting the Ondstrand applecart or any of those government-sponsored projects."

"Perhaps," I said, but I was skeptical. "Which brings us back to your original question: the relevance of this to our problem."

"And your view, now that you know what the hell I'm talking about?"

I shook my head. "I have no idea."

CHAPTER FORTY-FIVE

Tuesday Evening

I found Sandy Silber in the staff cafeteria, alone at a table with a bowl of soup and a thick file folder open before her. She didn't notice me until I was standing beside her. She looked up, blinking.

"Agent Myles—I didn't know you were still here." She wore jeans and a jumper over a polo shirt. Her cropped hair was combed back smooth, caught in place with clips shaped like butterflies. Her face was pale beneath her freckles and her eyes were large as she stared up at me, like a kitten interrupted at a milk saucer. "Is there something I can do for you?" she asked.

I sat down opposite her and spoke quietly. "I'd like you to pack up your things and accompany me outside. When we get there, you will have a decision to make: either you can tell me when and where you last saw Allegra Stans alive, or I can call a transport and have you moved off-site for more structured questioning. This will be annoying for me and decidedly traumatic for you, but with the inevitable result of you telling me what I want to know. I do recommend the former course of action, but the choice is yours."

Sandy Silber's face was completely still for a moment, and then her mouth opened but made no sound. I reached across the table and closed her file folder.

"Come," I said. I got up and started for the cafeteria entrance. When I was halfway there, I turned around. Silber was still at her table, still frozen, staring at me. I crooked a finger at her. She rose, shakily, and walked towards me, and it was clear that there was little connection between her mind and her body. I could see her knees quivering.

When she reached me, she took a stab at speech. "I . . . I don't know what—"

I cut her off. "Please, don't speak, Dr. Silber. I don't want you to compound your problems with more lying. I have a witness who saw you on the cliffs on the Saturday morning when Dr. Stans was killed, and saw you following her. So do keep silent until we get outside. Then you can tell me your decision."

I took her by the arm and led her from the cafeteria. She was trembling. We were nearly at the elevator when she spoke. "I have to pee," she said. Her voice was soft and flat. "I think I might be sick."

I nodded. "Common stress reactions. There's a washroom just ahead." I led her to it, and she seemed barely to notice when I followed her in. There was no one else there, and I held the stall door open for her. "I'll be right here," I said.

She did in fact have to pee and vomit and hyperventilate, and she spent perhaps twenty minutes at it. I made cold compresses from paper towels and helped her clean up afterwards, and I stood by while she sat on the toilet with her head hanging between her legs. When her breathing had returned to something like normal, she looked up at me.

"I don't want to go . . . off-site," she said. Her voice was small and impossibly young.

I nodded. "No one does." I put a hand on her shoulder. "The best thing for it is to tell me the truth."

She nodded. "I need air."

"We'll go outside, and you can show me where things happened."

saw her on that Saturday morning," Sandy Silber said, "but she didn't see me. I didn't speak to her or touch her or interact with her at all, and I doubt I was ever any closer than fifty meters to her." We were outside Ondstrand House now, on the terrace overlooking the beach. The sun was nearly gone, but light remained, and the clouds were pale calligraphy against the navy blue sky. The air had cooled considerably, and when Silber spoke, her breath was visible. She pointed south, to the far end of the terrace.

"I was out running—I go out nearly every Saturday morning, early. I was all but done, and was headed home, coming up to the part of the trail that runs along the cliff, just below the terrace. I usually take that to the end of the terrace, and then follow it around to the front of the main house. That Saturday, though, I saw Allie up ahead. I was at the end of the terrace when I saw her, and she was at the other end, by the stairs."

Silber traced the path with her finger, traversing the terrace, finally pointing at the top of the concrete steps. "She was taking it easy—just jogging—and following the trail that runs north along the cliff for a bit, and then into the woods. She didn't see me, and I decided to follow her."

She paused, expecting a question. "Go on," I said.

"There's not much else to tell. I followed her along the trail, into the woods. I didn't get much closer to her, but I could see her plainly. She went along the trail for maybe forty or fifty meters, and then, at the fork, she took the path that leads towards the Cottage. I saw her take that turn, and when I got there I took it, too, but I'd lost sight of her. I went down the trail, past the Cottage and the old chapel ruin and Dr. Hasp's studio, and I followed it to where it runs out of the woods, towards the main campus. The trail straightens out there, and you can easily see a quarter-mile ahead or more, but I didn't see Allie there. The trail ahead was empty, and she was gone."

I nodded. "And you saw no one else on the trail or in the woods?"

"No one."

"And no one on the beach?"

She shook her head. "I saw that boat—that launch—out in the ocean. It was *his* boat, I'm certain.

"And when you say '*his* boat,' whose boat do you mean?"

"I *told* you, Allie was seeing someone—a local. I told you about him when we first spoke."

"Yes, you did. In fact, of all the people I've spoken to, many of whom knew Dr. Stans much more intimately than you, you were the only one who mentioned her local boyfriend. I'm curious how you knew about him."

She seemed confused. "We . . . Allie and I were friends—*more* than friends."

"Were you? Dr. Stans did indeed have a boyfriend from one of the towns nearby, but she told no one about him. She certainly didn't tell you—isn't that right, Doctor? And, please, do keep in mind the consequences of lying to me at this juncture."

Silber's cheeks burned, and a shudder went through her. "She didn't tell me," she said softly.

"But you knew. How?"

"I saw her sometimes."

"*Saw* or *followed?*" I asked.

"Followed," she answered.

"Only sometimes?"

"Often."

I nodded. "Did you arrange your running schedule on Saturday mornings in the hopes of seeing her?" Silber nodded. "Was that effective?"

Another nod. "I . . . I saw her on the beach with him. And in the cave."

"And you saw her at other times out here, when he wasn't around?" Another nod. "Did you see her with anyone else any of those times?"

Silber shook her head. "No. She kept to a regular routine. She ran by herself, she ran fast, and she always ran the same route."

I nodded. "And did that route include the trail that leads past the Cottage and Dr. Hasp's studio?"

Sandy Silber shook her head again. "No. I never saw her take that route before, not any of the times I was with her." The wind picked up then, and Silber shuddered and hugged herself. "That's all I can tell you—really. Can we go inside now? It's cold here."

I looked at her and reached into my jacket pocket. "Soon," I said. "After you've shown me that trail." I flicked on my penlight and handed it to Silber. "Lead the way," I said.

CHAPTER FORTY-SIX

Tuesday Night

Ms. Mundt was packing up for the night when I appeared at her desk, and she wasn't pleased to see me. Karen Muir, tucking a file into a tote bag in her office, was even less so. Ms. Mundt asked if she could help me, in a way that suggested perhaps helping me off a cliff. I gave her no answer but stared at Muir through the glass wall. She stared back for a while with a look of weary resentment, then finally touched a key on her phone console. Her voice was icy as it came through Ms. Mundt's phone.

"Just send him in," she said. "Then you can go." Ms. Mundt opened the door in the glass wall, and I went through. When I looked back, the reception area was dark.

Karen Muir lifted her tote bag from her desk chair and dropped it onto her desk, next to her coat. She sat and sighed with resignation. "I supposed it would be pointless being irritated by the way you just materialize, with no appointment and no notice."

"Yes, entirely. I have some follow-up questions for you. It shouldn't take long." I didn't wait for a reply but forged ahead. "Last Thursday afternoon and night—I'd like you to account for your time."

She squinted. "The day I flew back from the conference?"

"From the time you landed until the end of the day—where you were, with whom, times."

She shook her head. "I'm not even going to ask why. Terry picked me up at the airport and dropped me at my house in Slocum. We made no stops. My flight arrived on time at two-thirty; he dropped me at home somewhere around five-thirty, I'd guess. I was home after that. I took a shower, put laundry in the washer, had a light bite to eat—soup, toast, tea—and went to bed. I was three time zones ahead, and I never sleep on the plane. I was really quite exhausted. That was my evening."

I nodded. "You saw no one during that time? Made no phone calls? No one called you?"

"No, I was blissfully alone and undisturbed. Is that a problem?"

"For you? Possibly. Do you know Ian Stiles, Doctor?"

Another practiced squint. "I do not. Is *that* a problem, too?"

I smiled. "You realize, I'm sure, that we will check your phone records to verify what we can."

She sighed. "If that's what you need to do. Who is Ian Stiles?"

"A murder victim."

Her eyes widened. "*What? Another* murder? Does this have to do with Allegra?"

"Of course it does, Dr. Muir. Why would I ask about him if it didn't? Tell me about your research into neurotoxins."

Yet another squint. "*That* research? That was years back. Three years? Five? Maybe longer. Fascinating stuff, but we hit a wall with it. Why?"

"But it was *your* research?"

"Yes. Piers helped out with stem cells, but I was the lead."

"I wonder why your brother would say otherwise."

She shrugged. "People do make mistakes, you know. And it was years ago."

"Did you retain a stockpile of the compounds?"

"We have the stem lines, certainly. And I imagine we have some product in a freezer somewhere—probably in R&D. Hardly a stockpile, I'm sure."

"And years ago was the last time you or anyone here worked with that material?"

She nodded. "Yes. Are we almost done?"

"Let's move on. To Special Project 1107."

She shook her head. "You know I can't discuss that project, not without authorization from the sponsoring client."

"I'm not asking about particulars of the project right now. Right now, I want to know why you removed all of the project documents from your servers."

Karen Muir clasped her hands in her lap, leaned back in her seat, and narrowed her eyes, and her demeanor shifted palpably, from weary, barely contained irritation to something more focused and decidedly colder.

"I'm not going to share my decision-making process with you, Agent

Myles—I don't believe I'm required to. Suffice it to say, I took steps I thought prudent in order to protect the IP of this firm and the interests of our clients."

"What happened three weeks ago that led you to believe either of those was at risk?"

She shook her head. "You were so eager to let me know, the last time we spoke, that you had access to confidential documents from this department, and so ready with your less-than-subtle suggestion that we don't take proper care of our IP here. Yet now you question steps taken for precisely that reason."

"I'm not questioning the steps, Doctor, I'm asking what—specifically—prompted them. What happened three weeks ago? The only thing I'm aware of is your meeting with Dr. Stans."

At the mention of Stans's name, something shifted in Muir again, from cool assessment to face-reddening anger. "There's apparently a great deal you're unaware of, and I'm not sure how it's my job to fill those voids—especially on topics so obviously far afield from the purpose of your presence here. Allegra Stans had nothing whatever to do with that dusty work on venom synthesis and was never involved with the project you named."

I held Karen Muir's gaze for a while, and then smiled. "Which brings me to my final question. The last time we spoke, I asked about Ondstrand House and its campus, and suggested that it was a less-than-obvious site for a corporate headquarters, especially given its rather sordid history. I didn't realize then that you shared in that history—that you had lived here for a period as a child. You neglected to mention any of that. I wonder why."

The color left Muir's face, and again she transformed. She was completely still, and her focus was on me entirely, though her gaze did not meet mine. Instead, she stared at a spot near the base of my neck, close to where my pulse throbbed against my shirt collar. Her office was perfectly quiet now but for the push of air through the ducts, the ancient shift of the ocean, and Karen Muir's uneven breath through delicately flared nostrils.

When she spoke, her voice was an icy monotone. "I suspect this is your technique when you're floundering on a case: you flail and thrash and cast absurd, provocative, or downright inflammatory questions on any topic, in every direction—all in an attempt to obscure your obvious failure." Muir didn't wait for a reply, or offer anything else on that subject, but rose, donned her coat, hoisted her tote bag onto her shoulder, and left the office. As she went, she said: "The lights will go out when you leave, and the doors will lock behind you."

CHAPTER FORTY-SEVEN

Tuesday Night

S uch full days, Myles," Director Mehta said. "And quite productive."
She was in her office, a cup of tea steaming at her elbow and the
nighttime city bright behind her—like holiday lights on black velvet.
"And ever so gently done—with no broken crockery, to speak of."

"If you call bullying a drunken man and terrifying a woman who's
already unsteady 'ever so gently.'"

The Director sighed. "You could've had both Witmer and Silber under some very bright lights indeed if you'd chosen, and no one would've
thought twice of it. No one here, certainly."

"My way was quicker."

"And it had the added benefit of protecting your delicate sensibilities."

"Not entirely," I said.

The Director smiled and drank some tea. "And now a Wednesday in
the city for you?" she asked.

I nodded. "Ivessen located Prather there, at a biotech private-equity
firm. I want to speak with him in person, and also with Jacob Hanro.
Ivessen has had trouble connecting with him, which raises all sorts of
questions."

"Indeed, and, given your conversations with Hasp, Vroman, and Witmer, Hanro's testimony may be particularly relevant. Still, no thoughts
on how Dr. Stans re-entered Ondstrand House?"

I shook my head. "Nothing that makes sense. I wondered for a while
if I was overcomplicating the problem and considered the possibility
that Stans had re-entered in the usual way, but perhaps with someone
else's ID, or that she'd somehow slipped in behind someone else and
avoided the turnstiles. But I re-watched the security footage for that
morning, and there are no breaks in any of the video feeds, and no

sign of her. And Ivessen tells me there are no obvious anomalies in the security logs. And so . . ."

"A question mark still."

I nodded, and was prepared to sign off when the Director sat back and sighed. "And speaking of your porter . . . When were you planning to mention his raid on Domestic Security?"

"I suppose I hadn't quite decided."

"I've saved you the trouble, then. I must say, I'm a bit surprised at Goss. Our brethren in Domestic may not inspire awe, but I thought he'd know that it's best not to provoke them simply for the abundant pleasure of it. Perhaps it's my own fault, though—I should've realized that once a pirate . . ."

"It wasn't simply for his own amusement. They were stonewalling us."

"Something I'm well aware of, Myles. Or did you think that that had somehow slipped my mind?"

"I didn't."

"That's some comfort. So, then, I gather that you and your porter thought my judgment flawed somehow." I shook my head. "Simple impatience, then?"

"That's probably the closest. And, just to clarify, this was on *my* initiative. Pirate or no, Ivessen was following my—"

"*Please*, Myles, let's agree: no ridiculous theater of nobility. Ivessen called me earlier; I'm well aware that you had no idea what he was up to. Which, to be clear, is a good deal more troubling than if you had. And it joins a long list of problems that arise when agents operate alone."

"I'm hardly alone."

"By which I mean without partners." I said nothing, but looked at the screen, which was preferable to meeting her gaze in person. Director Mehta shook her head in disgust. "Do you care to share your thoughts on the fruits of your transgression?" she said.

"As Ivessen might've told you, neither one of us knows quite what to make of it. It's not surprising that Hasp—or anyone, really—might want to distance himself from that kind of history. I find it a bit odd that Domestic Security would assist him in cordoning off that chapter of his life. I find it odder still, with the kind of baggage this property must carry—the personal baggage—that Hasp and Muir would choose Ondstrand House as their headquarters."

"And Dr. Muir offered no enlightenment, it seems. Nor did she seem particularly intimidated."

"Not at all," I said. "But she did remind me of someone."

"Did she?"

"Not of a particular person but ... When I was at Conservatory, there were a handful of students—one or two every year, it seemed—who were too fond of the live-fire exercises and the full-contact training. They'd get *overstimulated* by things—a bit carried away—and would have to be removed from the cadre. Almost always after more than the usual amount of blood had been spilled."

"I'm aware. What does it have to do with Dr. Muir?"

"There was something about the look in her eye when she was looking at me that reminded me of those students."

The Director nodded, though I wasn't sure if it was in agreement or simply contemplation. Finally, she said: "Enjoy the city, Myles." And then my screen went blank.

CHAPTER FORTY-EIGHT

Wednesday Morning

Allegra Stans's car embraced the motorway. It settled comfortably into its top gear, was fast and confident on the unspooling straight-aways, and sure-footed on the sweeping curves. At high speed and with the top down, the airflow carried off the world's sounds and left the cabin in a muted bubble. The road signs swept past, and evidence of civilization, mostly in the forms of filling stations and roadside fast food, proliferated as the distance to the city dwindled.

I'd been up at dawn, and out to where I'd walked the night before with Sandy Silber. The trail was lovely in the rising light, breezy and bright where it ran along the cliff, quiet and shaded where it veered into the woods, and quieter still at the fork, where it wound between mature pines and ran past Hasp's residence, the Cottage. The wood was manicured there, and it looked like the fantasy of a forest, an illustration from a children's book. But just past dawn, there'd been no halflings out strolling on the trail—no one at all, in fact.

I'd walked to where the woods thinned and the path straightened and found that Sandy Silber was right about the sight lines: they were unim-peded for at least a quarter-mile. I'd walked back toward the Cottage again and stopped where the running trail met a brick-paved footpath that I hadn't noticed the night before. It was the path I'd taken a week before, when I'd interviewed Hasp in his studio.

The bricks were uneven and bordered by a line of ancient lampposts. In one direction they curved towards Ondstrand House, and in the other toward Hasp's house and the cement slab of his studio. I walked the fifty or so meters of path, first towards Hasp's place and then towards Ondstrand House, and found nothing either way. In both directions they petered out just short of reaching a destination: consumed by pine needles at one end and lawn at the other.

I'd stood at the end close to Ondstrand House, looking at the north wing, then turned and looked towards the Cottage. Then I'd pulled out my phone and called Goss Ivessen. If I'd woken him, he gave no sign.

"That book you mentioned—the one by the local reporter, about Ondstrand Hall and Hasp's father . . ."

"The title is *Horror on the Headland: Ondstrand Hall and a Legacy of Terror.*"

"No wonder it was self-published."

"Which is why it took so long to find copies. It reads much better than its title, I must say."

"It couldn't read much worse. Who wrote it?"

"Matthew Veddar, and he did a yeoman's service on the research. A bit obsessed with his subject, I think, and likely carrying a grudge at having had his story pulled out from under him."

"Is he still alive?"

"Long gone, sad to say."

"Can you send me a copy of the book?"

"I'll arrange for a courier."

Far ahead, the new towers of the city seemed to float above the motorway. They looked delicate at this distance, like ice or spun sugar at the horizon. I started paying attention to the signs, and saw I was approaching an interchange—an exit to the ring road that would loop me around to the Dockyards district of the city, to the offices of Membrane Capital, and to Dr. Alan Prather. I downshifted and drifted across to the off-ramp.

Membrane Capital had offices at a bend of the river, on a cobblestone street, in what used to be a warehouse. It was now a brick-and-glass temple to gods of money and design. Despite all that, the place still smelled faintly of raw wood, damp rope, and creosote. It was late morning when I arrived, and few people were in the lobby besides uniformed security. They edged away at the sight of my ID, though one of them held the elevator for me.

Membrane was on the topmost floor, and its offices were like the pocket of an expensive suit—soft, quiet, in shades of gray. The better to meditate on investments in nascent biotech companies, no doubt. The receptionist was a slim young man in a white shirt and gray flannels, who became very still at the sight of my ID. I spoke softly so as not to alarm him further, asked for directions to a conference room, and asked that he call Alan Prather and direct him there as well. He pointed me down a quiet gray corridor.

"Third door on the right," he said in a whisper, and picked up his phone.

The conference room was mostly windows, with expansive views up and down the river, which was running high and fast that morning. There were, as always, whitecaps on the coffee-colored water, and much traffic amidst them—ferries, barges, and the quick neon-yellow boats of the river patrol—like exotic blossoms transplanted from the tropics. I looked to the west and could see, just a few miles away by crow, the tower that was headquarters to Standard Division. It was undistinguished architecturally, just another new spike of steel and glass against the blue sky. It seemed like a lifetime since I'd been there.

The door opened behind me, and Alan Prather came in. He looked like his pictures: young, rangy, handsome, callow, with close-cut blond hair and an opportunistic glint in his pale eyes. He stared from the doorway, a mix of irritation and curiosity on his narrow face. He wore a trim gray suit, a blue shirt, and no tie.

"Reception said I had a visitor. Do I know you?" His voice was deep but nasal.

I took out my ID and slid it across the table. Prather peered at it without picking it up. He squinted and looked at me. "Shit," he said. "What do you want with me?"

"Shut the door, please," I said, and Prather did as he was told. Then I sat, and Prather did the same. "This concerns your time at Ondstrand Biologic."

Prather scowled, and his face colored. "Ondstrand? I just talked to you people about that a few days ago."

"Which 'you people,' Dr. Prather?"

"Okay, not *you* people—I've never spoken to one of *you* before—but someone from Domestic Security called me out of the blue, like two days ago, at home. A woman from some director's office, reminding

me of the stipulations of my security clearance, and the nondisclo-
sures I'd agreed to when I hired on and separated from Ondstrand. I
don't remember the woman's name. She was from Director Elkhorn's
office."

"Elkort?"

He nodded. "Elkort—that's it."

"And what in particular did your caller want you to remember?"

"That I can't talk to anyone about anything I did at Ondstrand without written permission—in advance—from the Science and Technology Division, under penalty of fine and imprisonment. She also noted
that my separation agreement from Ondstrand forbids me from discussing the terms of my employment or reasons for separation from the
company with anyone for any reason, and that Ondstrand has the right
to sue for damages and penalties should I violate."

"Stern stuff," I said. "What did you say?"

"That I'd been over all that with my legal counsel before I signed,
and that I hadn't forgotten. How could I? The guy scared hell out of me
with stories of what they could do if I violated. So, if you're here to ask
me about any of that . . ."

"I'm not. I'm here to talk to you about Allegra Stans."

Prather leaned away from the table. His face was frozen, and color
rose in his cheeks; he glanced behind him to confirm that the door was
still closed. "What about her?"

"I'd like to know about your relationship with her."

"Relationship? What relationship? I haven't seen her since I left Ondstrand, and haven't exchanged a word with her since months before
that. Why?"

"And before? What was your relationship before all that?"

He colored more deeply. "This is really out of the blue, Mr. Myles—"

"'Myles' will do."

"As I said, this is coming out of nowhere. Yes, Dr. Stans and I know
each other—you know everybody at least a little in a place that small,
but—"

"Is that your answer—that you know her a little? Because we both
know that's not true. And while whoever called you may have blan-
dished threats of lawsuits, fines, and prison, I can assure you—the consequences of lying to me can be considerably more upsetting and occur
with much less notice."

Prather raised his hands in something like surrender. "I didn't say I didn't know her at *all*. But to say we had a *relationship*—"

"You slept with her, yes?"

Prather closed his eyes and sighed. "Three or four times maybe, like eight months ago—the biggest mistake I ever made. Why—what is she saying?"

I nodded, let some silence grow, and let Prather squirm a bit. "I have to imagine you've made plenty of mistakes in your life, Dr. Prather, even allowing for your youth, so I'm curious as to how sleeping with Dr. Stans qualifies as 'the biggest mistake.'"

Prather rubbed the back of his neck. "Is she saying something? That *I* did something? Because it was all the other way."

I smoothed my tie and brushed nothing from my jacket sleeve. "Let me ease your mind—Dr. Stans isn't saying anything at all about you or about anyone else. Dr. Stans is dead."

A small parade of emotions marched across Prather's face: surprise, relief, regret, perplexity, and fear. The last brought sweat to his hairline and brought his eyes back to mine. "What happened? You don't think I—"

"I don't, Dr. Prather, at least not yet. And your continued cooperation will give me no reason to change that view. So . . . your relationship with Dr. Stans . . . ?"

Prather wiped his brow and stared at the table. "I'm not trying to be difficult, but this *does* get into areas I'm obliged not to discuss. Obliged by Domestic Security."

I sighed. "I'm sure, Dr. Prather, that a fellow as clever as yourself can thread this needle. He might, for example, restrict his narrative only to his interactions with Dr. Stans, and only to the immediate circumstances of his transfer from Special Projects to Trials, and he might never utter the words 'Special Project 1107.' And, having heard such a narrative, I could truthfully attest that this fellow hadn't violated the obligations of whatever leash is fastened to his collar, and then that bright lad could go change his underpants, get back to moneymaking, and never see me again. Do you think my faith in you is well placed, Dr. Prather—do you think you can thread this needle?"

Alan Prather looked at me for a long moment, wiped his mouth, and nodded. "It *was* the biggest mistake I ever made—it's how I ended up here. But she was just so incredibly . . . And she was *so* damn smart.

If she wasn't, I wouldn't have opened my mouth." But he had, eight months back.

"I'd just started training with the running club, and I struggled to keep up with her—she was so fast, and so tough. Like a machine. And she hated to lose—even a training run. She barely said a word to me at those first workouts, until the evening she asked what I was doing after my shower. That was our first time." Prather sighed, shook his head, and continued.

"The second time was a few days later, after another run, and that time we didn't bother to shower first. It was just as intense, maybe more so. Afterwards, I wanted to talk. Not about any particular thing—I wasn't looking to profess my love or anything. I just thought perhaps a bit of pillow talk might be . . . I suppose I just didn't want her to leave. Stans wasn't big on conversation, though—not with me, anyway. Maybe that's why I went on and on, talking and talking. I think I was trying to hold her interest.

"We weren't supposed to discuss the project at all, not with anyone outside our immediate team. Prohibited. Strict rule. But I knew Stans had a background in AAVs, and all my problems had to do with them." He looked at me. "AAVs—those are adeno—"

"I know what they are," I said.

Prather nodded. "Well, Stans had tremendous experience with them—much more than I—and she was *smart*. My problems had to do with increasing their gene-carrying capacity—an area she'd worked in extensively. So I talked to her about it—that night and the next time we got together, and the time after that. Told her about my problems, and all about the clever solutions I was devising. . . . I was very impressive, I thought. Impossible to resist." Prather laughed bitterly.

"Was Dr. Stans duly awed?"

Prather shook his head. "Beyond a few questions, she didn't say much. She certainly didn't offer any solutions—not to me. But apparently she had plenty to say to Muir.

"A couple of days after my last time with Stans, Muir summoned me to her office and flayed the flesh off my bones. Said that I'd violated the confidentiality mandates of the project, that I was being transferred out of Special Projects immediately, that I was lucky I wasn't fired on the spot, and luckier still that the government security goons—no offense—weren't being called in.

"They moved me to Trials that afternoon. I left Ondstrand a couple of months later."

I thought for a while and nodded. "And you're sure that all of that came about because of your conversations with Dr. Stans?"

"I don't know how else to explain it. Outside of my most immediate co-workers and Karen Muir herself, Stans was the *only* person I'd ever discussed the work with. And all this took place within days of our talk. Plus, she was transferred out of Special Projects at the same time I was. How else would you interpret all that?"

I had no answer for him. "Assuming she did speak with Muir, what might her motive have been? You must've given some thought to it these past months."

Prather's face tightened. "I really try not to think about it—it does bad things to my gut and my head. But, yeah, early on I spent a lot of time on *why*."

"And?"

"And I don't know, not really. My best guess is, maybe she was trying to curry favor somehow—with Muir, or the management team as a whole. Maybe she had some ideas about the problems I'd laid out—about my approach being wrong, about a better way. Maybe she saw something I didn't and took it to Muir in search of—what?— a promotion? Not a great idea, it turned out." Prather shook his head and laid a hand on his stomach. "But I don't know what was in her head. I really didn't know her at all."

CHAPTER FORTY-NINE

Wednesday Afternoon

Dr. Jacob Hanro lived in the north of the city, in Saint Gobain Park, on the elegant western edge of the vast park itself, and due east of the New University Hospital. The hospital, its medical school, and Hanro's offices were two miles from his house, along Avenue Betten-court, a wide and handsome street flanked by wide and handsome stone houses and apartment buildings, well-tended linden trees, and a broad meridian park down its length. The park had crushed-stone paths and graceful benches, and the air, as I walked towards the hospital grounds, was redolent of roasted nuts and fresh coffee from the vendors' carts. There were joggers, lively dogs, and old men drowsing over newspapers. I was surprised at the longing I felt, seeing it all, after just a week or so on the stony coast.

It was still early afternoon when I parked near Hanro's place, on a quiet street just off the avenue, a tall, narrow house of brown brick, with a glossy black door and a wrought-iron fence. It was meticulously kempt, but for the first twenty minutes that I'd watched it, from my parking spot across the street and two houses down, there'd been no sign of a living thing within. Then the front door had opened and a maid in a gray-and-white uniform emerged and swept the low stone steps and the stone walk that ran to the front gate. Then she'd disappeared inside. Several minutes later, another woman had emerged.

She was tall, with strong shoulders and slim hips, and she was dressed for horses, in paddock boots, brown riding pants, a fawn jumper, and a quilted green vest. She had a leather rucksack on her shoulder and a black riding helmet under her arm. She'd walked down the block in my direction, but paid me no mind. I'd taken pictures of her as she unlocked a pricey estate car, gotten in and driven off. Then I'd sent the pictures to Goss Ivessen.

"Mrs. Hanro," he'd said after much rapid typing. "It's her house, too, and her horses, on her family's estate out amidst the gently rolling hills. It's her daddy's bank that endowed the chair at the medical school that Hanro's arse is currently keeping warm."

I nodded. "Quite a bit to lose," I'd said.

Ivessen chuckled. "Is that why he didn't take my calls: he thinks we lack sensitivity?"

I'd laughed at that and started my walk to the hospital.

New University Hospital was a complex of sleek glass-and-steel structures, interlinked by glassed-in walkways, and surrounded by an arboretum that, regardless of what the calendar said, was fully committed to springtime. The security people looked at me, my ID, and me again, then waved me through the gates and onto the grounds without comment.

I wandered amidst the first greens and yellows of the specimen trees until I found a bench in the shade of a dogwood that was still contemplating blossoms, and that had excellent sight lines to the medical school's main pavilion. Then I sent a message to Ivessen. Five minutes later, a man in a white coat, pale blue shirt, red-striped necktie, and navy trousers came down the pavilion's steps. He scanned the landscape nervously as he did. I stood, and his eyes locked on me. His steps, as he approached, were hesitant.

Hanro was a fortyish, medium-sized man whose tailor had kept pace well with his thickening waist. His chestnut hair, lightly touched by gray, was cut short and smooth around his ears, his face was clean-shaven and pink-cheeked, and his jawline had only just begun to blur. His mouth was a self-satisfied line, his nose was straight and narrow, and his blue eyes were wary. He made a show of checking his watch and adjusting his cuff links.

"Are you the fellow who's been calling?" His voice was deep but chilly.

I shook my head and showed him my ID. "That fellow works with me."

Hanro glanced at my card, as if a quick look would hasten our encounter to its end. "He said if I wasn't outside in five minutes he would send someone inside to take me into custody."

"I told him to say it."

"It was melodramatic and unnecessary."

"Melodramatic, perhaps, but true nonetheless. As for its necessity, your lack of cooperation dictated that. Have a seat, Doctor."

He eyed the bench with some suspicion, then sat. "I don't have a lot of time."

"Nor do I, so let's not be wasteful. I'd like to talk about the evening of a week ago last Friday. I'd like to know how you spent it, where, and with whom. With as much detail as you can provide, please."

"This is about Karen, isn't it? Karen Muir."

"Is it?"

"That's who I was with that evening, for drinks, dinner, and afterwards. Is that what you need?"

"I just described to you what I need, Doctor. If you were with Dr. Muir, I need to know the times and places you were together, what you were doing, if you saw other people, and when you parted."

Hanro swallowed. "I was with her all night, all right? We met for drinks and didn't part until the next day, after midday."

I sighed. "I'll say it again if I must, Doctor. I need details: times, places, as much detail as you can provide. If you need a quieter place to gather your thoughts, someplace without all these lovely distractions, I can certainly arrange that." Hanro stiffened, and his eyes flitted away from mine. "Is there a problem, Dr. Hanro?"

"No, no problem," he said impatiently, and he told me his story.

It was simple enough, at first. He and Muir had met for drinks at a hotel lounge in Colonia. Drinks had become dinner at a nearby brasserie, which had become cocktails at a cozy spot around the corner from the apartment Muir kept in the city. It was in Muir's apartment where they'd decided to open a bottle of champagne, or two. Possibly three. They had spent the night there, and parted after noon the following day, the Saturday when Allegra Stans was murdered. Hanro had returned to his house—his wife's house—in Saint Gobain Park; Muir had gone to the airport.

"There," Hanro said when he'd finished. "Now you know all of it." He rose and brushed off his white coat. "So, if that's all—"

"That's not remotely all, Doctor. Please, sit down."

"I've told you—"

"I said *sit down*." Hanro sat. "Where was your wife while you were on your date with Dr. Muir?"

Color flared in his cheeks, and his mouth turned hard. "Is that necessary?" he said. I didn't respond and he continued. "Ellen was away, at her parents' place," Hanro said. "She's there almost every weekend. She rides." He made it sound like a chronic illness.

"And who organized this cozy evening?"

His eyes flitted away again. "She did—Karen. She called me."

"When?"

"It must've been nearly four weeks ago now."

I nodded. "And when had you previously heard from Dr. Muir?"

Hanro turned towards the medical-school pavilion, but his gaze was much farther away. "It had been quite a while."

"Meaning months? Years?"

"Nine years."

"Quite a while, indeed. Was that before or after your marriage?"

"Before. Just before. I was engaged at the time."

"I assume your fiancée was unaware."

"She was," Hanro said, his voice all but disappearing in his throat.

"How did you come to know Dr. Muir?"

"Medical school. We first met in medical school."

"What kind of medicine do you practice, Doctor?"

"I'm a psychiatrist."

I nodded again. "How long did your relationship with Dr. Muir go on?"

"We saw each other in medical school and afterwards, on and off. Things . . . tapered off when I got engaged. I suppose, all told, it comprised about six years."

I nodded. "But she wasn't married when you met."

"No. She was Karen Jolley then."

"And somewhere along the line, she married Marcus Muir." He nodded. "So . . . let me make sure I understand this. You started *seeing her*, which I assume entailed sleeping with her, in medical school; you continued *seeing her*, though less regularly, afterwards, though you did continue to *see her* after she married and after you were engaged to marry. In fact, you *saw her* throughout the entirety of her marriage. Is that correct?"

Hanro's nostrils flared. "I know what it looks like: an engaged man—a physician—carrying on an affair with a married woman, one whose husband is dying. I'm not proud of any of this. Nothing like it had happened before, and nothing like it has happened since."

"Not since ten days ago, anyway," I said, and Hanro cringed. "When *exactly* did you and Dr. Muir end things?"

"It was nine years ago, just after her husband died."

"Who broke it off?"

Hanro looked at his polished shoes. "She did."

"And no word since?" He shook his head. "Had you tried to contact her?"

He nodded. "Years ago. She didn't respond."

"You must've been surprised to hear from her, then." Another nod. "Pleased?"

"I suppose."

"Did she say why, after so long, she felt moved to be in touch?"

Hanro colored. "She said she'd been thinking of me, of our time together. That she'd thought of me often over the years and felt badly that things had ended in such a *muddle*—that was the word she used. She wondered if I'd like to have drinks sometime and catch up. She said she'd be in the city for the night in a few weeks."

"Had things ended in a muddle, Doctor?"

He swallowed hard. "The death of her husband, my impending marriage . . . It was a difficult period."

"No doubt. And of course, there were inquiries following Mr. Muir's death." Hanro's cheeks burned. "I expect those might've been awkward for both of you. As you put it, a physician and the wife of a dying man . . ."

"I wasn't his attending, and there was *nothing* untoward about Muir's death. It's actually amazing he'd survived as long as he had—the shape his lungs were in."

"And, despite the muddle of nine years ago, you had no qualms about seeing her? No hesitation?"

He shook his head. "I'd thought much about her, too, and . . . Karen is a very compelling woman."

I nodded. "Have you heard from Dr. Muir since you last saw her on that Saturday?"

Again, he studied his shoes. "She left me a message the following

Friday, saying the authorities might be in contact with me to confirm her whereabouts on the previous Friday and Saturday. She didn't say it would be you people."

"Was that your only contact with her? You didn't call her back?"

More shoes. "I did."

"And?"

"It was a brief conversation. I told her I'd rather not get involved with . . . anything. That I had my marriage to consider. She said that I should simply tell the truth, and that nothing else would come of it. That it was simply routine."

"'Simply routine.' But, despite such comforting words from Dr. Muir, you were reluctant to speak to us. Why was that?"

Hanro looked up, and back to the medical school. His face was very still and pale. "It's not just my marriage I have to consider. It's my career. My wife's family—her father—is quite influential at the university. And he's quite vindictive. He's never been fond of me. Never trusted me. He also has extensive political connections. I was worried that somehow . . ."

"We are capable of discretion, Doctor, even in the face of political pressures. If that's any consolation."

"I'm pleased to hear it. Now, if that's all . . ."

I said nothing. Hanro rose and turned towards the medical school but didn't walk away. I could hear his breathing, which sounded effortful.

"I wonder, Doctor, if Dr. Muir happened to share with you the context of our questioning. Did she tell you what kind of investigation we're engaged in?"

His voice was brittle. "No—why should she? That's your people's concern, and Karen's maybe, but not mine. Not my business."

"As long as you've told us the truth."

"She said it was routine."

I sighed. "If you consider murder routine." I heard a sharp intake of breath, and a stiffness overtook Hanro's limbs. A shudder went through him, and he stepped backwards and sat heavily on the bench. "I will, of course, be reviewing the records, Doctor, public and otherwise, of the investigations that followed Mr. Muir's death. If you participated in those in any way and were perhaps less than candid—less than truthful—now would be the time to tell me. Similarly, if you've not told me the truth about your recent evening with Dr. Muir—"

"I did tell the truth! I told it then and I've told you the truth now, as best I could. The problem is . . . The problem is I don't *know* what's true—not with certainty—not then and not now. I'm just not sure."

"Doctor, I don't—"

He bent forward and buried his face in his hands. "I can't believe she's doing this to me again," he whispered. "And now she has pictures."

I took a deep breath. "I want you to compose yourself, Doctor," I said. "And then I want you to explain."

Eventually, he did both of those things, though it took him some time.

CHAPTER FIFTY

Wednesday Night

It was late when I left the city, and on my way to the ring road I was
caught in traffic in Zoological Park. Despite the hour, or because of it,
the streets there were busy: noisy, full of young people laughing in the
glow of neon, leaning in to one another, crowding the takeaway counters, making losing arguments to the gatekeepers at the clubs. Music
tumbled from the doorways, along with drunks and the smells of food
and smoke and bodies. The giddy jumble was hypnotic somehow, and
only an irritated driver behind me, leaning on his horn, moved me along.

I checked my phone as I crept forward, but there was nothing yet
from Ivessen. After my chat with Hanro, I'd called him, told him what
I'd learned, and asked him to pull any records of the inquest into Marcus
Muir's death—the official one, or anything sponsored by his heirs or his
company. Ivessen had started typing immediately.

"Poor Dr. Hanro," Ivessen had said as he typed. "I feel a bit sorry
for him."

"He's less sympathetic in person. And, of course, he had no actual
proof. Without which, we're left with—what?—a cheating husband who
can't handle his liquor and so can't entirely corroborate a legitimate
alibi? Who instead tells a silly story of conspiracy? That would be the
counterargument Muir's legal counsel might offer."

Ivessen had laughed softly. "If you let it come to that. Still, you had
quite a day in the city. Two pieces in place that weren't before."

"Perhaps a piece and a half," I'd said.

A flock of blurry-eyed kids, the oldest no more than twenty, staggered across the road and into and around the bumper of my stopped
car. They shouted in my direction, but it quickly dissolved into giggling
and off-key singing. When they'd crossed, the way ahead was clear.

Then I was through to the ring road, going fast, and faster still when I made the motorway. Night and the rush of wind engulfed the car, and I chased twin cones of light into what seemed an endless dark. I glanced in the rearview, and the city behind me was nothing more than a golden glow, fading like a memory. I sighed, and it sounded like a sob.

CHAPTER FIFTY-ONE

Thursday Morning–Night

Payment was exacted for the taste of spring on Wednesday, by a late-winter storm on Thursday. The storm sent hammering surf, scouring winds, and sleet like a lash up and down the coast, under skies that seemed to drain the will to live, or at least the will to rise from bed, from all who gazed upon them. I was one such, and I struggled mightily to make it to the shower, and then to the cafeteria for breakfast and a carafe of coffee. I carried a full carafe back to my rooms afterwards, settled myself on the sofa, and contemplated the notes I'd made days ago: the flowcharts and time lines and lists of questions. I poured some coffee and found some blank pages.

Goss Ivessen had been right: I had more pieces now, and with them the makings of a narrative. It began eight months ago or so. . . .

Allegra Stans, out of boredom, curiosity, habit, or nothing more complicated than lust, had taken Alan Prather as a lover. Though they had both worked in the Special Projects Department, under Karen Muir, Stans and Prather had not previously known each other. Stans was much senior to Prather and had her own set of projects to worry about, while Prather was cloistered on the secretive and highly compartmentalized Special Project 1107—forbidden even from knowing what his colleagues on the project were up to, and from discussing his work with anyone apart from Karen Muir. That changed when Prather started training with Stans's running club, and the two started sleeping together.

Stans had described Prather to Leila Vroman as "eager to please," and so he was. Eager to please, eager to impress—sexually and otherwise. He knew that Allegra was an expert in the use of adeno-associated viruses as vectors for vaccines and genetic therapies—a subject Prather also knew something about—and he thought that this was intellectual common ground between them, and perhaps an opportunity to dazzle her. So, in a postcoital collapse of judgment, he'd shared his problems on Special Project 1107—his failed efforts to increase the gene-carrying capacity of the vectors, his thoughts on possible solutions. But whatever connection he'd sought with Allegra was not to be. Not that she was uninterested in what Prather had to say—she'd simply been uninterested in discussing any of it with him. She'd set her sights higher.

As to why Allegra had gone straight to Karen Muir with whatever was on her mind regarding Special Project 1107, I—like Prather—could only speculate. And my speculation, like his, suggested personal ambition. Perhaps Allegra envisioned a scene of the sort she'd orchestrated with Witmer, in her earliest days at Ondstrand—a bold initiative to reinvent the status quo. Or perhaps it was something more selfless— a team player seeking to support the team. Whatever her motives, though, things hadn't worked out well for her or for Alan Prather.

Within days of his last pillow talk with Allegra, Prather had had the flesh flayed off his bones, as he'd put it, for violating confidentiality regarding Special Project 1107, and been reassigned to Trials, under Piers Witmer, in what was essentially a job washing bottles. Two months later, he was gone from Ondstrand Biologic, embarked on a new career in private equity.

Allegra's conversations with Prather and then with Karen Muir were, I was certain, the precipitating events. By asking questions about Special Project 1107, Allegra had unknowingly stepped into what Karen Muir considered forbidden territory, and the result was transfer and demotion for her as well. But whereas Prather's part in the story ended with separation from the firm and a career change, Allegra's ended rather differently.

I didn't know precisely when Allegra had met Ian Stiles, how or on whose behalf he had recruited her into corporate espionage, or if indeed she'd needed recruitment at all, but I knew that her systematic theft of Ondstrand secrets had commenced soon after her demotion. I thought of what I'd learned from Petra Witmer, about the blunt-force solution Allegra had seized upon for the problem of how to break things off with the clingy Piers, and felt secure in my assumption that the theft and sale of Ondstrand's intellectual property was Allegra's response to Karen Muir's derailment of her career.

I sighed and poured more coffee. I felt on solid ground with that part of my story, but as I moved on, the footing grew less sure. Allegra's thefts had proceeded quickly. In a few months' time, she had plundered nearly all of what Special Projects had to offer. And then, after stealing Karen Muir's security credentials, she had come to Special Project 1107, at first stealing the standard set of documents associated with the project, as she'd done with all the projects before. Then she'd come back and taken much more.

I stood up, stretched, and drained my coffee mug. Outside, the wind was gusting and flinging sleet and frozen rain at the window, and it made a sound like chattering teeth. I went to the window and looked out. The fountain and its statuary were coated in gray ice, like a second skin that made them even more alien and bizarre.

I still had no idea of what Stans had found in her pillage of that project, but whatever it was, it had changed things. And, I thought, it had set in motion the beginning of the end for her and for her handler, Ian Stiles. I reached for the time lines I'd created for Allegra and for Karen Muir.

Six, nearly seven weeks back now, Allegra had made her first pass through the Special Project 1107 documents; a week later, she'd come back for more; a week—more or less—after that, she'd met with Karen Muir to discuss, according to Muir, the status of some projects that had traveled with Stans to R&D.

That was the start of a busy period for Karen Muir. Immediately following her meeting with Allegra Stans, Muir had taken steps to remove nearly all of the Special Project 1107 information—documents, data, correspondence, backups, and most everything else—from Ondstrand's servers. A week after *that*, according to Jacob Hanro, Karen Muir had contacted him for the first time in nine years, to arrange a date—a date that had begun on the evening before Allegra's death, and ended on the day of.

It sounded compelling in my head, but of course it was all circumstantial. Karen Muir might come up with any number of explanations for her actions, and no doubt they'd all sound plausible.

Her explanation of why she had rebooked her flight overseas on that Saturday, and taken a late-afternoon flight rather than a morning one, had certainly sounded plausible at first. She'd spent a long, somewhat drunken night with an old lover, and woken up with a hangover. All very reasonable, until one spoke with Jacob Hanro, pressed him a bit, and discovered that, though he had indeed woken up in Karen Muir's apartment in the city at around noon on Saturday, in her bed, while she was in the kitchen brewing coffee, he couldn't actually recall anything about what had happened that morning or the evening before. His memory was a blank, he said, from the time they opened that second bottle of champagne, and all Saturday he'd been nauseated and his head had felt like a board with nails being pounded in.

In fact, Hanro said, he felt as if he'd been drugged—was all but certain he had been. And it wasn't the first time he'd felt that way on a morning after with Karen Muir.

The first time had been nine years before, on the morning after Karen Muir's husband, Marcus, had passed away at home, in his sleep, succumbing finally to the chronic respiratory problems that had plagued him for years.

Not long after his death, Muir's other heirs had begun asking questions about the circumstances of his passing. Suspicions were voiced, allegations were bandied about, and an official inquest was made. In the course of that, possible anomalies were found in certain toxicology results; metabolites were present—or *may* have been present—that could, under some interpretations, suggest the presence of a toxin, though the amounts involved were minute. It was all quite equivocal, but, still, where *had* the widow been?

Thus Karen Muir had been called to account for her whereabouts on the night of her husband's death. It turned out that she'd been in the company of the sympathetic Dr. Jacob Hanro, with whom she'd been managing the stresses of her husband's long decline and relieving her anticipatory grief for several months prior to her husband's actual death. She'd been in Hanro's bed, in Hanro's room, which was next door to the suite that Karen Muir had long maintained at the loveliest hotel in the lovely little town that was a mile or so from Marcus Muir's country estate.

Of course, Dr. Hanro was asked to corroborate this, but it was a delicate matter: he was engaged to be married, after all; he'd had much to lose, and was naturally reluctant. Still, Karen Muir was persistent and persuasive. Not without resources, she had arranged that Dr. Hanro's testimony would be handled discreetly, confidentially, his name masked in the official record. Hanro remained hesitant, but Muir was not to be denied: she'd made it clear to him, without ever quite coming out and saying it, that one way or another—confidentially or very publicly—he *would* corroborate her story.

And so he had—though his testimony was a brief thing. Yes, they'd been seeing each other for years; yes, their usual routine was to meet at the hotel, where he would take the room next to hers; yes, they had done so on the night in question; yes, they'd had room-service dinner that night, and breakfast the following morning; yes, the waitstaff would recall them; yes, they'd stayed in Dr. Hanro's room all night; no, to his knowledge, she hadn't left until morning.

To his knowledge. That was the thin reed Hanro had hidden behind, and it remained the sweat and pallor and shame-inducing thing that, years later, he tried never to think of. Because the truth of it was, he *didn't* remember much about that night—didn't remember a single thing from drinks after dinner—a split of champagne, as was their habit—until Room Service came knocking the next morning. He could, in fact, barely remember much from that morning, given the nausea and the blinding headache that had gripped him. Like a board with nails being pounded in.

So his most recent night with Karen Muir—as much as he'd looked forward to it, fantasized for nine years about one more such night, consigned his fear of her to the back of his mind and his desire for her to every other part, as much as he'd ached for her—that night had had a sickening familiarity. The pounding in his head that Saturday morning, his memory, or lack thereof, his nausea—he'd been through it all before, though now there was a new twist: the pictures.

When Hanro pushed back against corroborating a story he couldn't remember, Karen Muir hadn't bothered to cajole or threaten. She'd merely shared with him pictures she had taken of the two of them together that night—quite explicit photos—and asked if they refreshed his memory. She wondered aloud if she should share them with the authorities, but then pretended to think the better of it because, once they were out in the world, who knew where such photos might turn up. Then she made a show of dismissing these thoughts entirely, as she knew that Hanro's corroboration would make the photos entirely irrelevant and unnecessary.

Karen Muir's alibi was decidedly less plausible in this context, and less so still when I thought about the last things Hanro had told me.

He'd been all but spent then, exhausted, red-eyed, and I didn't envy the patients he might see later that afternoon. He'd struggled to rise, as if he were chained to the bench we sat on, or caught in a whirlpool. He took an unsteady step towards the medical school and stopped. He spoke again, but couldn't turn to face me.

"She's sick, you know. Karen. There's something quite *wrong* with her. It's an antisocial personality disorder without doubt, likely a form of psychopathy, though not like anything I've read about in the literature. Certainly not like anything I've seen." Hanro took a deep, shuddering breath, and I found myself holding mine.

"Is this a professional opinion?"

"Amongst other things. She did her residency in medical genetics, you know." I nodded. "Did you know that before that she'd begun a residency in a different subspecialty?"

"I did not."

He chuckled bitterly. "Anesthesiology. An odd choice for someone who'd already earned a doctorate in molecular biology, no? And who'd go on to earn another doctorate in genetics, and a business degree besides. Off at a ninety-degree angle, don't you think? She transferred out of the program after six months, but it speaks clearly of her . . . *enthusiasms*.

"Agency negated; will made irrelevant. She was particularly fasci-nated with paralytics—compounds that suspend physical activity while preserving consciousness. Not for her, of course, no—but inducing that state in others. The power it gave her . . . That's what she most enjoyed." Hanro's breath deserted him then, and he struggled for a moment to get it back. When he spoke again, I strained to hear him. "She wanted to try them on me, more than a few times. She insisted, really. And I'm ashamed to say I indulged her.

"There's psychosis there, and sadism, and . . . I'm not sure what else. Something broken, the result of some early trauma, I think. I never succeeded in getting her to speak of it, and I realize now that I was in danger just making the attempt. I always suspected it had something to do with that stepbrother of hers—Hasp. They were *close* when I first knew her, though I was never sure how close, or in what ways."

Pieces found, steps forward, but still no proof. Not yet.

t was near nightfall when I went to the window again. The winds
howled on, the sleet whipped down, the clouds boiled, and the fountain statues hid their faces behind gray masks. I stretched, yawned, and
reached for the parcel, wrapped in brown paper, that had been waiting
for me when I returned to Ondstrand House the night before. I tore off
the wrapping.

Horror on the Headland: Ondstrand Hall and a Legacy of Terror.

It was a weighty volume, with a thick section of illustrations in the
middle, lengthy footnotes, an extensive index, and on the cover a stark
black-and-white photo of Ondstrand House looming large against a
threatening sky, and spattered liberally with vivid, wet-looking, blood-
red spots. But despite the cover and the crazy title, it was a serious
piece of journalism. I opened the volume, read the table of contents,
and started skimming.

Aside from bathroom breaks and another trip to the commissary—
more coffee and sandwiches—I didn't put the book down until nearly
midnight.

It was fascinating, deeply disturbing stuff—a story of multigenera-
tional abuse, with Hasp's father, Jerome Roeg, first as the victim of his
own father, Potter Roeg, a bishop of the church, and then as a perpetra-
tor himself. Around this central strand, the author, Matthew Veddar, had
woven other stories as well. Some were about children whose allegations
were ignored, and who were traumatized again by official indifference.
Some were about cover-ups—of Potter Roeg's crimes by church elders,
and of Jerome Roeg's by the trustees and influential alums of Ondstrand
Hall. Some were about the police, local and national, who were either
too incompetent, too lazy, or too politically compromised to do much
more than lift a corner of the rug so the truth could be swept beneath.

Terrence Hasp and his stepsister appeared in the book, but—
disappointingly, from my perspective—only briefly. They were walk-
on characters, and Veddar noted—in the same epilogue in which he
discussed the purchase of Ondstrand Hall by the pair—that neither
Hasp nor Muir had agreed to talk to him. This didn't seem to surprise
him much.

I recalled what Ivessen had said to me when he first told me about
what had happened here: "grisly tales of Headmaster Roeg, complete

with all the gothic flourishes: ghostly apparitions, midnight visitations, dungeons and secret passages, threats of death, all quite lurid." And Veddar hadn't skimped on any of that. Though he'd taken pains not to sensationalize, the plain facts did that work for him. There were indeed midnight visitations, with some of Roeg's victims claiming that he'd seemed to materialize from thin air in the nighttime corridors. Others reported that they hadn't seen him at all—had been aware of nothing before waking up to find themselves bound in some sort of chamber, variously described as a dungeon, a crypt, a cellar, and a vault. According to Veddar, the authorities, in their rush to do as little as possible, as quietly as possible, had failed to investigate the particulars of these claims, and had never located a dungeon, crypt, cellar, or vault, or determined if such ever existed.

I sighed and poured the last of the carafe—room-temperature now—into my mug. I carried it and the book to the window and looked out. The courtyard was dark and, with half a dozen exceptions, so were the windows in Ondstrand House. I put my mug on the sill and opened to the illustrations section, in the middle of the book. There were maps of the coast and the grounds, sketches that showed Ondstrand House and its environs.

I paused when I came to the end of that section. I was leafing through photos from the school's late history—the administration of Jerome Roeg. Most of the photos were of school life: sporting events, theatrical productions, meals, holiday celebrations, school outings. The one I was staring at was from an outing: a trip the students made to do horses. They were kitted out for riding: hard hats, thin gloves, boots—and they were gathered, ten of them, in front of a stable, though not the stables on the Ondstrand campus. And yet somehow familiar. I peered and peered. I carried the book to some better light, pulled a magnifying glass from my briefcase, and peered some more. And then, in an upper corner of the photo, I saw the edge of a sign, and on it, fragments of two words: *ping Equest.*

I stood up straight and laughed. *Little Storping Equestrian*—the abandoned horse farm where I'd found Ian Stiles's body. Terrence Hasp wasn't in the photo, nor was Karen Muir—that would've been too easy—but still . . . It wasn't a message from Matthew Veddar from the great beyond, I knew, but it was enough to rouse me in a way that coffee hadn't—to take me back to those descriptions in his book of midnight abduction, back again to the photos and illustrations, and back, finally, to the notes of my last interview with Sandy Silber.

It was after one in the morning when I pulled a black jumper over my white shirt and pulled a flashlight from my bag.

CHAPTER FIFTY-TWO

Friday Morning

I took the stairs down, rather than the elevator, and I was careful about noise. But there wasn't much I could do about the motion-activated lighting that shuddered on as I proceeded down the white corridors of the north wing to the old Ondstrand Hall classrooms. I started in Latin class. I felt along the wall for a switch, found one, and flicked it on; the old fluorescent tubes struggled to life.

The room was unchanged since the first time I'd seen it, though bleaker under the flickering light. I ignored the shabby furnishings but went directly to the cupboard. It was fitted with shelves but otherwise empty, save for dust and a stack of yellowed exam books. I rapped on the cupboard walls and ran my fingers around the shelves, and then moved on to geography. This room had even less to offer: sicklier lights, no shelves in the cupboard, and no exam books. Again I knocked on the cupboard walls and felt in the corners, but again found nothing. And so to chemistry lab.

There was the same scarred furniture, the same clouded labware, the same sad lectern, and the permanently smudged chalkboard that ran across the front of the room. The same nostalgic and vaguely nauseating smell. I looked up at the small windows—black now—set above the chalkboard. I went to the front of the room and placed my palms on the chalkboard.

From close up, I saw that the board was actually several chalkboard panels, identically sized and set side by side, with the seams all but invisible between them. Below them was a chalk tray that looked like chair-rail molding, and that also ran across the room. It, too, was actually several chalk trays, each just as wide as the section of chalkboard above it. Below them, running from the tray to the floor, were panels of wainscot, whose widths also matched that of the chalkboards. Each was about thirty inches wide—the width of a narrowish door.

Which of course is what they were. The latch mechanisms were set in the chalk trays, at the right edge of each section, and required only a push. I pushed one, and the right edge of the door popped out several inches. I opened it to find a shallow supply cupboard—with shelves not even a foot deep and full of dust and, in the first instance, some dead flies, a length of old tubing for a gas burner, and a box of glass pipettes with one shattered straw still inside. I went across the front of the room, pressing and opening, and found more dust, more dead bugs, more ancient bits of labware, a wooden meter stick, and one unopened box of chalk. I walked across the front of the room again and rapped on the walls of the closets. I heard and felt no difference amongst them.

I went around the lab bench and pushed aside some glassware. Then I picked up a one-armed desk and placed it on the bench. I leapt onto the bench and climbed on the desk and looked out one of the windows. Too much reflection. I dropped down, went to the classroom door, flicked off the lights, and climbed up again. Better.

Balanced precariously, with one foot on the desk's writing surface and the other on its back, I looked through one of the narrow windows. I saw the corrugated steel of the window well, a slice of angry sky, and the very top of a leaning lamppost. I climbed down, switched on the classroom lights, and went to the second closet from the right. I took out my flashlight and knelt.

I saw a faint line where dust had been disturbed along the floor. It took me a bit longer to find the mechanism—on the left side wall of the closet, hidden beneath one of the closet's lower shelves. It was impossible to see on casual inspection, but not difficult to find by feel once you knew it was there. Find the slot cut into the wood, slide back a small bolt, hook a finger in a ring, give a sharp pull, and presto.

There was no organ music, no ominous creaking, no bats flapping or rats running free. Just a rush of cold, damp air that smelled of wet brick and mildew, as the rear wall of the closet, shelves and all, swept back several inches on the left, and revealed itself to be a door. I took a deep breath and pushed some more. The door swung quietly away.

Beyond was a low passage, with a stone floor that sloped downwards.

I ducked my head as I moved forward. There were bare bulbs strung on the right-hand wall, near the ceiling, and I looked for a switch. I found one a few paces in and flicked it.

The corridor curved gradually to the left, and the bulbs hung at wide intervals along it for as far as I could see. The bulbs were dim and yellowed, and several were burnt out, but still I saw that I stood in a neat bit of engineering, albeit one much in need of repair. The passage was brick-lined and topped with a brick barrel-arch ceiling. But the stone floor was wet, and had been for some time, and there were puddles and mold patches in spots along the seams of floor and wall. Water dripped here and there through the clever brickwork of the ceiling, some of which had buckled, and some of which was on the floor. The passage, I was certain, was original to the house, though I couldn't guess what the builder had had in mind. But whatever its original purpose, it had found much darker use. I turned off my flashlight and went forward.

The sharp downward slope leveled off after a dozen paces or so, and the passage maintained its steady leftward curve. It went on for fifty meters or more, then straightened out for ten more, until it ended in a brick-lined room of about twenty by twenty feet.

A wooden table stood there, and two wooden chairs with arms and ladder backs, and there was a daybed with a thin, bare mattress whose ticking was black with mold and in the last stages of decomposition. Leather restraints, stained and cracked with age, hung from the corners of the daybed. Against one wall was a glass-fronted cabinet. Inside were several amber, glass-stoppered chemical bottles. Most of the labels were gone or had faded with age. I suppressed a wave of nausea.

This was without question a crime scene, though I wasn't sure how recent. And, like the classroom at the far end of the tunnel, it was also a sort of museum display. Or a memorial. I shook my head.

On the far wall of the chamber, the brickwork gave way to a stone foundation, and the height of the ceiling rose. A folding wooden ladder was affixed to the ceiling there, to the threshold of a large hatch door made of thick timbers and brass bindings. A rope hung down to eye level, and I pulled it. The ladder extended downwards, smoothly and without noise. I brought out my flashlight, took hold of a rail, and stepped up.

The door had a thick brass ring set into it, and a sturdy chain to keep it from swinging fully open on its hinges. I grabbed the ring and put my back to the timbers. The door was heavy, and I was careful with it, as I wasn't sure what might be above.

What was above when I raised the door was darkness. I stood at the top of the ladder, flicked on my flashlight, and ran the beam over a massive black table, a pair of gray leather chairs, a large fireplace with a surround of rough-hewn slate, a wall of bookshelves that rose to the ceiling, and a wall of sleet-spattered glass that looked onto black woods and the stone ruin of a chapel. An impressive space, even in the dark, but I was not impressed just then.

The black-and-blue-striped rug that had hidden the trapdoor in Hasp's studio had slid away when I opened it, and I had no way to replace it when I left. I found that I didn't much care. I gave another look around and then took the weight of the door again. I stepped carefully down the ladder, easing the door closed as I went.

My journey back was quicker. I closed the passage door when I returned to the classroom, and all the closet doors, and lifted the one-armed desk from the lab bench, and returned it to its place. Then I turned out the classroom lights and stepped into the white corridor, and nearly collided with Nadia Blom as she came around the corner.

"What are you doing?" she demanded. She was in jeans and a white roll-neck, and her wicked braid was looking a bit frazzled.

"Working," I said.

"It's very late."

"It's been quite some time since I've been subject to a curfew, Ms. Blom. I work when there is work to be done. What's your excuse for being up at this hour?"

"You're not the only one with things to do. I was taking a break, and on my way to get a coffee. What kind of work needed doing in that classroom?"

"Schoolwork," I said. "A bit of history, a bit of current events. You should go back to your chores, Ms. Blom. Or get some sleep. That's what I intend to do." Then I stepped around her and headed down the corridor to the stairs. All the way, I felt her gaze on my back.

CHAPTER FIFTY-THREE

Friday Morning

I'd lied to Nadia Blom. I had no intention of going to sleep, and probably couldn't have had I tried. I was awash in adrenaline—from the discovery I'd made, its implications, and—after reading Matthew Veddar's book—from the surge of anger it provoked. But I'd been trained to be wary of this adrenal rush, trained to control it, to direct it. Back in my rooms, I drank several glasses of water, did some breathing exercises, and took another look at my notes.

My story was almost there: I knew *how* Allegra Stans was killed, and *where*, and now I knew how she'd gotten back into Ondstrand House without going past security. And I was pretty sure I knew *who* had killed her—and by extension who had killed Ian Stiles, though I was less certain about who else might have assisted the killer. Still missing was the full story of *why*. I knew the broad strokes, certainly—in her theft of corporate secrets, Allegra had come across some information related to Special Project 1107, information she'd attempted to exploit—likely monetize—by way of "wrapping things up," prior to decamping to Playa Arcadia. That information, and that attempt, had gotten her killed. But I didn't know the specifics—didn't know what she'd learned, what made it worth killing for, and what interest Domestic Security had in the matter.

That said, I didn't need to know. Strictly speaking, I had enough now to call a transport, and if Director Elkort or her Minister had an issue, they could take it up with Director Mehta. Though Director Mehta might see things a bit differently. More information is always preferable to less, and in whatever political games were roiling the thin air of the security bureaucracy, I suspected that Director Mehta would probably appreciate as much information as I could provide.

Which brought me around again to Special Project 1107. Allegra had recognized the significance and potential value of what she'd stolen—she was attempting to cash in, after all. Given that, it was hard to imagine that she would've handled that material in the same way she'd handled the other things she'd stolen, and nearly inconceivable that she wouldn't have maintained a copy of whatever it was. But where?

I read over the notes from my many interviews with the people who knew her, one way or another, and pulled out the photos I'd removed from her apartment.

Allegra preparing to race, Allegra racing, Allegra at the finish, and afterwards, with her fellow runners. I looked again at the racing photos. Allegra's cropped hair, spiked and darkened with sweat, her singlet rippled with speed, her necklace flying behind her, the thin gold chain and the locket catching the sun. Her red-and-black cloisonné locket, with a deer leaping against a black wood. The locket that I'd never found, that had not turned up on her person, in her apartment, or in her car, but that she wore in every photo of her I'd seen.

I looked again at the photos of Allegra's body in the refrigerator. The pink-gold chain was plain to see. I looked at the photos from the autopsy, and there was the gold chain amongst her personal effects—its links and its clasp clearly intact.

If the locket had been taken by force from Allegra, either prior to or after her death, would whoever had taken it have bothered with the niceties of unclasping the chain, removing the locket, and clasping the chain again? Unlikely. Which suggested that Allegra had removed the locket herself and . . . done what with it? I had no idea, and no real idea of why it was important. Just a feeling that it was, and a gnawing irritation at not having found it.

I took a closer look at one of her racing photos, applied my magnifying glass, and tried to judge the locket's size and what it could accommodate. Too small for a memory card—certainly for the kind of card that her cameras would've used. Maybe Ian Stiles had supplied her with something more specialized. I sighed. Maybe many things.

The adrenaline was fading now, and my very long day had caught me by the collar, was shaking me as a hound might shake a fox. It was near dawn, and my eyes were full of grit. I kicked off my shoes and was asleep before I hit the pillow.

CHAPTER FIFTY-FOUR

Friday Morning

I was up early on Friday, and surprisingly alert given three hours sleep. After a shower, and breakfast in the staff cafeteria, I stepped outside to call Director Mehta. The sunshine had returned, if not the mild temperatures, and the façade of Ondstrand House, along with the fountain and its figures, sparkled with a skin of ice that peeled away and shattered when the wind blew. Surprisingly, I was not able to reach the Director immediately—a rare occurrence—and got her assistant, Mr. Nguyen, instead.

"Called to the Ministry, Myles, first thing," Mr. Nguyen said.

"And due back when?"

"Didn't say. Have her call?"

"Please."

I pocketed my phone, found the keys to Allegra's car, and headed for the parking lot. I stopped when I saw a blond head in my peripheral vision, and a bald one. I turned and saw Nadia Blom, in black pants and a short black jacket, her braid fully disciplined, by the porte cochere, talking to Dr. Hasp. Their heads were bent together, and it was impossible to say what passed between them—news, orders, or intrigue. They looked up, saw me, and moved inside.

The drive to Fiskdorp was bright but perilous, as the sun was not yet warm enough to have melted the patches of black ice on the roadway, mostly at the curves. But traffic was light and Allegra's car was game, and the sliding and skidding did at least as much to wake me as the coffee had. I called Jens-Edvard Neumann on the way, and we met near the harbormaster's office.

He looked thinner and older than when I'd seen him last: shadow-eyed, sallow beneath the scruffy beard, with his broad shoulders slumped. He seemed mostly indifferent to the cold, wearing only a gray jumper and a watch cap, and with a black woolen scarf around his neck.

"It's early," he muttered.

"Not that early. Besides, I thought fishermen were up before the sun."

"My da's the fisherman, not me, and he don't want me on the boat now. Says I'm a menace. Says I should stay ashore till I get my head straight." I nodded. "What you want me for, anyway? You find something out about Allie, about whoever . . . ?"

I started walking slowly down the waterfront, and Jens-Edvard followed. "I'm nearly there, I think, but I need your help again."

Jens-Edvard squinted. "I've told you all—more'n I thought I knew."

"It's a few questions, no more," I said, and took out my phone. "You remember I asked you about this?" I showed him the picture of Allegra's locket, and he stopped and stared.

"I remember. What about it?"

"You told me that she got it from her father, that it was the only thing she had from him."

"Besides the car. I remember."

"You said she wore it all the time."

"Yeah."

"And that she'd been wearing it the last time you saw her, on the beach."

"Yeah, and . . . ?"

I spoke very softly now. "And I still haven't been able to find it. Not in her apartment, not in her office or her car, not in the place she died or where her body was discovered. No one who knew her knows anything about where it could be."

"I get it—it's lost. Why you keep asking me about it? And why you give a damn where it is? What does it matter, anyway?"

"I'm not sure that it does. But it's a missing piece, and it might be important, and I honestly can't think of where else to search."

Jens-Edvard stared at his boots. His voice grew small. "What you want it for? It's just a little thing—too damn little to hold anything."

"You're probably right about that. But I need to have a look, to be certain. I wouldn't need to keep it, or even take it anywhere."

Jens-Edvard looked at me, and then looked out at the harbor and let out a slow, shaking breath. Then he unwound the scarf from his neck and reached down his sweater. The locket was on a length of fishing line, and it was tiny in his rough hand. He reached behind his neck and found the knot—a sailor's knot—and deftly set it free.

"It's all I have of her, you know," he said. "She gave it to me in the cave—said I should hold on to it. I thought you were gonna take it."

I shook my head. "I just need to have a look."

He placed it in my palm. It was warm from the heat of his body. "There's nothing but a picture of her da," he told me.

I nodded and pressed the tiny catch, and the locket popped open. It was pink gold inside, and the left half was engraved with initials and a date, both rubbed too faint to read. In the right half was a small picture, no larger than a postage stamp, in black and white—a handsome young man with short, fair hair and something elfin in his smile.

"Her da," Jens-Edvard said. "Just that."

I stared for a while, then reached in my pocket, pulled out my knife, and flicked it open. Jens-Edvard looked alarmed and caught my wrist. "What're you doing?"

I looked at him. "I'll be careful," I said softly. He met my gaze and nodded and released my wrist. I worked the sharp point beneath the photo and lifted it out. Behind it was another stamp-sized piece of paper, white, folded in half. I unfolded it, and we both were quiet as we stared at the cluster of colored dots.

CHAPTER FIFTY-FIVE

Friday Morning

I called Freja Berg from the car, and by the time I returned to Ondstrand House, she'd sent me the software my phone required to scan and interpret the optical code on the ribbon of paper Allegra had secured in her locket. Back in my rooms, I used it, and the colored dots became a Web address and a password.

I spent an hour reading what I found there, though I could've spent many hours more on the documents she'd stored. Then I went to Piers Witmer's office. When I learned that he was out ill again, I headed for Allegra's car. On the way, I stopped by my rooms, sent the Web address and password to Director Mehta and Goss Ivessen, took my handgun from my bag, and put it into my pocket. The adrenaline was back again, bubbling now, singing through my arms and legs.

Shards of ice were melting in Piers Witmer's courtyard when I arrived, and his green sedan was there, along with a car I hadn't seen before—a quick-looking silver two-seater with a convertible top. I rang the bell, and in a moment the door opened to something else I hadn't seen before. Karen Muir stood there in white yoga togs, holding a soup ladle. Her hair was pulled back in a ponytail, her symmetrical cheeks were pink, and she was smiling. There was music playing, something lively, with violins.

"Myles! I thought it might be you; I hoped it would be. Do come in."

She didn't wait for a reply but bustled off through the foyer, and so did not see the look of surprise—possibly shock—on my face. As I stepped inside, I smelled chicken soup. I followed the aroma to the left, into a parlor. It had a low, beamed ceiling and a brick fireplace, and it was furnished with a lumpy sofa along one wall and a leather club chair and small round table by the hearth. Karen Muir had gone through to the dining room and into the kitchen. I called to her from the parlor.

"Why did you think it might be me at the door, Dr. Muir?"

She laughed, an odd, broken-glass sort of sound. "The tunnel, of course. Terry told me someone had been in the tunnel last night, and I told him it had to have been you. Who else? And if that was so, then it stood to reason you'd turn up here eventually. It's not another hangover, by the way. Piers, I mean. He really *is* under the weather today. And all by himself now, more's the pity. But you know that, don't you? That's why Terry and I stopped in—to see how he's faring and bring him a hot lunch."

"That's kind of you. Where is Dr. Witmer?"

She leaned at the kitchen door and looked at me across the dining room for a while. "Terry is helping Piers get squared away," she said eventually. "They'll be right out." She looked at me a moment longer and then turned back into the kitchen.

I turned, too, back to the club chair and the round table by the hearth, and to what I'd seen on the floor beneath them. It was peeking out from under the chair, resting on the bricks of the fireplace—the leather corner of a thick, bound document. The covers were black and soft-looking and had the Ondstrand Biologic scarlet-shield logo on the upper-right corner. I knelt and picked it up. There was a title printed in scarlet on it: "Special Project 1107." I sat in the club chair and opened the document.

I was ten pages in when Muir reappeared. "So you found it," she said, now leaning at the dining-room door, holding the ladle and a glass of wine. "I guess you've been hunting it for a while. Lunch will be a bit longer, so take your time. Can I offer you some of this?" She proffered her glass. "I'm not much of a wine person, but Terry tells me it's quite a good claret."

"Neither am I," I said, looking up. "A wine person. And your ladle is dripping."

She seemed surprised that she still held it. "Is it? Well, if not wine, then something else to drink—something stronger? Or weaker? An iced tea? Some water?"

"Really, nothing."

"But you will join us for lunch, won't you? There's honestly plenty."

"I think not, Dr. Muir."

She looked at me for a moment and shrugged. "Suit yourself," she said, and returned to the kitchen. "Still, you're welcome to the project report. You've gone to such trouble, after all."

"As it happens, I managed to read a number of the project documents just a short while ago."

There was a long silence from the kitchen. "Did you, now?" she called finally. Her voice was bright and brittle. "I suppose you found Allegra's little cache, then."

"I did. The project documents, correspondence between yourself, Dr. Hasp, Dr. Witmer, Director Elkort, her Minister, and much more besides—all on a password-protected Web site. It was not at all a *little* cache."

"Good for you, Myles, *good* for you. I was never able to find it. Never sure it existed, actually. But, still, you may want to browse that report. Allegra was really quite untrustworthy, you know."

"Was she?"

"Oh yes. All that business with her associate Mr. Stiles. A really horrid man."

"So you met him?" Karen Muir's only response was a short, harsh sound—possibly a laugh—that raised the hairs on the back of my neck.

I flipped back to the document's title page. "Special Project 1107: Field Operator Physical and Cognitive Optimizations: A Genetic Therapy Approach."

I read the title aloud to Karen Muir, and said: "Does this tell a story different from the material Allegra left behind? Something other than that this project was always more fantasy than reality? That it was doomed to failure from the start? That, for all the years of its existence, it's been nothing but a highly lucrative fraud that Ondstrand Biologic has perpetrated against the Science and Technology Division of Domestic Security?

"I say Ondstrand Biologic, but that's not quite right, is it, Dr. Muir? It wasn't the company so much as it was Dr. Hasp, Dr. Witmer, and you. Though you did apparently have some help from within Domestic Security, did you not? One thing that wasn't clear to me, though—have Director Elkort and her Minister been in this from the start, or were they latecomers?"

Karen Muir chuckled from the kitchen; she didn't sound unhinged, though I had begun to think otherwise. "Latecomers. We were years into the project by then, and they'd passed on glowing reports of our progress to their masters, signed off on all the costs with nary a question, and had seen their careers blossom as a result. When, finally, they started to ask questions, to demand to see, in person, the results of the human trials we'd been reporting on, we brought them fully into the status of the project."

"That must've been a tense episode."

"Oh yes. They were quite upset at first, threatened all sorts of things. But when we pointed out their own culpability—how much they themselves had to lose—and when we further pointed out how much, on the other hand, there was to be shared . . . well, they soon came around."

"I'm surprised they didn't do a better job of shielding you from our investigation."

"That surprised us, too. It wasn't supposed to be you lot that came down here; it was supposed to have been theirs—Domestic Security. I imagine that's down to your masters. They jumped on this before Elkort could lace her boots. She wasn't exactly sure how that happened. She's quite frightened of your masters, you know."

"She's not a *complete* idiot, then."

Muir snickered. "Well, we'll see about that. It *wasn't* fantasy, you know—this project. Yes, we got out over our skis a bit, oversold it, and got people a bit too enthusiastic about our line of super-mice. But there's no reason it *couldn't* work in humans, given a bit of time, despite what that arrogant bitch Allegra thought. There are viable vectors other than AAVs, after all. I'm confident we'll get there."

"I hate to disagree, Dr. Muir, but you will certainly *not* get there. The only place you'll *get* is into the transport I'm going to call, and the only place they will take you is off to our shop for quizzing. You do understand that, don't you? I'm here to take all three of you into custody."

Karen Muir came out from the kitchen then, and she had traded her soup ladle for a surgical mask and gloves. She was holding a large, heavy-gauge zip-top plastic bag. She crossed the dining room and leaned in the doorway of the parlor, her arms folded on her chest. There was an odd light in her eyes—curious, excited, and cold.

"I hate to disagree with *you*, Agent Myles," she said softly. Then she walked towards me and carefully took the document from my hands, which dropped like two stones into my lap. Muir placed the document in the zip bag.

"I think you've had quite enough of that by now," she said as she sealed the zipper. She leaned the bag against the fireplace bricks, then took my hands in her gloved ones, turned them palms-up, prodded the meaty parts, and peered at them. She dropped them in my lap again, peeled off her gloves, and took off her mask. She was smiling. "I expect by now you can't move your arms or your legs very much."

I tried to nod but couldn't, and I focused on keeping my breathing under control. "Not at all, actually," I said.

CHAPTER FIFTY-SIX

Friday Afternoon

t's because you're in good shape and your reflexes are good," Karen Muir said. "It takes hold faster in subjects like you."

"The synthetic venom?"

She nodded. "An engineered version of spectacled-cobra venom," she said, and patted me down. She found the gun and put it on the little round table.

"In the document covers? Through the skin?" I asked, and she smiled and nodded again. "I didn't feel a thing."

"And that was *not* easy to achieve with molecules of that size, if I say so myself. I've worked at it for years."

I tried to shrug my shoulders but couldn't. I took in a slow four-count breath through my nose and let it out at the same rate through my mouth, and kept doing that while I recalled my training. There'd been hours and days on end of it—from when I was quite young, in surroundings that ranged from schoolroom to field, under a variety of diabolical conditions, which, unfortunately, had not included snake venom. Still . . .

"I knew your brother had lied about that—about it being Witmer's research," I said, "about it having gone nowhere."

She shook her head in disgust. "Half true—the research went nowhere commercially. It *was* too expensive to synthesize at scale. But in every other way it was a tremendous success, and fascinating to work with. As you know, I was able to engineer the toxin molecules for trans-dermal absorption. But before that, there was the extensive tuning of how, where, and at what pace the molecule attaches to nerve sites. That's why it doesn't behave like the natural compound; it's why you can't move but you can still breathe and talk. For the moment, at any rate. It was stupid of Terry to lie about it. I said as much to him—that it was unnecessary and would make you suspicious."

"Don't be too hard on him. I was already quite suspicious. That business of scrubbing the servers of the Project 1107 documents . . ."

Muir frowned, and something haughty came into her voice. "That was *perfectly* understandable—perfectly defensible. There were indications of a data breach, and I took steps to protect our most sensitive research. I protected government interests as well as our corporate ones."

I managed a sort of laugh, though it sounded ghastly to me, perhaps because my breathing had become labored. "Things might've gone better all around if you'd thought that way when your fraud started. A little more security back then might've saved a lot of trouble in the end."

Karen Muir's cheeks colored, and I found some breath to continue.

"But your brother's lie about the neurotoxin—that it was Witmer's research—was heavy-handed. It made me consider whether he was trying to construct some narrative in which Dr. Witmer was behind all this—Allegra's murder and Ian Stiles's. It made me wonder if that's why Allegra's phone was left with Stiles's body, and Stiles's phone and gun were taken away. It seemed that someone was leaving a trail of breadcrumbs. Your brother made me wonder if that trail was intended to lead to Dr. Witmer."

She laughed derisively. "Well, *of course* it was. The phone and the gun are here, as is Piers, naturally. As are you now, too—all the important pieces together. If you hadn't come, I would've called you—or, rather, had Piers call, or send you a message. Perhaps from Mr. Stiles's phone. Perhaps we just would've switched on his phone and had you come on your own."

"You're quick to improvise, Dr. Muir, but not good at it, I'm afraid. You're too impulsive. Just like your plan to dispose of Allegra's body in the construction bin. It might've seemed ingenious at first glance, but it was never going to work. You've been careening around from the start, from impulse to half-plan and half-stories that could never hold water."

I took a deep breath then, and my head spun. Karen Muir squinted at me, came over, and placed two fingers on my carotid artery. They were like ice.

"Starting to feel it, are we? Not to worry—we can titrate with antivenin, and keep you breathing as long as needs be. Amazing you're still talking so much, though. You must enjoy the sound of your own voice. You really *are* an arrogant prick—just like her."

"By 'her' I assume you mean Dr. Stans."

"She also loved the sound of her voice. Especially when she had something to lord over you."

"Is that what happened seven months ago, when she came to talk to you about the project?"

Muir reached behind her and fiddled with her hair tie. Her ponytail came loose, and she swept a hand through her blond hair. "That bitch couldn't keep her legs together, and that fool Prather couldn't keep his mouth shut. And then she comes swanning into my office as if she's just invented gene editing. Starts lecturing me about cassette size limits in AAVs and chattering on about all the work she's done on it, and the other approaches we should consider. . . . Arrogant."

"Offering suggestions—that was enough for you to derail her career?"

Her face clenched. "Of course it was enough! I couldn't have her sticking her nose into that project, raising questions. It was more than enough."

"Is that when you decided to kill her?"

She retied her hair, more tightly this time. "That came later," she said matter-of-factly, "about a month ago, when she told me with such smug satisfaction all that she had discovered about the project. That cunt."

"What was she asking for?"

"Money, of course. A *ridiculous* amount of money, and to be released from her non-compete. In exchange for which she would keep her mouth shut, return what she'd stolen, and go away. And I should take it on faith that she'd be true to her word. She was a liar—a thief and a liar."

"As far as I know, she really was planning to go away, right after she met with you. But that meeting was never going to go well for her, was it? Though I imagine it didn't quite go to plan."

Muir stood in front of me and picked up the wineglass. She took a sip and nodded appreciatively. "She was an arrogant cunt, and she screwed things from the start that Saturday. After the trouble I'd taken in the city, with dear Jacob, that fucking drive back, hiding my car on an old walking trail and hiking to the Cottage before the sun was up—*she* decided that *my* word was the one that wasn't good enough, that *my* representations couldn't be trusted. She demanded to hear from Terry directly before she would give us anything. She insisted on speaking to him, *in person*. And she wanted *his* signature on the release."

My chest was leaden now, and every breath was a weight up an ever-steeper hill. "Is that why you two went back into Ondstrand House?"

She took another sip of wine. "I told her we'd meet Terry in the executive dining room. I was going to call his office on a house phone once we got inside. I certainly didn't want to turn on my phone to do it, or use his own phone from the Cottage—how would that look? Allegra and I went through the tunnel—I couldn't go through security, after all. As it was, I took a big risk, just going from the classroom to the dining room. I knew not many people were around, and we took the stairs, but, still, it was just sheer luck we weren't seen. Of course, she thought it was a big joke. She even laughed at the tunnel."

"Did Dr. Hasp meet you in the dining room?"

"Not in time to speak with her," Karen said, chuckling. "I told her he'd meet us in back, by the wine room, and I asked again for the documents she'd stolen. She refused. She said that if she was satisfied with what Terry had to say, then her partner would arrange delivery, but only once payment had been made. *Her partner!* It was the first I'd heard about any partner. She saw my surprise and laughed at me again and handed me her *fucking phone.* She said that I should keep it—that her partner would be in touch on it. That he'd text me."

I was dizzy now, and my vision was darkening around the edges. My chest was too heavy for my lungs to move. Still, I managed a few words. "That can't have gone well."

Karen Muir laughed again, bitterly, and carried the wineglass to the parlor windows. She took another sip. "She was a thorn to me from beginning to end, but that was the worst. Meanwhile, Terry was nowhere to be found, and I left her waiting by the wine room to go fetch him. I risked all, creeping down the hall to Terry's office, and when I retrieved him and Piers, and we made our way back to the dining room, what do we find—that bitch, *dead* on the bathroom floor!

"I honestly didn't know what to think. I hadn't seen a single soul about, and I had no idea who'd done her in, but out of nowhere it became my problem to solve. Well, mine, Terry's, and Piers's—though, truth be told, those two were mostly useless, dithering and sputtering and suggesting—practically insisting—that it was I who'd laid her out. As if! I'd had things worked out nicely, thank you, and if they'd gone to plan she would've turned up at the old stables in Little Storping after many days and long searching. But no, not Allegra Stans. As I said— a *cunt*, and a thorn to me from beginning to end."

I wanted to look at her but couldn't. I tried another laugh. "Dr. Muir, are you seriously telling me that you *didn't* kill Allegra—that you'd planned to but were robbed of the opportunity?"

"Terry and Piers didn't believe me, either, the bastards. They wanted to debate the matter with her cooling at our feet. I had to point out that, regardless of who had actually done it, we were on the hook for it, and had to deal with it."

"I think you're a bit mad, Dr. Muir," I said softly. "And more than a bit impulsive. Scrubbing the servers, killing Allegra, dumping her body, your alibi with Jacob Hanro—it's all as leaky as cheesecloth. Hanro didn't survive ten minutes of questioning, by the way, before he completely surrendered that story. And not just *that* story, I should point out. You're all impulse and bad improvisation."

Muir came around in front of me and flung what was left in the wineglass in my face. Then she clamped a strong, chilly hand around my lower jaw and squeezed. "I *swear* you are just like her," she said. Her face was close to mine and her voice was low and harsh. "I look forward to watching you—"

With whatever force I could muster, I slammed my forehead into her face.

Sadly, I couldn't muster much.

But it did surprise her. *"Fuck!"* she shouted; she stumbled back and rubbed the bridge of her nose. Then she wiped her mouth, and there was blood on her hand. "And you cut my *fucking* lip." She balled her fist, but stopped, stared at me, and shook her head. "You shouldn't have been able to do that," she said softly. "I'm going to want some samples from you, Agent Myles. Before you leave us."

Muir went into the dining room and returned with a medical bag, but she stopped when Hasp appeared. He wore a surgical mask hanging down on his black tee shirt, surgical gloves, and blue coverings over his shoes, and he was pushing a wheelchair in which Piers Witmer sat, bound at the wrists and ankles. Witmer's mouth was gagged, and his eyes were wide and wild with fear. Hasp looked at me and frowned.

"Hell, Kar, what are you two playing at, and what have you done to poor Myles? The man's cyanotic. Needs antivenin if you're gonna keep him alive to die of a gunshot."

CHAPTER FIFTY-SEVEN

Friday Afternoon

And what the hell have you done to his head?" Hasp continued, as he examined my face. "He's got a contusion like a golf ball, and apparently he's been bathing in claret. How you gonna explain that in an autopsy?"

"He's fine, for God's sake," Muir said. "It'll all be fine. I've got a syringe loaded with antivenin."

Hasp clapped me on the shoulder. "Hear that, old man? Relief on the way!" His voice sounded a long way off now, and as if it were coming through leagues of water. My vision had contracted to a clouded keyhole, and my mind had started to reel backwards and sideways, wandering to unlikely places: to Conservatory and my first classes with the Major—the barking and the beating, the ice water rushing up my nose, wandering to Tessa, and my first weeks of field training—the cool steadiness of her voice, the ever-present look of skepticism, the distractions of her hair and her hands, the scent of her. . . .

Karen Muir knelt beside me, and I was aware of her doing something to my left leg or foot, without actually feeling it. There was something that might've been a pinprick, though I wasn't sure where. And then, suddenly, my chest lightened, and breath returned.

"Good on you, Myles—you're pinking right up," Hasp said, cheerily.

"You might want to bind him," Muir said. "The bastard butted me in the head."

Hasp laughed. "Really? How'd you manage that, mate? Your limbs should be mostly sand now."

"Contrarian," I said, with effort.

Hasp laughed again. "Careful with that—Karen's *not* fond of contrarians, are you, Kar? She prefers strict compliance."

Muir was still kneeling, examining my bare foot. "Injection site's invisible," she reported, and stood. She looked at Hasp. "He's got Allegra's copy of the documents," she told Hasp. "At least, he says he has."

"Do you, Myles? That's tremendous. Where'd you find it?"

I managed a smile. "Stuck on her fridge with a magnet."

Hasp smiled, then frowned when Witmer's wheelchair rattled. "Piers, settle down." He spoke as if to an insubordinate pet.

"'Stuck on her fridge' won't please Karen, and I think you've seen she can get testy."

"Little problem there. Hard to know how best to threaten someone once you've promised to kill them."

"To be blunt, old man, the threat has to do with how uncomfortable you are along the way. And, honestly, Karen can make you very uncomfortable indeed."

"Point taken," I said. "But I can't help feeling you're missing the forest for the trees. As I've pointed out to Dr. Muir, the story you're telling—her alibi, Stiles's killing, whatever scenario you have in mind for Dr. Witmer and myself—it won't hold water. Certainly my division will not be convinced, and they will not let my death pass without comment."

Hasp shrugged. "Worry not, Myles. All due respect to the vaunted Standard Division—and I'm sure your death will devastate them—all we need is a *plausible* story. It need not be bulletproof, merely plausible, and Director Elkort will take care of the rest. Putting a lid on things, taking over future inquiries, et cetera."

"You have a great deal of faith in her, but can even she sort out the hash you people have made of this? It seems some bit of planning went into Allegra's killing, and even so that went to shit. You don't believe that story of your sister's, by the way—that Dr. Stans was alive when she went to find you?"

Hasp colored and looked embarrassed. "Best not to bring that up, mate," he said in a whisper. "Truly. Gets her a bit wild."

But I continued. "And Stiles's killing was even worse. She didn't have an alibi for his death—not even a shabby one."

Again, Hasp shrugged. "Stiles was a surprise—didn't know he was in the picture at all before Allegra mentioned him. Bit of a shock, really. And Allegra's nonsense about him delivering her copy of the

1107 documents—utter fantasy, that. He had no clue about the project, though we didn't know that before Kar questioned him. Do you know that Allegra told him that Kar was another recruit for his little corporate spy ring? Can you imagine? Worked in our favor, though—made it easier to arrange a meet with him in an out-of-the-way spot. Put it down to the new recruit being nervous. Poor fella thought from those texts we had Piers send on Allegra's phone, from Soligstrand, that he'd be seeing Allegra and Karen together, but it was Karen only."

Karen Muir was into her medical bag, removing syringes and laying them on the little table beside me. She looked up and looked disdainful. "He was a horrible man, like a used-car salesman. But certainly more cooperative than you, Agent Myles. In the end, he couldn't tell me things quickly enough. Hard to shut him up, really. But he did tell me all about what Allegra had stolen for him, all those files which, you may be interested to know, may yet destroy this company."

"I'm actually not interested."

Another shrug from Hasp. From somewhere he produced a handgun, a black semiautomatic. A Voda 9. Hasp dropped the magazine out, worked the slide, and checked the chamber. He dry-fired the gun and looked at me. "Young Explorers. Gun-safety badge. Dr. Roeg insisted."

"I'm sure he set a fine example," I said.

Hasp looked at me, stone-faced. Then he grinned widely. "I enjoy you, Myles—really, I do. I shall miss you." He stepped over to Witmer and freed his right hand from its restraint. He placed the gun in Witmer's hand and wrapped Witmer's fingers around the grip and on the trigger. He lifted Witmer's hand and aimed the gun at me and dry-fired again.

"That should do," he said, "when the time comes."

"It didn't work with Stiles, you know."

Hasp scowled. "What are you on about now?"

"It was better when he was cyanotic," Karen Muir muttered, examining a needle.

"Shooting Stiles didn't obscure things. We picked up traces of the synthetic snake venom in the toxicology screen."

"That's old news, Myles," Hasp said, shaking his head. "You all but told me that when you asked me about venom in my office. Fact is, it worked perfectly. The traces were meant to be found, just as the venom vials here at Piers's place are meant to be found. Piers is central to our story. There'll be evidence of his stealing the venom from Ondstrand House; it'll be quite convincing."

"Or at least plausible," I said.

"He's wasting time," Karen Muir said. "Let's be about it, shall we? Either he'll tell us where the documents are, and die simply and without pain, or he won't."

I took another stab at a laugh. "You two do understand that my management knows what I know, yes? They'll have seen the project documents by now. They will not accept whatever story you're selling—regardless of how plausible. And your story isn't."

Hasp shook his head again. "Our story won't be materially different from yours, actually. It will simply omit anything about Project 1107, and it will star Piers as Allegra's partner, along with Mr. Stiles. Piers as a deceived and angry partner, then as a murderous partner, then as the desperate, cornered killer, then, finally, as a suicide. You will feature as the brave but doomed investigator, who got his man but gave his life, et cetera, et cetera. A moving story."

Karen Muir slipped a blood-pressure cuff around my left biceps, and a pulse oximeter on my finger.

I looked at Hasp. "You should really think things through a bit more. You have some leverage here, you know. My division would stop and listen if you could tell them about corruption in Domestic Security, particularly at a high level. You could expect a fair amount of consideration for that."

"Really?" Hasp said with sarcastic breathlessness. "We'll have to give that serious thought."

"If I could shake my head, I would," I said. "Your solution is rash, Dr. Hasp. You said that Allegra and your sister were very much alike—that they had the same kind of mind—and I see your point. The same impulsivity. The same recklessness."

That hit. Karen Muir straightened and looked at Hasp. "*Same kind of mind?* Really? *Really,* Terry? What the hell does that mean?"

"He's just trying to get under your skin, Karen—ignore him. You're right, we should get on with things."

"No—I'd appreciate an explanation. The same kind of mind as that arrogant, lying cunt? *Really?*"

"God, Karen—it's just something I said to him, that's all. It doesn't mean anything."

"Were you sleeping with her, Dr. Hasp?" I asked.

Hasp went white. *"What?"*

Muir glared at him. *"Sleeping with her*—with that *bitch?* Were you, Terry? Is *that* what you've decided you prefer?"

"Of course not. Damn you, Myles—shut the hell up. Karen, he's winding you up, though I'm not sure why. Unless it's just to buy himself some time."

Muir was about to say something when her gaze shifted to Witmer, bound to the wheelchair. His body was rigid, his face was a color I'd not seen before in human flesh, and he'd begun to shake and thrash.

"Good God, Terry, he's seizing," she said impatiently. "Did you not top up his antivenin?" Witmer's flailing sent his chair rolling out of the parlor and into the entrance foyer, and Karen Muir scooped up a syringe and followed. "I can't trust you with a damn thing," she muttered.

Hasp shrugged and looked at me. "Shape of things to come, Myles. You don't want to go that route."

I spoke fast to Hasp, and in a whisper. "You realize that something's wrong with her, don't you? Jacob Hanro says she's psychotic, possibly related to some trauma she experienced when she was young. Is he right about that?"

Hasp was horrified. "My God, man," he whispered, "don't let her hear that stuff, not unless you want to go out screaming."

"Was it something that happened at Ondstrand Hall? Something your father did to her, in that tunnel?"

Hasp took a step back and looked at me as if for the first time. "Dr. Roeg didn't *do* anything to her. Not the way you mean. He never touched her; he never even knew we were in there. It wasn't anything he *did* to Karen, but I suppose . . . it was what he *showed* her, without knowing it. What we watched him do. I'll tell you the truth, Myles, what he did to that boy, I pissed myself. If the place hadn't already stunk of urine, Dr. Roeg would've rumbled us for sure. I could barely draw breath, but Karen . . . For her it was some kind of . . . revelation. As if something she'd been waiting for her whole life had finally arrived. A missing piece. An answer. She wasn't the same after that."

Hasp shook his head and shook off his reverie. "Why do you think she insisted we preserve that goddamn tunnel, and his fucking chem lab?" he asked, grinning.

Karen Muir returned, pushing Piers Witmer in his chair. Witmer's flesh had regained a recognizable color, and his bound limbs were no longer quivering. Muir squinted at Hasp. "What are you gossiping about?" she asked.

Hasp chuckled and shook his head. "Not a thing, Kar. I told you, he's just buying time."

Karen Muir took a deep breath, shook her head, and returned to the table beside my chair. She slung a stethoscope around her neck and picked up a syringe. She knelt by my bare foot. "Well, he's run out of it now. This is the last opportunity you'll have to avoid what I understand is excruciating pain, Myles—something like drowning, except it goes on for much longer. For as long as we say, actually."

Hasp stepped in front of me. "What about it, sport—a bit of rationality in the midst of this madness? Want to tell us where those documents are?"

They needed me alive, I told myself, so that they could shoot me while Witmer held the gun. I shook my head. "Contrarian," I said.

"Have it your way," Hasp said with regret, and I felt something that might've been a pinprick, somewhere south of my knee.

"I'll warn you, Myles," Karen Muir said, "this hits faster than the transdermal variety."

She wasn't lying. Suddenly my chest felt as if a piano were parked there, and panic built rapidly with my carbon dioxide levels. It did feel like drowning, but, thanks to the Major, it wasn't my first time.

"Focused dissociation," she called it—the opposite of being present; absenting oneself from, well, physical reality. Slow the heart rate, slow the breath—that was happening regardless—lead the mind . . . elsewhere. Anywhere.

Which was backwards and backwards and backwards again . . . to Tessa, and my first day in the field—a surveillance exercise, a simple observe-and-report, and somehow I'd botched it; back to Conservatory, and that first, terrifying week, flung into a perpetual war of all-against-all for survival, and an endless series of unannounced up-or-out exams; back further still, to the last of the state homes, the Myles Van der Wees Home, a giant toilet mostly, and to the morning when Director Mehta paid a visit there, like a creature floating down from another world. To this day, I had no idea of who Myles Van der Wees was or what sins he'd committed to merit the attachment of his name to that green-and-beige latrine, and I was only grateful that Standard Division hadn't seen fit to rechristen me Van der Wees when they took me into Conservatory. And backwards, backwards again—to the looming, terrifying shade of my grandmother, as wide across as she was tall, so quick with a pinch, a scratch, a callused backhand for offenses that were entirely obscure, yet always the same: that I existed at all, and that she was burdened with me—to the wraithlike, shadowed memory of my mother, her fair, lank hair, her ancient eyes, her poor, tattered arms. Tumbling backwards, backwards, backwards off the highest of cliffs, the sky rushing away but the ground never any closer.

My vision was gone now, and everything I heard was a whisper in the surf. Something squeezed my arm, and I felt a cold circle on my chest. Someone hit my face, and there was a bright light in one eye and then in the other. Someone said, "He's crashing, Kar," and someone said, "Find a pulse," and someone said, "Was that a car," and someone said, "Was that the door." And then the pressure on my arm, the cold circle, the bright light, and all else were lost.

CHAPTER FIFTY-EIGHT

Two Weeks Later

Hospital again. Not for the first time. Likely not the last. The same non-place of a place, in a time out of time. The casino quality—no days, no nights, artificial air, dubious food, a parade of strange faces, a string of incongruous questions, recitations of numbers and impenetrable vernacular, no dignity, no silence, sleep the only succor but nearly impossible to sustain and somehow never restful.

I assumed that I was back in the city, but had no idea of where, nor had I any idea of how long I'd been wherever I was. If I could have spoken, I might've asked one of the strange faces, but speaking—even to ask that the curtains be pulled back—was too much effort. And, in any event, my periods of consciousness were really quite brief.

Then came a day when I could speak, could remain conscious, and when a familiar face appeared. Jane Wilding was there when I woke. She was slouched in a chair, with her stockinged feet propped on the end of my bed. She wore jeans and a striped shirt with a boat neck. A laptop and a plank of sunshine lay across her thighs.

"How long?" I asked.

"Couple of weeks. There was significant nerve insult, but your neurologist says it's temporary."

"Comforting. Where are we?"

"Sisters of Solace, special ward. You've been here before—remember?"

I nodded. "It was winter then, and the curtains were different."

Jane closed her laptop, rose, and pulled the curtains fully back. I saw blue sky and the branches of a tree washed in pale, budding green. "It's springtime now," she said.

She sat beside me on the bed, produced a penlight, and shined it in my eyes. "Much better," she said.

"Good to hear. Have you been here long?"

"I've been in and out. I do have a job, you know. But, for the conquering hero, the Director makes some allowances."

I winced. "What did I conquer?"

Jane put her hand on my cheek. Her palm was warm and dry. "Death, for starters. I'll let the Director go through the rest. She'd have my head otherwise."

"Can't have that," I said. "Too nice a head." I closed my eyes.

It was dark when I opened them again, and my phone was buzzing. It took a good deal of concentration to answer—like playing tennis with the wrong hand.

Ivessen's cat spoke before Ivessen, and I fancied I detected some feline concern. "Rumor has it that you're again amongst the living," Ivessen said. "Thought I'd see for myself."

"I'm touched. What time is it?"

He laughed. "Less than spry, are we?"

"Just a shade. You got my last message."

"And fascinating reading it made."

"I take it you notified the Director."

"As soon as I saw what Dr. Stans had stored on that Web site. The Director had already seen your note and mobilized some assets, lucky for you. You could have reached out sooner, you know—when you discovered the tunnel, for instance, or when you found the locket."

"Had the bit in my teeth. Too much adrenaline, I suppose."

Ivessen laughed again. "We'll keep that from the Major," he said, and then he was gone.

The Director came the next day—at least, I thought it was the next day. She wore a dove-gray suit and a white blouse, and at her neck a scarf with a pattern of green leaves. Her black hair was shining. She stood in the doorway for a moment and surveyed the room, then came in and sat. She studied my face and smiled.

"Much improved," she said, nodding. "Feeling better?"

"In that I'm feeling something again. Also, I am apparently no longer dead."

"Let's not rush to judgment. They do tell me you're eating well, though."

"It's not the quality of the kitchen."

"When the medics approve, I'll have my cook fix you up. The Major sends her best, by the way. She's really *very* proud. It's actually quite sweet. She was even talking about stopping by for a visit."

"Please, no," I said.

The Director smiled, crossed her legs, and sighed. "No doubt you want to know what you've missed while you've been sleeping."

"I'd like to know what I missed before that as well."

She raised an eyebrow. "Not so very much," she said, "but let's catch you up on recent news. Working from the top down, Director Elkort and her Minister are no longer in their old posts, and Domestic Security—particularly the Science and Technology Division—is undergoing significant reorganization. I expect this will continue for some time."

"'No longer in their old posts'—that sounds ominous."

"Very much so—particularly for the late Minister. Ms. Elkort, on the other hand, has been eager to cooperate. She's identified a pair of auditors who were a part of the conspiracy, and she's participating in the recovery of funds. For which assistance she will earn what will effectively be a life sentence. Which, in the scheme of things, constitutes a good deal of mercy, I think.

"As for the management team at Ondstrand Biologic, Piers Witmer is also assisting the authorities, for the moment from a hospital bed."

"And Hasp and Karen Muir?"

"With us no longer," she said, and the spark of something—satisfaction, amusement—glinted in the Director's eyes. "They died shortly after you did, though more permanently." I raised an eyebrow, and she went on. "Ondstrand Biologic itself continues, though, under the temporary supervision of our division. Dr. Pohl is acting as the interim chief executive and is certainly on the short list in our search for a permanent head. Our Minister is assembling a temporary board of directors, on which she will serve as chair. There are many valuable assets there, and with luck we'll be able to preserve those, and possibly make use of some."

"Such as synthetic snake venom?"

She smiled. "Our R&D people are eager to have a look."

"Any intellectual property of the company will be less valuable if it turns out to have been stolen and sold by Dr. Stans and Ian Stiles."

She nodded. "Freja's people are attempting to trace the stolen material, with support from your Ms. Drucker. A very competent woman, she. Does that about cover things?"

"It does not. I assume you've known about the goings-on at Ond-strand for some time."

"'Known' would be overstatement. 'Suspected' is closer to the truth. But, yes, we've had an eye out for some time. Years, in fact. With Dr. Stans's death, an opportunity presented itself."

"Though not, apparently, an opportunity to tell me what the hell was actually going on."

"I detect frustration, which I'm told is not conducive to a speedy re-covery. You were there to investigate a murder—two murders, as it happened—and you acquitted yourself admirably, as you always do. Would it have helped you so very much to know that we've had suspi-cions? That our Minister harbored doubts about her colleague oversee-ing Domestic? That we'd investigated discreetly but with no results?"

"It might've helped me to avoid that last unpleasantness—the one that killed me."

The Director pretended to consider it, then shrugged. "Let's not waste time speculating. And as for that last part, it was essential. Not the dying, of course—that was unfortunate—but it was from that last bit that we got Hasp's and Muir's confessions, including the unambigu-ous implication of Elkort and her Minister. That recording, and the e-mails in amongst the Project 1107 material you found, simplified mat-ters greatly when we confronted the two of them."

I frowned. "Perhaps I suffered some brain damage, but, while I re-member Hasp and Muir confessing, I don't recall recording anything."

The Director smiled. "Don't fret, Myles—your brain is no worse than usual. Of course you didn't record them, but you did have your phone with you. Which, by the way, was also quite useful in tracking you."

I looked at her for a while, and she held my gaze. "Under the circum-stances," I said finally, "I suppose I should be grateful."

She smiled. "That goes without saying."

"But you must've had a team nearby that afternoon." The Director tilted her head in a way that was nearly a nod. "Any people I know?"

Director Mehta sighed. "Yes. Which brings us to a conversation we must have again, Myles—about a partner."

I rolled my eyes. "I'm fairly certain I feel a relapse coming on."

She ignored me. "We will have this conversation again, and for the *last time*."

"I really don't see why, Director. I did my job; I did it *admirably*, as you yourself said. I don't see—"

"You *died*, Myles. The outcome was admirable, yes, but your death was not, and, had it been a permanent affliction, it would have meant the loss of a significant asset for us. An expensive one to replace."

"That's very moving. But that said—"

Her voice hardened. "This is not a debate, Myles. And it's not a conversation we're going to have again. I've indulged you in this for far too long. I understand what you suffered when we lost Ms. Lake, but this is policy, and you are not exempt."

I looked out the window at the greening branches and sighed. "Yes, Director."

She brightened. "As it happened, we *did* have an asset quite nearby that afternoon, which accounts for why you're still with us. And that is who I have in mind for you."

"I'm sure whoever it is will be adequate. I just hope that he or she has some field experience."

"Yes, though not the same sort as yours, and not as much. Her assignments to date have been cover."

I grimaced. "What sort of cover?"

"Corporate."

I rolled my eyes. "You're partnering me with an accountant?"

The Director smiled. "She's a bit more than that, Myles. She made short work of Hasp and Muir, after all—right there on the spot, before bringing you back from the dead." The Director rose and smoothed her skirt. "She's waiting in the hall, by the way. I thought you might like to thank her personally, and as I must be off . . ."

"Now? *Really?*"

The Director patted my hand. "Really, dear boy," she said, and left.

And then the door opened again.

Her wardrobe was still vaguely martial—a short jacket in brown leather with a mandarin collar, a crisp white tee shirt beneath, black riding pants, and brown boots. Vaguely martial or vaguely dominatrix. The white-blond hair was gone, though, and so, too, was the riding-crop braid. Now it was a wing of coppery chestnut, caught in a loose ponytail. Nadia Blom stood at my bedside, at parade rest, and regarded me with cool gray eyes.

"You're looking well," she said. "Breathing on your own, and so forth."

Her voice was different, too—more relaxed, less brittle, a subtle change in accent.

"The Director says I owe you thanks, and I rarely argue with her. So—thank you, Ms. Blom." She smiled minutely and shook her head. "Not Blom?" I asked.

"Van der Wees," she said. "Astrid Van der Wees."

I raised an eyebrow. *Van der Wees?*

"Van der Wees," she repeated, and a smile flickered on her lips and then was gone.

"Well . . . my thanks, Ms. Van der Wees."

"'Astrid' will do," she said, and this time the smile lingered.

CHAPTER FIFTY-NINE

Two Weeks Later

Tuesday Afternoon

Ondstrand House was lovely in the high spring sunlight, amidst velvet lawns, trees in full leaf, and raucous flower beds. Its façade glowed gold, its ornamental scrolls and fluting looked freshly etched and flossed, and its many windows shone like mirrors. Water leapt and splashed in the courtyard fountain, and even the fountain statuary, still melting and strange, looked more benign now—merely odd rather than sinister. It was nearly impossible, as I pulled into the courtyard, to imagine the place as the scene of murder. Nearly.

The forecourt was empty of people when we stopped just short of the porte cochere, though there were several sedans—government cars—parked beneath it. We'd had the windows down since Slocum, and the sea air had sparked an unexpected appetite in me—an urge to roll up my trousers and run into the surf, though running was still out of bounds. I got out, stiff and unsteady, stretched, and looked into the car.

"I shouldn't be long," I said, and Astrid Van der Wees nodded, and stared at the fountain. "You mind being back?" I asked.

She shook her head, but her gaze didn't waver. "That was Nadia Blom," she said evenly. "Not me."

"Okay, then," I said, "half an hour and send in the search dogs." Astrid nodded.

After all the sun, the darkness of the lobby was dizzying, and I took my time crossing. I used my Ondstrand ID at the barrier, and the guards said not a word.

It was another indulgence on the Director's part, this trip—a nod to my sense of order, and perhaps to her own, even if the larger security apparatus was satisfied with the narrative it had been given, and largely indifferent to details like truth.

"I've always suspected you of being a completist, Myles," the Director had said before I set out from the city, early this morning.

Standing before her desk, I shook my head. "You sent me to do a job. I think we'd both like to know it was done."

She shrugged. "It will be good for you to stretch your legs, I suppose, and for you and Ms. Van der Wees to spend some time together."

"Is that the only reason you've authorized this?"

The Director did not look up from her reading. "I listened to those recordings again, as you suggested," she said. "You may have a point." Then she waved a hand in a gesture that might've meant, *Begone,* or *Quit while you're ahead.*

Sandra Silber was alone in her small, shared office, two floors above the executive dining room, and she looked up from her computer screen when I opened the door. She went white and stock-still when she recognized me, and if I'd taken her neck in my teeth at that moment I doubt she would've moved or made a sound.

I closed the door behind me and leaned against it and crossed my arms. "Dr. Silber, I'd like to continue our conversation where we left off several weeks ago. You lost sight of Dr. Stans in the woods, where the trail went by the Cottage. Having finished your run, you returned to Ondstrand House. Tell me what happened next."

Sandy Silber opened her mouth, but no intelligible sound came out for a while. I could hear her struggling to inhale, and finally she managed speech. "They're *dead.* They told us—Dr. Hasp and Dr. Muir are *dead,* and *they* killed Allegra. They did it."

"Except you and I know that they didn't, and we're not going to pretend otherwise. Things have gone wrong for you, Sandy, and they're going to get worse—I won't lie to you about that. You can't stop it, but you can influence how bad it gets. And right now is the time to exert that influence. If you are honest with me, I can see to it that your case is referred to the local authorities, and you'll have legal counsel and all the due-process protections. The alternative is for Standard Division to handle things. And that, Sandy, is something you do *not* want."

Silber went from white to gray, and she began to hyperventilate. I took her hand, leaned close, and spoke softly. "You need to breathe, Sandy: in through the nose, out through the mouth, a four-count each way, with a two-second pause in between."

She did as I instructed, and after a while she finished her story.

"I didn't go right inside," she began. "I stretched first, in the court-yard. Then I went in, to my office. I had run some simulations overnight, and I wanted to check the results. I took the stairs up, as I always do, and just as I reached my floor, and was about to leave the stairwell, I heard her voice.

"Of course I knew it was her—I could recognize her voice anywhere, and it carried clearly in the stairwell. She was with someone else— I couldn't tell who, and I couldn't make out what they were saying, but I heard them climbing the stairs and opening an exit door below. I went to my office then, but I didn't go inside. I paced up and down the hallway and wondered who Allie was with, and if her voice had sounded, I don't know—tense, I suppose. I don't know how long I paced there. A few minutes, probably. Then I opened my office door, but I just stood in the hall and didn't go in.

"Instead, I thought about going downstairs for coffee. I'm too junior to eat in the executive dining room, but the coffee machines are always on, and it's so close, and no one had ever said anything. I thought I could just go down there and have a cup, and if I happened to run into Allie and whoever she was with . . . I stood there thinking about it, for a few minutes probably; then I closed my office door and went downstairs.

"When I went into the dining room, I thought somehow I'd missed her—it was dead quiet, and there was no one in sight. I don't know what made me think to go in the back—I don't know why I did it. But I did, and there she was, in the hallway. She was really startled to see me—to see anybody there, I think—and she practically jumped when I opened that door. And then she got angry. And *so* mean.

"I hadn't said a word to her in weeks—months, even. Hadn't sent her any texts or . . . anything. But before I could say anything—even hello—she started screaming at me. She was like a *crazy* person, really. What was I doing there? Why was I always following her? What did I want from her? Why couldn't I just leave her alone? Why did I have to be such a nosy cow?"

Tears were streaming down Sandy Silber's cheeks now, and her nose was running. She didn't seem to notice. "She . . . she called me a *cow*, and then she pushed by me and went into the bathroom, and I followed her. I opened the door, and she whirled around and said: 'Can't I even pee in peace? Or do you want a few drops for your fucking hope chest? My God, Sandy, you are like gum stuck to my fucking shoe.' I hadn't said a word to her—not a word. And she said those things. . . .

"I grabbed her—by the arms. I don't know why. I suppose I wanted to make her listen, or make her stop yelling. But I couldn't. And I was just so hurt and angry that I *pushed* her. She went backwards and hit her head on the wall, and then she stood there with her mouth open, and I thought she was going to yell again. And so I pushed her again.

"I don't remember clearly what happened after that. I suppose I ran out of there and went back to my office. And I suppose, for a while, I was waiting for Protection or the police to come for me. When her body was discovered and there was all the ruckus, I thought they'd be at my door at any moment. But then I heard that she'd been found in the kitchen, and I . . . I didn't know what to think. Maybe I hadn't . . . Maybe she wasn't dead when I'd run from there. Maybe . . . I didn't know what to think. And then you came, and I was just so scared. I just didn't want to . . . I was just so *scared*."

The breath seemed to leave her at the end, and her body was spent and slack. There was a box of tissues on the desk, and I brought them to her and helped her clean up before we left.

I spoke to the locals on the phone and had an odd-job, one of our contingent at Ondstrand, transport her to Soligstrand. Then I called the Director and told her about it. She seemed mildly amused that I'd turned Sandy Silber over to the locals, but not otherwise fussed. "You are nothing if not consistent, Myles," she said, and rang off.

Astrid Van der Wees was leaning against our government car, watching me. She, too, seemed mildly amused. "As scared as she was, Dr. Silber managed to deceive you for some time," she said. "She was quite an effective liar."

"Certainly a motivated one," I said. "As for effective . . . perhaps I'm just not terribly astute."

A tiny smile flickered across her lips. "Well, yes, there's that."

Tuesday Evening

It was nearing dinnertime when I parked Allegra Stans's car in Fisk-dorp, near the north end of Beacon Square. There was a breeze off the water, and as I crossed the square it carried to me the smells of baking bread and grilling meats from the restaurants, and the dizzying aroma of roasting coffee beans from the espresso bar. Tables were set up on the cobblestones outside the eateries, and there was a couple at one sharing bread and cheese and a bottle of wine. Gulls spun above and squawked in anticipation. The sky was deep blue but still full of light, and a few clouds drifted around like blossoms or daydreams. Jens-Edvard Neu-mann met me in an alleyway off the square. He wore black pants, a white shirt, and a bar apron. He was on break before the dinner crowd came, and he smoked a cigarette with nervous energy.

"Didn't think I'd see you again," he said.

"You almost didn't."

He squinted at me. "You been sick?"

I nodded. "Dead, actually."

Jens-Edvard shook his head. "Why you call, then? You find who did for Allie, or did your lot just call it quits?"

"We found them."

His eyes widened. "Them? More than one?"

"More than one."

"What's gonna happen to 'em?"

"To the ones still breathing—nothing good."

He looked down at his boots and kicked a pebble that skittered down the alleyway. "Some are dead?" I nodded. "Should that make me feel better?"

I shrugged. "I don't know about *should*. My own experience is that it sometimes does—though not much better, and not for very long."

"Can you tell me who? Or why? Why she had to . . . ?"

"I can't," I said.

"Can you tell me *anything*?" I shook my head. "Then . . . what am I supposed to make of it all?"

I thought about that for a while and shook my head. "I don't know. And even if I could answer your questions, I don't know that the answers would be of any help."

Jens-Edvard scowled and flicked away his cigarette butt. "Screw it," he said angrily. "And screw you. What use are you?"

I shook my head again. "I definitely have no answer to that," I said. Then I tossed the keys to Allegra's car in a long parabola over to him. He caught them in both hands, looked down at them, and back at me.

"What's this?" he asked.

"The keys to her car."

"Why the hell you giving 'em to me?"

"I can't think of what else to do with them, I suppose."

"She has family somewhere. A brother or sister or some such."

"As far as I can tell, you're her family, as much as anyone."

His cheeks burned, and he stared at the keys in his hands. "What am I supposed to do with a car?"

I shrugged. "If I were you? I'd sell it and take the money and get the hell out of this town. I'd get myself down to Playa Arcadia and into that art school. Between the tuition waiver and what you get for the car, that should see you for the first term, maybe longer. After that, you'll have to figure something out—work the problem, as Allegra might say. Anyway, that's what I'd do. But, as you pointed out—my usefulness is questionable."

"I . . . I don't—"

"Don't think too much," I said. "Just get out of here. I won't say it's what she'd have wanted, because I have no idea of that. But just get out of here. The car's parked off the north side of the square."

I turned and left the alleyway and crossed the square again, headed for the waterfront. I found Astrid Van der Wees leaning up against our sedan, which she had parked up on a sidewalk. She was watching boats in the harbor, and her face was a mask. She stood up straight when I approached. She had a paper sack in one hand and the sedan's keys in the other, and she held both aloft.

"Fish and chips," she said. "You want to drive first or eat first?"

"Eat first," I said, and Astrid nodded and tossed me the bag.

Acknowledgments

Like Myles's world, ours has seemed more than a few degrees off-true of late, what with plague, climate catastrophe, authoritarian threat, and other resurgent evils casting weird shadows everywhere. Or perhaps it was our recent history that was the anomaly, and the past couple of years just a brutal reversion to the mean. . . . Either way, March 2020 to March 2021 was a weird time to be writing a book. And so, I find that I owe more than the usual thanks to many people.

I was fortunate in being able to write at all during that period—in having had the health and general wherewithal to do my work. And while I am always grateful to my family for their support, that year they exceeded all precedents and expectations. I am especially grateful—beyond words or measure—to Alice Wang, whose desert island credentials are without equal. As I've said to her often: "thank you" doesn't begin to cover it.

Work was a blessing during that endless year (honestly, who wouldn't have welcomed the chance to escape each day into a gothic landscape of conspiracy and murder), but, like so much else, it was touched by change and sadness. First, the change: my literary agent of twenty years, the wonderful Denise Marcil, elected to retire in 2020—an eminently sensible decision, carried out with the professionalism and grace I've so valued throughout our relationship. Even as she saw to the disposition of her business, Denise took the time and care to introduce me to my new agent. I thank her for that, as I do for so much else.

Many thanks, too, to the excellent Vicky Bijur—a perceptive and knowledgeable reader, a vigorous and effective advocate, and a reliable voice of reason. *A Secret About a Secret* was our first book together, and it was a pleasure throughout. I look forward to many more.

Thanks also to Edward Kastenmeier, at Knopf—an astute and deft editor. His insights and pointed questions made this a better book, and I am deeply grateful for his input and support.

Which leaves the sadness. Sonny Mehta passed away at the bitter end of 2019, and I was still processing that loss the following March, when everything went ass over teakettle. Sonny was the only editor I'd had at that point, but he was much more than that. It's not hyperbole to say that he changed my life—I'm one of many authors who can say this. And it's a simple statement of fact that the world was larger, richer, more interesting, and generally more civilized with him in it. I am fortunate to have known him, and grateful to have felt his presence whenever I sat down to work on this.

Peter Spiegelman is the author of *Black Maps*, which won the 2004 Shamus Award for Best First P.I. Novel, *Death's Little Help-ers*, *Red Cat*, *Thick as Thieves*, and *Dr. Knox*. Prior to his career as a writer, Mr. Spiegelman spent nearly twenty years in the financial services and software industries. He lives in New York City.

A NOTE ON THE TYPE

This book was set in Janson, a typeface named for Anton Janson, but is actually the work of Nicholas Kis (1650–1702). The type is an example of the sturdy Dutch types that prevailed in England up to the time William Caslon (1692–1766) developed his own incomparable designs from them.

Typeset by Scribe,
Philadelphia, Pennsylvania

Printed and bound by Berryville Graphics,
Berryville, Virginia

Designed by Betty Lew